The Seventh Word

S.L. Smith

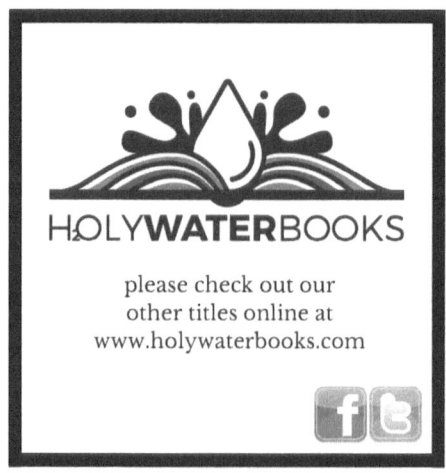

HOLYWATERBOOKS

please check out our
other titles online at
www.holywaterbooks.com

A Warning

A handful of pecans made a clacking sound as they fell into a white plastic bucket. The man leaned over, reaching down to collect another handful of pecans.

"Isn't that a lovely sound?" The woman asked, as she, too, dropped a scoop of pecans into the bucket. Unlike the man, she had a tool to pick the pecans. It was a long wooden handle attached to a metal can. The can had once been painted barn red, and its mouth was crossed with wires. The wires had just enough give. The pecans just popped through and were trapped inside the little can.

The man smiled as he nodded and dropped a handful of pecans into the folded hem of his sweatshirt. He exhaled as he bent down and watched his breath condense before him in a cloud. "Like pennies falling into a piggy bank." He answered.

The man – Jim was his name – had been picking pecans deep into the furthest recesses of his memory. When he was still very young, his Gran had taken him to a small metal building beside the place where the railroad tracks crossed Patin Dike. There, he had hefted two grocery bags full of pecans onto a great ceramic scale, like an offering to a seated idol. The scale had been nearly three times his height and bore a massive face with a springy red needle. The needle seemed to wobble forever over the final weight.

It must have been a poor year for harvesting pecans, because the forty or so pounds that he had managed to collect were replaced by a crisp twenty dollar bill. After seeing the startled look on President Andrew Jackson's face, he had collected pecans ever since. A crisp November breeze and the feeling of hard shells bulging through the thin soles of his shoes always reminded him of that first primordial moment.

They were slowly making their way along the outskirts of a thick green pasture overhung with rows of pecan trees. Beyond the lines of trees, their small red car sat parked at an incline in the ditch beside a shoulderless road, Parlange Lane. Their faded blue Chevy Chevette sagged towards the hatchback end with the weight of buckets filled with the striped nuts. The field stood near a bend in the road that cars inevitably took too fast. Jim's wife, Anne, had a childhood friend die on this road, not far, maybe another mile, from where they were standing. It was a memory that Anne kept safe and buried. There were sharp whipping sounds as cars flashed by. Away from the road, beyond the lines of trees, the field curled gently upwards into a levee, beyond which lay the swampy outskirts of the Mississippi River.

Anne shivered in her red down vest. There was a nip in the air, but only very slight. They were both preoccupied by the same thought. It was the same thought, it seemed, they always had these days. A child. Anne and Jim were nearing their first anniversary, and they still had not conceived. All their friends seemed to be getting married, and all of them seemed to be returning from their honeymoons pregnant. Anne and Jim had also wanted a honeymoon baby, but it just hadn't come. It still hadn't come.

Though Jim was an only child, to his everlasting disappointment, Anne was from a large family. That was one of the many reasons why Jim had fallen in love with her. Anne was one of six, and she had been born from a family of large families. All of her uncles and aunts had been exceptionally fruitful. It was almost unnatural, Jim thought, as he counted Anne's cousins at their Mamou's annual Christmas party. There were hundreds *and hundreds*. At least, this seemed unnatural to Jim who had grown up in the tractless wilderness of suburbia with so many other only children – if people even decided to have children.

"We're doing this for the baby's college fund, right?" Anne asked.

"Not that I think he'll – I mean, *they'll* – need one, but yes." Jim answered with a wink. Jim liked to pick pecans along Parlange Lane because of the rumors that had always swirled about the plantation. Most people kept their distance, because of the dark clouds that had long hung over the place. Jim had mostly ignored that sort of talk in favor of the rumors of treasure. It was told that the matron of Parlange Plantation, after catching word that the Union Army was marching through the area, had ordered her slaves to bury three trunks of gold and silver coins. Two of the trunks had been recovered, but the third was never found.

"You think all your babies will be geniuses like you, don't you?"

Jim flushed at this and his smile faltered. But his smile flared up again, as he said, "Maybe not geniuses, but *nerds*. Like us. A whole bunch of them, too."

Anne batted her eyelashes at him, playfully. He smiled at her and reached down to grab a small clutch of pecans. As he did, he started humming *dummm-de-dum-dum, dum-dum-dum*. It was "La Vie en Rose." She had played the record of it on the night they had started dating, when she had finally relented to his proposals. He had loved her first, and he never let her forget it. She had played it that night on his uncle's pier, which she had filled with candlelight. He had grabbed her hand and kissed her on the cheek, but they had not kissed for real, that is, on the mouth until their wedding day. They had waited for Father to say the words, "You may now kiss the bride." It had been the fulfillment of a promise Anne had made to herself long ago. Afterwards, they had danced to "La Vie en Rose," their first dance as Mr. and Mrs. David.

"Now, now, you're getting a-head of your heels, Mr. David." Anne's sly expression faltered as Jim nearly doubled over laughing. "Oh," she said. "I did it again, didn't I?"

"Another Anne-urysm," Jim whispered, barely able to breath he was laughing so hard. It was the term Jim had coined for Anne's peculiar talent for mixing and inverting idioms. Jim loved this sort of thing about Anne. Mistakes that he would be so embarrassed by, she bore with such grace and charm. He had even taken to writing down some of her best lines, like "you're gonna kick yourself in the foot" and "that hits the nail on the hammer."

Any further laughter was suddenly squelched in Jim's throat as his ears pricked up at the sound of a quick gasp. It was Anne. He turned and saw her standing at the bucket of pecans where she had been emptying the can of her tool. She stood perfectly still, like a startled bird. Jim turned quickly to see what had stilled his wife.

There was a man staring at them. He was standing on the far side of the road, just inside the tight line of trees that hemmed in the narrow roadway. Jim had no idea how long he had been standing there, just watching them. The man was dressed in a black coat and a black suit and wore a starched white shirt buttoned all the way to the neck. As he watched the man, Jim could feel a tightness grow in his own throat as his eyes followed the line of buttons to the man's neck where the collar seemed impossibly tight, though the man wore no tie.

As his eyes reached the man's face, Jim suddenly understood why his wife had gasped. The man's mouth was not right, and his eyes filled Jim with a terrible sense of foreboding. They would later ask themselves whether they had seen a mouth at all, or whether the man had been maybe missing a mouth or just the lips. They would decide later that night, even though they could not remember the man's face, not exactly, anyway – that they just knew he had no lips and that his teeth had been impossibly long, as though the roots themselves had been exposed. However, even these shared memories would fade unnaturally fast.

But it was the eyes that made the two young people question the reality of their happy life. Staring into those eyes, Jim's world felt paper thin. He could not say if the whole eye had been black, like those of a bird – a raven – or if it was the sickly white of the rest of the face that had made the eyes look so dark. To Anne, the eyes looked wet and bulging, like goggles. They were like two protruding pools of viscous tar. They swirled like eddies in a river, but did not pour from the head, though the otherwise sickly white face was marred by flecks of splattered tar.

There was a sudden, deathly screeching far above their heads. The two found that their minds resisted looking away with great force. Had the sound overhead been any less shocking and terrifying, they felt they may never have looked away. When the two young people did look away, the image of the man's face was left imprinted on their retinas. The negative of the man's face was even more ghastly for the pure whiteness of the empty eye sockets in the sea of blackness. The man's face was superimposed into the overcast sky, as they looked skyward. They searched the sky nervously, but found nothing, though the sound of feathers was distinct and close, as close as the screech had been.

Jim's mind was overcome in a flash. He was hardly aware of the rush of oncoming memories, when his conscious mind succumbed to the bitterest moments of his childhood. He was suddenly at the side of his father's fishing boat again, watching and waiting for his father to resurface. Watching and waiting. Watching and waiting. It was the day his father had drowned. He had dove into False River and never resurfaced. His body had never been found.

Jim's mind suddenly cleared again, and they were both searching the sky for the sound which had seemed so close. "There," Anne said pointing. Though the sound seemed almost at their faces, the bird was across the field beyond the levee. It was a white heron. As they watched, the bird was snatched out of the air by an arm of dirty river water. The mucky water suddenly filled with bright red strands of the bird's blood, as its body was crushed within an ill-formed fist. When Jim remembered it later, he thought he had seen a neck of water with a mouth and fangs.

When at last their eyes darted back to the figure across the road, he was gone.

"Jim?" Anne asked.

"No, no, it couldn't be." The young man answered, pulling his wife to his side.

Even as the images faded from their eyes, the echoing cries of the heron changed, growing lighter. It changed into the cry of a child. It was a baby crying in the woods. Jim could feel his wife in the crook of his arm. He could feel her body moving towards the sound even before he was sure of what he was hearing.

Jim's arm tightened around his wife's shoulder, as though she might float away like a bundle of birthday balloons. "Let's get out of here," he said, giving his wife a gentle tug. But Jim could see the sound working on the young woman.

"But what about the pecans?" She said, letting her arm drift backwards absentmindedly over the bucket of pecans. As she did it, her whole body remained aimed at the sound of the child crying. The sound was coming from within the woods on the far side of the field.

"Forget the damn pecans," Jim said, as the floodgates of fear finally opened in his belly, mixing there with boiling anger.

"Don't curse." A flutter of disappointment crossed the girl's face. She said it as though waking from a dream.

"I mean it. *Anne*, let's get out of here."

The woman grew suddenly willful. "We are *not* leaving that baby."

Jim's face reddened with the madness of the situation. "That's not a baby, *dear*. There's something wicked out there or across the street. Don't you get that? What's wrong with you? Snap out of this! Somehow we've stumbled across hell's doorstep while innocently collecting pecans – perhaps while illegally trespassing – but whatever, nothing inviting *this*. We're getting out of here, and we're going NOW." As he finished, Jim grabbed his wife's hand and yanked.

The next thing Jim knew, he was again staring into the sky. His wife's slender, delicate forearm turned suddenly into a rod of iron. His wife's sudden immobility jerked him violently backwards and he slammed into the earth on his back. A wave of delirium swept over him along with the first pangs of a concussion. "What the –?" Jim said rubbing his head, as he picked himself back up.

He reached up for his wife, but she was already halfway across the wide field. Had he blacked out, Jim wondered. She was beside him only a moment ago.

By the time Jim had caught up with her, she was into the woods. It was about this time that Jim realized that his wife was not here right now, not exactly, and if he didn't break whatever trance she'd stumbled into, something very, very bad was about to happen. Jim scanned the woods around them. He took one cautious glance through the woods to his left, where he could just see the outline of the road. There, beyond the black of the asphalt, stood an even darker figure whose head glowed sickly white.

"Uh, honey?" Jim approached his wife from behind. She was standing still in the open woods with her back to her husband. She made no indication that she heard his voice. She didn't move at all. Jim reached for her shoulder, but hesitated. What if he turned her, he thought, and it was not his wife. What if she had *his* face? The man in the road. The one whose lips had withered away, which he knew but could not see. My God, he thought, what if he turned her to him, and she had *no* face.

Jim realized that he had this chance – this one moment – when he could leave. He could just turn around. He could almost hear the idea being whispered into his ear. He could just turn around and leave. Yes, he'd be leaving his wife to almost certain obliteration before the howling hounds of hell, but he would be free. It would be easy, so easy. So good. She would, in fact, want him to do this for her. Just make like a good boy, the voices were whispering, and we'll pretend none of this mess ever happened.

Just then, he was back in a place he had long forgotten, or at least that was what he told himself. He was just leaving school. The bell had rung. There was a chill in the air. It was that miraculous time, when freedom and excitement was so thick you had to brush it away from your face. It was the beginning of Christmas break. He was walking home from school warmed by the thought of Amy Claire Ryan. She had smiled at him that day, igniting embers of hope that she may like him – *like* him, like him.

He was threading his way along the path beaten between the chain link fence behind the recess courts and the dark, untended brambles that lay beyond. His mom had told him so many times to walk home along the sidewalk, but this way was so much *faster*. Besides, all the kids did it. The path was strewn with must have been a hundred years' worth of cast off candy wrappers and cigarette butts. This was also where the older kids hung out when they ditched.

Behind the recess court and the chain link fence, where the fence disappeared into the darkness of the woods beyond, he heard something. It could have been a strangled cry for help. He imagined himself as Lieutenant Theo Kojak. Just another day in the NYPD Eleventh Precinct – "Counselor, you tell your client to behave, or he's a prime candidate for a get well card."

He strode back to that dark place. The roof of the school's tool shed overhung the fence just there, and it was dark. So dark. "Hey you," he called out to the empty darkness. He sucked at his imaginary lollipop. "Get your damn hands off her!" It was then that Jim's younger self realized he had not just imagined that muffled cry earlier. The darkness was not empty, but rather filled with a hulking figure. Jimmy's eyes widened even as his pupils dilated adjusting to the dark. The figure swung towards him out of the darkness. It was Mitch Bowers, or "Hackface" as the kids called him when they were sure they were far, far away from him and safe. Hackface said something to him, but all he heard was a snarl and the throbbing of his pulse above his ears where his glasses rested. Jimmy thought for an instant that he had startled Hackface while he played with a doll, thus bringing down wrath upon himself. Hackface was nearly sixteen and still mouldering in the seventh grade. Jimmy knew that he had a touch of mental disability, but playing with baby dolls like a little kid was –

Jimmy shook violently when he realized that it had been Hackface's massive size that had made it look like a baby doll. It was no doll hanging from Hackface's meaty fist, it was a girl. It was – oh, God, no – it was *her*. Jimmy felt a warm sticky wetness spread across his pants leg. It wasn't because he stood in the shadow of the monster. It was the infinite potential of the moment he had pined for and dreamed about. Here was the moment to rescue the damsel, *his* damsel: Amy Claire. It was that same potential which now drained out of him, as he realized he had no strength, no courage, not even a voice to scream out and save her. It was what he saw in Hackface's eyes – his intent and what he meant to do to the girl. Things Jimmy had only guessed at. It all made him small. His reality ripped apart then like torn paper. The girl looked at him. The one who had smiled at him, igniting a whole world of light and possibility, looked at him now with fear and pleading. Jimmy could see that dead leaves were stuck in her hair. She was screaming silently for help, for *his* help. Words were whispered into his ear.

8

He ran. He turned and ran. He could hear the girl's muffled screams behind him and he pounded them away with his feet beating across the sidewalk, the same sidewalk his mom had been nagging him about. He did nothing. He ran straight into his Gran's shed and hid there behind the stacked lumber until long after sunset. Nothing ever happened. He never saw Amy Claire again. He heard when he returned to school, that her parents had decided to move away.

The rush of the memory faded. He was back with the pecans – back with Anne. Here, again, he could almost see Hackface's broad back and misshapen face rising from the mounds of dead leaves beyond Anne, the love of his life. His ears were again licked with the same yellow words. "Just walk away. Let it be." "This can all be over, if you just walk away." He heard it all at once, a thousand whispered excuses.

Forget "almost." He could see Hackface himself now rising from the black rot of the forest floor. He wore the same red flannel shirt with the same torn sleeves. They reached for his wife. Soon, his wife would be hanging like a baby doll from his arms with dead leaves in her hair. Only now, the red flannel shirt was melting away. The colors of the plaid bled together, each growing darker until Hackface wore only black. Hackface rolled back onto his haunches with jerky, animal-like movements. Hackface's broken face stretched and melted, too. Soon, it was only the mouth that Jim could see. A widening snarl without lips. Maybe the lips had been eaten away by rats. Maybe they had just rotted away. The thing's jaw dropped impossibly far from its skull. It was then just a waiting mouth in a black suit. There was a sound of chattering teeth, but the jaws were only widening. The impossibly white collar had snapped. It was then that Jim realized what it was doing. It was waiting between his wife's legs. It was waiting to devour something – a baby. But that's impossible, Jim thought, his wife would never, *could* never –

The dust of a thousand broken dreams suddenly erupted from the darkened corners of his mind. Jim roared not from his throat but from somewhere inside his bowels. The sound screamed from his belly, bypassing his vocal cords entirely. In the moment when Hackface's slimed arms or this new thing's widening jaws would have reached around his wife's soft lavender sweater, Jim did not run. He plowed into the thing, reaching his long fingers around the ridges of the thing's lower jaw, lifting it by its mandible and slamming its now-shrunken, vestigial arms and exposed spine against the round trunk of a cypress tree.

Jim stood over the disappearing carcass of his childhood nightmares and the stuff of entirely new ones. He was panting and shivering as adrenaline coursed through his veins. He realized that his wife had shifted from the delivery position and was staring into a cradle of leaves. He could hear a baby crying there, but he could only see the leaves.

"Come on!" He half-screamed, as he stood bent over and panting. Whatever had just happened and why, he had no clue. But Jim found that when he tugged at his wife's arm, she was soft again, and not the inflexible iron statue. He grabbed her and ran. She screamed as she was pulled away from the impromptu manger. Together, they caught a last glimpse – which was also Jim's first glimpse – of the wailing child. The child's scream seemed to splinter into hundreds of little pieces, which scurried into the undergrowth.

And as it disappeared back into impossibility, the baby said six words.

The Defense of Ivy Williams

The Tafts' maid stood frozen inside the home's wide bay window. A man was staring at her from the far side of road. He wore a black suit and starched white shirt, which looked gray against his flesh.

The woman fit, in every respect, the stereotype of a Southern maid. The Tafts were well-grounded in their stereotypes. Her name was Ivy Williams, and for the last hour she had been shifting her weight from one foot to the other. The tight white shoes that the Tafts made her wear were too small. She could feel blisters welling up against the insides of the shoes, making the shoes even tighter. Her pinkie toes, especially, burned like a pair of hot pokers.

But for the last ten, maybe twenty, seconds, she had forgotten entirely about her feet, her arms and legs, as well, for that matter. Her head swam and could not be turned from the face of the man who stood across the road. He came nearer. His leg brushed against the front fender of her beat up 1979 Ford Escort, which she had parked in front of the house against the Tafts' express wishes. Had she not been transfixed by his horrible eyes, she would have noticed that his pants leg collapsed completely inward when it brushed against the car's metal bumper. In a moment, he had crossed the street and was resting white swollen fingers on the short picket fence which wrapped the front yard.

Ivy could hear whispers humming just outside her ears: "Let me inside, Ivy." "I'm coming to you, Ivy." "Ivy, where are the butter pats?" "Would you get the door, dear?"

Had the Tafts' grandchild not chosen that exact moment to start wailing, Ivy felt she might have lost herself in those whispers, as down a long, dark hallway. She clapped her hand to her chest in fright at the sound of the child and blinked. When her eyes snapped back open, the man at the fence was gone.

When she was halfway up the home's narrow servant staircase, the blazing pain in her feet returned. Ivy thought about her daughter, Aricka. She often did this at work when pain bloomed in her feet or during one of Mrs. Taft's ferocious tongue-lashings. She and her daughter had moved to St. Maryville, Louisiana from their home in Gloucester, Mississipi not long ago. They had moved to escape Aricka's father, a massive man most people just knew as Kiki. Aricka was not yet ten, but was just emerging from childhood cerebral palsy. Her father had shaken her when she was two, because she had knocked over his can of Schlitz. The seizures started not long after that. Ivy would have fled – should have fled, she would tell herself – before then or at least as soon as he hurt Aricka, but Kiki was a savage man and the seizures had scared her terribly. There was no money for medicine or doctors. Aricka would have grand mals almost hourly for the next several years. Ivy could barely leave her side, so they were forced to live like slaves in Kiki's trailer. Ivy had prayed and prayed, and eventually her daughter's small body had quieted, though she would always walk with a heavy limp. Ivy escaped with what little money she had managed to hide from Kiki late one August night. She had stolen Kiki's truck, and she knew he would pursue them relentlessly, if only to recover his truck. She had ditched it near the Louisiana state line, where she was sure it would be found, and she and Aricka had hitchhiked the rest of the way.

Eventually, the winds had carried them to St. Maryville. It was a place Ivy had never heard of. She had made sure of this. She knew Kiki's fury would extend to her family, and Kiki would know instantly if their ignorance of Ivy's whereabouts was real or feigned. From time to time, Ivy sent back unmarked postcards to her momma. They had been able to re-start their lives in St. Maryville. Ivy had stumbled across an old friend from middle school, D'Laika, almost as soon as she arrived in town. "Dee" didn't have much to offer, but Ivy and Aricka were able to sleep on her couch for as long as they needed. It was Dee who had helped Ivy find a spot at the Taft house, after the Tafts' baby was born. It would be Dee, only Dee, who would later speak up for Ivy's innocence.

With every step she climbed, Ivy winced with pain. The servants' staircase was narrow and without handrails, so she pushed against the walls on both sides to steady herself. This helped little when she was carrying up trays of food, or – God help us – the babies. There were deep grooves worn into the middle of each wooden step, bearing the imprint of two hundred years of climbing and descending servants and nursemaids. In this cursed house, not a few of these lives had ended grotesquely.

"Hush now, baby-child. Ivy's coming. Ivy's coming." The maid peeked her head around the door to the baby's room. It wasn't horror that swept across Ivy's face then – not yet, anyway – but bewilderment. The baby was standing up in his crib, holding onto the bedrail. This should not have been possible. It *was* not possible. The baby was barely three months old.

The only way a baby that old could be standing along his crib-rail, barring highly advanced motor skills, would be for someone to lift the baby and hold him steady just there. Ivy knew this, but there were no arms and no hands holding the baby. That she could see.

She had heard the other maids speak of the mysteries of this old house. Never seeing anything out of order herself, though, Ivy had dismissed their superstitions. She had tried.

The baby was crying as if it had been long-abandoned, and his screams were growing hoarse and erratic. Its entire body was shaking. His little fists were white, curled tight around the rail of the crib. No, that was wrong. Only one of the fists was clenching the rail. The other arm was lifted above the baby's head and was swaying at odd angles. All these things might have been fine, and Ivy might have handled all of them. She could have suppressed this new strangeness along with all the other oddities of the house. She could have, that is, if not for the line of red dots creeping across the baby's onesie. They were like little red ants wriggling through the fabric.

Ivy could not see, then, but could feel the heavy hideousness of what she was watching. There were only the little red ants and the odd stance of the baby who should not have been standing. And then there was more, and Ivy opened her mouth to scream but she could squeeze no sound from her throat.

Teeth suddenly grew from those little red dots. Teeth like needles. The needles grew flesh and bone and a face without lips, and a head appeared atop a black suit. The thing in the black suit was feeding on the baby. Ivy would later say, after repeating her story endlessly to more men in suits – suits with badges – that the last things she could remember before passing out was the sound of the baby's bones crunching inside the monster's throat. And those six words. Six words.

****

Ivy was found only a half hour later by Stephen Myriad, the grocery delivery boy. Stephen knocked and knocked and eventually let himself in through the servant's entrance at the rear of the kitchen. He called for Ivy in the kitchen for about five minutes before following a shadow and some smothered whispers up the stairs and into the hallway. There he saw Ivy lying unconscious on the threshold of the baby's room. Stephen tried shaking Ivy awake, but he eventually caught a glimpse of the splashes of spilled red paint that covered the baby's room. It was not paint, but Stephen was unable – maybe unwilling – to see this for several moments.

There were very few people willing to testify on Ivy's behalf at the trial. The Tafts were an exceedingly cruel family under normal circumstances, but following the gruesome disappearance of their only son, they became a lynch mob. Their money had helped to put and keep the District Attorney in office, so they could choose anyone they wanted to pin the murder on. Stephen Myriad was lucky to escape with his life, such as it became – Stephen grew old in Angola prison waiting for parole that never came. Ivy Williams became the last woman to be executed by electrocution in Louisiana. Somehow, Aricka Williams found her way without her mother.

Though he was shouted down every time he mentioned it, Assistant District Attorney Kerry Rivere insisted on pointing out the oddities of Ivy's testimony. Originally, Ivy had cobbled together a fake story when she realized no one would believe what she had seen. The fake story did not hold up long under interrogation, and Ivy quickly began to understand the darkness that awaited her. She gave up her fake story for the truth, if only because it was easier to remember. Changing her story, of course, didn't do her any favors. But it was too late for that, anyhow.

Ivy had told the officers with their barely-hidden smirks about the man in the black suit with teeth like needles. She had told them how, at first, she had only seen the little red ants of blood, and that the moment she realized the child was being eaten, she remembered no more. Rivere pointed out how, though her testimony varied widely prior to that point, Ivy never wavered in her story thereafter. Every detail became solid. A polygraph was impossible to administer, or should have been considered so, Rivere argued, because Ivy's was overcome with severe anxiety every time she described the man in the black suit.

There always came a point in Rivere's argument, in the defense of Ivy Williams which no jury would ever hear, when his colleagues were no longer able to stand his gaze, when they would start disappearing one-by-one from whatever office or break room they had first gathered in. It was the point at which Rivere compared Ivy's description of the man in the black suit to that given by a newlywed couple who had been attacked about the same time Ivy had fainted, but at the opposite end of the parish. In an obscure police report, Jim David explained how he and his wife had first seen a man in a black suit across the road from where they had been picking pecans and were later attacked by a man with a matching description. Both Jim David and Ivy Williams had described the same man in a black suit without lips and impossibly long teeth, and both – at this point Rivere would always pound his fist on the nearest desk – *both* independently described killers with a taste for a very particular kind of cannibalism. "And," he would say, always closing with the same line, like Muhammad Ali's phantom punch that downed Sonny Liston, "each account ended with those same six words."

Miss Tee-Eva's

Sometime after Ivy's conviction and sentencing, Main Street St. Maryville had again quieted. One cool fall morning, Deputy Vin Dabadie heard the first rumblings of the breakfast which had not quite filled his belly. He had parked his squad car facing toward the intersection of Main and New Roads Streets, where stood the idiomatic one stoplight of the town. Actually, St. Maryville had four stoplights, if you counted those on Hospital Road and Highway 10. Officer Dabadie had parked beside Florrick's Jewelry in the parking lot of the Barrett Insurance Company. Behind the insurance company, the ground dipped sharply down to Latterday's and Lesel's restaurants which overlooked False River. Ahead of him lay the intersection, and – what had caught his eye for the moment – Miss Tee-Eva's.

Miss Tee-Eva's shared a block with an empty lot, the LaCour Building, and another restaurant. The cinder-block building was painted with fresh shades of mauve and pink with blue-gray triangles scattered here and there. While the outside might have reflected an advancing aesthetic, the inside was bedecked with dark brown wood paneling and filled with linoleum covered tables.

Miss Tee-Eva had originally run a small praline stand in the French Quarter of New Orleans, but a terrible hurricane had led to her relocating upriver to St. Maryville. She had begun in St. Maryville selling pralines for a quarter apiece – add a bottle of Coca-Cola for another quarter – to the lines of cars waiting along the levee for the ferry which passed back and forth from St. Francisville.

16

Miss Tee-Eva would still pack up her yellow Volkswagen Beetle with pralines and bottles of Coke for the long lines of cars and trucks that formed in the early morning and after the five o'clock whistle. But for the rest of the day, Miss Tee-Eva and her daughter ran the diner at the corner of Main and New Roads Street, where she always had hot red beans or gumbo ready for the lunch crowd, as well as small foil tins of sweet potato and pecan pies. She also always had a fresh pot of coffee brewing. This was what, at the moment, was distracting Deputy Dabadie.

He toggled his radio and holstered his sidearm as he stepped out of his Ford Ace patrol car. He absentmindedly tried shutting the heavy door gently. He always felt sheepish taking a break in such a stereotypical fashion. Only he would not be having coffee and donuts, but rather coffee and sweet potato pie. *There was a difference*, he insisted to himself, shaking his head. *Besides talking to Miss Tee-Eva is just good police work.* And it was. The woman had her finger on the pulse of the city. She was a central conduit for gossip. Though no one knew it, as yet, it had been Miss Tee-Eva's information which had led to as many as three separate drug busts over the years.

The only other person in St. Maryville to offer such advice on a consistent basis was Mr. "Cigar" James. Mr. Cigar operated a gas station and wrecker service on the other side of the train tracks from Main Street. Bud-D was always the police and sheriff's offices first call after a traffic wreck. Mr. Cigar never failed to profit from his good deeds. His businesses always did well, and he was known to always carry large sums of money on his person as he distrusted banks. He was never mugged, though, because it was also known that his wallet had a derringer sewn into its lining and Mr. Cigar was itching for the opportunity to use it.

Miss Tee-Eva slid open her glass window. Her little diner had started as just a kitchen with a walk-up counter and a few banged-up aluminum picnic tables. Never wanting to disown a part of her business that had proved profitable, Miss Tee-Eva had decided to keep the walk-up counter with the sliding window into her kitchen. Usually people just came on inside the diner, but there were still some who preferred to lean against the worn wood planks of the counter and maybe carve in an initial or two.

"Don't say it, don't say a word! I knows just what you want, Officer. The *usual* – potato pie and black coffee!"

"Usual?" Officer Dabadie blushed, casting furtive glances about him. "I don't have a – have a – yeah, that'll do me just fine, Miss Tee." He leaned familiarly against the counter and scanned the comings and goings of Main Street from behind the twin mirrors of his sunglasses.

"That'll be two quarters, Mr. Officer." She said as she slid the sweet-potato pie in its wax-paper sleeve and white milk glass mug of steaming coffee across her wood-plank counter. "I just loves quarters. Listen to them just drop in my money bucket," she said as her aging black hand extended from inside her window to collect the coins.

"Thank'ya, Miss Tee." The officer said as he dropped the coins in her hand with a clink. "Mind if I stand under your awning for a spell?"

"Not at all, chèr. That's good for business! Keep those quarters rolling in."

"What you know, Miss Tee?" The officer asked as he stared down at the smiling orange sun announcing "Good Morning" which was stamped across the coffee mug.

"Oh, I knows a little of this and that. Maybe a little more or little less, depending. I tells ya this much. My floor ain't never got the shakes like this'n before."

"Hmgh?" A grunt escaped the officer's mouth which was filled with sweet potato. He took a long sip of coffee to wash it down, and said again. "How's that?"

"The *shakes*." She repeated. "My pies ain't settin' right, because of all the ground shaking."

"Miss Tee? What'd'you mean? There's no work being done 'round here – certainly no earthquakes."

"Maybe is and maybe it ain't, but I knows what I knows."

"Shakin', huh?"

"Sho is. And it's coming from under there." She hooked a curled thumb backward through her window toward the building behind her own: the LaCour Building.

"That building?" The deputy choked on a bolus of sweet potato. A thought stirred in his mind, as a few bits of the pie blew out from under his moustache. "Ain't nobody been in that building since the hardware shop shut down," he said coughing.

"Tha's not all. I've always been hearing queer sounds from thataway. It's in the pipes!"

The deputy was silent for a moment. He was stuck trying to grab at that thought. It had almost skipped his mind as he was coughing. It was something someone had told him, and he had no idea why he should be remembering it now. It was that Assistant District Attorney, he thought. *Rivere. He told me to look out for anything strange, out of place.* Dabadie cursed the attorney under his breathe for not being more specific.

"Well, tell me," Officer Dabadie asked trying to change the subject to something more productive. "You know anything 'bout ol' boy back there, what's his name? Spinner, I think."

"The Guichet boy?" Miss Tee-Eva let herself be distracted. "Oh, I shouldn't say much. Just small jobs right now." Their conversation gradually ebbed away, and finally ended when a pack of kids came walking up. Miss Tee-Eva also sold sno-cones for a quarter, and the kids would soon be leaving with cherry red-ringed lips or blue tongues, depending on the flavor. Miss Tee-Eva sold five delicious flavors, or so she had painted on the cinder-block.

By the time Officer Dabadie had returned to his squad car, he was just in time to miss what happened next on Main Street.

El Arca

A line of people were crossing Richy Street headed towards St. Mary's of False River for daily Mass. This wouldn't be unusual, except that they were all holding hands like a daisy chain. As they passed Chère Mama's restaurant, the windows rattled with people waving at the passing daisy chain. They were like a small parade passing through the town.

Suddenly, one of the links in the chain broke away. An older woman responded to the disturbance instantly. "Wally!" She called out. "Anne, can you go get him?" The woman, Ms. Peggy was her name, wore a close-cropped wig and glasses which made her eyes look like raisins hidden in the depths of her pudgy face. She was in the middle of her last battle with cancer, and had decided that she would keep working with the El Arca community. She had worked her entire life and she wasn't going to stop now just because it was ending, thank you very much. She was an uncommonly stubborn and wonderful woman, though few had taken the time to notice it.

"Blue car, blue car go down the street there," the middle-aged man who had broken free of the daisy chain cried out as he ran, half-stumbling towards the Christmas displays on the small lot owned by the city. This man's name was Wally. He was wearing a tight-fitting blue and red Superman t-shirt. He insisted on wearing it most days, especially church days. He was approaching fifty with the black and gray stubble to prove it – he would only allow Miss Peggy to trim his beard on Sundays – and had the mind of a four-year-old. His entire vocabulary consisted of about thirty to forty words, most of which

20

concerned the illusory blue car that was always winding its way down the street.

"At least he's not running into the street this time," Anne called back to Peggy. Anne made a small hourly wage working in the El Arca community, and it had helped support her and her husband Jim during his law school days. Truth be told, Anne would have worked at El Arca even if they hadn't paid her. The St. Maryville El Arca consisted of three houses where people like Peggy and Anne took care of persons with disabilities. Peggy was a "team member," that is, full-time staff who actually lived with residents like Wally. Team members did all the things for the core members, those with disabilities, that mothers do for their children and adults would shiver to do for one another.

"Wally did it!" An older black woman called as she, too, broke the daisy chain to point at the other man's antics. This was Miss Frannie Pearl who always carried the purse of a grandmother in one arm and a Raggedy-Anne doll in the other. She was very good at making friends and friendship bracelets, one of which was currently adorning, though nearly threadbare, Anne's own ankle. Anne had grown up in St. Maryville seeing Miss Frannie stroll down the street with her purse and doll. Most of the kids that Anne had grown up with loved to imitate Miss Frannie Pearl and the rest of the El Arca community, but Anne had always known that one day she would help care for these people. She was surprised to find out, not long after she had started volunteering at El Arca in high school, that what she gave and could offer was far less than what she received in return. Though the work could be hard – washing, clothing, feeding, repeat – Anne felt Miss Frannie, Wally, and the rest were doing more for her than she did for them. So it often was, Anne would come to realize, with the forgotten people of the world.

"Ms. Frannie Pearl! Where—?" Miss Peggy called out again. "Oh, Anne. You've got to help me better than this."

Wally had thrown his belly to the ground and was lying sprawled before a small weed with a yellow flower.

"What've you found there, Wally?" Anne asked crouching low beside Wally. He was soon trying to get back on his feet, and Anne eased in to help him. Wally's legs were very small and frail. It would not be long before such walking outings such as this would be impossible for him without a wheelchair. Wally also drank too much coffee and too little water, a habit that was soon to catch up with him.

"Rose for the lady," Wally announced as he raised aloft his plucked dandelion.

Chris was laughing and shifting quickly from foot to foot as Wally rejoined the line. "But Charlie," he was saying, "Star-Kist don't want tunas with good taste. Star-Kist want tunas that taste good!" Chris held Jonathan's hand, who was holding Miss Julie's hand. Miss Julie held a particular fondness for potato salad.

Chris was about Anne's age and loved Kolchak the Night Stalker, Rocky Balboa, and inquiries concerning Adam's apples. Anne had long become acquainted with Chris' inquiries concerning her figure. Peggy had long suggested that Chris and Anne work in separate houses, given Chris' over-fondness for her. Chris was autistic and his known idiot savant talents included an eidetic memory for the contents of television commercials, as well as the contents of any book he had ever seen, whether or not he had opened it, though this small detail had gone unnoticed.

Jonathan was another middle-aged man, but unlike Wally, whose mental retardation was likely the result of being mistreated in the womb or soon thereafter, no one knew for sure; Jonathan had Down's syndrome. He carried a teddy bear with him most places, including daily Mass, and rarely spoke. If the front door to 114 Pennsylvania Avenue, however, was not shut properly, Jonathan would heave one choice expletive from the insides of his toes straight out through his lungs.

Miss Julie was approaching seventy. She had suffered a traumatic brain injury as a little girl when someone had left her locked in a car one hot Alabama afternoon. She could still be very charming, though, even flirtatious. And she loved potato salad. Whoever was serving dinner on potato salad night would quickly learn just how persuasive she could be.

Peggy's shoulders visibly relaxed, as Anne repaired the daisy chain. But just as Peggy turned back toward the church, now so close at hand, and the parade resumed its happy march, a flashy yellow limousine slowed to a stop beside them. It was not a stretch limousine, just a Jaguar with a broad back seat. The car was painted in garish colors with heavily tinted windows.

Anne had begun the mental process of raising her hackles, anticipating that some rich slob was about to taunt her friends. Peggy, it seemed, was still headed towards the church thinking the daisy chain was still following her. Anne's mind was suddenly racked by a series of impossible realizations. Maybe it was because Anne had been distracted by the car's hideous colors, and now she could see there was even a red racing stripe. Maybe it was because what had just happened had been so far from Anne's perceived circumscription of the possible.

Anne realized first that the yellow Jaguar had not slowed to a stop of its own will. Before she had even realized the limo had slowed to a stop, the daisy chain had broken once more. About the time Anne had finished mentally raising her hackles, the daisy chain of the disabled El Arca members had reformed their line across Main Street, executing a blockade of the roadway with something approaching military precision.

About the time Anne understood that something very odd was happening, there was a fluttering of opening and closing car doors. Peggy, meanwhile, was still leading the way to church.

The occupants of the car were faster than Anne's optical nerves were able to process. They were standing toe-to-toe with Wally and the El Arca gang in the space of a quarter-blink. They wore black suits, black hats, and black sunglasses. They also wore black monogrammed scarves which covered the bottom half of their faces like bandit bandannas. Even so, Anne could see their faces were paler than she had previously thought possible. She thought she could even see the delicate throbbing lacework of blood vessels embedded in the translucent skin. It may not have been, Anne thought later, that the skin was pale, but that she was able to see straight to the curved bone of their skulls, muscle and sinew notwithstanding. At the time, Anne had space for just one thought and her heart filled with an icy coldness. She had time enough to remember the man's face in the roadway: the horrible visions, if they were visions, she and Jim had had while picking pecans.

It was about this time that a clicking noise started at the back of Anne's throat, as the electrical impulses of her courage began trying to fire but while speech was yet impossible. There was a moment when the two lines just stared each other down. Then, one of the men in black suits fumbled at the edge of his scarf. The hand was encased in a shining black leather glove. Otherwise, Anne was sure she would have been able to see the sharp bare bones of their metacarpals and phalanges. The man pulled down the scarf to reveal a nose that might have been eaten away by rats or the slow rot of time. All that remained were cavernous nostril holes. It moved its neck close to Wally's face with the quick darting movements of a bird. Then the man in the black suit took a long languishing breath near Wally's neck and mouth. Wally's scent must have startled the man badly. Anne wondered incongruously whether Wally had allowed her to brush his teeth that morning. The man reeled backwards and glanced quickly at his black-suited brethren. Actually, Anne now noticed, they may not have been all men.

"Blue car go down the street there!" Wally suddenly blurted out, and then his thick arms suddenly raised the limp dandelion flower above his head like a broad sword. He brought the flower down against the man's skin. While Anne was about to wonder at the outrageous mismatch of the threat and the weapon of choice, the black suits stumbled backward in fear racing back to their car at their incredible speed. But even such speed could not save the man who had taken such a luxurious draught of Wally's musk. Wally brought the flower down against the side of the man's head, and Anne realized that Wally meant not simply to strike the man with the flower, absurd as it may sound, but to slice him in half with it. With one long slicing motion, the dandelion swept down through the man's head, into the suit, and exited somewhere beneath where the hip bone was supposed to be. The top half of the man toppled backwards from Wally and had dissolved into a slimey dust before it hit the pavement of Main Street. Only an untidy mess of suit, scarf, and accoutrements remained.

Then Anne must have blinked or shifted her head just slightly, as one might do during a dream, and the whole scene vanished. The daisy chain was again lined up on the street. They were milling around a bit but still in good order. The yellow car, the empty suit, it was all gone. Wally's dandelion, Anne saw, was beginning to hang limply from his fist, as the plucked weed gradually lost water pressure and wilted.

Anne put her hand to her head and exhaled sharply. She realized she hadn't breathed during the whole incident. Even now, she was starting to question if any of it had actually happened. It was about this time that Peggy finished crossing the street onto church property and looked backward to see she was alone. A shocked cry escaped the woman and she slapped her worn handbag against her hip. "Anne!" She yelled with eyes wide even behind her thick glasses. "We just don't have time for this! Where's your head? The church is *this* way."

School Mass

The students from St. Joseph High School shuffled into the church building, class-by-class. They were mostly filling in from the side doors, as these were the closest to the school. The El Arca Community came in through the front doors which faced Main Street. They sat at the pews along the back of the church. It wasn't that the El Arca team members were embarrassed at the core members' sudden and often very loud outbursts during Mass, or even embarrassed by the waves of snickering from the school kids. El Arca sat at the back of church because it was closer to Main Street if an ambulance needed to reach one of the core members, which was not an uncommon occurrence. Also, there was better wheelchair access at the front.

Ms. Cathy Ranger's seventh grade class was the last class to shuffle through the east side doors of St. Mary's. Mass was scheduled to start at 11am, so they were still five minutes early. The less time the children had to wait before Mass, Ms. Granger believed, the less time they would have to be idle. Ms. Granger was the natural enemy of idleness. She had already caught one of her seventh graders, Chris Nolen, carving his initials into the pew in front of him. Every time she went to Mass, now, she was greeted by Nolen's graven mark: "C.J." *What a little jerk*, Ms. Granger had thought. *But honestly*, she scolded herself, *it wasn't really all his fault*. Chris had the absolute shortest attention span of any child she had ever taught. Chris had probably – as he had begged Ms. Granger to believe – carved his initials before noticing what his hands were doing. Other than that incident, Ms. Granger had few behavioral challenges from her seventh graders. They all called her "Danger Granger," based on a reputation she had carefully cultivated over the years.

Though Ms. Granger might have worried about being the last of the classes to arrive, she needn't have worried because Monsignor Regenswood operated entirely on his own schedule. He was a truly holy and virtuous man, but somehow punctuality and memory had been omitted from his long list of gifts. He was known to miss entire marriage ceremonies. The bride and groom and all wedding party would just be looking around, tapping their feet, asking themselves what was missing. So the wise would always leave him plenty of reminders.

Mass did eventually start. Students had been selected to read and serve at the Mass, as per the usual. The commentator, a freshman named Elton DiSalvio, shuffled out carrying a green binder of readings which looked extra large between his small hands. He walked past the altar without bowing, and was stopped in his tracks by a sharp clicking sound. This was Ms. Alice Boudreaux who directed the children's choir and helped make sure – really all the teachers and teachers' assistants were needed for this – the Mass flowed smoothly. She knelt hidden in front of the first pew, whispering hushed instructions and clicking. At Ms. Alice's fine-tuned clicking, Elton reversed course dramatically back to the altar, bowed clumsily, and finished shuffling over to the lectern. There was a green-carpeted, to match the rest of the altar, box behind the lectern for the students to stand on while reading; otherwise, they would simply disappear behind the faux-marble painted stand.

Once the commentator had finished a few lines of announcements. He scurried off the altar to a flurry of clicking noises. He returned sheepishly a moment later to bow again at the altar. This cued Miss Lindy at the piano at the front-right of the church. Behind her, about a dozen students in neat lines sang the opening hymn and a line of altar servers, the lector, and Monsignor processed up the main aisle of the church. These students were mostly all practiced hands, so the level of decorum noticeably improved with Monsignor's entrance.

Sam Pitre, a new kid – a sophomore – had just moved from around the Houma-Thibodaux area. He had been asked to be the lector that morning, as his old principal had sent him to St. Maryville with a glowing report. After Monsignor had finished the opening prayers, Sam Pitre walked up to the altar, bowed, read clearly and precisely, bowed at the ambo, bowed at the altar and returned to his assigned seat with nary a click from Miss Alice.

The second reading was an ordeal for poor Elton, though, sending Ms. Alice into a fit of clicks. Eventually, Elton ran back into the sacristy crying with Ms. Alice running after him. After a stiff moment of awkwardness, Monsignor nodded at Sam Pitre. Without missing a beat or a bow, Sam took care of business on the altar. It was no easy task for him, either. The large lectionary had been knocked off the ambo by the hapless Elton and all the ribbon bookmarks had rustled out of the pages. But, somehow, Sam had managed seamlessly, like the Vatican's own majordomo. Though he could not see it since he was sitting in the front pew, he was receiving a favorable round of whispers from the students and teachers seated in the pews behind, especially among the girls.

There was one girl in particular – she had already caught Sam's eye in the short time he'd been there. Though discreet about it, she had already taken notice of Sam, as well. Her name was Erin Bellefontaine. She was a tall, slender girl with long blond hair, and she moved with the grace of trained dancer. Most every one of the boys had a crush on her, but she had never dated any of them seriously, just accepting an invitation now and then to prom.

There was one student, however, that was less than thrilled by the new kid's early rise in popularity. This was Rock Bellelo. He, too, had an eye for Erin and had been pursuing her since the fifth grade. It had been in the fifth grade, as well, that colleges had started pursuing Rock for their offensive lines. Rock was massive and could have just as easily been called Boulder. He'd had to contend with a five o'clock shadow since elementary school. Being unusually thick in limb and mind made him fine bully material. His father had cut and run not long after Rock's birth, and his mom, who worked multiple jobs including waitress at Tee-Eva's, had been left to fend for the family. Rock usually walked home from school to an empty house where his mom had left him a can of franks 'n beans for supper.

Rock made up for all this by beating up whatever smaller creature wandered into his path, and he was about to make sure Sam Pitre wandered into his path.

St. Joseph High School was just two blocks from St. Mary's Church on a lightly trafficked road so the students just walked back *en masse*. The idea was to walk back to the school single-file, but clumping and scattering was inevitable. It was pretty easy, even for a kid as big as Rock, to get lost in the shuffle. Rock knew that the students who helped with Mass walked back on their own or with Ms. Alice. With very little strategizing, then, Rock was able to position himself easily for an attack on the new kid.

Fifteen, maybe twenty minutes after Mass, like clockwork, Sam Pitre, Elton DiSalvio, and five or so other kids, including Erin Bellefontaine, rounded the chain-link corner of Poydras Street and First Avenue. There was an overgrown Azalea bush there which all but blocked the sidewalk. The teenagers returning to school would have to go single file at this bottleneck, and there Rock lay in wait.

Though Erin hadn't been a part of the Mass, she had nevertheless found a way to hang back with the others. She thought it might be a good time to meet the new boy. While still twenty paces from the azalea bush where Rock would spring his trap, Rock could just hear the sound of their voices.

"Don't feel bad about it, Elton," Sam was saying. "Maybe we could work together on it."

"What's the point?" Elton was saying. "They'll never let me up there again."

"Maybe they will and maybe they won't. Somehow, I think you'll get your chance," Sam said, knowingly. "And so what if you had a bad start? If you keep trying and getting better, people will forget how it used to be."

"Really? Think so?"

"Oh, yeah. I'd set my seal on it."

Elton looked up at Sam a little confused at the expression. The younger boy could see what Sam meant from his eyes, though, and nodded vigorously in agreement.

"Do people talk a little funny in Houma?" Erin said, smoothly cutting into the boys' conversation.

Sam's heart twisted a bit in his chest. His lungs were suddenly incapable of carrying enough air to sustain human life, or so he felt, and his mouth dried up despite the humidity. Nevertheless, the boy kept his head. "I don't remember mentioning where I moved from–?"

Erin felt a wave of heat flash across her face. She had been listening for details about the new boy, and he had caught her in it. She smiled slyly, as though a secret had just been shared between them, but gave no other outward sign of her embarrassment. "After you," she said, as the sidewalk was narrowed suddenly by a giant azalea bush.

"M'lady," Sam said bowing regally and returning the girl's sly smile. "After *you*."

Sam followed the girl around the azalea bush. His mind was swimming. He had caught an intoxicating whiff of her perfume as her hair caught in the wind. *What would he say next? Come on, man! Think of something. Gotta be good. Or, at least not dorky or—*

Rock hadn't really decided what his first move would be. He decided he would just see what felt right. When he saw Erin walk past him and the azalea bush, he suddenly realized who the new boy had just been flirting with – his girl! *Oh, he's gonna* GET *it!* The heat of his blood rushed to Rock's head. The slurry of rage, heat, and hormones erupted within the boy. When Sam finally rustled past the azalea bush, Rock took a wide stance and shoved Sam. Sam was launched into the street, tumbling tail over tea kettle. He landed as a sprawling mess and skittered across the rough asphalt. He managed to land so horribly that patches of skin were torn from every side of him. He skinned both knees, ripping holes in his new uniform pants. His face, too, looked like ground meat.

It wasn't fear or pain that quickened Sam's pulse at that instant. It was anger, the ferocious, gnawing kind of anger that can only arise from facing humiliation in front of a girl. If Sam had been aware of himself in that moment, he would have realized the significance of the anger boiling over inside him. The sheer power of it could only mean that, in just the space of a few seconds, he had begun to care very deeply for this new girl. They had only exchanged a few sentences, but the hook had set.

It was ironic given the way the next few moments would affect the rest of his life that he saw Rock in that moment and not Erin. If he had looked at Erin just then, he would have seen the look of concern in her face. Erin's face was betraying her. She wasn't looking at him as a friend, but as a lover.

Rock stood with his fists on his hips, surveying his cleverness. He thought he'd add a dash of wit to his show of force, saying "Watch where you're walking, fag-boy!" The rest of the kids had grouped around to watch how the event would unfold. Word had traveled fast up the line of kids walking back from Mass. Entire grades were now pouring back out of the school.

Elton made a move to run and get a teacher, and Rock quickly clapped one maw of a hand on Elton's frail shoulder. The boy's chest and shoulder felt like a trapped bird inside Rock's meaty hand. "Why don't you just stay and watch, Elmo? Wait, no – let's practice your bowing!" Rock roared in laughter, surprised at his own cleverness.

"Bradley, no!" Erin screamed. She was the only one whom Rock let address him by his first name.

Satisfied that Sam had bit it hard on the asphalt, at least enough for a little multitasking, Rock shifted his attention to the boy who was finding it as hard as ever to bow. "Forgot how to bow, again, Elmo? Let's see if I can help." Rock wrapped his meaty hand around Elton's neck now, and was making perverse movement with the boy's head.

Erin pushed Rock away from the poor freshman. Rock laughed crazily at this, lapping up any attention – good or bad, usually bad – that Erin directed his way.

Elton and Erin had provided just enough of a diversion for Sam to dust himself off and regroup. The crowd of kids watching would later describe Sam getting back on his feet in much more dramatic terms. Manny Trudeau of the seventh grade would say it was like he was "blown" back onto his feet, "like Dracula rising out of his coffin or Bruce Lee."

Sam needed little time to formulate a plan of his own. He was very good at thinking on his feet. He always seemed to find his way out of a jam, whether by talking his way out of it or by the acute application of force.

There was plenty of space between him and Rock. He dipped his head and bull-rushed the much larger boy. Sam aimed his head for the side of the bully's knee. Hopefully, Sam thought, he would have enough time afterwards to fall back a few paces.

With a soft crushing noise, the impact of Sam's head bent Rock's knee joint into an odd angle and the boy went sprawling against the chain link fence with the crash of disturbed metal links.

But Rock, too, recovered quickly from his tumble. "You're gonna pay for that, fags. Gonna make you eat grass."

Sam had the time he needed to walk back a few paces. He watched the rest of his plan unfold before him with lethal cunning. He noticed a bright yellow Jaguar was hurtling down First Avenue. The hoard of kids had somehow managed to avoid blocking or even setting foot on the road. Sam saw that this yellow Jaguar was hurtling straight for him and would soon hit him, *if* he didn't move. But Sam saw more than that, too. He saw that the car would hit him at precisely the same spot in the road that Rock was about to flatten him. Rock, too, was hurtling at Sam, running Sam's bull rush with his own. The idea flashed into Sam's head with cold ruthlessness. He rattled off a quick 5-4-3-2-1 in his head and dove forward and to the side of Rock.

Rock had already left his feet when he realized how the boy had out-maneuvered him. In the space of a millisecond, he turned his head to see Sam's hasty leap. It was then he finally saw the approaching yellow Jaguar.

Rock's head collided with the side of the sedan, even as Sam's head had collided with his knee moments before. If Rock had leaped any sooner, he would have likely been decapitated. As it was, though, he hadn't fared much better from the impact.

****

Word had traveled fast that there was a fight between Rock and the new kid. When Sam had finally looked up from Rock's still body, he saw nearly the whole school had swarmed into the street. At least it seemed that way. Before any of the teachers could respond to the commotion, much less push through the crowd of kids that now filled the street, Rock had been taken away. Strange-looking men had filed out of the yellow car and scooped up Rock's unconscious body.

Once he was again aware of his surroundings, Sam began to look for Erin, but she was lost in the crowd. The teachers had hurried Sam off to the school's front office. They told him to sit down on one of a line of molded yellow plastic chairs. He could hear worried voices and the sounds of an argument coming from inside the principal's office. A group of some younger kids, probably middle school, were staring at him slack-jawed from outside the office's reinforced glass window. Sam watched as these kids were shoved out of the way by some of the older kids, who also wanted a turn staring and pointing at Sam, who was squirming uncomfortably in his yellow plastic seat. Elton eventually wandered into the office, too. He came and sat next to Sam, not knowing what else to do.

Sam would spend the rest of the day in his bedroom. He had been sent home from school, there to wait as the principal and staff and later the police continued to argue over his fate. The school wouldn't say if he had been expelled, but they apparently didn't know what else to do with him. Sam's mom didn't know, either. She just waited between her front door and the phone, hoping for some direction. She thought maybe Sam's dad could sort it all out when he got home.

Sam, too, was sitting and waiting. He sat at the edge of his new bed, half-heartedly trying to find something to distract himself with.

Unlike the rest of the house, which was still full of boxes waiting to be unpacked, Sam's room looked normal. Very few of Sam's possessions remained in boxes, except for one on the top shelf of his closet. He had unpacked and put his room together within a day of moving in.

His Star Wars collection – he was just beginning to feel too old for this – had already been arranged meticulously. Most of it stood in neat rows of Imperial Stormtroopers, droids, and bounty hunters along the bench of his window seat. At the center of it all was a little cardboard diorama.

His parents had had the foresight in the winter of 1977 to buy Sam an Early Bird Certificate Package. However, to the horror of children everywhere, there were no Star Wars toys that Christmas. Sam had survived the nationwide famine through the strength of his imagination. Nevertheless, he had rushed home every day for two months to check the mailbox to see if

Kenner had at last mailed him the figures he was owed. Eventually, a small white box arrived. Inside was a gleaming white tray – as white as the hallways of Bespin, the city in the clouds. Inside the white tray had been four bagged action figures: Luke, Leia, R2-D2, and Chewie. It was the beginning of a beautiful friendship.

The four figures were set in their place in the diorama and soon joined by Han, Darth, and the others. This sat at the center of his collection, which had grown quite a bit from the original four. Somehow all of it had survived the intervening six years of childhood adventures in immaculate condition.

The rest of his room also bore signs of the galactic struggle. The Millennium Falcon hung from fishing line from his ceiling. He had moved to his desk to fiddle with his current project. It was a scale model of the Degobah swamp. Sam had quickly adopted Yoda as his favorite – this Louisiana boy obviously preferred the character who lived in a swamp to those from desert planets.

Sam's plan was for Yoda to be able to use the Force to lift the X-wing out of the swamp, just as in the movie. He had accomplished this with a lever arm and some more fishing line. He would just pretend the muddy water part, though, as he kept his X-wing in far better condition than Luke did.

Sam's walls, too, unlike the bare walls of the rest of the house, were covered in posters. Strangely, none of the posters had anything to do with Star Wars. He had a *Dark Crystal* poster, if only for Frank Oz. At the center of his wall was his *Lord of the Rings* poster. It wasn't that he particularly liked the animated movie; it just didn't compare to the books. It was the poster's artwork that struck him. Gandalf towered over the little bite-size hobbits. Not only was he holding the massive sword, Glamdring, but Gandalf was shooting bolts of power from his forefinger. It seemed to Sam like the good version of Emperor Palpatine's finger-borne lightning bolts. Sometimes he lay awake imagining the great, final battle between the Emperor and Gandalf.

These were things he would never dare share with Erin or any girl, for that matter. Even now, what he had felt for her was beginning to make all these things in his room seem faded. For now, though, his thoughts had turned to which elven maiden Erin looked like. She was tallish and blonde, so she was probably more of a Galadriel, he thought. No, he didn't like that – he had no use for Celeborn. He wanted her to be an Arwen, the kind of elf that fell for a mortal man, such as himself. Rock, on the other hand, would have to be a balrog. *No! Better yet,* he snickered to himself, *a troll.*

Later that day, Sam heard his mom return the handset of their phone to its cradle. It had been the police. Rock's mom had decided not to press charges. She knew how her son was, what he had become since Rock's father had left them. This was not the first time Rock had been in a fight, not by a long shot. She was usually the one waiting and wondering whether the other kid's parents would press charges. It gave her a little relief, despite everything, that she could give another mother some peace.

Rock would spend the rest of that month in the hospital healing from a skull fracture and a swollen brain. He had also crushed a vertebrae in his cervical spine.

Rock's mother was unable to pay for the medical bills, but the Jaguar's owner, whose employee had been driving, graciously offered to pay the bills and even attend to the boy. The owner, it turned out, was actually a doctor of some sort. He made nightly visits to Rock's hospital room to check on his recovery. Despite all the medical attention he received, Rock would die a month later under mysterious circumstances unrelated to his head wound.

The Ship

Isaiah Harris had decided a long time ago that if the early bird gets the worm, then a really late worm gets the fish – or something like that. He shut off the engine of his white 1975 Ford Courier compact pickup truck, on the driver's door of which was hand-painted "B&G Janitorial." A floor polishing machine and an industrial vacuum stood tall in the bed of his truck and an assortment of spray bottles and empty Coke cans rattled around them. Isaiah let his truck coast down the steepest hill in all of St. Maryville. It had been at least three hours since the last car left the parking lot adjacent to the St. Maryville docks, where stood Lesel's and Latterday's Restaurants. Isaiah didn't want to chance disturbing the fish, which he believed had spent the last several hours slowly creeping back toward the docks after all the noisemakers had left.

After gently gliding into a parking space, Isaiah softly pulled up on his emergency brake with a whisper of a crank. Slowly, he slid out of the driver's seat and out the door. He took a whole extra minute dropping his tailgate, because it squeaked something awful. He pulled out his fishing poles. He had one with a reel and one crappie pole – pronounce "croppie." The crappie pole was just a bamboo pole with a fishing line and lure attached to the end of it. He set these poles on the asphalt of the parking lot next to a 5-gallon bucket. Isaiah would either sit on the bucket or fill it with water by pressing his chest down on the dock and tipping the bucket into the water. He'd be able to keep his fish alive longer by dropping them in the water bucket.

Isaiah set down his tackle box next to his poles and bucket, and let out a sigh, relieved that he'd made no noise whatsoever while unloading. He turned back around and slammed his tailgate door closed. "Son of a –!" Isaiah growled as the slam echoed across the parking lot and across the lake. "Piss!"

Isaiah shook his head in disgust and picked up his gear. He had lost all pretense of stealth. A hollow sound rang out under the boards of the pier as he walked. Isaiah was not especially tall, but he was thick with muscle. It was rumored around town that Isaiah, while working at Pourciau's Body Shop, had lifted an entire engine block out a car.

He dropped his bucket onto the graying, weathered boards of the pier. The pier paralleled the boat ramp into False River and then made a sharp ninety degree turn toward Lesel's Bait Shop and Restaurant. Isaiah sat down softly, slowly returning to silence. "Feels like a good night for sac-au-lait," he hummed to himself, grabbing the long red-dyed bamboo pole and dropping the casting rod to his side. He rigged up the pole with a bit of live worm he had tugged out of his tackle box, and swung the line out over the water. He secured it in place with the metal handle of the upturned bucket, and went about setting the hook of the casting pole. He would cast again and again with this pole while the tip of the bamboo bent up and down rhythmically.

Isaiah thought that he would just let the bamboo pole do its thing for a minute and hold off on casting. He shivered. "Man," he said rubbing his sides with his crossed arms. Louisiana mornings were typically always comfortable, but not this morning. Isaiah looked back longingly at his white truck, still visible in the half light. He regretted having left his jacket in the cab. He was only wearing an old t-shirt worn thin in the most important spots.

But just then, the tip of the bamboo arched down sharply. It was a sure sign of a bite. A solid bite. Isaiah lifted the cane pole from the grip of the bucket handle with a practiced hand. The soft shine of fish scales gleamed briefly from the dark water. As he fought with the fish, he barely noticed the water beginning to ripple all around him.

Isaiah plucked the fish out of the water and laid it on the wood planks of the pier to remove the hook. As he did though, he noticed that something was wrong. The fish was laying strangely still. Fish don't always flop around noisily after leaving the water, but this was somehow different. Before Isaiah could understand what he was seeing, he heard another thud on pier. And another. And another. And another. It was then that Isaiah finally noticed the water churning with fish.

"What the hell?" Isaiah grumbled. Fish were popping out of the water all over now and thumping along the pier. It was as if they were going mad. Isaiah saw the wealth of fish covering the pier, and he suddenly realized his good fortune. He scooped up his white plastic bucket and began filling it with the fish. It was like being at the Piggly-Wiggly and being told that, for the next five minutes, everything you can put in your shopping cart is free. Isaiah was in the midst of a shopping spree. He darted around scooping up the fish, and forgot to wonder at the cause of it all. It was no matter, though. He would soon learn why the fish had suddenly gone mad.

Isaiah was standing on the first few planks of the pier, and quickly brought the bucket to his chest, hugging it tightly. His eyes were fixed on a figure rising out of the deep blackness before dawn. His eyes darted to his poles, left at the far end of the pier. He snatched a quick look at the Ford Courier parked some distance behind him. He could run away now and still have all the fish. But he looked back to his poles. He was caught for a second looking back and forth.

The thoughts drained from his head. The greater fear soon cleared his mind of lesser fears. Isaiah's eyes grew wide and unbelieving and his veins opened up wide to receive the increased flow of blood from his quickening heart. If he had been a white man, his face and body would have flushed red with the heat of the blood.

The first tongues of a coarse fog licked at his head and rushed passed him, up the hill where the church stood guard. It emerged from the darkness, and Isaiah could just see its outline traced by the sliver of moonlight. Isaiah's jaw dipped a bit. Had he put air to his mouth, he would have whispered a single word: "Pirates."

It was a ship with black, moldering sails, like an ancient widow's pall. It was a triple-masted galleon with the mizzen mast rigged as a brigantine. Isaiah was watching a seventeenth – maybe sixteenth – century ship sail past him, bold as brass. More than that, where had it sailed *from*? The lake was entirely cut off from the main artery of the Mississippi. Though Isaiah was barely aware of it, he could just hear a thin, warbling sound rising from the water.

Though his eyes were fixed on the ship, Isaiah's nose twitched in discomfort. He looked down despite himself. He was still hugging the bucket of fish against his chest. As he watched, the fish liquefied into gore and then rapidly desiccated into crisp skeletons. The smell of it felt like a physical assault, and he stepped backward catching his sneakered heel on an uneven plank. He dropped the bucket, which rolled off the pier with a splash, as he slammed down on his tailbone. Isaiah saw fish mess putrefying up and down the dock. Below, also, fish were rising to the surface. From beneath the perch or sac-au-lait which kept close to the lake's edge, larger and larger creatures were boiling up. There were large bass and ancient catfish. There were unspeakable things, as well, all churning up from the depths of the lake.

Isaiah looked up from his supine position back to the passing ship. Its stern and rudder were now visible. Isaiah squinted into the darkness. The ship's name was written there in long-faded paint that had been partially burned away. He thought he saw six letters. The first letter was an 'E,' and its name ended in 'os' or 'as' – he couldn't tell for sure.

Moments later, Isaiah's poles and bucket were forgotten behind him, as he turned the key in the ignition of his Ford Courier. His tires squealed out of the parking lot, and the truck's small engine bleated up the steep hill towards the church and Main Street. Isaiah's truck squealed again as it turned broadside at St. Mary's and sped down Main Street. Main Street circumscribed the lake until it turned into Highway One which continued its tight course around the lake.

The noise made by Isaiah's truck should have awoken all the homeowners on the lake side, like something out of Longfellow's poem of Paul Revere, but all of St. Maryville, save Isaiah, slept deeply that night. Isaiah wasn't just squealing his tires, but honking his horn, as well. He wanted to wake up the whole town to see what he'd seen. But it was no use. The darkness which rolled out from the black ship like coarse tendrils of fog might well have been the Angel of Death, itself, for the depth of the town's slumber.

Between the houses and sometimes over the rooftops, Isaiah kept sight of the black ship. A thought had lodged in his brain, from where he did not know, he would not lose sight of this ship – not tonight, anyway.

The ship's course curled to the south matching the crescent shape of False River. Though Isaiah's speedometer needle was hanging past forty, he was just barely keeping up with the ship. The ship's sails were full despite being filled with rips and tears and the wind having died off with its approach.

Isaiah could hear soft thuds along and beside the roadway over the sound of his whining, almost mutinous engine, but he couldn't see what was making the sound. The sliver of the moon was the only light fighting the early morning darkness. The night was rarely interrupted by streetlights along Isaiah's road. He thought to himself that there seemed to be a lot of burned out bulbs tonight – and had the stoplight at Hospital Road even been on when he'd passed it? Now that he thought about it, there hadn't been a red, green, or yellow light back there. Not that he would have paid it any mind. *The whole damn world's turning black!* He thought to himself, miserably. It was as if he'd lost himself in one of those nightmare tunnels. He didn't want to be here. He didn't want to be chasing this black specter down the lake. *What am I doing?* He shouted in his mind, but found himself powerless to deny the compulsion of the chase.

WHUMP-*cccrishh!*

Isaiah learned suddenly what the thumping sounds had been. The body of a fat blackbird – those they call castle rooks – crashed into his windshield. A thick smear of dark blood gushed across his line of sight, blinding him from his quarry. He let his foot off the accelerator, and thumbed his windshield wiper switch on and off, on and off, rapidly. The blades knocked the bird inch-by-inch towards the hood, and smeared gaps of light red in the tar of the blood wash. It was no good. Isaiah put his foot to the brake pedal – only the pad of the pedal had long-since fallen off leaving just a stub. The Ford Courier drifted to the shoulder of the road.

Standing on tip-toes at the edge of the roadway, Isaiah found that he'd lost sight of the black ship. He left the truck behind him, and ran down a steep driveway on the far side of the road which fell away through some random fellow's yard to the lake. Isaiah hopped – a little too noisily – the locked gate leading to the same random fellow's pier. His feet pounded echoing thuds along the weathered boards to the end of the pier.

Isaiah leaned his belly and his body over the railing at the roofed end of the pier, like some comical imitation of an Edward Hopper painting. He squinted into the distant darkness, trying to mark the outline of the ship. It seemed at once to be drawing darkness to it and releasing it as the dark, spreading fog. Seeing no outline of the ship, Isaiah instead looked for the darkest spot on the horizon. His eyes traced the ripples of moonlight on the water, until the light seemed to wink out. *There!* It was now just a smudge, maybe a full mile away and hiding in the shadows of the curving shoreline. He thought it looked as though it had stopped – laid anchor, or whatever ships do. He thought, too, that he knew where it had stopped. If he could just notch a landmark along the shoreline. He leaned as far as he could from the railing, squinting as hard as he could …

A door slammed shut behind him. Isaiah whirled around to see a man – the random fellow who owned the property on which Isaiah was trespassing – running towards him holding something in his hands, the outline of which Isaiah knew all too well being a black man in the Deep South. The man was too far away for Isaiah to hear his pounding footsteps. If he didn't move fast, though, he was going to be trapped on the pier by a man rudely awakened in the middle of the night, likely as not with an itchy trigger finger.

Isaiah ran down the pier with his arms reaching high in the air. He knew that a man as big as he was would look mighty intimidating barreling towards you in the middle of the night. Isaiah didn't want his actions wrongly interpreted as aggressive, or else this man might shoot first, think later.

"I'm leaving – I'm leaving. Don't you mind me none!" Isaiah shouted, knowing that the best way to mollify white men was to play to their expectations of colored folk, crudely formed in their minstrel shows.

"Fella, you picked the wrong yard to get high in!"

If this man thought he was on drugs, Isaiah thought better than to mention the black ship he'd been following. *Good God!* What excuse could he possibly come up with to explain himself? Just then God provided inspiration. A bird landed – *PLUNK!* – between them on the pier.

It stopped the fellow with the rifle in his tracks. "What in the hell?" And then, the man was knocked backward by another falling bird. If the bird hadn't knocked him backward, the mounting stench of dead fish would have. Isaiah didn't wait for another opportunity. He saw his chance and ran for it. Going back up the steep hillside and driveway was much harder than coming down, and Isaiah felt like he squeezed five pounds of belly fat out through his sweat glands. He just lay stretched against the door of his truck for a moment breathing the free air. Isaiah need not have worried. The fellow with the gun never looked back once Isaiah hurtled again over the locked gate. He had walked over to the retaining wall that separated his property from the lake. He stood on the stacked timbers for a full five minutes watching the rising tide of dead fish.

Isaiah kept quiet about what he saw that night for several months, but all the while he felt like somebody was watching him. There would be shadows at the edge of his vision. He would turn half expecting to find a man in a suit, but there would be nothing and nobody. Isaiah, for his part, would be keeping watch, as well.

The Young Solicitor

Jim was walking home from the courthouse for lunch. He turned at the corner of Main Street and Pennsylvania Avenue where Deville's Grocery stood and smelled of paper bags and produce. He walked up Pennsylvania Avenue to the yellow house that he had bought for his new bride and they had renovated together. The yellow house, which Anne had christened Honey House, lay across the street from Aunt Charlotte's house, Anne's aunt, and a white house with green trim that Jim's great-grandfather had built. His grandparents and Aunt Bitsy lived in this house.

Jim and his wife had still not been able to conceive a child. The stress of it had worn on both Jim and Anne, though Anne had borne the stress of them both. Jim hadn't had time for stress – after failing the Bar Exam the first time he took it, he'd been forced to support his family on a clerk's salary, tutoring on the side, and studying for the next Bar exam with all the time he had left.

The stacks of flash cards had never left Jim's side. They rode shotgun with him during his long commutes around the 18th Judicial District for the Honorable James West. It just so happened that from the northern tip of Pointe Coupee Parish to the southern line of Iberville Parish, the 18th JDC was the longest in Louisiana.

Jim had dammed up the shame of not passing the Bar exam on the first try. Louisiana was the same state that the legendary counterfeiter and con-man Frank Abagnale had passed the Bar Exam without ever attending law school. Though all together it was one of the hardest exams in the country, the Louisiana Bar Exam could be passed sections at a time. That's what old Frank had done.

Jim had tried not to notice when all his buddies from law school would talk about their new experiences as practicing lawyers, though Jim had had plenty of experiences of his own as Judge West's clerk. The trial of Ivey Williams had been the worst of it. He had, of course, known she wasn't guilty. He'd known that what had happened to her had something to do with what happened to him. He'd done what he could. He'd spoken to – that is, *pestered* – Judge West more than a man without other job prospects ought to have dared. It never did any good. Jim succeeded only in changing the way Judge West looked at him. For all his efforts, Jim had only succeeded in increasing the number of resumes crossing his desk for his own position.

He had retaken the Bar Exam not long after the incident that happened when they were picking pecans. Jim had mostly repressed the whole encounter. He had to – a far grimmer prospect lay before him than the phantoms and the visions. Not passing the Bar *again*.

It was entirely possible, and Jim knew it, that the letter could come today – the letter on which Jim knew his whole future would hinge. The results of his second attempt at passing the Bar.

The front door of Honey House opened the instant Jim put his key to the lock. Anne swung the door open and jumped into Jim's arms. Jim held his briefcase and coat up in awkward surprise.

"Jim!" Anne said through choked-back tears. "You did it, Jim. You did it."

Jim pushed his wife backward and let his things drop to the concrete stoop of their house. He just looked at her, reading her face. "The letter came?" Jim asked, slowly catching up to reality. "You read it? What did it say? Let me see it!"

"I have it right here." Anne said, reaching into the folds of her apron. She gave it to him, biting her lip excitedly and brushing the loose strands of her hair behind her ears. Before Jim could finish unfolding the letter he had so long been waiting for, Anne again threw her arms around his neck. "Jim, you did it! I love you, and you *did it!*"

"This is just, it's just…" Jim said, trailing off and reading the letter behind

Anne's back. "I just can't believe it. I'm in shock. But I can feel something. It's like a whole car sliding off my back."

"Mine, too, Jim!"

"Have you told anybody?"

"No, I thought I wouldn't be able to wait, but I did."

"I've gotta tell Gran; she can finally stop worrying. This'll add years to her life. Go, make your calls, Anne. Let me listen in on the other line when you call your mom, okay?" Jim was dragged into the house by Anne, who also collected the items he'd dropped. "Anne! My love, *we did it!*"

"We did, honey. We sure did. Now, I get my husband back, too."

Jim threw himself onto the living room couch. "I'm just gonna lay here for a minute and let it sink in."

"You do that, baby." Anne said unlacing Jim's brown Oxfords. "I've got lunch ready for you."

"What's this?" Jim said reaching for another envelope that was sitting on top of their coffee table. The envelope was made out of a fine linen and cotton material. His name had been drawn in tight script on the envelope in dark black ink. There was no other address and no postage.

"That came just after the mail. It was dropped off."

"Did you see who brought it?"

"No, but, gosh, I'd forgotten all about it in the excitement of it all – I'd have sworn I heard hooves clopping down the street afterwards."

"You mean, it was brought by horse and buggy?"

"Yes, Jim." Anne smiled. "The eighteenth century just rang our doorbell."

Jim turned to his wife and wrapped her up in his arms. He smiled at her and brushed a few loose strands of hair behind her ears. "Sometimes, I think I must forget how beautiful you are."

She looked down and smiled. "You're making me shy." Then, tapping on his chest, "Come on. Open it. Let's see what's inside."

"Yes, ma'am." He said, kissing his wife on the forehead. Turning the envelope around, he said, "Would you look at this thing?" Jim and Anne stared in wonder at the red wax seal at the back of the envelope.

"Are those initials?" Anne asked.

"If it is, it looks like the central letter is a capital 'T' with an 'o' tucked in on either side."

"Oliver O'Malley Templeton?" Anne suggested.

"Or, Oscar Otis Trumpkin?" Jim smiled.

"Or, Octave O … oh! Just open the thing!" Anne laughed, tugging at Jim's arms.

"Okay, alright." Jim tugged lightly at the wax seal, hoping to open the envelope without breaking the seal. He succeeded, but not without making a mess of the envelope.

"Why didn't you just break the seal?"

"Breaking a seal just felt ominous. You know, like in *The Seventh Seal,* that Ingmar Bergman movie, and Revelation?" Jim put the envelope on the mantelpiece. Jim and Anne had what would be considered an odd choice of mantel decorations. Above the mantel, there was an icon of the Holy Family which they had bought during their honeymoon in Rome. Along the mantel, there were statues of the saints, a collection which Anne had been building for Jim every holiday. There was also at the center of the mantelpiece a first class relic of St. Martin de Porres, which, while Jim had still been a teacher, had been given to him as a gift by one of his students. Jim tucked the envelope behind one of the saint statues, and slowly unfolded the letter. It was just a single page. The paper was of the same kind and quality as the envelope.

Anne leaned her head against Jim's shoulder and they read the letter together:

> My friend Jim,
>
> Congratulations to you on your admission to the Louisiana Bar of Solicitors. I trust you will soon know the reward of hard work and perseverance. I am writing to engage and retain your services for a series of transactions as I acquire new residence in your charming town. I am anxiously awaiting meeting you. Sleep well tonight. At three this morning, my business associate, Mr. Edward Teach, will be back to deliver you to my new home. You may thereafter decide to forgo your current employment, as I assure you,

you will be generously compensated for your services to me. I ask – nay, require – only one thing in return: your strictest confidence. You may tell no one of our arrangement, except for your wife, Anne, as I anticipate she is currently at your side reading this letter, as well.

I trust that I will enjoy my stay in your beautiful land. Again, my warmest congratulations –

I remain,
LaColt
Principal, LaColt & Teach

They just stared at the letter for a few minutes. They each read it a couple times, not knowing what else to do. "Well," Anne finally said.

"Yeah, 'well' about does it," Jim answered. "How the hell did this LaColt guy already know I'd passed the Bar?"

"Maybe he just knew the day results came out, and assumed you'd passed."

"He seems to know quite a lot about us – both of us: he knew your name, that you'd be standing next to me. It was like he was speaking to us directly. None of it makes any sense. But I guess I'll learn more when I go see the man."

"Whoa … wait." Anne said, going to sit at the edge of the couch. "You mean you're actually gonna meet this guy, ride in this *carriage* at *three* AM? What are you, Kolchak the Night Stalker?"

"A job's a job, Anne." Jim said, leaning back against the mantelpiece. "It's not like there'll be clients knocking down my door five minutes after I've passed the Bar exam *and* having failed it once already. Plus, it says 'generous compensation' – I have to at least see what this is about."

"Jim, I just don't know. I've got a really bad feeling about this. And *three* AM? That's the …"

"The witching hour, I know. Strange choice of day to be sure. He sounds foreign; maybe he's still getting used to the time over here."

"Who is this guy?" Anne said, holding her head. There was something, a memory, stirring at the edge of her consciousness. It was like she had just forgotten something extremely important. "Can you ask to postpone your meeting? I think we should pray about this first. 3AM is the opposite side of the clock from 3PM, the hour of Christ's death."

"I *know*, Anne. But just think about it – how would I even postpone? It's not like we have a phone number. We don't even have an address."

"Call the operator. She may know."

"No, Anne. I've got to do this." Jim said, turning to lean both arms and his head on the mantelpiece. "This could be really good for us, for our *family*, and I'm not spoiling a first impression by being disagreeable."

"You may not want to sound too eager, either, Jim."

"I'm supposed to just play it cool? A starving young lawyer without prospects?" Jim had sprang from the mantelpiece and spoke with his arms spread wide in question.

Anne looked away, straightening the pillows at the far back corner of their hand-me-down couch. "Well, I can see there will be no talking you out of it."

Jim watched her then, but she wouldn't return his stare. He smiled a little at the corner of his mouth. Anne stood and walked across the room, after having fixed her pillows. She walked right up to her husband and straightened his lapel. Then she gave a little tug at his tie. "Kiss me," she said. "Just in case I never see you again, kiss me."

He did kiss her. He kissed her long and good, as he had not kissed her for over a year. In that kiss, they could both feel layers of stress melt away, like the scales of St. Paul's eyes. Jim didn't return to work until later that afternoon, and when he did, there was still a little smile at the corner of his mouth.

The Witching Hour

Jim was waiting under the light at his doorstep when he heard the clop-clop of horse hooves coming down Pennsylvania Avenue. Anne was awake. She'd woken up around midnight and hadn't been able to fall back to sleep. Not long thereafter, Anne's stirrings had awakened Jim. He had tossed himself out of bed towards the coffee pot, and managed to stumble back into the bedroom with two steaming mugs of coffee. Anne had called it a coffee date; she usually did. Dread irrevocably returned to their minds, however, as the hour drew nearer to three.

"Can you see it, Jim?" Anne asked from behind the screen door. She was clutching it as if it were a battlement. "Does it look like a Nazgul? God, this must've been how Farmer Maggot felt. Jim, you can't go. I won't let you."

"Anne, was that fog there a moment ago? You've got to be kidding me; this is like something out of a movie."

Together, they watched as pale rings of light formed around the streetlamps in the growing fog, and the sound of hooves drew nearer. They thought they could dimly guess a dark shape in the mist, ten yards or so ahead, approaching the end of their gravel driveway.

All of a sudden, a team of four horses charged into the driveway and the air filled with the sound of hooves grating on gravel. They pulled a gleaming carriage. By the light of the street lamps, Jim could see the horses and carriage were coal-black. On it sat a large man, who seemed to crouch in the driver's bench, wrapped in a great black cloak and hood, so that only his boots showed below. The rider's face was shadowed and invisible, except for a black beard and a pair of very deep set eyes. The eyes gleamed bright when they turned toward Jim, and they seemed to shine red in the electric streetlights.

"Give me your luggage, sir." The driver said to Jim, who was suddenly keenly aware of how he was cowering at the corner of his porch.

"Jim!" His wife whispered urgently. "You can't do this. This is too weird. Get back in here before one of those things gets you … Jim!" She tried pushing the screen door back open, but found it wedged tightly into the door frame and immovable.

"I don't care what all this crap is. This anachronism or nightmare or whatever. It's a job. And God knows I need that right now."

"I love you, Jim." Anne whispered again from behind the screen. Jim looked back at her, and blinked as a splash of something came through the screen door. "Holy water is all. Come back to me."

"I will." Jim promised. "I love you, Anne."

"And buckle up, if that thing has buckles." And then she added in a whisper, "For the dead travel fast."

Jim handed the driver his briefcase. "Is this all, sir?" As he spoke, the driver smiled, and the street light fell on a hard-looking mouth, with very red lips and sharp-looking teeth, as white as ivory.

"Y-Yes," Jim stammered. "I had assumed I would only be gone an hour or two."

The hooded figure nodded. "Very good, sir. So you may." And then with exceptional alacrity, an uncommonly long arm reached down to where he stood on the porch, gently removed the bag from Jim, and settled it atop the carriage. Then, the arm returned to Jim. The driver's hand caught Jim's arm in a grip of steel and lifted him up to the driver's seat beside him. The strength of the driver must have been prodigious, because he scooped Jim up and placed him at his side as a girl might return a fallen doll to a tea party.

Then the driver cracked his whip and clucking sounds issued from deep within his long beard. The carriage and team of horses retreated mournfully out of the driveway.

"It is a chill night, young master. My Lord bade me keep all care of you."

Jim nodded beginning to shiver. Whether it was from the chill or otherwise, he couldn't say. He thought to himself, *If your Lord had wanted you to take care of me, why am I sitting on the driver's bench?* He had seen the deep leather seats – empty seats – within the carriage.

"If you need it, sir, there's a flask of tequila under the seat. That should keep you warm enough."

"No, thanks." Jim laughed nervously.

"Is it a religious proscription?"

"What? Oh, huh. No. I'm not Baptist, if that's what you're thinking. I'm Catholic; we haven't stopped drinking since Cana."

"A Christian," The driver remarked from deep within his cloak. The driver turned minutely toward Jim, and he felt like he was being sniffed. More than that, Jim felt like his scent was being studied, analyzed.

"Yes. What of it?" Jim answered, having quickly shifted from meek and insecure to steely. Words flickered across his sleepy mind: *Always be prepared to make a defense for the hope that is within you.* But something told Jim that such a pursuit would be hopeless. Jim was chilled by the feeling that no common ground existed between himself and the cloaked man. That maybe an abyss separated them. It made his prepared defense of his faith, which seemed so strong when shared with his wife, seem like a silly, inconsequential thing.

"Begging your pardon, m'lord. I meant no offense."

"None taken," Jim began to smile, but was cut short. They were now passing through the heart of town and under one of the few traffic lights that hung in the town. It was drifting harmlessly through its colors, and the carriage driver apparently felt no compunction to heed its stops and starts. Not that it mattered, the street was empty of any movement besides the changing colors of the streetlight. The town seemed to click between different colored lenses.

"I just think it odd that a man, a Christian man, could think that he could overcome the weight of his own sin." As the driver spoke, the traffic light clicked from yellow to red. At that moment, the driver turned to Jim, and he could see reflected within the driver's pall two red eyes. They were passing now by the LaCour Building and the church was growing tall before them.

"I don't think *I* can overcome the weight of my sin." Jim answered, looking up to see the church's steeple swelling in the moonlight, untinged by the traffic light. "It's Christ, of course, who paid that price with his own blood."

The driver then decided to veer away from Main Street and took the side street on the far side of the restaurant, Chère Mama's, which shared an alleyway with the LaCour building. They passed a quiet laundromat and the church was obscured from Jim's view by tall dark trees. The horses' hooves echoed less in the tighter space of the side street.

"Ah, yes." The driver said. "The perfect man, who paid the perfect price with his perfect blood. Perfect satisfaction, yes?"

"Yes." Jim nodded, slightly taken aback by the man's unlooked for insights. The way the driver spoke, the light of the great deeds seemed to pale.

"But what of the inperfect man? Not Christ, but what of his Christians? What of you? What have you done for this man, who did everything for you?"

"I've fasted, I've prayed, gone to Mass, done good works. I'm trying to be fruitful and multiply."

"And that's supposed to make up for the sins you've committed? Do you think that's even made up for one sin, even the smallest of your sins?"

"Well, maybe just the smallest." Jim considered the question. "And yes, all of them together, in the sacrifice of the Mass and a solid confession before it, of course." Even though Jim was feeling weak under the hooded man's gaze, the words kept coming. They were not the best words, Jim knew. He was no St. Thomas before the gallows.

"Do you understand the weight of sin? One small sin was enough for all mankind to fall, enough for Adam and all mankind bound up within him. It hadn't been the fruit, it had just been a smaller thing, if God had willed that man should just look at Him and not look away. One small dart of the eyes in any other direction, that would have been enough for the whole race of man to fall."

Jim looked away from the deep set pinpricks of eyes, which still shone red despite the long-eclipsed stoplight. The driver took the carriage away from town, and they were soon riding along the lake. It was black with one long streak of rippled white in the moonlight.

"Sir," Jim said. "I see you understand the weight of sin, but do you understand the weight of the Mass? One small sin of Adam and all of mankind fell. But not all, not really. The Virgin was conceived without corruption and so was her Son. And it was enough – I'd say more than enough – that that perfect man didn't look away. It was enough to, not only restore mankind to the place of Adam, but to greater glory. And this happens again and again at every Mass, like someone clubbing the devil in the face again and again and again." Jim smiled, "Now, isn't that a pleasant thought?" His smile grew, surprised at the power of his own lungs next to this chilling man, and then Jim laughed. "I think I just might have a swig of that tequila. A thermos of coffee would be better, of course."

"I think you will do just fine, sir." The voice grated from beneath the hood.

"How's that?" Jim asked, his smile contorting.

"Nothing sir, nothing. Only that I think my master has made a fine choice for his solicitor."

Jim's smile faltered at this, but did not fade completely. He uncorked the brown and tan jug that he had pulled from under the driver's bench, and nipped a bit of the cactus juice from within. Jim coughed a little as the fire rolled up his throat and through his nostrils. "That is good stuff," he said, and moments later he had drifted off to sleep. His head lolled and Jim gradually leaned until his head was resting against the cloaked man's shoulder.

****

Jim awoke when the team of horses drifted from the smooth roadway to a gravel driveway and the grass lawn beyond. "That was some tequila," Jim said groggily.

The carriage began to lurch back and forth, rumbling along the grass lawn. Jim's eyes opened slowly. Gradually, he recognized the huge shapes of trees on either side of the grass lawn. It was an oak alley, he realized. The carriage lurched madly, and Jim's head swung down to look over the side of the carriage. The ground was coated with a film of fog. The horses seemed to be pulling the carriage along the ridge of a cloud.

"It's the roots, young sir. The roots of the oak trees. They've grown and grown."

Jim looked back to the driver, and as he did, he caught side of a ghostly whiteness at the end of the alley. It was a house. "Hang on, I know this place. This is Parlange Plantation."

"Why are you taking me here, driver? Is Master LaColt a guest of the family?"

"Until very recently, yes."

When the carriage stopped, the driver jumped down and turned back to Jim as the fog gusted away from his billowing cloak. The driver rummaged within his breast pocket for a moment, and then removed a bundle of papers with a flourish. He handed them to Jim, saying, "I think you'll find all these in order."

Jim took the papers and looked back at the driver in bewilderment. As he did, the driver closed the small metal door of the carriage lantern, which had been shining forward into the fog as a headlight. As he closed one of the lantern doors and opened another, light spilled across the driver's bench illuminating Jim and the papers he was now holding in his hands. "Go ahead," the driver repeated. "Inspect the transfer of title and associated documents. Then, sign where indicated for the notary. I'll sign as mandatary for Master LaColt. All other signatures have already been provided."

Jim looked through the papers carefully in the lamplight. He touched the papers lightly, as though inspecting an ancient manuscript. All the documents had been written by hand in a careful and measured stroke. Not a one of them was typewritten. Jim admired their beauty.

Jim read and re-read the papers, while the driver had stood by waiting patiently and without moving. "Well." Jim finally said, nodding. "This is all very finely drafted. But what do you need *me* for?"

"There is the matter of the Notary's signature."

"Sure, but why hire an attorney-notary, when the documents were already drafted? A notary would have been more than competent to review the documents."

"That is a matter you will have to take up with the Master. He is waiting for you in the house."

Jim relented without having his question answered, knowing full well that he needed this job and the generous compensation that had been offered. Jim took a pen from the inside of his jacket pocket. It was a fine silver pen that his grandfather, Charlie, had given him when he graduated law school.

Jim took a moment for himself, letting the fact sink in that he was signing his first document as an attorney. And then his stomach lurched. He panicked suddenly. "Oh no," Jim said gravely. "In the rush and excitement of the day and LaColt's letter, I forgot that I haven't been sworn in yet. I don't even have my bar roll number. I can't sign any of this."

"Your number is 15,842. My Master has already seen to that. Congratulations, sir."

Jim's jaw muscles loosened and his mouth hung open. "What?" He mumbled. "But you can't … how could …?"

As Jim jabbered, the driver rummaged around in his other breast pocket. He again produced a bundle of papers, and handed them to Jim. "I trust you'll find they're all in order."

Jim thumbed through the second set of papers without really seeing what he was pretending to look at. He did manage to find the paper with his bar roll number stamped across it. He looked at it, and confirmed the number: 15-8-42.

"Good, sir. Now, if you would finish with the papers. Dawn is approaching and my lord is waiting."

Jim fumbled around with his pen, and managed to scribble his first signature on a legal document. It was sloppy, but his hand eventually remembered its work after the third or fourth signing. LaColt had even seen to it that the documents included a hold harmless form for the young lawyer. Everything appeared to be in order, and Jim handed the papers back to the driver. He thought he might need to indicate the places for the driver to sign, but he quickly saw that his guidance was unnecessary. Against the polished wood of the carriage, the driver stood and signed the documents holding a slim quill in his thick hand.

"Very good, sir." The driver said, leading, almost lifting, Jim out of the driver's bench. The man's prodigious strength was unsettling. "Now, I'll be off and you're to meet the Master in the house." Moments later, he shook the reins and was gone.

Soon, Jim was standing with his leather briefcase slouching against his feet. There was silence except for the sounds of the horses and carriage rumbling over the thick, raised roots of the oak alley. Jim soon felt doubts and fears crowding upon him. *What sort of grim adventure have I gotten myself into? Was this a normal incident in the life of a law clerk? Listen to me: law clerk. Anne would correct me, if she were here. Attorney. Maybe it's all just a nightmare after last night's drinking, and I'll awake at home with dawn struggling through the windows in my bed next to Anne.*

Jim looked up the wide staircase leading up to the veranda which ran the length and breadth of the house and to the wide front doors. He saw that he was not sleeping. From where he stood, he looked onto the dark brick basement and brick columns which were hardly visible in the moonlight. The white staircase, though, gleamed, as did the slim white colonettes reaching up to the hipped roof. Just before him, the house was encircled by a small picket fence. Slowly, he leaned forward, mustering his courage, and he swung open the short gate.

"15,842." Jim mumbled to himself. "It's not bad, as numbers go." He kept an eye on the house, as the hand which was not carrying his briefcase guided the gate back into place behind him. His feet seemed to boom like the cannons of the *1812 Overture* as he mounted the steps one by one.

As he neared the top of the steps, Jim failed to notice that the rhythmic booms of his feet were being matched by another set of approaching footsteps. As he stilled, standing on the veranda, Jim finally noticed the heavy step approaching behind the plantation's great doors. He saw through the uneven waves of the glass window panes the gleam of a coming light. There was the sound of rattling chains and a bolt sliding backward. After the slow creak of a turning doorknob, long fingers curled around the edge of the door and the door swung inward. Light spilled across the veranda, illuminating Jim and a tall old man. He was clean shaven and clad in a long red robe which reached to the ground. His smile was broad and long white hair was pinned back behind his white face. Beneath the folds of his robe, a ruby amulet twinkled from the center of a stiff white collar.

He held in his hand a silver lamp in which the flame seemed to burn without a wick and threw long quivering shadows as it flickered in the draught of the open doorway. The old man motioned to Jim with his other hand and bowed in a courtly gesture. He moved easily, without any hint of stiffness, and said with strange intonation, "Welcome to my house! Enter freely and of your own will, my friend." The old man stood fixed in his bow. Jim, too, was frozen, staring at the man in odd fascination. He wondered suddenly whether it might not be better to drop his briefcase and run madly back down the oak alley, never looking back. He thought he could even hear Anne calling to him in warning, but it was the thought of Anne and the dream of a family which urged him forward. As soon as Jim leaned in, making to step over the threshold, the old man snapped back up and pivoted backward, beckoning the young man. "Good, young master. Come freely, and leave something of the happiness you bring."

As Jim crossed the threshold, the old man moved impulsively, taking the younger man's hand in his own. He grasped Jim's hand with a strength that made him wince. *Like the driver*, Jim thought to himself and shivered for the icy coldness of the man's hand. Jim recoiled at the touch and LaColt did as well. Jim looked away in shame and embarrassment, thinking the old man had snatched his hand back because of him. "Sir," he said. "Your hands, sir. They're cold as the grave."

The old man's gaze never wavered, though his smile grew broader. "Welcome to my home, Mister David."

"Mister LaColt?"

"I am LaColt. Come in, sir, there is a chill to the morning air. There is a table prepared for you, and you must eat." LaColt led Jim by lamplight through a series of rooms. He stopped in a room near the center of the house. The room was dark, untouched even by the moonlight. LaColt left Jim at the doorway with the lamp and glided into the darkness. The old man's white face again appeared in the far corner of the room. Smoke filled the globe of the lantern, and Jim watched as the old man trimmed the wick. The light crept across the room until it fell across a plate of food covered by a silver dome. Had he not been distracted by the prospect of breakfast, he might have noticed the way LaColt's shadow danced its own course along the wall. And many things might have gone differently.

"I pray you, be seated and eat. You will, I trust, excuse me that I do not join you. My diet is too irregular even for breakfast, and I have dined already."

Jim, who had been standing with a hand along the back of the chair, rested the silver lamp on the table and took the seat readily. Though there had been many points along the way when he had lost his appetite, he was ravenous. He lifted the silver dome from its place and looked for a moment at his own face reflected in the curved silver surface. He looked older somehow and worn.

"Allow me," LaColt remarked, as he took hold of the silver dome and placed it on a carved side table. Jim furrowed his brow at the breakfast. He tried quickly to disguise his surprise, but he could feel the old man's gaze upon him. The plate was full of eggs. They weren't rolling around uncooked, but it was odd nonetheless. There were scrambled eggs, fried quail eggs, a poached egg, and eggs hollandaise, as well.

"Eggs it is," Jim laughed nervously.

"Yes," his hosted smiled. "I'm afraid my appetite for them is nearly …" LaColt paused looking around for the right word. "Insatiable," he finally said. "There's wine, as well. A bottle of old Tokay."

"Tokay?" Jim asked. "Not that I'm picky. I've just never heard of it."

"Oh, err. Tokay d'Alsace? It's also called Pinot Gris, I believe."

"Is that a breakfast wine?" Jim smiled weakly. While he ate, LaColt riddled Jim with questions about St. Maryville and Louisiana law and customs. The man's appetite for knowledge, too, was insatiable. After two full glasses of the wine, Jim had almost been bled dry of information. At some point, the old man had drawn a chair beside the room's fireplace. He had first lit the fire, then an incredibly long, slim cigarette. It was like a cigarillo, but even narrower. It reminded Jim of the man's long white fingers, and almost seemed to get lost among them as he held the cigarette aloft. When offered, Jim had politely refused as he did not smoke. "Not cigarettes, anyway."

In the mild haze caused by the wine, Jim studied the lines of the old man's face. The outline of the face was illuminated by the fire and the rest of the face would brighten from time to time as light spilled from the glowing tip of the cigarette. The bony structure of the man's skull seemed overgrown, as though the bone had thickened with age. He had a lofty domed forehead, and his long hair might have reached even to the floor had it not been meticulously rolled and pinned back. The man's brow was prominent and descended into the high bridge of his nose. Jim's mind had grown foggy, and he was struggling to find the right word to describe the man's strange features. *Tourmaline? Aquamarine? Aqua, aqua,* aquiline*! That's it.* Jim leaned back in his chair, resting in his triumph. He began then to notice the man's mouth as it took impossibly long draughts of the cigarette. The ends of his mouth seemed fixed. They curled like twin scars into a cruel grin. The bony overgrowth of the man's skull continued into his teeth, which protruded here and there over his bottom lip. The single most distinguishing feature of the man's face, however, was its utter lack of color.

As Jim looked on, there came a sound of many animals growling near the house. "Listen to them," LaColt leaned forward in his chair by the fire. He finished the cigarette with one last long pull leaving no butt. "Do you hear them? What music they make! The children of the night."

Jim must have looked at LaColt strangely, for the old man added: "Ah, young man, you who dwell in the cities cannot truly enter into the feelings of the hunter."

Rising, he added, "Their voice marks the end of the night, and with it, I must retire. A bedroom has been prepared for you. Sleep as late as you will. I will not return until nightfall."

Jim would have protested, but his mind had grown fuzzier still. He watched as his host receded from the room, and nodded impotently. He was left half-dreaming in a sea of wonders and hypnotized in the light of the fire.

Real Estate

Phyllis Malchaud was leading a gaggle of ladies sashaying down the street at break-neck speed. It looked like somebody was fast forwarding a video of models walking down a catwalk. They were "power walking" based on the best-selling advice of exercise guru Steve Reeves. Phyllis had nearly zoomed right past the windows of her real estate office when a quick sidelong glance revealed that, though it should have been empty and dark, it was not empty.

"It's *only* seven o'clock in the morning," Phyllis shouted in surprise as she came to a sudden halt, creating a pile-up of skinny women behind her. "And it was locked!" Phyllis walked without power to the front door of her office, sidestepping the entangled pile of women she had created. She was clad, as were the other ladies, in a spandex leotard worn on top of a spandex body suit with knee socks pushed down to her white Addidas shoes. No two pieces of clothing were the same color. It was a maddening mix of reds, yellows, hot pinks, and pastels, and all of it shining at a high gloss. They could have all fallen right out of an Olivia Newton-John music video: "Let's get into physical ... let me hear your body talk."

The bells hanging from the front door clanged wildly back and forth as Phyllis slammed the door shut behind her. "If you're an intruder, I'll shoot you. You just see if I don't, rapist!"

A man was sitting in one of the two chairs facing the broad desk at the center of the office. He would have seemed like any other customer, but that he was sitting alone in the dark. There was a briefcase laid across his lap, and his back faced the door that Phyllis had just clanged through. His back was still facing Phyllis, and he had not moved.

Phyllis flipped the lights on, after she was done raving at the unmoving man. She had begun to worry that he was actually dead, as he had yet to make any sound or movement whatsoever. Phyllis thought perhaps that her habit of absentmindedly forgetting people waiting for her in her office had finally caught up with her, that this gentleman had waited for her so long yesterday afternoon that he had had a heart attack, dying from lack of patience or a panic attack or God knows what.

She sniffed the air to check for the stench of decay, as if a body left for dead all night would have a characteristic smell. Instead, there was a sweet, earthy smell which must have been the man's cologne. *He still hasn't said anything!* Phyllis' thoughts screamed in her head, mixed with a sudden rush of emotions. She took a quick look outside the wide office window where she had hoped to still find the other ladies as backup in case something was about to go horribly wrong. Unfortunately, they were off power walking and were probably passing in front of the church by now. She was, given the hour, suddenly all alone except for the unmoving man sitting in the dark.

Then, slowly, the man in the armchair raised his arm and beckoned her pointing a long white finger to the seat behind her desk. An image of the Grim Reaper or maybe it had been the Ghost of Christmas Future appeared in Phyllis' mind. Nevertheless, she found herself doing exactly as the hand had instructed. Slowly, she walked around to the back of her desk, finally seeing the man's face. He was smiling at her pleasantly. He had a handsome face, a narrow portion of which was covered in a close-cropped black beard. The beard accentuated rather than hid a sharp and prominent chin. His eyes were set very deep into his sockets, so that only glints of light shined beneath the man's brow.

Phyllis made no sound until she finally slid into her office chair where the springs whimpered softly. Her vibrantly colored leotard and accompanying spandex stood in sharp contrast to the man's black suit and starched white shirt, which was buttoned all the way to the collar though the man wore no tie.

"Do sit down. I really must be moving on, *ought* to have moved on already." Phyllis would later recall that, though the man had no real accent, it sounded as though he had once had a British accent that was now long forgotten. It was true of the man, a native of Bristol, that with certain words the heavy bloke accent still shone through.

Phyllis' normally overloud voice cracked as she said, "Excus—uh-hmm— Excuse me, do I know you?"

"I come to transact a purchase of real estate, as well as a lease of commercial property. You are an agent for such matters, are you not?"

"Well, yes, but ..."

"Very well, my name is Edward Teach. I speak on behalf of my business partner, Mr. LaColt, as well as myself. I will be purchasing a parcel of land with all improvements thereupon." As he spoke, Phyllis was scrambling around wildly for her yellow pad of paper and pen, amid a staccato of opening and closing drawers.

Phyllis caught a glimpse of the property address written on the papers Teach had spread before her. "Parlange? But that's the address of Parlange Plantation! But that's owned by ..."

"Clara Parlange. Yess, of course. It was Ms. Parlange who signed this Bill of Sale to Teach & LaColt only last night." As he said it, he pulled the document from his briefcase with his slender white fingers. "I hope you will find the document in order. I have retained the services of a young lawyer named Jim David."

"You've bought Parlange Plantation? I can't believe it. It's been in that family since, well, the Civil War, at least. And how did you know about Jim? He only just passed the Bar."

"It has *always* been in the family's hands. Before the War between the States, before even the Revolution. Two hundred fifty years ... right up to midnight last night. Odd coincidence, do you not agree?"

Parlange Plantation was one of the many antebellum plantation homes wrapping St. Maryville like a string of pearls. There was Austerlitz, Wicliffe – which had been built by Frances Lorio's grandfather and Jim's great-great-grandfather – Ramsay, Labatut, Alma, and several others. Each had their own stories. Parlange, however, may have the only story known to outsiders.

Marie Virginie de Ternant is the reason Parlange Plantation survives. She is also the reason her youngest daughter, Julie Eriphile de Ternant, can still be seen on certain moonlit nights running through the oaks in her wedding dress – the Lady in White.

Lady in White

Claude Vincent de Ternant, later the master of Parlange Plantation, set sail for Louisiana with his older half-brother Jean Baptiste in January 1777. Jean had recently passed the entrance exam for Mézières, the French Academy of Military Engineering, but had been denied entrance to the school. Jean had hoped this would be his path to a commission in the Royal Army of France. Instead, he and his younger half-brother journeyed to America seeking a commission from the Continental Army. Again, Jean was denied his commission. The Commander-in-Chief of the Continental Army, General George Washington, refused to employ the young man who was without experience or social rank. While Claude Vincent was the son of the Marquis of Dansville-sur-Meuse, Jean had been born into a bourgeois family of merchants and tanners. However, upon the urging of the Baron von Steuben, Jean was appointed to the office of sub-inspector, a civilian post without military rank. It was all Jean needed. Beginning with the Baron von Steuben, Jean would leave lasting impressions on a succession of influential men. Through John Laurens, Washington's aide-de-camp, Jean was commissioned a Lieutenant Colonel and Chief Inspector of the South. He became General Benjamin Lincoln's Adjutant General during the Siege of Charleston, where he would be taken as a prisoner of war. While imprisoned, he befriended Anne-Cesar, Chevalier de La Luzerne, the French minister to the United States. With Anne-Cesar as his patron as well as the Marquis de Lafayette, Jean, himself, later became the Minister-Plenipotentiary to the United States from the court of King Louis XVI. Jean remained true to the ideals of the French and American Revolutions, believing in a monarchy limited by a Constitution, and refused to rejoin the French Army as an officer in Napoleon's Regime. While the tanner's son rose to international prominence, Claude Vincent became the Marquis of Dansville-sur-Meuse living in a humble farming community and relative obscurity. Jean died in 1833, two years before his half-brother lost his wife in childbirth and married his second wife.

Claude Vincent lost not only his wife in 1835, but the child she was bearing, as well. He allowed himself little time to mourn the deaths of his wife and only child, a son. His eyes turned to his young second-cousin Marie Virginie, the daughter of white French Créoles. Marie Virginie was possessed of such beauty as to help any man forget his mourning. The aging Marquis had not been alone in noticing Marie Virginie's beauty, nor would her beauty long remain hidden from the rest of the world. She married Claude Vincent on a Wednesday that same year, not long after her seventeenth birthday.

Though Marie Virginie's marriage only lasted six years, she bore the Marquis four children, Henri, Julie, Marius, and Marie Virginie, only two of which would survive to adulthood. She was known to be a strong-willed mother, who allowed very few people to have contact with her children. Though she allowed almost no one between her and her children, her life would be forever marred by those select few whom she allowed to infiltrate her close family circle. The first to do so was a Nanny for the children, named Samaria Arceneaux.

While Marie Virginie was pregnant with Marius, she had hired Samaria Arceneaux because she believed her to be as fiercely protective of the children, as she herself was. And she was, unerringly so. But Samaria Arceneaux was a young woman, who had been hired from among the Cajuns of Avoyelles Parish. She had been loathe to leave behind a suitor in Avoyelles, but had never looked back. Her suitor, however, would not give up so easily. It was said that he went mad after being spurned by the young woman. Several months after Samaria wrote to him, ending their courtship and any further communication, the young man traveled to Pointe Coupee Parish.

One day, as Samaria Arceneaux was leading Marie Virginie's children on an outing beside the Mississippi River, the bend that would later be cut off to form False River, Henri ventured off on his own, as young boys are want to do. Samaria did not immediately notice the boy's absence, as just then one of the babies, Julie, began to wail. As Samaria set to work pacifying the baby, her spurned suitor fell upon the child. The next time Samaria saw the child, he was floating face down along the riverbank. The body of the small boy was recovered, and at Marie Virginie's insistence the body was inspected by the Ternant family doctor. The doctor confirmed Marie Virginie's suspicions: the body had been dead before being thrown into the river. The boy had been strangled to death first. Before cooler heads could prevail, and despite Marie Virginie's desperate efforts to prevent it, Samaria Arceneaux was convicted by a lynch mob of the child's death and hung from the stiff arm of a live oak tree which stood before the plantation home. That night, Samaria's suitor came upon the body of his lover still hanging from the live oak and in a fit of madness killed himself. He climbed the live oak and lifted Samaria's body, laying her along the wide branch. Taking the same noose around his neck, he threw himself off the branch. They were found the following morning by a Camille LeJeune, the overseer of the formal gardens which surrounded the house.

It would be from Marie Virginie's second husband, Colonel Charles Parlange, that the plantation finally received its enduring name. One son was born of this marriage, Charles Parlange the younger. Marie Virginie's two boys, each from a different father, would end up having very different lives. Marius, who was born not long after the deaths of Henri, Samaria, and her suitor, would also die young. After too many days of drinking himself to sleep and drinking himself awake, Marius died of alcohol poisoning at the age of twenty-five. Charles Parlange the younger would serve Louisiana as State Senator, Lieutenant Governor, and eventually, Federal Judge, after being nominated by President Grover Cleveland.

Long before any of her remaining children had grown to age, though, Colonel Charles Parlange died and Marie Virginie was made a widow for a second time. The family was living then in Paris, having moved there sometime after the lynching of their nanny and the suicide. The children experienced terrible dreams following the three deaths, and often complained of seeing their nanny in the oaks. But then Paris also became hostile to them following their stepfather's death. Marie Virginie moved her family back to Louisiana in 1861 believing, like so many others, that the War Between the States would be short-lived.

The Civil War quickly moved west to Louisiana following U.S. Grant's victories at Forts Henry and Donelson and David Farragut's sea battles along the Gulf Coast. The Union was poised to wrest control of the entire Mississippi River Valley from the Confederates, but the port of Vicksburg was stubbornly resisting Grant's siege. To tip the scales, Farragut convinced General Nathaniel Banks to make a diversionary land attack at Port Hudson and lay siege to it. Port Hudson lay just upriver from Baton Rouge and almost directly across the river from St. Maryville and False River. Union and Confederate troops were soon slogging all around Pointe Coupee Parish causing skirmishes here and there.

In the rolling heat of the Summer of 1863, General Banks and his regiments came upon Parlange Plantation. The General marched right up the front steps of the plantation and to its front door, which was swung open wide for him by Marie Virginie. General Banks and his officers found a sumptuous feast had been already prepared for them, and the infantry was invited to make camp in the formal gardens which surrounded the house in neat rows. By her wit and charm, Marie Virginie saved her plantation from the torch and General Banks made the home his headquarters for the duration of the siege. Marie Virginie made similar preparations for the arrival of Confederate General Richard Taylor, the only son of President Zachary Taylor, and he, too, spared the structure, despite its earlier alliance with the Union general whom he would pursue along the Red River. Taylor's forces eventually defeated Banks' at the Battles of Mansfield and Pleasant Hill, but his commanding officer would prevent his pursuit of Banks' retreating armies, earning Taylor's lasting enmity.

Though Vicksburg fell not long after General Banks' arrival and with it Port Hudson, no army would ever succeed in catching Marie Virginie unawares. Warned of the infantry's advance towards Parlange, Marie Virginie had led her own army of children and slaves in removing all the valuable furniture from her home before it could be besieged by looting armies. All of the plantation's more valuable furniture was hidden, as well as the Limoges and Vincennes porcelain and a priceless collection of silver pieces made by Robert-Joseph Auguste, the silversmith of King Louis XVI, who made the king's own coronation crown. The silver pieces were called the Ternant collection – an entire *service à la française* of twelve place settings – which was brought to Louisiana by Claude Vincent de Ternant. Marie Virginie also asked her two most trusted slaves to fill three trunks with her entire fortune in gold and silver coin, and to bury them in secret across her property. Two were later recovered from the formal gardens, but a third was never found. It remains lost to this day. In all, the three trunks contained nearly half a million in gold and silver.

Though Marie Virginie saved her home and fields from the worst of the war, the plantation's fortunes flagged following the war. It was then that the family was again visited by tragedy.

****

Julie Eriphile de Ternant was born the same year as her sister, Marie, who was named for their mother. Following the Civil War, with the family's fortunes in decline, Marie Virginie the mother sought to make advantageous unions for her daughters. The mother had worn a deep callous in her left middle finger scribbling notes to the Parisian relatives of her dead husband, Charles Vincent de Ternant. Despite remarrying, she still signed her name Marquise of Dansville-sur-Meuse, as she hoped her small indulgence would attract suitors for her daughters.

Charles Vincent's brother, Jean Baptiste, and following his death, his heirs had by that time cast a long shadow over the Second Empire of Napoleon III. Marie Virginie had access to a formidable network of contacts throughout Paris.

Ever resourceful, Marie Virginie had brought her lovely daughters by carriage ride down along the River Road to the New Orleans. There, at a photography studio at 64 Carondelet Street, she had a supply of cartes-de-visite portraits made of her daughters. Marie Virginie had then carefully wrapped these photographs in wax paper and sent them across the Atlantic. She knew the beauty of her daughters would have its effect.

Marie Virginie chose Lieutenant Lucas Rochilieu a young man of noble birth for Julie. From the beginning, Julie was caught off guard by the arranged marriage. She had been expecting her mother to arrange a match first for his sister, who was older than her. This was still the way of things, even though Julie shared her birth year with her sister.

Far worse than this, however, was the problem that Julie Eriphile had already given her heart away to another. His name was Simon Barrow. He was a fine man, a rich man with a long pedigree and great fortune. Simon Barrow's lands and plantation lay across the Mississippi River from St. Maryville, near the town of St. Francisville, which John James Audubon had already begun making famous with his *Birds of America* series.

Marie Virginie knew of Mr. Barrow and his intentions for her daughter. However, she also knew that he was of British, not French, ancestry and, worse than this, was an Anglican. Barrow was a *Protestant*, by God, and, Marie Virginie believed the mixing of cults was unwise, much less with an Anglican. Her fears would later be validated, though long after her death, when Barrow's descendant went on a spree of bank robberies with Bonnie Parker in the 1930s which ended when they were both gunned down in Bienville Parish. During Marie's life, however, Barrow's life would suffer such tragedy, as to validate even the horror that she helped cause.

Julie Eriphile was told by her mother, in no uncertain terms, that she would see the Barrow boy no more. Whatever promises and plans had been made between the two young lovers were now to be broken. Normally, a quiet and frail child, Julie raged over her broken engagement. Marie Virginie dismissed her child's tirades as the storms of young love which quickly pass. She would later regret how deeply she had misjudged her daughter.

Despite her mother's strict orders, Julie did not stop seeing Simon Barrow. Barrow would cross the river every Friday night and ride on horseback down the lane to Parlange Plantation. Julie would slip from the house, running in her white nightclothes through the moonlit oaks, and meet her lover along the lane. It was rumored that on one of these nights, Simon took Julie between the high rows of sugarcane and laid with her, consummating in secret the fate which they had been denied.

Eventually, the boat bearing Lieutenant Lucas Rochilieu, who was now betrothed to Julie Eriphile, landed in the Port of New Orleans. There, Marie Virginie's black carriages had been waiting to carry him, the aunt who accompanied him, and his servants up the river to Parlange Plantation. Wedding plans proceeded as scheduled by Julie's mother. In the meantime, she had posted servants at Julie's door to guard against future midnight excursions and trysts in the canefields. Julie's will was adamant and she responded accordingly. The trays of food that were sent up to her room were each returned to Marie Virginie untouched. The whole household grieved over the terrible rift between mother and daughter. Even the servants, who affectionately referred to Julie Eriphile as "Mam'selle Pom Pom," dared not defy their mistress. It seemed Julie had inherited her mother's steely will.

The already frail woman, when her wedding day arrived, had withered almost to the bone. No expense had been spared by Marie Virginie for her daughter's wedding dress. The seamstress who had made the dress of the finest satin and lace had to be summoned the night before the wedding to make emergency alterations, narrowing further the dress' already narrow waist and bodice. The seamstress later said she could have made a second dress of the satin she had to cut away.

The wedding plans proceeded without affair even to the reciting of vows. Few noticed the listless manner by which Julie pronounced her lifelong commitment to the young Lieutenant Rochilieu. Julie's niece, her sister's daughter whose story would also grow strange, described the hapless Lieutenant as an ugly toad of a man with an unsightly mole and patched eye. The eye was patched not from a wound he sustained on the battlefield, but from the accidental discharge of his weapon while cleaning it.

Marie Virginie had prepared her home for the reception, filling it with thousands and thousands of cut blossoms, not even one of which had come from her own gardens. There were so many blossoms, it is told, that one guest remarked that the reception had the air of a funeral.

In the midst of the lavish feast, grander still than the ones Marie Virginie had prepared for the generals, no one noticed that Julie's plates were left untouched and her crystal wine glass untipped. The last lingering guests eventually retreated for the night. Garlands of white flowers were still hanging across the mansion's wide porches and across the wide oak alleys. They were swinging softly in the still night, and the newly christened Master and Mistress Rochilieu were ushered into the bridal chamber. Though it may have been an ancient tradition for the best man to guard the bridal chamber on the wedding night, it was not the custom of the house. For the first time in many months, the door to Julie's room was left unguarded.

Still wearing her wedding dress, the young wife slipped quietly from the home. She leaned from the west veranda of her home to listen for the clop-clop of hooves that had always signaled the approach of Simon Barrow. She must have waited there against the porch railing for hours, until her frail arms could support her no longer. Then, slowly at first, she descended the wide stairs of the porch, and glided like a white ghost through the oak trees. The still breeze could have lifted her away then, so slight had she become. She saw then the image which had so long haunted her childhood. Among the garlands of white flowers, there hung the single noose which had snapped two necks. Hanging from the noose was her old nanny, Samaria Arceneaux, and as her body twisted in the still breeze, the bloated eyes stared at her charge of old. Twisting and twisting, Samaria's face changed and her dead, staring eyes changed into the snarl of her suitor. And so together, as in a lover's pact, they hanged the same noose and the same oak limb forever.

Julie was too weak to scream, but she found the power to run. It cannot be known whether she was fleeing the spectre of her nanny or seeking desperately with the last of her life for her own spurned lover along the lane. And it cannot be known whether her brittle feet tripped across the thick, exposed roots of the oaks, or if she intentionally threw herself against one of the ancient trees in a futile attempt to preserve her maidenhood for all time. The result was irrevocable, no matter the reason. Julie Eriphile was found smashed against the base of one of Parlange's massive oak trees, shattered like a fallen wine glass. When they prepared her broken body for burial, there was found within her the baby of Simon Barrow, who had died many days before his mother, malnourished within her womb.

And so, like her nanny who preceded her, Julie Eriphile can still be seen in the moonlight among the oak trees. She is the Lady in White, the ghost of Parlange, who is still running, always running, among the great oaks of the plantation.

The Fog Barrier

Jim awoke with a shock. His arms and legs twitched with surprise, as though he had been dreaming of falling down a bottomless hole. He had first expected to see his bedroom at home and Anne. Then, that reality was quickly banished and he expected to see the chair and the fireplace where he had been drowsing the night before. That thought, too, scampered away. He was frozen for a moment or two longer staring at his surroundings in confusion.

He was in a bedroom full of sunlight. He had been moved from the chair to the bedroom, *but who?* He thought, and then mumbled, "My clothes!" He was wearing nightclothes of some sort. He felt very odd thinking about who had undressed him and re-dressed him. He rubbed his forehead. He was suddenly aware of a pressing heaviness somewhere within his skull. "That would be the Tokay," he mumbled again to himself as he slowly raised himself up on his elbows.

Remembering the Tokay, he suddenly remembered the old man, as well. LaColt. The sunlight carried with it a certain amount of sobriety. He needed to get out of this place, even if it meant walking home. He could hitchhike, too; he was only on the far side of the lake from his home.

Jim knew that his mind had found solutions to questions he had yet to ask. Among these, getting out of this place and fleeing whatever evil LaColt represented – for Jim knew now at all levels that the man was not right – was paramount. He should have, but did not, consider how many hours of daylight remained to him.

Jim swung his legs through the soft linens of the bed and over the bedside. He hung his legs over the side of the bed and quickly discovered that, strangely, his feet did not touch the floor but were only dangling over the edge. He was tempted for a moment to retreat back under the covers. They felt like the softest he had ever touched. But before he could fully form the idea of creeping back within the magnificent bed, he caught a glimpse of the floor beneath him.

There is no floor. No floor, no floor, no floor! The idea reverberated inside Jim's head. Even as he glimpsed the strange emptiness beneath him, the vision faded. In the space of a blink, there had been a hole beneath his feet. Or a tunnel reaching down, down. *Or a gateway.* "It was there. God help me, it *was* there. Tell me this isn't another Tokay thing. Probably had absinthe in it, crazy old codger."

Jim decided to jump from the foot of the bed, instead. He landed as softly as he could, which was still hard enough to send everything in the room wobbling. Luckily, though, he was near the chair where his briefcase had been placed. He looked around and found a hangar stand where all his clothes had been neatly arranged. He was surprised that he hadn't noticed the clothes sooner – it looked like a hollow image of himself standing across the room from him. Soon, his nightclothes were draped haphazardly over the hangar stand, and the bedroom door was slowly closing behind Jim.

Jim found the house surprisingly easy to escape. He could hear a distant tinkling. It was likely a maid dusting or preparing a meal. For the most part, though, the house seemed still and empty. The house would have been filled with light streaming in through the tall parlor windows, but thick draperies were closed tight against the sunlight. Thin lines of light still crept around the edges of the drapes and where they met at the middle. It was enough light to cast a dull haze over the great rooms. The rooms were full of glittering silver and gold pieces. He crept past wooden packing crates left in a state of hasty unpacking. It would have been a beautiful home even in the half light, but for the dark presence that Jim felt beneath it all. He could almost feel the air jostle back and forth as if the whole house were the lungs of a terrible sleeping thing.

At the front door, he let his hand drop softly onto the oval silver knob. It was silver and engraved with flowers. Ever so slowly, he gripped the silver knob and turned. He bit his bottom lip tighter and tighter as he slowly rotated the knob. It didn't squeak until the last. The knob squeaked just a little. It would have been no more than the complaint of a mouse, but at the sound, Jim noticed the house growing suddenly very quiet.

He bolted. He ran across the wooden planks of the porch. Each step boomed against the hollow underneath. He leaped down the wide staircase taking two and three steps at a time. A moment later, he was standing where the carriage had been before the dawn. He quieted and crouched where he was, like a man told to lay down his weapon. He listened for signs of pursuit. Jim should have heard the sounds of the South around him: birds and the thick buzzing of insects. There was only the returning quiet, as the booming sounds of his dash from the house fled into its recesses.

Jim loosened his muscles and raised himself from his half crouch. He let the briefcase fall to his side and he began wondering if he wasn't over-reacting. *No, God!* He shook his head as if trying to banish the whole fraudulent line of thought. *There was the hole by the bed, LaColt's obvious hate of the daylight ... the whole weird – no, terrible – feeling of the place.*

He spun on his heels, turning from the house to the oak alley. The feeling of dread did not lessen having turned from the house. The long oak alley seemed to stretch before Jim while the thick and torturous mat of roots seemed to swell in height. Jim also observed a strange fog as he walked into the alley. It was a low, creeping fog, but thick. Each gathering of roots seemed to be a smoking cauldron of unseen depth. And soon, his feet had disappeared below him. He had no idea now where he was placing his feet, and he began to stumble painfully step after step. *How had that carriage possibly ridden down this alley?*

Though his awareness was shrinking down to only the next step, Jim began to feel prickles on his neck as though he was being watched. It wasn't just the house; no, it seemed, for now, that the house had released him. It was the oak trees, themselves.

The fog seemed to thicken at the edges of the alley. Beyond the alley, Jim could see little of the oak trees which lay beyond. The fog quickly rose up beyond the alley into an impassable thickness. Jim shivered suddenly as he realized what he must look like scrambling over the roots and hemmed in on either side by the fog – *Moses and the Red Sea! Good God, it's Cecille B. DeMille, but I'm not Moses – I'm stinking pharaoh. And it's all about to come falling down on my head.*

Jim stubbornly refused to look back at the old manse. Besides, there was a growing feeling at his shoulders that something else was watching him. Something in the trees. Maybe even something *swinging* in the trees.

For what seemed like hours, Jim pushed on further and further – or was it deeper and deeper – into the alley. It was growing darker while he was growing tired. He knew he had a reason to fear the approaching dark. He began to feel very hot. The cauldrons of fog between the roots started to roil with flies and mosquitoes as though Jim had disturbed them from long hibernation. They became so thick that he was breathing them in, and worse they began creeping into ears.

Jim soon realized the source of the mosquitoes. It was the lake. He was nearly upon it. He could smell it. *But hadn't there been a road? Where's the road?* He spun around then, not believing that he had somehow missed the wide, smooth expanse of asphalt in all these godforsaken roots. *And the gate? There were whitewashed boards and brick columns!* And then he realized the path ahead of him, the only path that had been left open to him. His only way out. The river. He would have to swim out. It was then that an entirely new fear swept over him. His eyes swam with an inky, oily blackness. He would not swim – he *could* not – his *dad had died in that lake*. His dad had dove in, and never come back up. Never – even his body had never been found. There had been a great expanse of white satin. An empty casket. The lake had eaten him whole, the young Jim believed. Night after night of his childhood, in his dreams, the lake had eaten him, too. Much of his river boogey monster fears had been lost in childhood. What remained, however, may have been much worse. Now, the sloshing of the river water, like the last sound his father had made diving into the river, held only a faceless, de-personified terror. It was a pure black madness that lay below the waters. As he had grown older, the nameless terror had retreated to the level of his instinct, and there it had grown powerful. Roots had spread from there to other parts of his consciousness like a blind, groping mycelium. But the darkness had been held back, for both the boy and the man still honored the sacred mysteries.

The fog seemed to glow all around him. It caught the afternoon sun and scattered it. It was now like a dome, the only exits from which were the plantation and straight ahead, the lake. Great gray branches reached across the path ahead. Each step forward became more reluctant than the last. Whether it was the awakening inkiness of the fear, or true sleepiness, he could not tell. But the thickness of sleep seemed to be rising from the fog at his ankles. Sleepiness seemed to be creeping out of the ground itself, and climbing up his legs. Jim felt his chin go down and his head nod. He nearly fell forward on his knees. If he could just reach the water's edge and lean against the trunk of a tree in the cool shade, maybe even pull off his itching socks and dip just his toes in the water. Jim felt his chin go down and his head nod. He dragged his legs forward, staggering and almost falling to his knees.

Jim's mind was swimming. He was wiping thick sheets of flies and mosquitos from his face. They alone were keeping him awake. Then, suddenly, the insects were gone. There was a buzzing somewhere behind him, as if he has passed through the cloud. He now stood not far from the edge of the water. He looked back and saw that he had descended a steep slope without knowing it. The flies formed a wall higher up the slope, as if held back by a hand or else were limited by a specific elevation. Jim thought it bizarre. Beneath the buzzing, though, there was another sound. It was only a gentle noise at the edge of hearing, a soft fluttering as of a whispered song. It seemed to rustle in the leaves and boughs above him.

Jim lifted his head with great effort. Through bleary eyes, he saw leaning over him a giant willow tree, old and hoary. Its roots, like the ancient oaks behind him, were thick and braided. Its trunk was knotted and twisted. It was riven here and there by deep fissures that creaked faintly as the boughs swayed above. The tree's sprawling branches reached high in a gentle breeze like arms with many long-fingered hands. Jim was suddenly reminded of LaColt's hands and spindly fingers. Looking up, Jim lost his balance and collapsed. He lay there in the cool grass near the tree's creeping roots.

Jim let his eyelids drift down. Above him, grey and yellow leaves rippled in the gentle breeze and disappeared into the fog wall above and beyond. As his eyelids crept shut, he thought he could almost hear words, soft and cooling words, speaking to him of sleep. But even as the spell coiled around the young man's consciousness, there were the words of the water, too. These were stronger and more persistent. They could have been spoken by his father, whose voice, try as he might, Jim could no longer remember.

Confused by the competing voices, Jim staggered forward to the riverbank. There, great winding roots grew out into the water like eels descending into the depths, but these were withering and darkening. He fell and his knees splashed into the water. His arms and head fell forward into the water. Jim panicked for a moment, unable to see through the brown water to judge the bank's descent, but his hands sank no lower than his shoulders. It was just enough for the water to splash against his face.

The water, brown and dirty though it might have been, was sweet medicine. His drowsiness drained away like water droplets from his chin. The branches of the willow began to sway violently. The fog had darkened all around him without him noticing it. The light had now grown very thin. There was the sound of wind rising and spreading backwards to the oak alley. There, in the distance he could hear the whining timber of shifting trees. It was as if his touching of the water had sent out ripples disturbing the quiet slumber of the surrounding trees.

Without any clear idea of why he was doing it, or what he hoped for, he began calling for help. His cries began as a whisper, as though his vocal cords were caked with dust. Each time he cried out, though, his voice grew stronger, more resolved.

"Come out into the deep." He heard a voice say. The words may have only been in his mind, but they were clear and strong. Jim swung his head around up and down the slope in search of the source of the voice. He saw no one.

"Come out into the deep, beyond its reach." The voice again rang out in his head. He knew what the voice intended. *Of course it would*, Jim thought to himself ruefully. *Of course it would ask that. Of course* that *would be required of him.* Jim knew what the voice wanted: it wanted him to swim out into the deep. But the fear of the water flooded in on his thoughts, temporarily eclipsing the horror which lay behind him. Or did it? Did he really know what he thought he knew about LaColt? Or had it only been the nauseating mixture of excitement, strange dreams, and the tokay? "My God," he said, clutching the sides of his head. "Too many thoughts."

"Too many, indeed!" Another voice rang out from above. There were trees now huddled at the edge of the slop and thick swarms of buzzing flies, as well as a solitary, pale figure. Darkness had fallen. LaColt's scarlet robe cascaded in the rising wind. His shadow, in spite of the darkness, seemed to creep down the slope towards Jim. "Come back to my house. Eat and rest. And look, you've nearly forgotten, dear boy." As he said it, the wizened man raised aloft Jim's briefcase.

Jim loved that briefcase. His aunt had given it to him when he graduated from law school. It was fine leather. She had found it at an estate sale. It had been the only way Jim would have acquired such a fine case. And his letter from the Bar was still inside.

Without knowing it, Jim had begun walking up the slope. It felt like slipping back into a dream, from which he'd too soon been awakened. Even as he trudged forward, the voice at his back persisted. "Into the deep," it called. The voice dislodged, momentarily, LaColt's hold on his mind. Jim was distracted and the heaviness returned to his legs just in time for one foot to trip the other. He stumbled and slid back down the bank.

It was then he finally saw the source of the first voice. Perhaps it had been there all along. Far out onto the glittering surface of the lake, where the fog could not reach, there stood a solitary figure. The moonlight illuminated a silver lining along his shoulders and head, but he was otherwise in shadow.

Jim blinked his tired eyes slowly, not believing what he was seeing. It was a man standing in the middle of the lake. Out, on the water. "Whaa…?" He muttered.

LaColt's voice came louder behind him. There was a hidden ugliness to the sweet voice, a disguised screeching, that was rising to the surface. Jim ignored it. He was transfixed by the sight of the gentle moonlit figure. The silhouette was somehow familiar to Jim, as was the voice, come to think of it.

"Can it be?" Jim whispered.

"Come into the deep, my son. My boy."

Jim began to weep. He knew the voice. He had never truly forgotten it. He never would again, he promised himself. It was the voice of his father. "I don't ... I can't," he said. "It'll kill me! Like it killed *you*."

"It won't. The water is holy tonight, James. Swim to me, Jim. It's the only way. You'll be his forever if you go back. You'll be gone to all those who wait."

Jim knelt at the water's edge. His head was swimming again with the uncorked, primal fears of his childhood. He vomited in the grass, and suddenly felt much better.

"Just take the first step, James. You'll grow stronger, Jim. I promise you."

Jim snapped his teeth together in resolve, and stuck his first foot into the cold water. The water was black now in the gathering dark. He could have been walking out into open space for the myriad of stars above him and reflecting below him.

A squall of sound erupted behind him. The shrill shrieking was now filling with the low rumbles of some hidden predator. It didn't matter now. The sudden sound caused him to rush forward into the water. But he did not sink. He walked forward another pair of steps. Surely by now, the slope had fallen away even more and he was overlooking deeper water, but how?

"Come to me, son. Follow me into the deep." The shadowy man beckoned Jim on. He was gaining confidence. It was exhilarating, and he was relieved not to be swimming in the cold blackness of the river. The wails of the old man behind him were soon lost in whipping of the rising wind. Waves of water came splashing rhythmically across his feet and legs. But it was nothing, like walking along the seashore, only without the sand conforming to the soles of his feet beneath him.

Jim kept his eyes on the figure ahead of him, trying to make up the distance between. But again, his eyelids grew heavy. Eventually, he began to sink into the water. Sinking into the lake and passing into sleep were now indistinguishable for the young solicitor. He eventually woke up in his own bed the following morning. He woke up asking Anne, again and again, who had delivered him to the house. Had he just been left at the doorstep? Had she seen the one who had dropped him off? What did he look like?

"Well," she said. "It was still pretty dark, and I wasn't in a good place emotionally – having been worrying about you all day. But, I'm pretty sure it was Monsignor."

Rock's Body

Sometime that night, Cedric Newton pulled a clipboard from the nurse's station to read his instructions for the night. The orderly for the day shift would make notes about what still remained to be finished from his shift. Cedric cussed aloud as he read over Freddy Sprole's barely legible notes. *He left me morgue duty! 'Course he would, that turd. That's the last time he crashes on* my *couch after a fight with Misty.*

"Don't like dealing with the dead, Ced?" One of the nurses smirked at him. This was Mary Jack. She and Cedric had sort of a thing going, though Cedric had yet to make a move. The two of them each pulled the night shift at least half the week and these nights *coincidentally* always seemed to overlap. Very little happened during the night shift, so it a prime time for flirting.

"It's at the tippity-top of my crap list, if that's what you mean," Cedric answered. "It's just above scrubbing live patients which can't control their bowels. Know why? Because, first of all, dead bodies are *dead*."

"Quite an assessment there." Mary nodded.

"It creeps me out, man. Not only that, I gotta roll that gurney into the elevator, where it's just me, the corpse, and the sweet tones of elevator music. Weird. And then, down to the morgue where there were even more dead people."

"*And* their ghosts!" The nurse hissed with laughter.

"Hey! I swear to you I saw something that one time. It was a legit ghost sighting. Make fun, whatever."

"And number two?"

"Huh?" Cedric asked, thinking she meant the other kind of "number two."

"You said 'first of all,' so what's 'second of all?'"

"Oh, right – *second of all*. Apparently, the last step in kicking the bucket, before your foot actually hits the metal, is crapping. Death row inmates have their last meals. Everyone else has their last craps. And not just a sweet little baby crap, these corpse expel Thanksgiving dinner five years back, and – I swear – every piece of chewing gum they've ever eaten and never processed."

"Come on, Ced. That's nasty. Now I'm gonna be thinking about that all night."

"You think you've got it bad? I'm the one that has to go deal with Doublemint down there."

"Here you go, then. Double your flavor, double your fun!" Nurse Mary said pushing out a piece of foil-wrapped gum to the orderly.

"Nice touch. Chew some for me, will you? *Duty* calls."

Cedric left Mary Jack smiling, which had been his goal. It would set him up for their next conversation that night, where, he hoped – he planned – to finally ask her out. He had been working on a couple witty lines all day.

Cedric was still thinking about Nurse Mary as he selected a spare gurney from the hallway, and started wheeling it down the hall to the room where the boy had died. The wheels squeaked at even intervals as the orderly pushed the gurney down the tiled hallway. Cedric had nearly maneuvered the gurney fully into the room when he noticed that the bed sheets looked odd. They looked odd because there was no body beneath them. Absentmindedly, he knocked on the bathroom door, asking if anybody was inside. The thunderbolt of realization hit him, and he jumped backwards to check the room number outside the door. The door read "8-15." Cedric checked the clipboard again, and then looked back to the door. "Must be some kind of mistake," he whispered to himself.

He left the gurney in the room, and jogged down the hallway back to the nursing station.

Nurse Mary Jack watched him approach with a smirk, until she noticed the worried look on his face. "What is it, Ced? If you've got another ghost sto—"

"Listen, Mary. You gotta tell me something. You gotta tell me I'm not going crazy." Cedric swallowed and took a breath. "What room number was the boy in? The dead one?"

"It was 8-15. Why?"

"Check that, okay?"

The nurse turned and grabbed a room list. Her finger moved down the page, matching the movement of her eyes, as she scanned the page. With a double-tap of her finger, she confirmed the number. "Yeah. 8-15. What's wrong?"

"Come with me and make sure I've got the right 8-15."

Cedric followed the nurse down the hallway. He was so out of sorts that he even forgot to check her out, as he walked behind her. "This is the one. 8-15."

"Fine," Cedric said. "Now, go inside and tell me what's wrong with all this?"

The orderly stayed in the hallway, as the nurse went inside. After a delay, there was a scream. And another scream. And another.

"Jeez, Mary. It's just a missing body. Probably just Freddy playing a—" Cedric stopped when he saw the woman standing over the hospital bed. He could barely hear himself speak over the din of her scream. Her voice was like a klaxon bleating its warning again and again, ceaselessly.

Cedric saw that Mary Jack had pulled down the sheets of the hospital bed, perhaps in an attempt to make sure the boy wasn't there. The nurse's back was to Cedric and she kept screaming, as if she couldn't pull herself away from what she had found there. Between the sheets.

Slowly, Cedric steeled himself to look over Mary's shoulder. He hoped it wasn't blood. He was imagining one long smear of blood. It was probably mixed with the crap of the dead boy's final poop. That would be nasty, but nothing to scream about.

He reached around Mary's waist to try and still her, and as he did the woman turned on him. Her eyes were filled with madness. Nurse Mary flung herself onto Cedric. She was scratching at his face, as if he was an attacker or worse. She was like a banshee, no longer recognizable as the girl he flirted with, and, apparently, he no longer was recognizable to her.

But just before the nurse had flung herself onto Cedric, he had caught sight of what lay between the sheets of the bed. He dismissed what he *thought* he saw immediately, because that was impossible. Nevertheless, he found his mind slowly untethering. He felt a coldness gnawing at the edge of his perception. It was as if the steady ground was slowly being pulled from his feet and he was nearing the verge of a vast emptiness filled only with cries of madness.

Nurse Mary eventually fell off of him. Her rage dissolved into whimpers, and she lay curled up on the floor with her back against the wall. Cedric stood then to get a second look at what lay in the bed. He was driven less by curiosity, and more in an attempt to salvage his sanity.

Cedric saw something terrible in the bed. *God, why couldn't it have been just crap or blood!* He thought to himself. His hand fumbled towards the light switch near the head of the bed, one last desperate hope that his eyes were somehow playing tricks on him.

With a tinkle of the expanding filament, light spilled across the dead boy's hospital bed. Cedric saw that he had been wrong. That the boy had been in the bed all along, sort of. He realized also why he had first thought the bed was empty, *because the boy was empty.* The boy's dead body looked like it had deflated like a stale party balloon.

Cedric's mind was suddenly filled with a memory from his childhood. His buddy and he had been fooling around in the library during a class trip. Mike – that had been his buddy's name – had found a book titled *Death in Yellowstone.* He was reading about this guy whose dog had accidentally dove into a hot spring. The dog had started whimpering in pain, and the man decided to dive in after his dog. There had been others there that told the man he was crazy and to stop: Don't do it! But the man wouldn't listen, and he dove into the boiling water headfirst, as though from a diving board. The man actually succeeded in reaching the far side of the pool *and his dog* before the people watching noticed the first signs of trouble. The dog was already dead when he had reached her, so the man left it behind and tried swimming back to safety. Somehow, the bystanders had pulled him back and out of the hot spring. They walked the man over to the wooden boardwalk, which visitors were prohibited from leaving. As they walked together, the man kept mumbling how stupid he had been. It was then – this part of Mike's book had always stayed with Cedric – the men knew they were walking beside a dead man. The man had sustained third degree burns over one hundred percent of his body. His eyeballs were pure white, like cotton balls. The bystanders tried to take off the man's boots and stopped when they saw his feet were coming off with the boots. The man was airlifted to the nearest hospital but it was too late. He was dead on arrival.

Cedric realized then why this stupid memory had cropped up just at the moment. When the park rangers had returned to the boardwalk, they found what appeared to be a pair of white gloves. They had been the skins of the man's hands. What Cedric was now looking at, it was like those "white gloves." It was the soft glove of the dead boy's skin.

Cedric was suddenly shaken out of his reverie by the sound of Nurse Mary's klaxon-like screaming. Still sitting down against the wall, she had again started her siren's wail. It had started seconds after Cedric had flipped the light switch. As Cedric turned toward her to see what she was screaming at now, he saw with a violent shiver of revulsion what the nurse had seen when he'd turned on the lights.

She dove into his arms first. Then, apparently thinking better of it her defender, ran out the room and into the hallway beyond. She kept running, and as far as the log books at Pointe Coupee General would later report, she never came back.

The thing they saw only after Cedric had illuminated the room had presumably been using the darkness to grope blindly at the hospital window and to slowly open it. Even before the lights had gone on, had Cedric been paying close attention, he would have seen the glistening trail of silvery mucous the creature had left behind on the wall and window pane. The thing which had been slowly sliding across the wall and into the window was about five feet in length. It was some kind of massive slug or perhaps just condensed mucous. By the time Nurse Mary's screams could no longer be heard fading away down the hallway, down the stairwell, and across the lawn to the employee parking lot, the thing had pried open the window with its single length of gelatinous muscle and was gone from the room.

Star in the Window

The sale of Parlange Plantation as well as the leasing of the LaCour building proceeded with Jim's signature appearing as notary or counsel of record on all the documents. It happened that the Taft family were the current owners of the LaCour building. The building, however, had a long and complicated history. For one thing, it was one of the few buildings in St. Maryville with a basement. In southern Louisiana, a basement was typically synonymous with an indoor pool, as the water table was so near the surface. St. Maryville, however, had landed inside a bend in the Mississippi River. It would have been a peninsula but the river had adjusted its course leaving behind an oxbow lake named False River. The whole town was perched on the lake with its back against the Mississippi River. Levees had been built along either side of the Mississippi over the course of generations, but mostly during the Great Depression and the years of Roosevelt's New Deal and Huey P. Long. During certain times of the year, the Mississippi River stage, which is the height of the water in the river, was taller than the town and taller still than False River.

There were some spots along False River that could manage a basement, but the LaCour Building was older than the levees. It had been built when the Mississippi River still flooded annually, depositing rich alluvium across all the farmlands. A basement from this time period was very odd. But there were many odd things between the river and False River.

One week after Jim's reappearance on his doorstep, the breakfast patrons of Miss Tee-Eva's Diner were buzzing with news of the new business moving into town. A radio was playing in the kitchen in the back. Above the din of silverware clattering against thick ceramic plates, a song could be heard — "It's gonna take a lot to drag me away from you" — wafting in and out as the kitchen door swung back and forth.

Mr. Gremillion, one of the town's inspectors, mumbled from a mouth and moustache full of grits, "What'd he look like?"

Brian Freemantle of the Clerk of Court's office stood at the counter filling his morning coffee with half and half from a metal creamer. The lid to the creamer, as it clapped open and shut, always seemed to give him fits. He had confirmed that someone had come to the courthouse the day before to file the Lease Agreement in the conveyance records. "Johnny, to be honest, I felt like I was in a bad dream the whole time. He looked like … His eyes were sort of sunken under a deep brow. You know what? He looked like Rasputin. Yeah, he really did. Only with an English accent." Brian wanted to mention, but wouldn't, the odd way the man had treated him. Brian barely even noticed any more when people took offense to his skin color. But it was as though the man wasn't used to seeing *free* black people, let alone one serving in a public office.

Jim was also at Tee-Eva's that morning. Though Anne had forgotten none of her time spent worrying over him, Jim's memories of his time at Parlange were steadily draining away. It was now only a memory of a memory. Ever since their encounter while picking pecans the previous year, they had both been experiencing night terrors. They seemed to alternate nights, so one could usually calm down the other. They had never learned about Ivy Williams and what she had also seen that day, the day they had been picking pecans. Nor had they learned how their testimony might have been used to free her, if they could have somehow made people believe the impossible.

If Jim had looked down to the table to his mostly untouched food, he would have been surprised to see that his knuckles had turned white from grabbing the sides of the table.

The music again wafted across the diner:

"The wild dogs cry out in the night,

As they grow restless, longing for some solitary company."

"One of those New Orleans fellas, I bet." This was Boy Landry, who had recently retired from barbering after more than sixty years. He had given most of the men in Tee-Eva's their first haircuts when they were still just squirming toddlers propped up on red vinyl cushions and held still by their parents. He often thought fondly of the old chrome-coated barber chair at which he had so long plied his trade.

Brian Freemantle shook his head as his spoon clanked around inside the milk glass mug. An image of Buckskin Bill proudly promoted Morning Treat coffee from the side of the mug. "I don't know. He sure wasn't local." Brian let his eyes observe Jim as he glanced nonchalantly across the room. He had, of course, seen Jim's signature on all the documents that the strange Rasputin-man had brought to the courthouse. He was biding his time before bringing this up with Jim. He didn't know why exactly, but he knew he needed to tread lightly.

"Phyllis," Johnny said, "Tell us again about showing that fella the building." Phyllis Malchaud shivered at the memory. She had hated every moment she had had to spend with that Teach man ever since he appeared inside her office a week or so ago. She was a regular at Tee-Eva's though no one had actually ever seen her eat anything. She came in for expresso every morning following her power walk. It was only strong coffee, but Tee-Eva dared not correct her when Phyllis insisted on calling it expresso.

Tee-Eva made sure she or her daughter always had a cup of strong coffee waiting for Phyllis in the mornings. "That must be the most fidgetiest lady I ever seen," she would say. "Wound tighter than a tick."

Phyllis took a second to sip at her diminutive demi-tasse cup while gathering her thoughts. She normally spoke several decibels louder than anyone else, but she began in a whisper. "It was the oddest thing. I think. I did my normal walk-around, showing him the various amenities, pointing out structural features, you know, all that jazz. I'm not sure he heard a word of it. God, the way he looked at me. You can barely even see his eyes, you know. He could've been blowing smoke right into my face. I can hardly explain it. But here's the thing: I think he knew everything I was saying. Like he already knew the place. Or me," she shivered.

The group at the Diner considered all this for a moment. Brian Freemantle slurped some of his coffee, and sighed as though deep in thought. "And what did you say he looked like, again?"

"Me?" Phyllis turned her head in surprise. She had grown twitchy and distracted. "Oh, right. He – it's so strange – I try to picture him and I can't. It's like someone has smudged his face, except for those eyes, out of my memories. I'm normally very good with names and faces. Have to be, in my line of work."

"You can't remember their faces *at all?*" Tee-Eva called from the kitchen. She was scraping some hash off the grill, but always kept an ear on the conversation.

"*His* face, not 'their.'" Brian corrected the proprietor of the diner. "I don't think anyone has yet seen LaColt." He said it, keeping watch of Jim, who seemed to have let his mind wander.

Somebody in the kitchen was singing along with the radio. "I bless the rains down in Africa" –– the line kept ringing out from the kitchen.

"Except for the eyes, or the *feeling* of the eyes." Phyllis shivered again. "It was *really* unpleasant, actually. Trying to think about it. It's like I can look into their faces and they just smear in my mind, like they've been censored. You know how they do it on TV."

"That's so odd," Brain murmured. "That wasn't my experience at all, though I can certainly see what you're saying about the eyes. Freaky."

"Hey, hey. Look here." A man named Luis tapped against the *Advocate*, the daily newspaper from Baton Rouge. Luis had grown up in Nicaragua but had been brought to Louisiana by Doc Guidry, one of the richest men in St. Maryville and the state, as sort of a manservant. Luis was now approaching sixty, but in just the right light, he could still pass for man of thirty. Luis passed the paper to Brian who was slurping quickly on his coffee as the hour approached eight. "That's the address for the LaCour building, no?"

Luis was pointing to a quarter-page advertisement on the fourth page of the Features section just below the fold. Brian's eyes widened as he read the corner of newspaper, and he absentmindedly put his white milk glass mug down near the edge of the table. Luis just as absentmindedly righted the mug before a drop could be spilled. "I thought so," Luis said tapping a note of triumph on the table as he did.

"What? What is it?" Jim asked. He had been preparing to leave, having grown very uncomfortable with the conversation or the temperature or his biscuit; he couldn't be certain. He had stopped putting his blazer on mid-motion. At five minutes 'till eight, he and Brian would walk down to the courthouse, as was their custom.

"It's a want-ad posted by our new neighbors," Brian said with an unsettled tone. "It seems they're looking for certified health care professionals."

"Read it," Mr. Gremillion ordered as he brushed the grits from his moustache and pushed his napkin under his plate.

"Fine," Brian nodded. "Like I said, 'Wanted for Hire: Certified Health Care Professionals for Population Enhancement. Compensation Very Generous. OB-GYN, Nurse Practitioners. May assist or provide the following clinical procedures according to protocols: Medical abortion, surgical abortion, IUD insertion, implanon insertion, vasectomies, tubal ligations, colposcopies and biopsies. Contract bonuses may apply for qualified providers. Please call 225-638-6667 or mail inquiries to Happy Families, 148 Main Street, St. Maryville, LA 70760. Some travel may be required and must be willing to relocate.'"

A pall fell over the Diner. There was a slight rattle of silverware being laid down. Jim shoved his other arm in the blazer and grabbed his briefcase. A rope of bells clanged as the door closed behind him. His face had been a ghostly white.

"Abortion? Abortion!" Luis stammered, and then began raging in Spanish. A golden-brown glass ashtray wobbled across his table.

"Eh, what's the big deal?" Tee-Eva's daughter barked out from the kitchen. Tee-Eva shushed her.

"What?" Luis erupted. He nearly flew to the back of the diner. The sounds of the grill were soon overwhelmed by Luis' storm of Spanglish indignation.

"Don't worry," Mr. Gremillion waved his hand to Brian and the rest. "They won't possibly pass their inspection. I might just pay them a little look-see this afternoon, before they get too comfortable. Before they can buy their first batch of baby-sized biohazard disposal bags."

"*I* was the realtor," Phyllis said, suddenly getting to her feet. She didn't really feel any personal moral compunction about abortion, but she knew how people talked in a small town. Her hands were a blur, as she daintily dabbed her mouth with the napkin, opened her purse, and laid out exact change with tip on the table. "Oh my God, what will people think? They'll think I'm part of this. They will, of course they will. I got the commission, didn't I? Maybe it's not too late to get Sherika to put her name on this instead of mine. She's already known for this kind of stuff. Her husband's had a half-dozen procedures vasectomizing, undoing it, re-sectomizing. He's probably got a punch card by now." Her voice had risen back to her customary decibel range. She had soon slammed the door behind her.

****

Jim had not left Tee-Eva's for the courthouse. Instead, he stalked towards the chapel beside the church, still red-faced. His memories of the whole affair had grown unnaturally fuzzy and blurred, but he had known – yes, he had known – that something was very deeply wrong with the whole affair. That hadn't stopped him from accepting extremely generous payment for the nominal work he had done for the real estate transactions. And now, now, his name would be smeared across all the paperwork for the abortion clinic. Nevertheless, he had said many times before that there was no crisis, no anger, no catastrophe that wouldn't abate after a few minutes in the chapel.

Jim cut across the empty lot and passed in front of the LaCour building. He suddenly clutched at his chest, as though looking for something familiar there. *Did I sell my soul? Oh my God, I did! I'm Faust!* The panic washed over him. Moments later, he was even feeling silly at the thought of it. But then, the building bore down on him. The building actually seemed to be slouching towards him with its black window eyes leaning forward to inspect him. Jim wondered if this had been how Odysseus felt under the gaze of the Sphinx.

Jim moved to the far side of the street, walking along the Florrick's Jewelry sidewalk instead. The LaCour building would soon be busy with the rattles of construction workers, but it was preternaturally quiet right now as if veiled in a dampening cloth. Jim noticed a door to a side stairway. *Had the doorway always been painted red?* Jim thought with a chill.

Though he did not know it, Jim was traveling the same path the El Arca community had traveled the day it encountered the yellow Jaguar. After passing the future home of the clinic and Chère Mama's restaurant with its French Quarter-style balcony, Jim walked along the sidewalk beside the empty lot owned by the City and used for various functions during the year.

St. Joseph's Academy had once stood at the far back of the lot, but had been torn down to make way for a bank annex and – what else? – a parking lot. Jim's family history was intertwined with the old Academy, as he had generations of aunts who had been Sisters of St. Joseph, the order of nuns which started and ran the school. The school only occupied the first floor of the building. The second floor was a convent where the nuns lived, as well as a chapel.

Jim's great-great aunt had been Sister Anne Marie Lorio. The family called her and her sister, another nun, Tante Nanette and Tante Dunette. Tante Nanette had been a truly saintly woman. When she died, the sum total of her worldly possessions could barely fill the floor of a steamer trunk, and that included a second habit. But it had always been the manner of her death that stuck with Jim, though he had never known the woman.

Sister Anne Marie had been awakened in the middle of the night by the approach of a terrific storm. It was the kind of storm that rolls in from the Gulf showering the upper atmosphere with lightning and bending the trees backwards. She tried waking the other sisters. She had hoped to gather them into the chapel to pray for the intercession of Our Lady of Prompt Succor that the storm would pass. She was unable to awaken any of the other sisters, and instead prayed alone in the chapel. In the morning, after the storm had indeed passed, the sisters awoke to find Sister Anne Marie dead in the chapel. She had died on her knees on the morning of the Feast of the Ascension.

As he passed the now-empty lot where St. Joseph's Academy once stood, he looked up, as he always did, to wonder at the tall red-brick church building. The light always held a certain quality as it touched the steeple. Jim thought that maybe the steeple was less "here" than it appeared, like a ship's mast would appear to fish in the ocean below. As on ship masts, St. Elmo's fire was often seen dancing atop the steeple. The buzzing sound that accompanied the coronal discharge of electricity could often be heard along with the ringing church bells.

The steeple had been struck by lightning many, many times, but had never suffered damaged. Jim harbored a secret thought that, maybe, it marked sort of a passage between worlds, maybe even into heaven – maybe it had even been the spot where his Tante Nanette had been taken to heaven. The windows of the chapel where she died would have looked out onto the tall steeple, and St. Elmo's Fire, Jim imagined, would have been gathering at the points of the steeple that night.

The April 30, 1904 issue of the *Pointe Coupee Banner* stated that Father Francis LaRoche had engaged New Orleans architect Theodore Brune to draw plans for the new church building to replace the old St. Mary's building which had been built in 1823. However, on May 24 of the same year, the windows of Father LaRoche's rectory were found to have been broken by vandals. Tied around one of the rocks that had sailed through the priest's home was a written threat that if construction did not begin within thirty days the priest would be attacked. The June 18th edition of the *Banner* showed Brune's plans for an 80-foot Gothic Revival structure topped by an 80-foot spire steeple atop a belltower. The spire and steeple were to remain uncompleted for more than twenty years. In the meantime, Father Alfred Bacciochi succeeded Father LaRoche as pastor. No stones were to be thrown through Father Bacciochi's windows, a lion of a man and kinsman of Napoleon Bonaparte. Father Bacciochi was part of a long pedigree of warrior-priests called to serve the small Catholic community of St. Maryville.

Jim passed in front of the church, crossing himself. The history of his battleworn parish was not yet known to him. But if he had turned just then and squinted his eyes, he might have just been able to see the two inscriptions at the base of the stained glass windows which hung above St. Mary's thick front doors, Romans 5:20 and Mathew 16:18: "Where sin increased, grace abounded all the more," and "And the gates of Hell shall not prevail against it."

As he opened the door to the Adoration Chapel he looked backward to the carport of the Rectory. Monsignor's vehicle was not there. He had suspected it would not be. Mondays were, after all, Monsignor's day off.

Soon enough, Jim told himself, he would need to go to the priest about the man LaColt, given the events unfolding in town. He had spoken to Monsignor after his vision or haunting or whatever it was back in the pecan grove. Monsignor did not look at him as if he were crazy, as the police had, though he had not quite understood Monsignor's expression. There was something there. It wasn't fear. Not quite. But he had felt a load lifted from his shoulders after telling Monsignor.

Jim dipped his fingertips in the cool water at the entrance to the room of prie-dieux, the kneelers that stood before the Monstrance holding the Eucharist. He nodded to the other man in the room. His name was Charles Lorio, an old bachelor who lived with his mother, Azema, along False River. Jim knelt and let his thoughts drift back over the night he had gone to see Monsignor. He had not thought over any of this in several months.

****

"Tell me again, what you saw, Joachim." Monsignor had said sitting at his desk in the Church office. Few people, besides Monsignor, called Jim by his full baptismal name. Jim wasn't short for James, but Joachim. It was a natural thing to do, as Monsignor had been the one to baptize Jim. Monsignor had been a priest at St. Joseph's Cathedral in Baton Rouge back then. "From start to finish."

Jim's eyes drifted over Monsignor's books and the odd assortment of knick-knacks. There was the standard fare of books for a priest's office: theology books, copies of the Catechism, breviaries, books of various liturgies, rites, and rituals. There were also some older-looking books in a glass case. What really caught Jim's eye were the autographed baseballs. He thought he had caught sight of a baseball signed, "Truly Yours, M. J. Kelly."

Jim forgot the baseballs for the moment, and told Monsignor how he and Anne had first seen the man in the black suit across the road. The image of the man seemed to evolve in his memory. Jim explained how at first the man had seemed just very pale, and then how the man's lips seemed to curl backward. "I didn't *see* that, not exactly." Jim said. "I saw the man's face in my mind, or maybe my mind was just filling in the details. I can't say. But there's more. I see more or I see him differently every time. I think – no, I *feel* like there were roots curling out of his body like teeth. Here and there. I don't know. It's crazy, isn't it?"

"Do you think you're crazy?" Monsignor asked. Jim answered him by shaking his head. He felt good. He wasn't trying to convince Monsignor of the truth, he wasn't forcing himself to sell the truth. "Tell me more about the bird, Jim. You said it was a white heron? Are you certain it was a heron?"

"Yeah, I'm sure it was a heron. I mean who doesn't know what a heron looks like around here, right?"

"Sit back, Jim, and close your eyes," Monsignor instructed.

"But I haven't told you even the half of it. You've got to hear me out! Please. I've got to tell you about LaColt. You really need to…"

"Fix the image of the bird in your mind. And when you open your eyes again, focus on my crucifix. You understand?" Jim relented and nodded. He leaned back in the armchair in front of Monsignor's desk. He fixed the flying bird in his mind. He focused on the bird's flight before it had flown over the levee, where it had been crushed by the fist of water. After this, Jim remembered no more.

"Good. Open your eyes," Monsignor said, and Jim had an instant to notice Monsignor twisting the chain of his crucifix between his fingers so that the cross and the corpus spun around and around. Tiny pinpricks of light dazzled Jim's eyes as the spinning cross reflecting pulses of light.

"Jim," Monsignor asked. "What did you hear when the heron flew overhead?"

"Feathers." Jim answered.

"What else?"

"The baby was crying."

"What else?"

"The baby was crying. The baby was crying. The baby was crying. The baby was crying. The baby was crying. The baby was crying."

"Deeper, Jim. Climb down into the well. Look at the reflections."

"El niño busca su voz. La tenía el rey de los grillos," Jim whispered. He would have been surprised to hear himself speak Spanish, a language he had never learned.

After a pause, Monsignor answered, "En una gota de agua buscaba su voz el niño."

"No la quiero para hablar; me haré con ella un anillo que llevará mi silencio en su dedo pequeñito." Jim sang the words as a children's song.

"Me he perdido muchas veces por el mar," Monsignor answered, still twirling the crucifix. "What was the sound of the bird, Jim?"

"Lightning flashes across the water," Jim said as his fingers traced the jagged lines of the lightning.

"What did you hear, Jim?"

"Thunder. The bird's feathers were thunder."

Monsignor blinked hard at this and clenched his teeth, as though an old pain had resurfaced along his spine. "Jim," he said. "Describe the bird's eyes." Jim blinked but said nothing.

"The Throne commands you, Jim. Speak true. What were the eyes?"

"They should have been black. Black as spades. Black as the good earth."

Beads of sweat were forming on Monsignor's scarred forehead. There was a deep scar there, like an ice cream scoop had rolled away some of the man's vanilla skin. Monsignor carried the twirling cross closer to Jim's eyes. Lights paraded across the younger man's face. Jim's face shook minutely back and forth, pulsing. His pupils, too, were pulsing, but at a direction transverse to the motion of his head.

"The eyes bulged, protruded, Grave's disease, swimming goggles, Wink the hamster, monocles, coins over its eyes, coins for Charon, dead, swollen eyes, the Giver's eyes, the Green One's eyes."

"That's enough, Jim. Thank you," Monsignor said, holding his crucifix still with his other hand. "You will close your eyes and awake, feeling refreshed, that a burden has been lifted from your shoulders. This encounter will stop worrying you. You will go home and be a fantastic husband to your wife. God bless you in the Name of the Father, and of the Son, and of the Holy Spirit. Amen."

Shortly thereafter, Jim awoke and smiled. He stretched as though after a long nap. "How'd it go, Monsignor? Did it work? I feel much, much better. Monsignor?" Jim asked as he noticed the sweat dripping from the priest's brow. "Are you alright? Can I grab you some water?"

Monsignor grinned from the corner of his mouth, perhaps more grim than usual. "That's fine. I'm fine. I think it's about time for my mid-afternoon nap, is all. Lisa will be wondering what's happened to me."

"Thank you, father," Jim said. "I'll be heading home then. I have a sudden urge to kiss my wife and tell her I love her. I appreciate you making time for me."

"Of course. Hey, Jim, one quick thing. Do you speak Spanish?"

"No, why?"

Monsignor shook his head as if to dismiss the matter. "Jim, it was very important you came. You have a good sense of when things aren't right. You should trust that instinct, as well as the one that brought you to me. Go kiss your wife, kiss her once for me, as well. Just a peck on the cheek, though, don't go violating my vows!" They laughed together, as Monsignor led him out of the office and on his way. In just a few more short months after that meeting, Jim and Anne would finally become pregnant.

When Monsignor returned to his office, he closed the door firmly and locked it. His smile was quickly draining away. He took an autographed baseball from a holder and squeezed it until he could hear the bones in his hand whine with the stress. On the ball "Joe Jackson" had been scribbled by an unsure hand. He slammed it against the tile floor. It ricocheted from the floor to the wall, where it crushed the glass of a picture frame, from the picture frame to the ceiling, and from the ceiling back into his broad hand. But that wasn't good enough. The man of prayer spit on the ball and smeared it into the worn white leather with the heel of his other hand. He roared softly, "This is my parish, my post, my *flock*. You see this baseball, goat? I'm gonna teach your mouth *and that throat behind it* to praise Jesus with this baseball. You're not getting 'em this time."

Gone Fishing

"So, you and that girlfriend of yours gonna make it out this weekend?"

"Nah, buddy," Brad called out from the other side of the boat. "Get me a little closer, will ya, Roach?" The small pool of light cast by his flashlight was hovering around the exposed top of the next crawfish trap.

"Having problems reaching, Cookie?" The one called Roach snickered from behind the wheel of the fishing troller.

"I don't know, butt-head. Having problems steering after your *sixth* six-pack?"

"Remember last year, Cookie?" Roach said, ignoring the suggestion. "Huh? Remember?" Roach was prancing around at the back of the boat holding up his shirt which read, "Boozin' on the River, 1978." While he was prancing, the boat was veering slowly into a patch of green slime, nettles, and dragon weeds.

"Dude," Cookie said, giving up for the moment, and turning to watch his friend. This was the part of long nights like these that drove him crazy, but nevertheless he couldn't help but stare in fascination at his old friend. It had been like this since they'd dropped out of high school together sometime back in '74, or was it '75? They were Morganza boys. Nearly everybody in the small town by the spillway, down Highway 1 from St. Maryville, had long forgotten their original names in favor of nicknames.

"Show a little faith, little buddy," Roach said and his tapping, dancing feet began slowly rattling the bottom of the flat-bottomed aluminum boat, like a huge siren scaring all fish away. *Thank God we're just crawfishing*, Brad thought, *but I can say goodbye to those bullfrogs.* "There's magic in the night," Roach continued.

"Hey Boss," Brad crooked a smile. "This ain't Philly."

"You ain't a beauty," Roach crooned. "But, hey, you're alright."

"Yeah, whatever, just don't fall outta the boat this time." Brad – or Cookie, as he'd been called since grade school days on account of his almost cute, diminutive size – grabbed the paddle to direct the boat himself. Getting caught up in the nettles could be a nasty affair, and he knew it was best to let Roach spin himself out.

"Oh *oh*!" Roach continued, "Come take my hand.

We're riding out tonight to case the promised land.

Oh oh oh oh, oh oh oh … Thunder Road,

Oh, Thunder Road, oh, Thunder Road,

Lying out there like a killer in the, uh, *moonlight* —

Hey, I know it's late, we can make it if we run,

Oh oh oh oh, Thunder Road,

Sit tight, take hold, Thunder Road."

Roach soon finished playing his air guitar and mumbling "Thunder road, thunder road, oh, oh, thunder road." He sat down and rubbed his head, as Cookie finished pouring out the half dozen or so crawfish out of the basket and reloading it with a hunk of rotting perch and some guts. "Oh, hey, yeah. I forgot. Your girl's knocked up. I guess y'all won't be boozin' on the river this year."

"Nah, she ain't knocked up no more," Cookie mumbled, as he took over at the boat's driver seat. "Not no more."

"Huh, whazzat?" Roach said, belching. He was now laying over and across the ice chest, as if were about to do a forward somersault into the swamp. "She lost it?"

"Sort of," he answered.

"What? Like lost and found? Jeez, man, remember when he found Frankie's sister's dress in the lost and found?"

"No, not like lost and found, you frick-tard."

"Oh, like you flushed it, huh?" And then, after a few gurgles from his belly, Roach jettisoned a few beers into the swamp. "Ahh," he sighed. "Made enough room for last Natties. It's a death *trap*, it's a suicide trap, we gotta get out while we're young, 'cause tramps like us, baby, we were born to run."

"Something like that. Went down to that new clinic. Spoo-ooky place."

"Dude!" Roach suddenly hollered at him. "I just had a reveal – you know, a rev – *revelation*! I only know words to songs when I'm drunk. I could probably – yeah, I *know* I could – sing you all of 'American Pie,' right now." He began rubbing his forehead and he lay with his back against the top of the ice chest, rocking back and forth perilously close to tipping off the side of the boat. "Whoaa, this must be what psychics feel like."

Cookie put the small motor in neutral, and scrambled around to the prow of the boat. He stretched out length-wise and reached for the next crawfish basket. "Crap," he said, going back to get the frog gigging pole. He often used it to compensate for his stubby arms. He would hook the long rusty spike at the end of the pole into the wire basket.

"A long, long time ago," Roach sang out, resuming the serenade. "I can still remember how that music used to make me smile."

Cookie had begun tugging at the crawfish basket with the pole. "Damn thing's stuck on something." Using the pole, he was able to swing the prow of the boat over to the crawfish basket. "Weird. Thing's not budgin'." He crawled again up to the very front of the boat. Leaning over the side as far as he dared, which wasn't very far given his size, he was able to reach the basket without the pole. "The hell's going on … think it's tied down?"

"But something touched me deep inside, the day … the music died," he crooned in response.

"Nah, gotta be hung up on something. Only way," he answered his own question. So, he dipped his hand down into the dark water and began groping around down at the base of the basket. Suddenly, he whipped his hand backward and out of the water. He yowled quietly and shivered.

This was enough to distract Roach from his efforts. "What's up, dude?" He said upside-down, turning his head sideways from behind the cooler. "Dude?"

Cookie was rubbing his hand and staring at it. "It felt like – it was like something reached out to hold my finger."

"Something pulled your finger, eh?" Roach snorted and began rolling back and forth across the top of the cooler in mirth. "Drove my Chevy to the levee but the levee was dry, them good ole boys were drinking whiskey 'n rye, singin' this'll be the day that I die."

"It felt like a little hand reached around my finger," Cookie said, realizing he was again talking to himself. "Like a baby's."

Even as he said it, his neck was snapping in another direction as a sound bubbled out of the water from somewhere nearby the boat. "D'you hear that?" He called to his friend.

All Cookie got in response was, "This'll be the day that I die."

"I think it came from over here," Cookie said crawling across the width of the boat and leaning over the other side.

The sound came again. It *was* a baby. There was a soft voice, as from a toothless mouth, "Da-da, da-da-da." And then, there was a pitter-pat of little feet and a laugh, as from a slightly older child, a toddler.

Cookie was still scanning the water along the edge of the boat, when he noticed that Roach wasn't singing the next verse. "Roach?" He called to his friend. He couldn't see him just then, because the cooler had been stashed behind the steering wheel panel and the captain's chair. Still crawling, his hands splashed into a pool of water at the bottom of the boat. He looked down at his hands and realized that the water was dark and thick. He rounded the corner around the steering wheel panel and stopped.

Shreds of the boat's aluminum floor had blossomed outward. Cookie observed in silent horror that the second gigging pole had been stabbed upward through the bottom of the boat, through the floor and straight through his friend's skull. He had been pinned like an insect with his waist and lower back still resting on the cooler. The water spilling through the hole at the bottom of the boat was mixed with his friend's blood, black in the moonlight.

Just then, Cookie heard again the small peals of a toddler laughing. It was the last thing he heard before the first frog gigging pole, too, found its mark.

****

Deputy Vin Dabadie later recovered the bodies, after a fisherman noticed the half-submerged boat glinting in the morning light. "Just a couple of drunk boys," the deputy later explained to the receptionist at the sheriff's office. "You know, I grew up with these boys. Got into a scuffle, I'm sure, and somehow impaled each other with gigging poles. These two douches were always making swords out of yardsticks and whatever they could get their hands on. It was just a matter of time, really – what with lawn darts' ban lifted and all."

The Job Seeker

Jana Fiore clutched the newspaper to her chest as she walked away from her Ford Pinto. She hadn't even locked her car; "let 'em take it, if they can move it." She had just used the last penny of her last dime to drive out to St. Maryville, hoping to find a job. She was a nurse, and she held the newspaper in her arms which advertised that the new clinic was hiring.

She may have felt a sense of dread approaching the LaCour Building from the side street where she had parked. She couldn't tell, she had so many other feelings of dread bubbling up in her head. She rubbed absentmindedly at her ring finger which bore a white smear of untanned skin.

She swung open the front glass door of the LaCour building to a slight tinkle of chimes. Maybe it was the brightness of the day, but for a second, she felt like she was walking into a wide open mouth. She put her hand up ready to pull away the black curtain hanging just inside the doorway. As she stepped inside, she was startled to discover there was no curtain. Her eyes adjusted rapidly and unnaturally to the light. She blinked and rubbed her eyes, stumbling across the thin metal threshold.

"Dear, dear, I'm sorry about that, missus! Happens *all* the time! But the Big Nurse won't let us change a thing."

Jana was relieved to hear a kind voice inside the building. It was a high-pitched black woman's voice, which dimly reminded Jana of Butterfly McQueen from *Gone With the Wind*. Jana finished blinking to discover the harsh fluorescent lighting of a waiting room.

"But, I thought –" Jana said, pointing backward. "I thought there was a curtain at the door … how?"

"Oh, isn't it the weirdest? Ain't nothing for it – you'll just learn to snap your eyes closed when walking through that do'. It's alright, honey child. You here for an interview, I expect?"

"Yes, yes. I'm a nurse."

"Nurse Jana?" The receptionist asked.

"That's right. How did you—?"

"Oh! We expecting you. Didn't you call just the other day?"

"Well, yes, but …"

"Not that it matters none. I'm Fixie, by the way. I'll just buzz you in. I'm sure Nurse Fletcher will be expecting you. That one, she always seems t'be expecting on everybody." Jana watched through now-adjusted eyes as the shorter woman hurried back behind the receptionist desk, and pressed a button with a loud *chirrup!* "You just set right down … right there. That's nice."

Jana waited quietly for her head to stop spinning. She felt like she had been spun in on a whirlwind, the latest in what seemed like an unending succession of whirling about. She felt the black leather strap of the seat's modern armrest under her hands, and she realized how her hands were sweating. She rubbed them into the leather and looked around for a distraction.

Just as she was leaning over to reach for a magazine, she was stopped short by a voice. "No, my child. There will be no time for that."

Jana looked up to see a smiling white woman dressed entirely in white from her nurse's cap down to her stockings and shoes. There was a driving, pulsing quality about her eyes, as if she had just been called away from the battlefield. "Please follow me back to my office."

Jana stood up a little too quickly and nearly lost her balance. She flushed, but was relieved to see that the nurse – whom she presumed to be Nurse Fletcher – had already strode away back down the hallway. She quickly collected her things and jogged after the older woman.

The hallway had emptied before her. The nurse was gone whom she had been following. She seemed to have just disappeared. Behind her, she had already in the space of a couple lefts and rights lost track of where she had left the receptionist's desk and Fixie. How big *is* this building? She asked herself, as she stood alone in a brightly-lit gray, sterile hallway. She kept walking forward and turned a corner, and rounded on a door that had been left ajar. She hoped that she would find Nurse Fletcher just on the other side, and so she pushed it open.

She found a long tiled room of hospital beds behind the door. In one such bed, there was a woman, obviously drugged and unconscious. Around her bed, stood a bevy of nurses in white coats and at the front of the bed, sitting between the unconscious woman's stirruped legs, was a doctor wearing a facemask. He was holding forceps which pinched bloodstained wads of gauze.

Something was very wrong with the whole thing, but Jana couldn't understand what. She looked nervously from face to face and finally realized what it was. One of the faces – a nurse – was she? Was it? The face of a *bird*?

A face suddenly crossed before Jana's, near enough to kiss her. It was the steely eyes of Nurse Fletcher. She had stepped in front of Jana and closed the door behind her. "My child," she wagged her head slowly. "You had better keep up," she smiled sweetly and furiously "—or we'll have to put you away. With the dear ones."

"D-d-dear ones?" Jana asked.

"Of course." Nurse Fletcher nodded, but she was no longer standing in front of Jana in the hallway. Nurse Fletcher was at her desk, and the interview – Jana realized – was nearing its end. Jana looked around suddenly. She didn't remember the hallway or how she had found her way to the seat in front of Nurse Fletcher's desk. She was vaguely aware of the missing time, but even that was drifting away and would soon be gone.

"Of course," Nurse Fletcher continued, "for such a salary, we will demand quite a lot out of you. It is a great work, you see, that Mr. Teach is accomplishing at this clinic, and it is a privilege for us to be a part of it." Nurse Fletcher held Jana's gaze for a moment, and then continued. "You will have one day off a week, and, honestly, very few holidays. We work Easter and Christmas, for example, though you will be free for the solstices, of course."

The words "of course" kept pounding through Jana's head, and she found herself nodding and signing a small stack of paperwork. All the while, Nurse Fletcher was still smiling sweetly and furiously.

Monsignor's Day Off

A tall man in a long black overcoat sat beside a small fire at the verge of the forest. He wore a knitted cap over his bald head. It was Monsignor. With his back to a long stand of bloodweed, he surveyed the wide expanse of swamp before him. It was the Morganza spillway, and not counting the odd rotting shell of a tree sticking skyward, it was flat as far as the eye could see. It was lakes and tall grasses for miles and miles. It reminded Monsignor of the Dead Marshes that Tolkien had written about. The clouds fringing the horizon, he mused, could have been a tsunami or a wall of water. These clouds and others made for a muggy, gray day.

Ever since that day in his office speaking to Jim while under hypnosis, Monsignor had been spending his days off walking the levees near where Jim had said he and Anne saw the white heron. "I'll need to be physically, as well as spiritually, fit for what's coming," Monsignor often told himself in those days.

During nearly a year's worth of off-days, he had seen hundreds of white herons and caught his fill of catfish in the marshes and borrow-pits, which were created long ago to form the levees. He always left the fish for his housekeeper, Miss Lisa Chustz. At first, she had appreciated the fish and had cooked them for the priest, but she had grown increasingly concerned that the old man was out fishing by himself. *If she only knew the half of it.* Monsignor would think to himself, as she nagged on and on.

But Monsignor wasn't just fishing, he was hunting. The creature which now stalked the Louisiana moors was no imagined Baskerville hound. He had seen plenty of evidence that something strange was prowling the spillway. There were more mangled bodies of white herons. These were often just slop and feathers when Monsignor came upon them, but there was never any blood left. Still more disturbing than this was the flaying of the larger predators. Monsignor had found the bodies of coyotes, deer, and even alligators – big ones. Every one of them was over ten feet, with some pushing fifteen, which he knew would be a record in this parish. Alligators had held no fear for him since his childhood long, long ago, when he and his brother had faced the deep-dweller, the mother of all the great spinetails, whose slow twists and turns were felt through all the swamps. But that was another story.

Monsignor was just finishing a bit of catfish he had caught earlier. He had cooked in a bit of aluminum foil he had brought with him. He wiped off the foil and folded it back together to re-use. He didn't like to waste things, though he usually found that the bits of foil he had managed to save were all quickly found and tossed out by Miss Lisa. While eating his lunch, he had watched as birds slowly circled in the distance, marking the location of a fresh kill. Monsignor left his fishing pole behind to be collected later, and trudged down the slope of the levee. He had big, wide feet that steadied him despite having knees that had begun to wobble a bit. Around a bend in the long hill from where he had lunched, he spotted what the birds were after.

At the foot of the levee maybe another hundred yards away, there was the outer arm of one of the marsh's sprawling legs. There was a bulge in the surface of the water not far from the base of the levee. As Monsignor neared the site, he decided it was another slain alligator. This one was, by far, the largest he had yet encountered. It could have been just a massive pile of whitish-pink meat, as high as if Moby Dick had beached himself. The skinned meat was pale without blood to color it. The tough skin of the alligator had been slipped right off the beast, like a discarded snake skin. The flayed skin lay in a heap a bit further off. The alligator must have been over one hundred years old, Monsignor thought, because it was easily twenty feet long even without the skin.

Troubling still, the priest could hear that the thing was not dead, not yet.

It was laying on its side and its lungs still shook like a billows, jerkily spraying water and air out as from a diseased blowhole. Its jaws snapped occasionally, spasming with great pain, Monsignor could almost feel the pain, himself. "What could do this?" Monsignor whispered to himself, as he waded across the shallow water. Mud sucked at the bottom and sides of his rubber boots, as he stepped slowly into the lake. As he neared the thing, he could almost taste the spilled intestines. The smell of bile and partially digested food was thick in the air. Nearer the thing, he peaked over the side and confirmed that the alligator had been eviscerated and recently, probably that morning. There was a gaping hole where its belly ought to have been.

The giant alligator shook at Monsignor's approach from behind. Monsignor could sense it was afraid, and was probably fearing the return of whatever had been feasting on it. Monsignor laid a hand on the thing's skinned back, and it stilled. The thing sighed a long death rattle. The priest could sense the oppressive spirits that had taken refuge in the carcass. They had spread like fleas from whatever had been feasting here. He took a black leather purse from inside his overcoat. Glass jars tinkled inside of it. He pressed a firm hand on the dying animal and then spoke the words of the ritual against the blowing wet wind. The beast shook and then stilled again. Monsignor then spoke more prayers while removing glass jars of oil, salt, and water from the leather pouch. He poured a little of each on the bare meat and rubbed the slurry on like a marinade. He smeared it all with one hand while holding the pouch with his clean one. Then, collecting what remained, he let the mixture drip from his hand into the water, pressing more prayers into wind. With this, the entire lake became holy water.

Monsignor laughed as the water started boiling all around him with the kicking legs of disturbed frogs. The effect of the blessing spread across the face of the water in opposition to the wind, and the noise and racket of a thousand, thousand disturbed frogs erupted. "This evil multiplies quickly." Monsignor observed, as he concluded his prayers and hobbled slowly back to the base of the levee.

Monsignor stopped for a moment to stare at the levee he had walked down only a few minutes ago. He saw the green grass of the levee had been smudged and diveted by his wide bootprints. He saw something else, as well. He stood there just staring for a full minute, not fully comprehending what he was seeing. The levee was rent by a dark hole. There was a wide black mark of chewed up sod. Monsignor didn't understand how or what had made the hole in the levee, but he knew it had also been the thing that flayed the alligator alive and drained its blood.

As he returned along the levee to Morganza, the city just upriver from St. Maryville, where he had parked his car, he was dimly aware of a new presence watching him. He had an odd feeling like forgetting the name of an old friend.

Far away, hidden between the tall green stems of the bloodweed, something or someone *was* watching the old priest. It was short, and might even have been a child.

The Men of St. Maryville

A late middle-aged man slammed a red door being painted black behind him as he stalked up the worn wooden side stairway of the LaCour Building. The high frequency squeal of miter saw blades and the thud-thud-thud was thick in the air hazy with sawdust. It was still the same day that the newspaper had been read aloud at Tee-Eva's advertising the new abortion clinic.

"Ronnie! Where's Ronnie Fabre?" Fabre was pronounced like a watch "fob". Mr. Gremillion shouted gruffly through the bristles of his moustache, as a man is used to doing after living his whole adult life on a construction site.

One of the laborers swung his head away from his work and took the opportunity to squeeze out a few ounces of yellow tobacco juice into a used Coke can. "Super!" He called out to the back of the building, which was separated from the stairwell by a few temporary plastic walls. "Yo, supe! Somebody wants'ya!" Mr. Gremillion nodded without looking back to the boy. He could hear some more shouts traveling from man to man deeper into the building. Eventually they ended at a "What's that? Who's looking for me? Who?" And Mr. Gremillion listened as heavy footfalls banged and echoed against the wood floors heading in his general direction.

"Who's asking for me?" Mr. Fabre growled, tossing some plastic tarps aside as he made his way to the front of the building. The tarps fell back on the Assistant Supervisor who was close at Mr. Fabre's heels. The assistant recognized Mr. Gremillion and hung back.

"Johnny? That you?" Mr. Fabre then lightly slapped the laborer's head with a heavy hand. "Don't you know who that is, Greenie? Johnny's a parish inspector – you better give me a better heads-up if you see him come 'round again. Got it?"

"Sure, boss," the laborer said, squirting out a few more drops of shiny tar.

"Never miss a teaching moment, mm-hmm." Johnny nodded.

"What's that?" Gary said, turning the right side of his head to his moustached visitor. "That's my trick ear, Johnny. Speak to my good'un. And I ain't got no time for interruptions, so whatcha here for?"

Mr. Gremillion took off his foam and mesh John Deere hat, wiped a handful of sweat from his thick hair and scalp, and replaced it abruptly.

"Johnny?" Gary said, squinting intently at the man. "What is it? Why're you hesitating like that? If it's bad, tell me straight."

"Gary," Mr. Gremillion began and squared his boots to the slightly older man. "Do you know what you're building here?"

"Office space. What's it to ya?"

"Offices for a clinic, right?"

"Yeah, that's right. I remember something about that, come to mention it. What's it to—"

"Do you know what kind of clinic, Gary?"

Gary waved his hand at Mr. Gremillion to hurry it up.

"This is an *abortion* clinic, Gary." The Assistant Supervisor tucked his clipboard under his arm, and scooted back through the plastic. He returned not long after that followed one-by-one by other men, and the squealing saws and hammering gradually fell silent across the whole building.

"A what?" Gary shouted screwing up his face. "Say that again," he said, pointing to his good ear and leaning in."

"Abortion, Gary! You're standing in the future home of the Happy Families baby-killing salon and spa!"

Gary swiveled his good ear backward to the Assistant Supervisor, "You know anything about this, Red?" The man stammered, but did not answer the question. He just shook his head and then quickly broke off eye contact.

As he did, Mr. Gremillion took a folded piece of newsprint from his pocket, already swollen with a wadded pad and stubs of pencils. "Just read it, Gary." And he handed over the torn piece of paper. "One forty-eight Main Street, am I right?"

Mr. Fabre mouth hung open and he flicked his eyes back to Johnny. He handed the paper back. Mr. Fabre took his hard hat off, as Mr. Gremillion had done, and scratched at his scalp. "Dammit," he said hanging his head. "I really needed this job, too. I'm sure we all did, what with the falling price of oil and all. Sonofagun. Abortion, really?" Mr. Fabre suddenly gripped the rim of his hard hat so hard that his knuckles flushed white. He whirled it so hard against a new wall that the brim sank into the dry wall and the hat just hung there.

Mr. Fabre turned back to his men who had now all finished gathering on the second floor around the two men. "You heard the man. Show's over. Those of you wishing to stay can finish up your work. Your choice, if you can call it that. But Fabre Construction is rolling out of here, and you'll have to find your own tools."

By the time the sawdust had settled, there were over twenty hard hats embedded in that piece of drywall.

****

That night an emergency meeting was held between representatives of the abortion clinic; the city planner; the city attorney, Gene Ruby; as well as Ronnie Fabre and Johnny Gremillion. They met at the insistence of Edward Teach, the Chairman and CEO of Happy Families, Inc., who invited all parties to the first floor of the LaCour Building for the meeting. Edward Teach wore, as usual, a black beard and a black suit with a starched white shirt buttoned at the collar without a tie, as did his associates. His eyes, that night, glowed like a fox's deep in the woods.

The men from the city were outraged to find out what the building's new tenants had planned to open up on the Main Street of St. Maryville. Mr. Ruby lit into the clinic reps for nearly a half hour. He was gifted with deep-seated lungs and the will to use them, as his father, the Senator, had been before him. Throughout the nearly two hours of one-sided ranting, Edward

Teach and his colleagues remained serene and even nodded politely in agreement where appropriate.

When Mr. Ruby had finished his tirade, Mr. Gremillion started in. He stated matter-of-factly that under no circumstances would he or any other inspector in Pointe Coupee Parish approve the inspection of this building. Accordingly, no permits would be granted and the terms of the lease would be dissolved as of the end of the month.

Edward Teach nodded a final time at this, and said, "I assure you all and this lovely town that our company little appreciated the sensitive nature of our operations and their effect on the town. And for that we most heartily apologize. We have nothing to say for our actions, and I promise you, we are all surprised at this response." Edward Teach looked to his colleagues who all nodded vigorously and profoundly in agreement.

"You all must understand," Mr. Teach continued. "That where we come from –"

"Up north?" Mr. Fabre interrupted, squinting at Mr. Teach.

"Uh, yess," Edward Teach agreed, intersplicing his long pale fingers together like two picket fences. "Up north, as you say. Where we come from, we think of this procedure very differently – as any other medical procedure. But tonight, you men of St. Maryville have taught us something very important. Your courage is startling to us and very moving. It is time, I think, that we all seriously reconsidered our choices. The courage shown here tonight may well re-shape the future of this great nation." Edward Teach nodded gravely at this, and looked to each of the men in turn.

Mr. Gremillion, Mr. Fabre, and the others all relaxed visibly. Mr. Gremillion nodded and leaned back in his chair envisioning himself at Tee-Eva's Diner the next morning recounting his heroics.

"Gentlemen," Edward Teach began again. "As our situation is much removed from this morning, we would greatly appreciate any help you could offer us as we unroll our operations from your town." There was a general chorus of agreement and promised generosity from the men of St. Maryville. Edward Teach smiled then for the first time that evening. His smile was perhaps a little too wide, but attracted no further notice. "At least," he went on, "We will be able to say, years down the road, that we parted company without strife and with peace and amity." Edward spread out his spindly fingers to his sides like a skeletal bird.

"As a token of my appreciation for you all, that you came to us with your misgivings instead of taking legal action, allow us to treat you to a nightcap. This will serve as token of our appreciation to the Town of St. Maryville for its hospitality, albeit short-lived."

The men all clapped Edward Teach on the back as he led them all through a side door that led down to the basement of the LaCour Building.

"I had always heard this building had a basement," Mr. Gremillion smiled as he passed Edward Teach and began the descent of the stairs. "This is like a boyhood dream!" he exclaimed giddily.

"So it is. So it ever was." Edward Teach again smiled too widely as the last man passed into the darkness of the stairs leading down to the basement. And yet, they were not like the footsteps of living men.

The Women of St. Maryville

"Did you hear him come in last night?" Rosemary Plauche asked, looking at her slender thumb and forefingers as they held an empty white demitasse cup in tension. Rosemary sat beside her younger sister, Doris Ruby, whose husband, Gene, had met with Edward Teach the night before. News of the plans for the LaCour Building had spread fast in St. Maryville. Rosemary nodded at the black maid, who stood just outside the circle of ladies gathered in her front parlor for the monthly meeting of their reading circle. Rosemary returned the cup to its saucer with the barest tinkle and handed both to Daisy, the maid.

"I thought I did. I suppose I could've dreamed it." Missus Doris uncrossed and re-crossed her legs. Doris' hair was closer-cropped than that of the other ladies. She also wore linen pants while the others wore 'smart little skirts' as they would say, perhaps remembering their sorority days at LSU in the 1950s and the 'smart little skirts' they wore to the football games. Missus Doris' minor deviations were, of course, forgiven by the other ladies because she and her husband were both "old" St. Maryville. Nearly all the elected parish offices had been filled from the ranks of the Smiths and the Rubys for a century or more, though their grip on power had lessened of late. They were Catholics, as were most families in the parish, but there were still powerful Protestant families, as well, such as the Tafts.

"Well, what did he do that was so off-putting?" asked Mrs. Martha Smith, who played the piano at the St. Francis Chapel for the men's choir on early

Sunday mornings. Missus Smith was sitting beside Patty Gremillion, who had, as yet, contributed nothing to the conversation that morning.

"He – well, he …" Missus Doris fidgeted in frustration trying to think of the right words. As she did, drops of expresso came dangerously close to slipping out of her demitasse and onto Mrs. Frances Lorio's chartreuse shag carpet. She nodded reluctantly to Daisy, who quickly approached and took away the cup and saucer.

"Collect your thoughts, dear." Missus Frances had said, tapping Doris' knee lightly with her small hand. "And perhaps it's time for some brandy," she smiled to the ladies and to Daisy, who nodded and disappeared into the house.

"It's just that I hardly know how to describe it. It's not that I'm describing something, but the lack of something. Well, you all know Gene. He's equal parts scoundrel and saint, with an icy enough tongue for either." At this, the ladies laughed heartily as if Missus Ruby had made a joke, but Missus Ruby's face had only darkened. Moisture around her eyes threatened to become tears. "That man wasn't at my breakfast table this morning." She went on. "Gene didn't rant on about burnt toast – you know what a dreary cook I am – and the oil industry and Governor Edwards. He didn't rant about anything. He still looks like Gene, but the vigor has drained away. I'm sure of it."

"Maybe his coffee just hadn't kicked in yet, Doris." Rosemary suggested. "Also, you know how men will have their own cycle." The lady pursed her lips and winked at the other ladies.

"You said there was a meeting last night?" Miss Frances said trying to keep the conversation on course.

"Yes, that's right. It was Patty's husband who got the ball rolling in the first place." Heads swiveled away from Doris and towards the more taciturn woman.

"Is that true, Patty?" Missus Martha asked, "Then what about Johnny? Did he seem odd to you?"

Patty sighed and tried to smile politely, but found that her smile faltered with the uncontrollable spams of pent up tears. She folded her napkin to a point and dabbed at her eyes.

"Oh, dear, dear," Missus Martha said putting her head to the younger woman's shoulder in comfort.

Patty gathered herself together as she refolded her napkin. "It's actually something of a relief," she said, "to hear Doris talk about Gene. At least I know it's not just Johnny."

"*And* not another woman," Missus Rosemary added with a curt nod.

"No, no. It wouldn't be." Patty smiled, "Not with that mustache of his, anyway."

The women laughed despite themselves, and Missus Frances felt forced to bring the conversation back to productivity. She cleared her throat, and said, "Patty, are you saying Johnny was behaving similar to Gene."

Missus Patty nodded, "Johnny can certainly rant about toast and things, himself. And his temper can be extraordinary. But that's just it. He usually eats at Tee-Eva's in the morning, but this morning he made his own coffee and stayed home to read the paper."

"I'd hardly cry if my husband made his own coffee in the morning," Missus Rosemary smirked, striking a dissonant tone.

"That's not it. It's not just that he'd never done that. It was the way he had to ask where his clothes were. It was the way he left without his hat. It was …"

"The way he looked at you," Missus Doris stated icily. "That's it. You've put your finger on it. It was almost like when I would talk to my great-grandmother as a little girl. She had dementia. She would look at me as if I were a stranger. That's what Gene did. It was only an instant. Less than that. But it was there. It was like all our years together had vanished. Had ceased to exist."

"It was like *I* had ceased to exist," Patty added, and Doris quickly nodded closing her eyes before tears could burst out of them.

"But how can that be? What are we even talking about?" Missus Martha asked holding Patty's shoulder while searching the ladies' faces for an answer.

"Are you two saying that something happened at that meeting last night at the LaCour building?" Missus Frances asked.

"I think that's exactly what they're saying. Not that any of it is possible,"

Missus Rosemary said dryly. Her eyes flicked upward as Daisy re-entered the room. "Ah, yes. Just what we all need: some brandy. Thank you, Daisy. Better bring the bigger glasses."

Daisy looked to Missus Frances for confirmation, who nodded demurely. "If what you two are saying is true, we're all going to need *a lot* more brandy."

Protest

Miss Dot Poche had spent the whole night previous making posters and signs to protest the abortion clinic under construction. Despite her early morning shower, there were still marks and smudges left on her fingers. Her husband, Henry, had a Mr. Sketch marker smudge on his right cheek. He had stayed up pretty late himself, but his head had eventually slumped over on top of a poster. Miss Dot had taken a long moment to stare at her husband sweetly before tapping him on the shoulder and leading him to bed. She had slipped off her husband's socks and tucked him in. Then, she had hurried back to the poster Henry had been working on and wiped away the smear of drool.

Miss Dot had put together a group of people from St. Mary's and other local churches. She had gradually filled up her clipboards of time slots spanning forty days. She parked at St. Mary's and pulled out a couple posters at a time to half drag, half carry over to the sidewalk of the LaCour building. She left them tucked away beside the LaCour building, and returned to her car two blocks away. A couple minutes later, she returned to the same sidewalk dragging another couple posters.

"Jim! Hey, Anne! Y'all came! Good morning! Sorry about the smell, not sure what that's about."

Anne gave Miss Dot a hug. "Yeah, of course, we wouldn't miss it. Can you believe? Abortion right here in St. Maryville." Anne's hand slowly moved to her nose as she became aware of the smell.

Miss Dot gave Jim a hug, as well. After he had refilled his lungs with air following Miss Dot's characteristically strong hug, he asked, "You need any help with those posters, Miss Dot?"

"Oh, sure. And look, besides these two posters I'm holding, there are another two leaning against the wall over there. And we can say a rosary in a couple minutes."

Jim followed where Miss Dot was pointing. There was a mostly empty lot beside the LaCour Building. The lot sat at the actual corner of New Roads and Main Streets with the LaCour Building on its Main Street side and Miss Tee-Eva's on its New Roads Street side. There was a mural covering the entire side of the LaCour building that faced the empty lot. It was a painting over the brick wall of the cotton harvest, barges carrying cotton bales up and down False River, and of the church and other landmarks. The colors had faded over the years, but the image was still clear.

Miss Dot had leaned her first two posters – which were her favorites, actually, including the one Mr. Henry had drooled a bit on – against the wall covered in tall murals of the cotton harvest. Jim looked up and down the wall, but found no posters. He looked back to Miss Dot in confusion. She returned his gaze with an odd look. "Jim, don't you see them?"

Miss Dot walked around the corner to where she had placed her first two posters. "But they were right *here*. See? Right where that dirt's spilled over the grass. But, hey, there was just grass there when I put the posters down. Not this mound."

"Forget it," Jim said with a worried expression that meant he would not soon be forgetting anything. "They'll probably turn up. Things have a way of doing that."

"Yeah," Miss Dot said, still staring at the odd hole in the ground where her slaved-over signs had been. She shivered as her imagination began to wander. "I suppose so," she said, trailing off. She just stood there. Her head seemed to be slowly dropping to the ground, as though being tugged by an unseen hand.

Jim and Anne exchanged worried looks. Anne walked over to Miss Dot, "How about that rosary, huh?"

"Hey, look!" Jim said. "It's George and Luanda! Miss Dot, you better go get more signs. We'll hold on to these *very* carefully for you."

That was how the forty-day prayer vigil and peaceful protest had begun. The numbers of volunteers remained pretty steady throughout the forty days. The priests and pastors helped drum up support for it, and the sidewalk witnessed a modest increase in new volunteers throughout the event. The event was not without its odd happenings, though.

Nightly Visitor

In the time since Rock's head had collided with the Jaguar on First Avenue, Sam had settled into the social strata of Catholic High School somewhere near the bottom. Every kid in the parish had heard the story of how Sam Pitre had rid their pantheon of its Dark Lord. Despite his notoriety, Sam had still made few friends. A certain whispered word – "murderer" – had been nipping at Sam's heels wherever he went in the small town. Despite his initial success at the school Mass, he hadn't been asked again to serve as lector. Elton, on the other hand, had vastly improved with Sam's coaching. Elton had become Sam's one true friend, along with a handful of other social outcasts. These were often the only kind of kids who were able to assess a person honestly. They had been inoculated against the foolishness of popularity.

The teachers seemed to have reserved a blind spot in their vision for Sam. It was obvious and almost comical the way the teachers would blink across Sam as they scanned the lunch room crowds or their own classrooms. Sam had received his midterm report card almost two weeks late because his teachers just hadn't noticed the absence of Sam's name from the grade books.

Worst of all for Sam, his initial success with Erin had seemed to evaporate. Every day for a month following Rock's accident, Sam had been walking home almost seven blocks out of his way. This way, his path crossed Erin's for a solid three blocks. Every single day, the boy watched for her and she never looked his way.

It was so incredibly frustrating to Sam. He could bear the social ostracism, because who cares about being popular, anyway? His friends were the best of the lot anyhow. But the girl? He knew he had made a connection with her from that very first moment. It had never been that way with a girl before. He'd been noticing them for long enough, but the ones he liked never seemed to like him and vice-versa. But then this one came along. She was every boy's dream, and certainly his own. He didn't care that every other boy in school would both admire and hate him if he and Erin Bellefontaine started dating, but that made rejection all the more bitter. He could've lived the dream, but it had been snatched away. *And you what?* He screamed indignantly in his tussle-haired head – *I thought she was better than that. Different. But she's just like all the others. She can't even see me!*

"That's it," Sam said aloud, again walking home by himself. "I'm invisible. I'm the invisible freakin' man."

"Deciding on your Halloween costume?" A voice glided over to him. The boy turned to see Erin behind him on the wet leaf-strewn sidewalk. She wore a coy smile and the school's green and blue plaid uniform.

God, he thought to himself, *nobody moves like this girl.* Lost in his admiration, he nearly forgot to reply. They were lost in an awkward, inky silence for a time – the kind in which a boy is liable to question every plank of his existence. Fighting the desire to cut and run, Sam gave the girl a sly half-smile. "You're not about to mug me, are you?"

The girl laughed in surprise, scoffing at the suggestion. "*Never* on the first date, Sam."

Good Lord! Did she just wink at me? Sam felt like his heart was about to explode from his chest. "First date?" He asked, trying to keep his mind from falling apart. "A girl like you? No, way – a girl like you barely knows a guy like me exists."

"Is that so?" Erin said, distracting from the flush of red in her face by raising an eyebrow at the boy.

"It *is* so," Sam nodded seriously. They had fallen into step beside each other seamlessly. "It's been a month since you even loo—"

"I was letting *you* make the first move, Sammy." She pursed her lips in punctuation.

Sam didn't realize that he'd fallen a half-step behind the girl, as the galaxies behind his eyes had each chosen that moment to go supernova. His feet were on auto-pilot. A moment later, he was just standing there with a dumb look on his face, as though the Star of Bethlehem was shining across his face.

"Sam, you alright?"

The boy shook his head a little, bringing his focus back to the girl. "Is it possible …?" He began. "Is it possible that, for just a second – just one perfect second – a person can feel completely, maddeningly happy?"

Erin suddenly became very interested in the schoolbooks she was carrying with her hands clasped in front of her. They had arrived at the white picket gate in front of her house, though neither of them had realized it.

Still in his perfect moment, Sam's courage suddenly bubbled up to meet his clarity of mind. While the girl was still unable to return his gaze, Sam reached for the girl's delicate chin. He felt the smoothness of her skin as he lifted her face and pulled it to his own. He kissed her. He kissed the girl, thinking he'd never be able to pry himself from the girl's soft lips. He smiled at the girl, as she finally pulled away. They stood for a moment with their faces still close. Her eyes were still on his lips, though her own were curling into a smile. She flashed her green eyes at the boy, and turned briskly to the gate. She was through it and had climbed the stairs to her front porch before the boy had noticed he was alone. Her green eyes addressed him once more before she was gone.

An image flashed in Sam's mind that, after Erin had closed the door behind her, she had melted backward against the closed door, clutching her schoolbooks to her breast. He hoped to God that it was true. He couldn't feel the seven blocks of sidewalk beneath his feet walking home. But the Autumn had never smelled so sweet. He could smell the pecans in their shells still hanging from their branches. He could smell the pies and pralines they would become, too.

****

That night, still fresh from the shedding of its teenage skin, the thick slimey creature that had been Rock Bellelo inched across the yard of the Bellefontaine house. The creatures thoughts were rudimentary. It did not question how it crawled all the way from the hospital to this place. Or even, how long it had taken. It felt only hunger and desire. It had grown fat living in the sewer lines and consuming vermin. The eyes which looked dully from the shriveled face on its back seemed to have greater comprehension, but not the creature. It could feel the vibration of water pipes inside the cold ground against its wet belly. It could feel them even stronger as it began slurping upward along the house's vertical exterior walls. Waves of cilia fluttered at the creature's sides as it streaked cold slime around the second story bathroom window. Waves of warm steam curled against the glass panes and slick condensation formed on the creature's side of the glass.

The creature had no eyes, but its underbelly could smell the girl within. Eventually, the water was cut off, and the clink of shower curtain rings skidded across the shower rod. Mucous dripped in rivulets from the creature's body. It could feel the girl wiping off the mirror on the other side of the wall. It could feel, as well, her bare, wet footsteps as she came to the window. The louver window groaned open, as the girl rotated it upward to let some of the steam escape.

The thing, like congealed mucous, wrapped its body around the window frame and scurried through the cloud of escaping steam, sliding onto the moist walls inside the bathroom. The girl had since put on her robe and had set to work blow-drying her long hair. The thing did not know what would happen when it set its body on her, wrapping her in its slime – if it would destroy her – it knew only the desire of it.

It had climbed up and onto the bathroom's ceiling, coiling itself around the vent. It was slowly, almost delightedly, plucking away its cilia one by one. It would drop onto the girl, first sealing her head and mouth with its suffocating phlegm, and then he could set upon his work in silence.

While it was still attached to the ceiling and its head was slowly stretching down to the girl's golden hair – almost licking at her with its pseudopoda – it suddenly felt the call of its master. It was being pulled back the way it had come, following its own trail of slime backward. By then, the steam had cleared and the girl had closed the window. Nevertheless, the slug creature was being sucked through the narrow slit between the sill and the frame. Its insides swelled into its head as its tail and hindparts squealed through the thin gap. At this, the girl finally noticed her visitor waggling back and forth in pain along the edge of her window.

The devolved form of Rock's body was equipped with a very rudimentary digestive system, including a mouth, anus, and mostly gelatin in between. It was being pulled through the windowsill like a tube of toothpaste. Pressure was growing intense at the cap end of the creature and its head was swelling up like a balloon with dull circles for eyes. Goo was beginning to drip from its fluke-like mouth aperture. Then, its body fluids started flowing and gushing as a stream out of the mouth.

Erin started screaming as she was showered with the creature's acidic insides. She covered herself with her short robe and dove behind the shower curtain. A moment later, the creature's head exploded. Its now-completely deflated body slipped right out through the window sill. The bluish-grey mess which covered the bathroom walls in dripping splatters began to twitch. Slowly, the puddles and globs of the creature's insides coalesced. They formed together in narrow veins across the bathroom, marbleizing the wood-paneled walls of the bathroom. Soon, it had all slipped out the sides of her bathroom window.

Erin's parents were soon pounding on the locked door to the bathroom. When they found her, she was still huddled in the bathtub crying. It hadn't been the head which exploded that had left her so addled. It had been the shriveled, staring face on the thing's back that had left her feeling disconnected from reality. She had recognized the face.

Her dad, a judge, hadn't been able to find any trace of the thing that had attacked his daughter. There was only the caved-in remnants of a hole beneath his daughter's window. He would have to give the family dog a stern talking to, he told himself, if she had started digging again. If only the judge could find the dog.

Jaguar

The rain was pounding on the tin roof sheets of the Ennis community health clinic and growling down the galvanized steel gutters. The water flooded from the gutters into a frothy pool of mud, exposing buried layers of oyster shells. The rain had made a lagoon of the parking lot and road beyond. Beyond the road, the double row of buildings of St. Vincent de Paul Church seemed relatively high and dry.

Michelle Edmonds sighed, surveying the scene from inside the window of the community health clinic. This wasn't what she had expected when she volunteered for the rural health initiative out of Loyola Chicago's Medical School. She had imagined herself carrying a worn black medical case and stethoscope from house to shanty, delivering medical advice and lollipops, when necessary. She had also planned to deliver subversive advice on family planning to the sprawling families of the Louisiana back country. She would bring these Boudreaux's and Thibodeaux's into the twentieth century, delivering them from their "superstitious religious provincialism," as she had been taught in med school.

But this damned rain, Michelle thought, as she pushed against the window sill in frustration. The sill groaned dangerously beneath her – she may not have been the picture of health herself, given the roundishness of her figure. Time and time again, she had been silenced by the gentle nods of these country women, when she had made her subtle suggestions concerning birth control. It was the same knowing looks again and again.

She'd vent her frustrations to her med school classmates over the phone at night, twisting the cord tighter and tighter around her index finger. Michelle would blame it on these women's domineering husbands, though, in truth, she had seen very little evidence of this.

Michelle was staring through the window, in part, to avoid conversation with the nurse she had been provided, Cathy Leer, a local. She had decided long ago that she had very little in common with this nurse who spent nearly every one of her lunch breaks trudging across the road to St. Vincent de Paul for daily Mass. It was nearly time now for the nurse's daily excursion. The doctor was waiting to see the downpour's effect on the nurse's devotions.

"Listen," the nurse said.

"I hear it. Believe me, I don't need to be reminded of this blasted, unending rain."

"No," Cathy shook her head, tousling her long dark ponytail. "*Listen.*"

And then the young doctor heard it. It was another sound mixing with the rhythmic pounding of the rain. It was the oncoming Doppler shift of an approaching ambulance. "But they can't come *here*" Michelle protested. "We're not equipped for emergency care – what do those fools think they're doing?"

"The road across the spillway's likely closed due to the flooding," the nurse answered.

"Oh." The young doctor frowned.

"This is the only medical facility for miles and miles and miles." Cathy continued. Soon, there could see the green and white striped ambulance charging into view, spraying high walls of water in its wake. When it screeched to a halt out front, a wall of water crashed against the front of the building rattling the window in its sill.

The doctor waited inside as the nurse ran into the rain to meet the ambulance. She set about gathering what supplies she could to prepare for whatever it was that was about to barge into her clinic.

The door swung open with a spray of mist. The nurse rushed back in, followed by two black paramedics in yellow slickers who were carrying a limp body by hand.

"What happened to him?" Michelle asked.

"He was found by a hunter this morning. By Jim Lajoie." One of the black men answered. "He had been dragged deep into the woods 'round that way. Weirdest thing, Jimmy said a girl had brought the boy to him. How she could've carried him, I'll never know."

The doctor recognized suddenly that it was nothing more than a boy, the paramedics were carrying. *Maybe* sixteen years old. The kid was unconscious and pale, but shivering. There was a long rip in his shirt, soaked with blood, and another rip through his jeans.

"Why isn't he on a stretcher?" The doctor questioned the men, as the nurse led the men in laying the boy on the table in the center of the room. She had already started an intravenous line.

The doctor swung a light over the body to inspect the wounds closer. "Nurse, get the scissors, we're going to –" But the nurse was already busy cutting away the boy's clothes.

When the boy's shirt was pulled away, the doctor's and paramedics winced. Wide tearing rows of lacerations ran from the boy's shoulder. The flesh had been shredded. Down the bottom of the deepest laceration, the pale bones of the boy's rib cage could be counted. Another slash, probably a continuation of the first, led down into the meat of the boy's thigh. The gash was deep enough to see the boy's weak pulse trembling along the length of his exposed femoral artery.

"He's been mauled," the nurse observed.

"By what?" The doctor scoffed. "A dinosaur?" She had only seen one other mauling during her residency. It had involved a pit bull and a three-year-old child. The wounds were proportional in size to the larger boy. The doctor could not conceive of what may have caused this.

"He should be dead," the doctor went on, as she dabbed at the edge of the cuts with antiseptic. "Why didn't he bleed out? These wounds are *hours* old."

The nurse wrinkled her nose. "Do you smell that?" She asked the doctor.

The doctor shook her head. "Only the antiseptic."

"It smells like rotting, like death and decay. It's strange, though … never smelled anything quite like this."

"He couldn't've been out there long enough for necrosis," the doctor answered. "But I smell it, too."

"Mother Mary," the nurse suddenly exclaimed. She had moved on to inspect other parts of the boy's body. She was standing at his head now, and looking down in horror. The doctor and paramedics moved around the body to stand beside her.

"What in the hell?" Doctor Edmonds sneered, swinging the light around for a closer inspection. The boy's long hair had concealed the injury. There were *holes*.

"There's no blood," the doctor continued. She began wiping the boy's hair from the wound with a gloved hand.

"No, don't …," the nurse said, reaching out suddenly to stay the doctor's hand. Even as she did, they could all hear the sound as something fell from the boy's head, banged against the side of the metal table, and clattered to the floor. One of the paramedics ran into the bathroom at the back of the clinic, where he could later be heard wretching. The other paramedic just sat down at the windowsill as his knees grew weak beneath him. The nurse and the doctor exchanged horrified glances. Cathy held a trembling hand to her mouth. The doctor reached down to pick up the thick plate of skull and scalp which had tumbled from the boy's head.

Then, there was a thick gurgling from the other side of the boy's head. The nurse and doctor swung around the table in surprise at the sound. It was the boy. He was trying to say something, likely his last words, if he could manage them.

The boy's lips moved just a little. Obviously, the words came only with great effort. He whispered something.

"What? What was it he said?" The doctor asked.

The nurse had put her head to the boy's ear. Now, she pushed up from the metal table with a dazed, faraway look in her eyes. "He said," she began, shaking her head. "Garou."

"Baloo?" The doctor asked with a mad, wincing look on her face. "Like the bear, from the Disney movie?"

Cathy shook her head, distractedly. "No, *garou*. The boy means *rougarou*.

It's supposed to just be folklore. You grow up here, though, you hear whispers. Sometimes people just disappear, and it's probably just accidents. Maybe it's just the swamp, but maybe it's not, too."

"*What* are you going on about?" The doctor asked.

"Jag—" The boy gurgled out a second word.

"Jag? Jag-what?" The doctor asked. "Maybe he means 'jaguar'. Are there jaguars in Louisiana?"

But the nurse was ignoring the doctor, and backing away slowly from the table where the boy was laying. The doctor was about to order the nurse back to the table when the boy suddenly opened his eyes wide and sat straight up on the table. In one fluid motion, the boy sat up and blood exploded from his mouth. He fell back again to the table with a hard clank and began seizing. His body was vibrating and convulsing even as he continued to vomit blood. The doctor tried to grab him, but the boy's body toppled to the floor even as the table had begun to rock back and forth.

The body made a wet slapping sound and hollow bang as it fell to the wood plank floor below. He vomited again. The blood shot across the floor as if something had popped within him. It was likely some hidden pocket of internal hemorrhage. The smell that the nurse had earlier noticed now fell thickly across the room.

"What the hell is happening here?" A man yelled from the community clinic's door. In all the madness, no one had noticed the flashing lights and siren of the sheriff's cruiser pull in beside the silenced, but still flashing ambulance. It was Deputy Dabadie. When he saw the blood and the looks of horror, he looked down to the still-convulsing boy with the black hollowness peeking from the top of his head. He quickly turned away, his hand to his mouth.

The doctor was grabbing around dumbly for a stick to wedge into the boy's mouth as he continued to seize. The nurse was standing with her back to the wall, and the two paramedics were cowering out of sight. With a final rocking spasm, the boy relaxed and lay still.

The doctor bent over the boy to begin performing CPR, but the nurse, suddenly at her side, grabbed her and pulled her back. "No," she said. "Don't touch him. The rougarou, that smell — it crosses over."

"Oh, *hell*," the doctor said, pushing the nurse away.

"Yes," she said solemnly, regaining her balance. "*Hell*." The nurse, though smaller than the doctor, clapped one hand across the doctor's shoulder. "Stop, Michelle. You're not from here – you don't…"

The doctor wriggled under the nurse's iron grip, like a fly caught in a bell jar. The doctor looked back suddenly at the nurse, surprised at her hidden strength and resolve. After a few more seconds of squirming under her grasp, while the obscenities came dripping from her mouth, the nurse released her suddenly. "There, it is over," she said.

The doctor made to slap the nurse, and then she saw, below on the floor, that the boy had surely died. Even now, the body was in advanced stages of decomposition. The boy seemed to shrink and waste away. As the doctor watched, her entire sense of reality and possibility seemed to be collapsing in front of her. The doctor opened her mouth to scream, but found that the scream was too large to squeeze through her constricted throat. She scrambled backwards on her hands and feet, back against the wall. She began picking at her upper lip feverishly. It must have been a comfort to her that she had long ago buried away. It would be the last day that she practiced medicine.

The nurse was far more practical. As the doctor was careening down the rabbit hole beside her, she stood up and walked over to the sink. She began washing her hands thoroughly and then her arms. She removed all her blood-stained clothes and even her underwear. The blood seemed to have seeped through everything. She did her best to sterilize her entire body and then changed into the spare set of clothes she kept in her locker.

In just a few minutes, she had grabbed her purse and left. She passed back through the central multi-purpose room of the rural clinic. The others were all still staring at the rapidly decomposing body. They were all too horrified to move or even speak.

If the doctor had returned to her creaking window sill just then, she would have seen the nurse crossing the still-flooded parking lot and then the road. The church bells were ringing for daily Mass.

Nurse Jana

"Nurse Jana, please!" One of the protesters called. It had either been Miss Dot or the Landreneau girl visiting from LSU. They were calling to the newly-hired nurse from the short fence which marked the back parking lot of the LaCour Building. "Please don't go in there – please, if we could only talk …? I'll even buy your *lunch*!"

It had been days since the mauling of the Ennis boy and his death, and word had spread across the parish. The rumors of the jaguar had sparked a minor hysteria. There had been scattered reports of animal sounds around the parish and beyond. Every shadow in the woods and swamps was quickly becoming a jaguar. The Sheriff and his deputies were doing their best to dampen the panic.

The protest at the abortion clinic had continued uninterrupted by the rumors of the incident at the community clinic on the other side of the parish. Doctor Edmonds had requested a leave of absence, but had returned to Chicago before one could be granted.

Nurse Jana hurried into the side alley to where the employee's entrance stood. She hid her head behind her purse and walked swiftly. When she had arrived in the safety of the alley, she noticed that she was holding her purse up to her head and quickly put it back to her side. Her face quickly reddened, and she paused with her hand on the door handle before entering the clinic. Taking her hand from the handle, she turned her hand over and noticed that it was trembling.

The nurse shook her head and pushed forward through the metal door.

The cool air of the clinic washed across her face. She was relieved at least to be free of the smell that had been slowly filling the town. When the door clanged shut behind her, she was looking down a gleaming white hallway. Even now, after working at the clinic for several weeks, she still didn't know all the twists and turns of the hallways. She even thought that they might *shift* from time to time, if that was possible.

Nurse Jana stopped by her locker briefly to put up her purse and car keys. As the locker door, too, clanged shut, she wondered at the strange emptiness of it all. She knew she had seen a whole group of nurses her first day – and the one with the face of a bird – but where were they now? She barely saw anybody these days, except Nurse Fletcher – she shuddered – and Fixie.

Nurse Jana weaved down one of the only routes she had learned in the building, the path to the front desk. "Good morning, Fixie!" Nurse Jana managed a little excitement in her voice, as she turned into the waiting room. "I just wanted to tell you how thankful I am for you, Fixie. Sometimes, it seems like you're the only other human in this place."

But when Fixie turned her face to Jana, it was changed somehow. The lady's natural bubbliness had utterly dissipated.

"Fixie? What's wrong?"

"Oh, hi-yah, Jana." She said without hollow emotion. "Nurse Fletcher asked me to stay late last night. Must be tired. Mr. Teach came by."

"Mr. Teach?" Jana asked, again noticing that her hands were trembling as she groped for the coffee pot. She had yet to meet the enigmatic Mr. Teach. Her stomach was beginning to turn when she noticed the coffee pot was empty. She sneaked a look back at Fixie. She was staring forward at the door with wide, unseeing eyes. Every morning since her hiring, Fixie had had coffee ready and waiting. She loved the stuff, Jana thought. Jana went about fixing the coffee herself, choosing to keep her suspicions to herself.

Jana's hands nearly betrayed her suddenly, as a voice spoke up behind her. She clanged the glass coffee pot into place and spun around. At first, she thought her eyes had betrayed her, as well. A face like a white mask frozen in its dark, smiling features floated across her vision. She blinked, and saw it was Nurse Fletcher.

"There will be no time for *that* this morning, Nurse Jana," Fletcher said with derision. "Today's surgery day. Rooms 4, 5, and 6 all need to be prepped. Our ladies will begin arriving within the hour. No time for chit-chat and coffee –- you understand that, right?" Nurse Fletcher turned her head at the last comment, as if to suggest that, perhaps, she had mistaken the nurse all this time for an adult, when in reality, she was just the scum burnt to the underside of the coffee pot.

"Yes, mam," Jana nodded respectfully and laid down her cup inside the kitchenette adjacent to the receptionist's desk.

"That's a dear one," Nurse Fletcher smiled, suddenly sweet in demeanor. The older woman turned around suddenly and continued talking, expecting that Jana would stay close at her heels. "Now, listen close and take notes," Fletcher was saying as Jana jogged to catch up with her. Jana pulled a small pad and pencil from the pockets of her white dress. Room 4 requested a dressing and photographer – that should all be staged and ready by 10:45am. The dear ones should all be removed by 10:30am. You may need to remind the surgeon of that. The doulas will be here any minute …"

"Excuse me, mam. What's a *doula*?"

"They assist in the partial birth of the dear ones and help relieve the mothers of their emotional trauma." Nurse Fletcher now spoke indulgently to the young nurse. "All the mothers' past moral ruminations, lived horrors of sexual violence, imaginings of sin, and cravings for new life –- the doulas help deliver all this from the mothers, even as their children are liberated from the womb. The transformation is just remarkable," Nurse Fletcher's voice caught in her throat at this last, and she quickly rubbed a tear from the corner of her eye. Nurse Jana's head was swimming. She had meant to ask what "a dressing" was, as well, but she suddenly realized that she had lost track of their turnings down the labyrinthine hallways.

****

"Breathe, just breathe, Amy," The doula was saying.

An hour an half later, Nurse Jana was in the thick of an operation. She was holding gauze in place for the doctor, and dabbing away the fluids. The partial-birth abortions were always torture for her to assist with.

"How are you feeling, Amy? I just want to be here for you emotionally," the doula was explaining.

"Please," the patient, Amy, muttered in pain and annoyance. She was turning away from the doula, avoiding her eye contact. This was difficult as the doula was keeping her face within inches of the patient's face. "I don't need this. I just want *it* out of me and I'll be gone. I won't cause anyone anymore prob—" She stopped, grunting in discomfort, as her body was rocked by the doctor's jerking movements.

The doula nodded meaningfully at Nurse Fletcher. Nurse Jana, for her part, was trying to keep an eye on swabbing without looking at the partially-delivered body of a baby hanging limply in front of the doctor.

"You said it wouldn't be like *this*," the patient screamed, flashing daggers with her eyes at Nurse Fletcher. "You said I wouldn't *feel* anything! You *monster!*"

Nurse Fletcher's eyes were growing watery again. "But you are part of something so beautiful – the liberation of life," Nurse Fletcher said, wiping away strands of the patient's hair which were sticking across her face. The Big Nurse seemed not to notice when the women snapped her teeth at her hand, barely missing her outstretched hand. The patient's fury dissolved into weeping.

"I understand you're feeling emotionally saturated. I'm here to receive and hold whatever feelings you need to express." As the doula spoke, her hands crept down to the partially delivered child and was holding it between her fingers. Nurse Jana watched the slow caress of the fingers and felt her breakfast welling up inside of her. The fingers seemed for a moment to be too long, but she turned away in disgust before she could get too good of a look.

Like Arachne before her loom, the doula kept spinning her words. "It's important for you, as a woman, to feel in control of your body and your life. You must feel so feminine at this moment, this special moment."

"Are you stupid?" Amy barked at the doula. "This is hell!" She said before another wave of pain washed over her.

"I completely agree, dear. If that's where you feel you need to be right now, just *be*." The doula's words were almost hypnotic.

"Is it – almost – over?" The patient's body went limp. Nurse Jana's eyes darted over to the monitors, and she breathed a sigh of relief. The patient had only passed out.

"That's enough swabbing, Nurse." The doctor pushed away the long silver tweezers which held the nurse's gauze in place, as he prepared to complete the procedure.

"Quite right, Nurse," Fletcher said. "Prepare the little one for the dressing."

"For *disposal*?" Nurse Jana asked.

A flare of temper erupted into the older nurse's eyes. Nurse Fletcher snapped her eyes closed, letting the anger wash over her. "No," she said too quietly. "The *dressing*, Nurse Jana. Didn't you ever play with dolls as a child? You *dress* the baby."

Nurse Jana was shaking her head slowly. She felt trapped between the heaving nausea in her belly and abject fear. "Why … why?" she stammered. "Why would we dress it?"

"It's not an *it,* you beast." Outwardly, Nurse Fletcher had grabbed Jana's hands in a motherly gesture, but the younger nurse's knees began buckling with the pain of her bones bending within the woman's grip. "It's a child. *A person.* We dress the baby for the family photograph."

"A child?" Nurse Jana was weeping in pain and incomprehension. "Family pho…? But how can you say that as we kill it? You're – all of you – it's murder!"

Sweetness spread across Nurse Fletcher's face even as Jana's bones groaned within her grasp. "Murder? Ha! You sweet, silly thing. I love every child carried through these doors. That's why I so desire to *free* them. Don't you understand?" The Big Nurse waited a moment for a response. Nurse Jana crumpled to her knees, as her eyes began to roll back in her head. The nurse would later remember that moment and wonder if she had really seen what she thought she had seen: a flash of purple running through Nurse Fletcher's eyes.

"*Now,*" Nurse Fletcher continued, "I'll give you a moment to collect yourself, and then I expect you to go pick out a smart little outfit for this newborn."

"Oh! Maybe a sailor suit? You know how I love them in sailor suits!" The doula was pressing the lifeless body of the mutilated child to her face, like an adoring grandmother. "Oh, can we? Amy would love that, wouldn't you, Amy?"

Amy made no reply, though her monitors may have chirped in response. The patient's body lay as limp as that of her aborted child.

****

Nurse Jana stumbled out of the operating room, after making what excuses she could. She could feel her hand swelling unnaturally as she clutched it to her chest. Before she could leave, though, she was ordered by the Big Nurse to get needle and thread for stitching up the patient, more gauze, and an assortment of baby clothes from the rack. She had nodded obsequiously before leaving, even as she vowed in her heart never to return, to dash out of this godforsaken place now and forever.

As the pain drew her closer to fainting, she walked, half-staggered through the maze of hallways. She quickly lost track of her lefts and rights. Soon, she was completely lost and the light of the hallway had taken on a new, less-sterile complexion. She was looking from door to door. They all looked the same. There were no numbers. Some had light shining under the door and some didn't. Jana was growing equally afraid of both the lit rooms and the dark, and of what she might find in both.

Finally, she put her hand to one of the cheap brass door knobs. It turned beneath her grasp, and she wondered if any of the doors were ever locked. This room was lit, but only by a single light over a sink. Blue light spilled down. There were shelves on either side of the sink from floor to ceiling. The shelves were stacked two deep with jars filled with blue liquid. There were *things* preserved in the liquid, floating things, Jana saw. Her curiosity drew her closer, despite the mounting fear.

But she had failed to scan the whole room before getting distracted. The nurse didn't notice what lay beyond the sink and its small cone of light. They had turned to her and been watching her for seconds before she noticed them. Her whole body shook when she finally saw their small, sharp movements out of the corner of her eye. She didn't know whether her fright had been an instinctual revulsion to their strange movements or simple surprise, and she didn't have time to wonder.

They wore masks, white medical masks. She was frozen in place, as though caught between nightmare and reality. But in the strangeness idiocy of the moment, she stopped to wonder how they could wear the mask, the mask straps held onto the back of ears, but these things. They had *no ears*. Their faces were covered in feathers. Their heads were full of the black protruding bird eyes, and they watched her from the side of their brightly-colored heads. They had the hands of men, strong men.

Somehow, Jana pulled her gaze down from their heads to their hands, and what they were holding. What they were holding, it was nearly the last thing she saw before she blacked out. When she saw what they were holding, she realized what had been floating in the jars. At first, she hoped moronically they were just doll parts. But she knew darkly, they were not. *It was the fruit of her labors.* The clinic's trash, the remains of the unwanted.

As her knees began to buckle beneath her and just as her eyes began to roll backwards in their sockets, she realized that the babies *were* wanted. She saw what lay beyond the bird-men. There was a vast darkness, but the single bulb threw just enough light for the teeth to glint in the darkness.

A Gathering of Old Men

Warren David swiveled heavily out of his dark brown Lincoln Continental Town Car. He was carrying two McDonald's styrofoam coffee cups with rows of yellow, orange, and brown Ms stamped around the sides. He slowly lifted himself out of the deeply padded and well-worn plush mauve velour seats. He put the cups on the roof of the car as he leaned back in the car to pull out a newspaper and a grease-stained bag of donuts. He was a large man and always wore a herringbone paddy cap. He was terribly diabetic and his feet were numb nearly all the time now. Nevertheless, he drank his morning coffee with a single cake donut without fail.

He had parked his car inside a large paved area surrounded by a high chain-link fence which was, itself, surrounded by a tall hedge. Beyond the hedge lay row upon row of tombstones which grew into large family vaults of marble and granite the further one traveled towards the cemetery's front rod-iron gate. The front gate read "St. Mary's Cemetery" in iron letters painted black.

Inside the hedge, there was a small, white cinder-block building at the back of the paved area. On it hung a carved wooden sign which read "B&G Janitorial." The 'G' stood for Gremillion, Johnny Gremillion, who was a Parish Inspector, as well as a partner in the business. The 'B' stood for Bonnette, Charlie Bonnette, who mostly ran the place, and whose best employee and foreman was Isaiah Harris. It was Charlie whom Warren was paying a visit this morning.

"Whatcha say, sir?" Charlie asked Warren when he heard the door open and shut at precisely 7:00AM. The two men were Air Force buddies. They had served together and became friends while stationed at K. I. Sawyer Air Force Base in the Upper Peninsula ("UP") of Michigan. Warren had been an enlisted man, and was Chief Master Sergeant in charge of air traffic control operations. Charlie was a colonel in charge of a squadron of the Strategic Air Command or "SAC." They had become fast friends, despite one being an officer and the other an enlisted man. They had first bonded over baseball. Warren, having been raised in Taunton, Massacusetts, was a Red Sox man. He had been born into the long-suffering tradition of devotion to the Sox. Charlie had played baseball in college. He had been a pitcher for LSU. He had been good enough for the school to pay for his education, but little less. He was never scouted for the Majors, and instead entered the Air Force.

If they weren't friends already, they were stuck together after Charlie's daughter, Mary Frances, and Warren's son, Scott, were married. After retirement, Warren and his wife, Carol, had decided to move south to Louisiana, instead of returning home to Massachusetts, as Mary Frances had already convinced Scott to move to Louisiana. They now had a single grandson in common.

"Colonel! Hi, how are ya?" The last part was pronounced as the single New England conglomeration of "Hihowahya." "That smell outside, boy. It's a killah." Warren turned the corner into Charlie's office, where he was leaning back in his office chair with his hands behind his head and a broad, crooked smile on his face.

"Thank ya, Smitty," Charlie said as Warren handed him the hot-to-the-touch Styrofoam cup. "I'm gonna have to pay you back one of these days for always buying the coffee."

"Ah, now. There was that fishing pole of yours that got away from me last year." 'Year' sounded like 'ye-ah.' Most all of the man's 'r's softened into 'ah's. Smitty – that was Warren David's nickname – still spoke with the distinctive notes of a Massachusetts man despite over a decade in Louisiana.

Smitty had picked up the nickname back when he first entered the service. Charlie had once asked him about it when they were both stationed at the K.

I. Sawyer Air Force base in Michigan. "Smitty, why they call you that? I mean, your last name isn't Smith. It's David, f'God's sake." Charlie would never forget what Smitty said next. He had said, matter-of-factly, "Guess it's because I'm Irish."

"Eh, the pole was one of those Chinese jobs anyway. Or Korean," Charlie said distractedly. "Piece of crap." Both men had served in the Korean War. Smitty had even seen some action at the tail end of World War Two. He had been drafted just long enough for them to pull out all of his teeth. He had been wearing dentures since almost his eighteenth birthday.

"Maybe why it got away from me in the first place." Smitty made to re-fold the *Morning Advocate* so he could do his daily crossword puzzle. Then, he seemed to remember something.

"What is it?" Charlie noticed the look of disquiet on Smitty's face. "Your legs feeling numb again?"

"Well, yes, as a matter of fact – my whole right cheek as well, but no. It's that damned clinic."

"Oh, that," Charlie said. "Nobody's business as far as I'm concerned. At least they're adding to the tax base."

"I'd probably agree with you, but I can't get it out of my head. Out of my *dreams,*" Smitty said the last as though it took some effort to get out.

Charlie flashed a look over to Smitty, as though frustrated that the topic had resurfaced. Three, maybe four, times in all the time that the two men had known each other, Smitty had confided in Charlie about his dreams. He had never confided his secret in anyone else – there had only been Charlie and a man who had saved his life in the war, and whom he had named his first son after. Not even Carol, Smitty's wife, knew of the man's strange dreams that had a funny way of coming true. "Smitty, you know how I feel about that stuff. It's not really …"

"Look – you ever read about the Lincoln assassination? How he dreamed three nights in a row about his death? He dreamt, night after night, of going into the East Room of the White House and finding mourners weeping over a corpse. 'Who's dead in the White House?' He would ask. 'The President,' they answered. 'Killed by an assassin.'"

"I don't see what that's got to do with anything."

"I know, Charlie. But just hear me out. Suspension of disbelief, will yah?" Smitty removed his cap, smoothed down his gray hair in a gesture of rising anxiety, and replaced the cap.

Charlie nodded, seeing it was important to his friend. He took a sip of his coffee and leaned back in his chair with a short grating squeak. "Alright," Smitty said, taking a deep breath and pausing to find the right way to start. "Let me first tell you this, so if it happens you might finally believe me. You know the water tower out on Parent Street?"

"Sure, where the Major property meets up with the railroad track."

"Right," Smitty agreed. He had rustled open the little bag of donuts, reached in, and grabbed one of the felty brown cake donuts. He then held the donut with both hands, as though it were a tiny life preserver. Charlie was beginning to sense the fear in the man's words – a man not typically prone to fearfulness – and grew more attentive. Both men's jaw muscles tightened visibly. When next Smitty spoke, his teeth were clenched.

"It's always the same two dreams. The first one seems nearer" – he said it "near-ah" – "than the other, and the first one is more of an image than a dream. Like I said, it's the water-tower. Blood flows out from under it, like somebody's knocked the main support pipe from the center. It's pouring out blood, deep-red blood – almost black – like a barrel with er-uh bunghole knocked out. Then I see the same blood flowing out the faucets. Yours, mine, everybody's faucets. And there's uh – how do I describe it? There's a ..." As he said it, his hand started tapping on the arm of the chair. His wedding ring kept beating against the polished wood in a neat staccato. Tap-tap-tap-tap-tap-tap. Tap tap tap tap-tap-tap. Tap-tap-tap-tap-tap-tap.

Charlie's eyes narrowed in on his friend's hand. Smitty was saying something, or trying to say something. "Six," Charlie said, ignoring the other man. "Six. Always six."

"What's that there?" Smitty said, as though slapped gently out of a daydream.

"The beat. Every set of beats – there's six. Longs and shorts, too. Did you even know you were tapping? Bet that's code, too."

"What? Was I? Isn't that something. The mind sometimes doesn't know what the hand is doing."

"Keep it going. My Morse is a little rusty, but I'll get the long and short of it." Charlie grinned, but not just for his bit of cleverness. He loved a good riddle. Both men did. They were both intelligent men, though only one was college educated. And they both played down their intelligence, so they could, as Charlie would say, sneak up on the unsuspecting.

Smitty started tapping again, but couldn't quite get the almost maniacal rhythm. "You're thinking about it now. That'll never get it. Tell me more about your dreams. I'll keep track," Charlie said, tapping his pencil in explanation. The man used his left hand to write these days, as arthritis was curling his once-dominant right hand into a permanent fist, partly a result of years of playing handball. While in the Air Force and later during the Cold War, the men would be held on high alert for long spans of time. The pilots and their crews played handball to keep sharp during the sometimes excruciating-long waits.

"The ur-uh second dream, then. Well no, let me finish the first one. The water tower gushed with blood like a – well, hell – like you'd taken the cap off the reservoir of a tanker car" – pronounced 'cah' – "just dumping its whole load right there on the tarmac. But there was no tarmac beneath the water tower, no concrete – not even ground. It was just a black hole swallowing the blood. No, it wasn't a whole. It was a mouth. A giant mouth. But God help me it was blood. The whole damn town's blood. And through the faucets, too, like Moses, himself had slammed his staff into False River. And that was the worst of it, False River had turned a deep maroon, almost as if it had coagulated, crystallized, and scabbed over."

"I got it," Charlie interrupted.

"What's that?" Smitty asked, distracted. He seemed to be shaking images out of his head, like drops of water from a swimmer's ear.

"I got it," Charlie said, not looking up from the pad of paper he had been scribbling notes on while Smitty recounted his dream. "Each time you tapped your hand six times followed by a long pause. Six times total. Six different sets of Morse Code, almost."

"Can you make any sense of it? Were there any words – any words you can make out?"

"Yeah, yeah," Charlie answered. He was getting excited now at the prospect of the puzzle. "There's definitely something here. There may be no need for your crossword this morning, Smitty. I think we've found a puzzle of our own. Only, my Morse is a little rusty."

"Call 'em out, Charlie. If all I need is the alphabet, I should be okie dokie." Smitty held his pencil poised above the crossword, meaning to fill in the letters in the neat little boxes.

"Here goes." Charlie nodded. "Long. Short, short, short, short. Short."

"Bang a louey on that second one. What's that? Four shorts and then a short at the end?"

Charlie tapped his pencil against the paper, recounting his notes. "Yessir."

"That's an easy one, then. The first word is 'the.'"

"Okay, here comes the second one. Long, long, long. Long. Short."

"A-yuh, that's the word 'one.' Could've just used the number. No use spelling it out. Not for nothing."

In likewise fashion, the men went through the remaining four words. They dropped their pencils almost simultaneously, and the same confused expression wrinkled across their faces. "'The one man'?" Smitty asked.

"'Let man die' – what the hell does that mean?"

"What one man let all men die?" Smitty mused to himself, and almost instantly answered his own question. "Oh, well, I suppose there's Adam, the one espoused to Eve."

"Okay, but – I'll say it again – what the *hell* does that mean? I mean, what's it got to do with water towers and blood."

Smitty shook his head, and pushed his knitted cap down against his brow. He laughed to himself ruefully. "Now, you'll surely think me a nutter."

"We had a saying in Elmer," Charlie said smiling a little, and again leaning back in his chair with his hands folded on his chest. He had grown up on smallish farm in Elmer, Louisiana. A town which most people, even in Louisiana, would be surprised to know is in the state. It had been his wife, Frances Lorio, who had ensured that St. Maryville would be his forever home.

"Even a blind squirrel finds a nut every once in a while. No, Smitty, I don't think you're nuts – no more than any other man from the war days. Know how I know you're not crazy?" Charlie tipped his head toward Smitty, who raised his own head to meet his gaze. "Crazy people don't subconsciously tap out Morse Code when talking about their dreams. And not just code – there's a symmetry and a – and a – *shape* to it: six words, each of six longs and shorts. There's something going on, Smitty. There's been other funny things going on around town. Rumors. A heaviness. It's there for anybody to see. Honestly, I'd been doing my best to ignore it, but you come in here with your damn dreams – like the barn cat that drops mice at your doorstep."

"I haven't told you the second dream, Charlie. Knowing what we know now, it's probably a real pissah. God, I don't know – maybe it was those *Dune* books *your* grandson gave me to read. I don't take too well to that foreign stuff." By "your grandson," Smitty was referring to Jim David, their mutual grandson. And by "foreign stuff," Smitty meant any genre of books besides nonfiction.

"Did you say 'dune'? Like a desert?"

"Nevermind that. Maybe it's not sandworms. It begins with the ground moving like there's something big under it. The ground looks flimsy, like legs and arms moving under the sheets. Like waves even. The whole town is tumbling down except for one black building. Only it's not a building, not really. The people are all slouching toward it. Bowing and reaching toward it. It's like a huge black idol, like Easter Island but bigger. A monument to evil. And the black is like tar, liquid tar, but looming above everything like the John Hancock Building. And then a noose is tightening around the town and the people, all caught up in a frenzy around the idol, and smashed between the idol and the noose. It's like a necktie around the idol's giant black head, but it's not a necktie. It's a snake, biting its own tail. But it's no garter snake, it uncoils itself from deep under False River, hell, its body might even continue through the ground into the Mississippi. It's thick, thick as a triple-deckah. It shifts in the earth, like a long-buried thing, and slowly raises itself from an ancient grave. It leaves behind a whole new channel for the Mississippi turning St. Maryville into an island and returning False River to the Mississippi. As the thing slowly eats itself, the coil of its body tightens and tightens and that's how the dream ends."

The two men sat in silence for a time. After a long slurp of coffee, Charlie finally broke the silence. "You say the town and the people just get smushed between the snake and idol?"

"I, uh." Smitty looked down to his hands to eat the donut that he had been holding all this time, and realized that he was no longer holding the donut. "What'd I do with that thing? Must've put it down somewhere when I was writing." He patted his chest pocket and pants pockets. "Ah, there she is, little booger." He smiled, picking up the donut from the lid of his coffee cup.

"No, not exactly, there is something else," Smitty said, now munching on his donut. "It's hard to put my finger on it." As he said it, he looked down at the donut he was holding and then laughed. Still laughing, he raised the donut to Charlie. "Just like this thing, the serpent doesn't just smash the people against the idol. It feeds the idol. The people are all pressed into the thing's mouth. Its mouth is like a lake of tar. And the whole town's drowning in it."

"Well," Charlie said. "That's depressing."

"Ayuh, but it's just a dream," Smitty said sarcastically.

"Right," Charlie scoffed. "A girl's gotta have her dreams. Only I think we both know better than that. So, what's the play? What d'we do?"

"Hell if I know."

"You know, I think I will have a donut. You're making those things look mighty good." Charlie sat back munching on the cake donut. "I'll tell you this much, though, we're gonna need at least two things: more people and more donuts."

The Couple

"Are you feeling okay?" Sam Pitre asked Erin. Their romance had advanced rapidly, as only young love can, since that day when Erin had let Sam walk her home. "You – *God*, Erin – you actually look green."

Most all of their budding romance had happened in Erin's backyard. It was a beautiful backyard, for what it was worth. The entrance was marked by a Confederate jasmine-covered arbor which gave way to a pea gravel and brick walkway, which led to more vine-covered arbors and hidden corners. To Sam, it was the Garden of Eden. He was the smoothest he had ever been. In a week's time, every word he'd spoken had been inspired, or so he felt. Never had he lapsed into awkward teenage silences and goofiness. He hadn't even tripped over his own feet, as he was want to do.

It was magical, so magical that he hadn't even noticed Erin's declining health. Neither had Erin, for that matter. After the third day of their teenage swoon, Erin had stopped going to school.

Her mother and father, despite their fright at the incident in the bathroom, had almost completely forgotten the entire incident. Erin had, as well. An hour after the incident, they were all sleeping comfortably. The wool had been pulled over their eyes, even as they had pulled up their blankets.

When he had said that last romantic line, telling the girl that she looked *green*, it had been Sam's first stumble in front of the girl in an unnaturally long time. Erin looked at Sam suddenly after he had said it, as though he'd slapped her. She quickly pulled away, though, as her stomach lurched within her.

They were sitting together along a stone bench under a muscadine-covered arbor, which stood on five cast iron columns in Erin's backyard. Erin leaned over the far side of the bench, gripped the carved stone edge of the bench with white-knuckled clammy hands. She thought that she was about to do something which might stop Sam from ever kissing her on the lips again. She held her breath as the world spun around her. Eventually the spinning slowed – it might have been Sam's gentle hand rubbing her back between the shoulder blades – and she was able to sit back up again.

"What is it, Erin?" He asked. "That look you gave me. I'm sorry for saying you looked green, but that look you gave me. It was like something snapped in you."

Erin nodded slowly, still leaning forward and taking slow, delicate breaths. "I remembered something, Sam. I don't know how I ever forgot it. Probably a defense mechanism or something—but God!"

"Come on, you're scaring me. Tell me. Tell me everything."

"It's crazy," Erin said, as her green eyes were suddenly sheathed with tears. "Real crazy. Oh my God, it must be why I'm sick," she looked backward just then to the house, and to the upstairs bathroom window.

"Slow down, Erin. You're going too fast. I'm *totally* not following you."

"My parents," she moaned, grabbing her forehead. "They must've forgotten, too. But how could that even happen? What was that thing – oh, Jesus, *no*. That *face*."

"Erin!" Sam yelled, taking the girl by her shoulders. Her shoulders felt so small, so perfect in his hands. He pushed the thought out of his mind. "Tell me everything. I can help you. I fix things. It's what I do."

Erin took a few more delicate breaths. Sam watched her chest heave with the jagged breaths of choked-back tears and then it slowly settled down. Slowly, and with Sam's constant support, she told him the story of the thing that had come through the window.

Sam was quiet for a long time after Erin had finished her story. He kept shaking his head, and for a time, shook the cast iron bars of the arbor, too, as if this Eden had suddenly become his prison.

"So, your sickness. Your *nausea*." Sam slowly formed the thoughts. "Oh,

God, Erin!" And then he flew back to her, and wrapped his arms around her. "It got *inside* you. Erin, it must've … you must be … impregnated."

"You mean, you believe me?" Erin's wide green eyes stared into Sam's face imploringly, and the tightness at the edges of her face loosened.

"Of course I do," Sam blurted out. "I hadn't even considered not believing you. But, whatever, we've got to do something *right* now." He stood up suddenly and pulled the girl into his arms, burrowing his head deep into the space between her neck and shoulder. "I'm not losing you, Erin." His voice rose to her ears muffled through her sweater. "I'm not gonna let anything happen to you. I love you."

****

Sam had rushed Erin over to the Rectory of St. Mary's Church as soon as the weight of her story had settled on him. He knew taking her to the hospital would only be a secondary concern. Sam thought for such an unnatural happening he would need supernatural help.

"There you go. Just sit down right here, and I'll come back and get you," Sam said, as he leaned Erin back against the cool of the rectory's side porch. He could see the color again draining from her face. He ran around to the front door and rang Monsignor's bell, and then began tapping and then banging on the door as the seconds passed with excruciating slowness.

Finally, the heavy door swung open to the hallway and stairway beyond, and the old stooped figure of Monsignor stepped forward and eclipsed it all. Monsignor was smiling warmly, his crooked half smile. "Scott Pitre! How are you?"

"Sam, sir," He gently corrected. "Thank you for coming to the door, sir, and sorry for the banging, Father – I mean, Monsignor – anyway, please come, *please*." And Sam dashed around the corner of the house to where he had left Erin, trusting that Monsignor would follow. "Erin, he's coming," Sam said breathlessly. Sure enough, Monsignor came around the corner, hobbling slightly. His gentle smile had been replaced by a look of concern.

"What is it, Sam? Does she need a doctor?"

"Maybe, probably, but not yet. I think there's something worse. Something only you can help us with."

Monsignor took the girl's face in his broad hands, and looked into her eyes. "She's pregnant, yes?" It was more of a statement than a question. Sam nodded. "Do you mind?" Monsignor asked waiting for the girl's permission before he put his hand to her lower belly. He and Sam were both standing in the rectory flower beds, as Erin sat above on the porch. Erin did nod, and he pressed gently against her belly. At first nothing happened, and Monsignor just looked between the girl and his hand, back and forth, as Sam watched with growing anticipation.

Then, suddenly, Erin breathed in sharply, and looked to Monsignor in confusion. The old priest pushed off against the boards of the side porch and stepped out of the flower beds and back onto the sidewalk, nodding. "I'd imagine the same thing would happen if you wiped holy water on your belly." Monsignor nodded. "Come, tell me when this happened." He slowly mounted the stairs of his side porch and walked over to the girl. He held out his hand, and led her by his arm through the side porch's screen door into the rectory. "Come along, Sam."

Minutes later, Monsignor was pouring a kettle of hot water into the porcelain cups which sat in front of Sam and Erin on either side of his dining room table, and in his, as well, at the head of the table. "Let those steep for about three minutes," Monsignor instructed, as he laid the kettle on a trivet in the center of the table, and sat down with a groaning exhale.

"Is it medicine?" Erin asked.

"Oh, sort of," Monsignor smiled. "But no, it's not for your belly. Please, tell me how this all happened."

"It actually began that day the car hit Rock," Sam interceded.

"The day the car hit Rock, instead of you." Monsignor corrected mildly.

"Yes, Monsignor," Sam nodded. Then, taking turns, Sam and Erin explained the whole strange incident, as much as they knew to tell. At some point in the middle, Monsignor jumped suddenly. "Oh, dear," he said. "We've let the tea steep too long. Take out the bags now before it's too late." Monsignor turned over his hand a few times to encourage them to continue their story.

Soon, the story had almost been totally unwound. "And you say,"

Monsignor asked, "that you all just forgot the whole affair the next morning? Like a fog had fallen over your memory?"

"Yes, that's it," Erin said excitedly, before wincing in pain. "It was just like that. Like a brain fog."

Monsignor nodded, "I have seen a fog like this – only a physical one – not long ago. As if I needed confirmation," Monsignor added, speaking to himself. "Tell me, before the *fog* cleared, what had you thought about doing. Going to the doctor?"

"No, actually," Erin said drowsily, as though the thought was coming from afar. "My dad was actually planning to take me to the new clinic."

"The *abortion* clinic?" Sam asked with wide eyes.

"But," Monsignor interrupted. "You said the idea of being pregnant hadn't crossed you or your parents' minds, until today."

"Right," Erin nodded to Monsignor with a look of confusion spreading across her face.

"But then, why the clinic?" Sam asked. "That doesn't make *any* sense."

"It does, actually," Monsignor said, gulping down the last of his tea and sneaking a look at the bits of tea leaves that remained at the bottom. "It tells us that the idea did not come from you. That it came from somewhere else. That some*thing* else was calling you to the clinic."

There was a long moment of silence as the young couple mulled this over. Then, Sam looked up at Erin and met her eyes. Next, he turned to Monsignor. "So, what are we supposed to do?"

"I think, for *now*, you should not disobey that strange calling to the clinic."

Sam looked as though he'd been slapped in the face. "But it's an *abortion* clinic, Father, urr, Monsignor. How can we …?"

"Drink your tea, Sam." Monsignor nodded to the small cup on the table in front of Sam. Sam looked down at it, as if he'd rather toss it into the empty fireplace behind him than drink it, but he obeyed. He emptied the cup and set it back down. He winced a little at the bitterness from over-steeping. Monsignor reached for the boy's cup, and tilted it towards him. The old priest closed one eye and peered forward. He grunted in discomfort as he let the cup fall back into the saucer. Sam's mouth hung open as he watched the man, and then his head bobbed forward to see for himself what lay at the bottom of his cup. It was just a glob of black bits, he thought to himself.

Monsignor then nodded to Erin and her cup of tea. Monsignor grunted again after setting the girl's cup back in its saucer. "Well?" Sam asked as if in a daze. His head was swimming in confusion.

Monsignor looked at the boy in surprise. "Well, *what*?"

"Well, didn't you just read our tea leaves?" Sam asked.

Monsignor laughed in disdain. "What do I look like a mind-reader? Catholics don't read tea leaves." Sam looked across at Erin, who mirrored his look of confusion.

"You should go to the clinic," Monsignor was responding to the still-pending question. "And I am sorry about this. I wish there was more I could do, but, you say this all began less than a week ago?" Erin nodded, looking from Monsignor to Sam with wet green eyes.

Monsignor nodded, "The baby inside you is in its twentieth week, at least."

"But she's hardly showing at all!" Sam burst out. "How can that be?"

"Even if it were a natural baby, she might not be showing for a while yet, especially with a first pregnancy. And I'm not sure the baby will be the same size and shape as – uh – usual."

Erin's chest began to heave up and down uncontrollably and she was soon hiding her sobs behind her hands. Sam walked quickly around the table and moved another chair beside her to comfort her.

"And," Monsignor continued, albeit with hesitation. "I think those at the clinic – whose owner, by the way, I think, also tended to Rock in the hospital – will be very interested in seeing the baby is healthy and safely delivered. You must act as though you suspect *nothing*, do you understand?"

"So, uh – she'll be delivering this thing at the clinic in another *week*?" Sam whispered beneath the girl's sobs.

"No, no, *no*." Monsignor rose up full in his chair. "Yes, the delivery may happen that fast, but – whatever you do – she cannot deliver at the clinic. I'm afraid of what that thing might do to her once it's born."

A look of horror spread across Sam's face and the color finished draining from his cheeks until he looked almost translucent. He swallowed hard, and looked to the beautiful girl crying against his chest and at her flat belly below. "What about *before* it's born?"

After they had left, Monsignor half-hobbled back to the dining room table and picked up their tea cups. Inside his own tea cup, there was only the pure white of the porcelain cup's bottom. Inside each of his visitors' tea cups, there was an inky blackness filling the bottoms, as if a dark hole had opened up at the bottom of each cup, through the dining room table, through the wooden planks of the floor below, and down into the earth, without end.

Token Resistance

The local chapter of Louisiana Right to Life did all it could to prevent the opening of the abortion clinic on Main Street in the LaCour building. Henry and Dot Poche had held signs outside and hosted prayer vigils for forty days solid. Afterwards, though, the crowds slowly dried up. One by one, the protest grew cold and slipped away.

Anne ran across Miss Dot at the local Winn-Dixie shopping for groceries a couple months after the opening of the abortion facility, maybe twenty days after the conclusion of the forty day prayer vigil she had led. "Miss Dot!" Anne had called out excitedly, "What's next? We gonna kick in that clinic's doors?"

"How's that, dear?" Miss Dot smiled weakly, almost drowsily. She added, "I'm sorry, remind me of your name again." Miss Dot was a shorter woman, whom Anne had hitherto known as a near limitless source of energy. She knew every pro-life activist along the Gulf Coast. She had started working almost the same day *Roe v. Wade* came down. She even knew 'Jane Roe,' as the plaintiff of the case had been renamed; she had grown up nearby in Simmesport. Her sons, too, were deeply immersed in the pro-life movement. Anne had always thought of Miss Dot as a younger woman, but she seemed old now, much older than she had remembered.

"It's Anne, Miss Dot. You've known me since I was just a little girl in youth group."

"Oh yes, Annie. How are your folks doing?"

"They're fine. Miss Dot? Did you hear what I said?" Then, Anne's eyes grew suddenly wide as she looked at the woman. Anne had always admired Miss Dot's pale blue eyes. They were truly stunning, but now, "Miss Dot! Your eyes! What's happened to *your eyes?*" Anne looked down to find she was holding the woman by her shoulders.

Miss Dot, suddenly ferocious, threw Anne's arms from her shoulders and stormed off, casting hate-filled glances back at her as her shopping cart rattled away down another aisle. Anne just stood there for a long moment staring at the canned green beans and beets. Had she really seen what she thought she had seen? "No! They did, they really did!" Anne said suddenly aloud, startling a hapless stock boy who had wandered within range. "They were *purple*," Anne said, grabbing the stock boy's arm and pointing. "Purple! Miss Dot's eyes were purple!" The stock boy scampered off, as Anne was left to wonder if the eyes were truly purple, like Elizabeth Taylor's had been, or if they had just flashed purple. Anne grabbed a few cans and headed home lost in thought.

Later that night at dinner, when Jim was looking down and wondering at his plate of green beans and beets, Anne dived right into a description of Miss Dot's purple eyes.

"Could it have been contacts?" Jim asked. "I hear they've found a way to improve hard contact lenses, maybe they can color them now, too."

"No, Jim. I know they weren't. They were purple ... PURPLE!"

"Okay, fine. But what does it mean? So what if they were purple, plum, or zebra?"

"Well, it's not just the eyes, Jim. There's more. She seemed totally disinterested in the abortion clinic and closing it down. This is Miss Dot we're talking about. Have you ever known somebody more committed to anything than her?"

"Maybe she's just defeated. Broken. You know, like Patty Hearst and Stockholm Syndrome or something."

"More like *Invasion of the Body Snatchers*! She was like a whole different person – and if that's not enough – with another eye color completely? Don't you remember how blue her eyes were? They were like a whole shade unto themselves, like 'Titian Blue' – but this would've been 'Dot Blue!'"

"Anne –!"

"Don't you see what's happening?" She stopped suddenly. In her growing frustration and anger, she realized that she had only just put together what was happening. "Oh my God," she said. "Oh my God, why didn't we see it before? That smell in town, too."

"See what?" Jim said, forcing the beets down his throat.

"Jim! They're all disappearing. Before this clinic came, how many people could you have counted on to protest it? At least a dozen right off the top of your head, right? Twelve. Easy. But now, what? One or two, *if* you're lucky."

"Yeah, I guess so. Without Miss Dot, maybe less than one or two."

"Don't you see it, Jim?" Anne grabbed Jim's hand away from the last forkful of beets. "We're losing people. Something's *changing* them, making them something else."

"Something else?" Jim scoffed.

"It's time we circled the wagons," Anne said forcefully enough to put a chink in Jim's skepticism. "Tell me everyone you can still trust."

"Come on, Anne. Can't we do this in the morning? I'm really tired, and I just wanted to relax."

"Do it!"

"Okay fine. There's Monsignor, of course. He's as solid as they come. There's Brian Freemantle. He hasn't changed at all in the last year, or ever for that matter. Maybe Aquinas, too. He's former military, stays away from town, and already doesn't trust anybody."

"Good. That's three. And I've got Mamou and my brother Thomas. We need to come together. Form a team, you know? Like the Fantastic Four or five or seven."

"Oh," Jim said holding up his hand. "There's something else. Grandad and Grandpa have been going on about this, too. Grandpa has been having his dreams again, and Grandad actually seems to believe him this time."

Anne just looked back at her husband, clearly disturbed. She loved both of her husband's grandfathers. She treated Grandad Charlie like her own Grandad, as her grandfather, Mamou's father, had passed away before she was born. She was also particularly fond of Grandpa Smitty with his coffee and donuts. She thought his Massachusetts accent was like something out of a storybook.

"But Anne, what we do? You're not exactly at fighting weight. You're *pregnant*! You've got maybe a month left. Not exactly a perfect time to go gangbusters. And, we waited so long for this baby, I don't want to do anything that might put it in jeopardy."

"Jim, don't you see? All the babies are already in jeopardy, not just ours. And the longer we wait to make our move, the shorter our list of allies becomes."

"Well, what do we do?"

"First thing's first. Let's get everybody together for dinner at the Rectory."

****

Miss Lisa was taken aback when Monsignor gave her the night off. She spent nearly half an hour filling Monsignor's head with extra instructions, just in case Monsignor – or worse, the house – should fall apart in her absence. Monsignor politely listened to her litany of instructions all the while gently edging towards the kitchen door. Per Miss Lisa's instructions, Monsignor removed a white stoneware casserole dish from the refrigerator and placed it on the top rack of the oven. He set the oven to 350 degrees and turned on the rice cooker. He would be serving gumbo tonight; Mrs. Olinde always dropped off a gumbo for Monsignor on Tuesdays.

It wasn't long before Monsignor's guests started arriving. Of course, they weren't exactly Monsignor's guests – it had been Jim and Anne who had called the meeting at his house. Oddly, however, Jim and Anne were the last to arrive.

"Jim, what's the deal?" Brian Freemantle asked hurriedly, opening Monsignor's door when the couple rang the bell. He had been sitting nervously just inside the door, while the others carried on in the dining room. There was a parlor at the entrance to the rectory with armchairs and a telephone table. "I thought for sure you two would already be here? What happened? Why are you late?"

"Slow down, Brian." Jim clapped a hand on the smallish man's shoulder.

"Let a man get his coat off, will ya?" Jim had taken his coat off, and was helping Anne with hers. Even the simplest movements were becoming more and more difficult for Anne in the final stages of the pregnancy.

"Of course, of course, I was just thinking, you know. Over-thinking. Getting worried. Here, want me to take your cap?"

"It's alright, Brian. I'll keep it on. Just chill, okay? Brian? Actually, go check and see if Monsignor put on some coffee."

"Thank you," Anne told Jim, trying to catch her breath. At the sound of their entrance, other heads started popping up in the hallway leading from the dining room.

"You two look like you've seen a ghost," Monsignor said as he came walking down the hallway. Jim was always surprised at how tall he was. He towered over Brian as he hurried past to check on the coffee. Monsignor was backlit by the light of the dining room, but Jim could see he wore a smirk, though he was staring at them intently. The priest clapped a hand on Jim's shoulder and bent low for Anne's kiss.

Jim looked around the dining room after greeting Monsignor and his grandfathers. He felt layers of fear falling from him surrounded, as he was, by all his fathers. His father had died when Jim was only a boy. There had been a boating accident on the lake. Jim's dad and drowned and his body had never been found. Afterwards, the men in this room had stepped in serving as so many surrogate fathers for the boy.

There was also Mamou and Thomas, Anne's mother and brother. They both lived on the outskirts of town. Mamou lived in the family plantation, and Thomas lived far behind it down dirt roads with his new bride where he oversaw the maintenance of the family estate. Thomas was not a tall man, but he seemed to be made from timber beams. In his early teens, he could grip an axe one-handed at the end of the helve and hold it out, untrembling. His father, when he had still been alive, had hired the boy out for labor. It was said if you heard him felling trees in a clearing, you would say there were three men by the way the trees fell. For all his natural gifts, he was not a boastful man. In fact, he really spoke at all. But while his horse was resting or when he was waiting for his co-laborers to catch up with him, he could be found with a mouth full of prayers and a handful of rosary beads.

Thomas was one of thirteen children, almost all of which had been equally prolific. Jim had often said that, by marrying Anne, he had married into the half of the parish he wasn't already related to. It was no joke. Though his grandfather had been an only child, Jim's grandmother, Frances, a St. Maryville native, was one of eleven.

Mamou was a great bear of a woman. She seemed possessed of great strength, but her eyes were gentle and warm. She had married a Navy man in her youth, despite his being – in her words – "too little." She nevertheless provided great stock for her children, which remained unbraided through the generations. She had always tilled the ground, and – it was said – would pull her own plow when she outlasted the mule. Even now, she looked after the garden that surrounded her home, bounded on all sides by a picket fence. She called it her "Eden-place," and seemed even to walk with the Almighty there, an unblemished daughter of Eve.

Anne hurried over to her brother and mother and hugged them both, reaching over her belly. Thomas was busy with the land this time of year, and Anne hadn't seen him in weeks. He was still in his work clothes and dusty at the edges. Thomas squeezed his sister hard and kissed her.

"Not a ghost," Jim said. "Not exactly."

Anne laughed. "Yeah, I think Jim would have rathered a ghost."

"What was it, Jim?" Monsignor asked again, sitting down heavily at the head of the dining room table. The tone of his voice said that the meeting had begun.

Jim nodded and sat down beside Anne at the table. "Oh, who's this?" He was distracted for a moment and reached across the table to shake the boy's hand.

"This is Sam Pitre." Monsignor introduced the still-shaken boy. Sam had left Erin at her family's house for the evening, but his thoughts had stayed with her. He looked distracted and pale.

"Oh," Jim said, not knowing if he should recognize the name. "Good, that's fine. Glad you could come. Hey, Monsignor, what about my friend Aquinas? We're you able to reach him? I know he can be hard to …"

"No, unfortunately," Monsignor interrupted. "He would've been a good man to have with us, but no. I think he may yet have some part in this story, or the next." He ended mysteriously, and without further explanation.

"Monsignor," Jim went on, returning to Monsignor's still-hanging question. "We were pinned in the house for a good half hour. I went outside first to get the car started. Next thing I know, I was back in the house by the skin of my teeth with my back against the door. I was gasping and my heart was pounding."

"What was it, Jim?" Smitty asked.

"God, I don't know. It could've been a hallucination. You'll think I'm crazy, but something was growling at me from right there on the porch. It was a big something. The growl sounded like it was vibrating up out of a throat that went a mile into the ground."

"Like a bobcat?" Thomas asked.

Jim shook his head, and Anne said, "No, I heard it, too. It was bigger than that. Much bigger. But it was some kind of cat."

"Maybe a jaguar?" Sam piped up. The whole table turned to him, having forgotten he was even there.

"Why do you say that, Sam?" Monsignor asked.

Sam rubbed at his head briefly and then rubbed one hand inside the other, cracking a few knuckles. "It's just that. It's something that I've been thinking about. Kinduva loose connection, but somehow it feels right. Have you all been seeing those banana yellow cars driving around? They've been all over the place it seems like."

"Like the one that hit that boy, Rock?" Monsignor nodded, turning his hand for the boy to proceed.

"Yessir, it's just something I've been thinking about ever since that boy got ripped to shreds last year in Ennis."

"That's right," Thomas said. "I had nearly forgotten about that. He had been found near our land. God, I hope there's no connection. I've never heard of another animal attack like that 'round here."

Brian scoffed, "So, we're to believe a jaguar – a jungle animal – is just prowling the sleepy neighborhood streets of the Garden District?"

"It was just, uh," Sam stammered, feeling uncharacteristically self-conscious under the gaze of all the adults. "Just something that I'd had in the back of my mind."

"Oh no, Sam," Monsignor gently scolded the boy. "I think you're exactly right. There is a connection, most definitely. In fact, I'm certain of it, for other reasons, but I hadn't yet made the connection myself. That *is* very important, Sam, and I think there's an even greater lesson here: We – all of us – would be fools to discount those little thoughts in the back of our minds, especially at a time like this. This is why I've brought us all together tonight, in point of fact. There is something *terrible* ahead of us, *exquisitely* horrifying, not to put too fine a point on it. And I firmly believe that, if we are to defeat it, we will need every last puzzle piece dusted off from, as Sam has said, the backs of our minds."

"Now, Jim, what happened next?" Monsignor asked, turning his hand over a couple times as a sign to continue. The old priest sat back a little and crossed his arms before him as though to better weigh all he was about to hear.

Jim looked nervously at Anne, who, in turn, looked away avoiding eye contact. "I have no understanding of what happened next, but I'll tell you what I know." Jim shook his shoulders and arms, shivering. "My arms – my whole body for that matter – still feels sore from all the adrenaline. It was pretty terrible, which tells me, and let me just say, we are absolutely right in getting together tonight, if only because there's something evil out there that tried to stop us and nearly succeeded."

"I think you're exactly right, son," Charlie said. "I would never have believed I'd be saying it, but that's exactly what's going on."

Monsignor motioned again for Jim to continue. "If you're about to tell us what I think, not only are we right in getting together tonight, but speak quickly, as this may be the first *and* last time we are ever all together."

"It was crazy," Jim went on. "I really thought I was losing it. I could feel the thing growling through the door at my back, and then Anne comes at me. At first, I thought she was coming to help me secure the door. The thing outside might even have started pounding against the door. I could just hear the door splintering at my back. And then Anne does the oddest thing: she tries opening the door and pushing me aside. I saw her eyes then and I realized something was wrong. Like she was in a trance or something. And she was stronger, too. My God, I honestly thought it was all about to be over. I just hoped whatever it was would kill me before I could see it killing my wife and baby."

Jim was twisting his hair as he told the story. He took off his hat just then to grab at a bigger clump of his hair. It was his Red Sox hat, and it was dingy and well-worn.

"Jim," Smitty said pointing at his grandson. "Your *hair*, boy."

"What? What is it?" Jim said, pulling his hand away from his hair and inspecting it, half-expecting to find a large clump of his hair had fallen out. He twisted in his chair to get a look at himself in the mirror inlaid at the back of the rectory's buffet.

"Boy-o-boy," Thomas whistled.

"Jim," Anne said, reaching her hand to her husband's head and cradling it gently. "I did this, didn't I?"

"Did what?" Jim said, a little more loudly than he had wanted. Anne pulled her hand away. "I'm sorry," he said. "I feel like I'm going crazy all over again."

"It's your hair, frog," Charlie said. He had always called all his children and his only grandchild 'frog,' alternating at times with 'monkey.' "I'd say you've been skunked."

"I've been what?" Jim asked, starting to smile, relieved as he was by his Grandad Charlie's tone.

"You've got a white patch, dear," Mamou answered.

Jim laughed in surprise. "Really? Well, that's nothing. A small price to pay. I've always wanted gray hair, anyway. More distinguished looking."

"It's like Jean Valjean after his trial, after confessing," Brian pointed out. Most at the table just squinted at him in confusion.

"And I haven't even had my first trial," Jim laughed half-heartedly.

"That's not exactly true. Is it, Joachim?" Monsignor asked. His eyes never left Jim's face, as if watching for the slightest gesture there.

"I – I don't –" Jim stuttered, suddenly feeling very insecure.

"No, I suppose you wouldn't," Monsignor said gently, and Anne took her husband's hand under the table. Jim looked away from Monsignor's face first to Anne and then across the table. Most people turned away rather than look him in the eye.

"What is this? Is this an *intervention*? But why? I'm not a drug addict – maybe I'd been drinking a little too much waiting for the bar results, but that's ..."

"No." Monsignor put up a hand. "You've done nothing wrong. And honestly, I'm surprised you've lasted this long given what's arrayed against you."

"*Against* me?" Jim said, absentmindedly twisting his new lock of white hair.

"Jim, dear," Anne said, squeezing his hand. "You've forgotten. You keep forgetting."

"I *what*?"

"There's simple possession and then there's this. His flesh bears the mark of Baptism and so resists corruption, but this is different somehow. Maybe some special work of the sacraments *ad extra*?" Monsignor began again. "It's a very odd condition, indeed, but it's not one against which I've no experience or remedy."

"Monsignor, dear," Mamou said, "You're speaking in riddles. Tell him straight. Tell us *all* straight."

Monsignor nodded respectfully at the old woman. He leaned back in his seat at the head of the table with his hands steepled under his chin, weighing his words carefully before beginning. His great scarred brow shined brightly beneath the dining room chandelier. The table was still waiting for him to speak.

"This place," he finally began. "St. Maryville has always attracted attention. It's sort of a light that attracts things that buzz. It has a story that has never been told in its full, and though I know it – or think I do – it will not all be told tonight. But some and, hopefully, enough. *Only* enough."

A look around the table would have revealed everybody sitting perfectly still. Most were holding their breath without knowing it. Brian took a quick sip of his coffee, and his hand rubbed subconsciously at the pen and notepad he kept in his pocket. Jim was still twisting his hair. At Monsignor's voice, though, and without knowing it, they had all grown by degrees more at ease.

"It is a funny little place, isn't it?" Monsignor smiled his crooked half smile, as he leaned forward to rest his haunches on the edge of the table. "Bound on both sides by water, an island within an island that holds the island, as it has been called before: the middle ring in a tripartite structure. Without knowing why exactly, and thank God, evil finds its way here. And, for a reason I do not yet understand, this present evil has latched onto Jim. It is not possession. Not exactly. But something has been planted inside you, Jim. Something that can pass onto church land and within all my protections, as well. Something that speaks and, for now, does not grow. Something that has spoken to me, and I to it. Something that growls in the night. And worse still, something that does not know to be afraid."

"I'm sorry. You spoke to it?" Anne asked, daring to interrupt.

"Uh, yes. I have," Monsignor said, dipping his brow. "I began this exorcism over a year ago after your and Jim's experience picking pecans. The same day the Taft child was killed."

Anne looked away, embarrassed at the mention of the incident. "You told him about that?" Anne whispered to Jim.

"Of course," Jim blurted out. He was taken aback by the question. "Only, I can barely now even remember what happened."

"Don't be sore at him, chère." Mamou shook her head. "I told Monsignor, too, as soon as you told me."

"I *told* you?" Anne's eyes widened.

"You don't remember? No, I 'spect you wouldn't. And you didn't exactly tell me, either. Your Mamou just has a way of picking up on things." Monsignor smiled at the old woman, and they exchanged glances.

Anne was rubbing her forehead in confusion. "You mean you've known all along? I feel like you know more than me."

"I do, dear. We've been working in the background for some time now."

"Working?" Jim asked. "I feel like the rug's been pulled over my eyes."

"Oh, no," Anne smiled despite herself. "An Anne-uyrsm. *You're* mixing idioms now. You're starting to sound like me." Jim hardly responded. He just kept twisting at his hair. Anne looked again at Jim, not recognizing the expression on his face.

"Joachim, listen to me, son." Monsignor waved his hand to draw Jim's attention to him. The young man was growing increasingly drowsy. "There's something I've been wondering. When you were at LaColt's home, did you eat or drink something that seemed strange to you?"

Jim's head was lolling but he managed a nod. "Eggs," he mumbled.

Monsignor grimaced. "Always creeping into nests. That *monster*." The priest sat back and considered for a moment. He nodded to himself and then frowned suddenly. "No, no. That's close, but that's not it. Was there anything else, Jim? Joachim?" Monsignor snapped his fingers to wake up the nodding man. The sound was sharp and sudden, like a thick branch cracking in the undergrowth. "Something else," he asked, "maybe wine?"

Jim's eyes fluttered as he fought the oncoming sleep. He murmured something softly under his breath.

"What'd he say?" Smitty asked.

"I think he said 'token,' like 'token resistance,' or ..." Brian smiled sardonically. "The 'token' black dude in a horror movie." Several of them couldn't help but burst out laughing despite the mood of the room.

"He said," Monsignor said resolutely, "*Tokay*."

"Wait. Hungarian, right?" Charlie asked. "Knew a fella in the service, that's all he'd drink. Reminded him of a girl he knew once upon a time."

"I bet it did. A girl he would – *could* – never forget," Monsignor said. "He was likely as not infected, too. Tokay is made with botrytised grapes. *A wine which begins in death*. The grapes suffer from 'noble rot,' as it's called, a necrotrophic fungus. Think of a larva growing fat on the back of a spider, feeding off its blood. The grapes are parasitized. This would, of course, be LaColt's drink of choice. It was probably mixed with his own blood, such as he has. This explains much, but not all, I think."

"Monsignor," Sam said, raising his hand, as if he were in class. The boy waited until the priest nodded at him. "Sir, it reminds me of the slug thing, err, of *Rock*."

"What's he talking about, Monsignor?" Mamou asked.

"Monsignor said something about a larva growing fat on the back of the spider. It, uh, like the slug. It had, at least Erin said it did."

"Had what, dear?"

"His face. Rock's face. It was like some part of Rock was trapped forever in the slug. Until it exploded, anyway," Sam explained.

Several around the table exchanged looks with each other and looked to Monsignor's face to gauge the accuracy of the boy's story. "Sam," the priest said. "Why don't you tell them your part in this story."

Sam nodded, and told the tale, beginning with how it had been his fault that Rock hit his head and ending with the rapidly-developing pregnancy.

"I don't get it, Monsignor," Charlie said, rapping his hand against the table in frustration. "Are you and this boy suggesting that, at some point, the whole town will be turned into slugs?"

"Is that what's happening to Miss Dot?" Anne asked with fear mounting in her voice.

"No, no," Monsignor said, shaking his great brow. "I think that's just one permutation of what LaColt and Teach can do. Jim, poor boy, is another. With this boy – Rock – LaColt may have just revealed or intensified an existing condition of the soul. I do think, however, that soon – very soon, I'm afraid – this spreading disease, this *thrall* in which he already holds much of the parish, will reach critical mass, at which point it will become irreversible or worse, unstoppable."

At this, the group fell silent for a moment, as the thought of it all sunk in. Anne turned to her husband after listening to Monsignor's disturbing words. Jim's head was resting peacefully on his chest. She wiped the hair from his face and kept rubbing his head. She put her head to his chest. As the soft weight of her head pressed down on his chest, he exhaled a little. She thought she might have heard a few notes of "La Vie en Rose," as the breath escaped her husband's lips.

"Don't worry about him, Anne," Mamou said in soothing tones. "I think he's just going to rest for a while."

"Yeah, he should be fine," Charlie agreed, "I've seen fighter pilots do that sort of thing. Just let 'em be."

"I've seen some potheads do the same. Glassy eyes. Almost catatonic," Smitty grumbled.

"It's like a healing trance," Monsignor agreed. "Anne, your husband has mostly – to borrow a phrase from his grandfather – been running on auto-pilot for a while now. His subconscious fills in the gaps. He's barely aware of it. But he's fading."

"*Fading*?" Anne's voice was choked with tears. "What's that mean? Is he dying?"

"Yes and no." Monsignor scratched at his brow. "Remember, I said it wasn't a possession. There's no presence inside him, no demon. Yet. It's like a noose on his soul. Such a thing mimics mortal sin, which can leave him open – vulnerable – to further attack. It was intended that he become fully possessed. He's escaped that fate for now, but the poison remains in him."

"So, you knew about all this and you're just letting him 'rot' from the inside out? Is that it?" Anne was trembling.

"If I had acted sooner – please understand – I would have revealed myself to the enemy before the time was right. I'm afraid few of us may yet escape with our lives, so dark is this present evil, but many more may still escape with their souls. And, Anne, dear?" Monsignor paused, waiting for the young woman to raise her eyes to him. "That's because of your husband."

Anne turned to her husband just then. She saw a shine collecting at the corner of his mouth, and – at just that moment – she felt so overwhelmingly tender to him. She wrapped her arms around him, and buried her face on the inside of his arm. As she did, the baby leapt in her womb. The sudden pop of the baby inside Anne's belly made a thump against the table. Mamou clapped her old hands under her chin and smiled bitter-sweetly. Jim's grandfathers exchanged glances, and Monsignor's eyes shined deep under his brows.

Brian, for his part, didn't notice the thump against the table, and was looking from face to face in confusion. "Excuse me? I'm sorry. I feel like I'm understanding less and *less*."

Monsignor nodded patiently, "When Joachim told me about his vision – of the man with eyes like liquid tar, of the bird and the fist of water, and of the birth of a child and the beast waiting to devour it – I suspected then we were dealing with a very ancient and powerful demon. He was known to the Aztecs. His was the jaguar, the bird, the water, the tunnel, and the protruding eyes. And I will not speak his name. Demons are quick to hear their own names, like a whip cracking against their backs. I suspected all of this, but I did not know for sure until just a short time ago. I think by tonight our plan will be in place, but I would keep our doings secret from him as long as is allowed to us."

Brian's jaw hung loose and his mouth agape. He blurted out while everyone was still mulling over the news and the shock, "You're saying demons are real, and one has come *here*? To St. Maryville?"

"And it's not the first time, honey." Mamou tapped the young man's wrist.

"I should say not," Monsignor grumbled. "This has always been a treacherous post."

"So what's the plan?" Charlie asked, growing impatient with the indirect chatter.

"Right," Smitty added. "Just tell us how we get rid of this Masshole."

"Everybody needs to know what they're about to get involved with." Monsignor put up his hands to slow the men down.

"Losing our lives and probably our souls, too, right?" Smitty asked. "Ayuh, no delusions here. No disrespect, Monsignor, but get on with it. Missing the Sox game, okay? I'd like to see Ol' Pudge homer one last time before I die."

"Thus we are ministers of God's own wish." Monsignor nodded. "That the world and man for whom His Son died, will not be given over to monsters, whose very existence would defame Him. Already, He has allowed us to redeem a fair number of souls, and we go out as the old knights of the Cross to redeem still more. Like them, we will travel toward the sunrise; and like them, if we fall, we do not fail in vain." Monsignor held back his sleeve and marked the air with a cross, blessing them. "Does everybody understand this?"

"Punching a one-way ticket," Brian nodded, as the color drained from his face. Monsignor waited as one by one they nodded at him – even Jim, whose head was lolling in his stupor.

Monsignor nodded slowly, "Okay, this will have to do." Then, turning, he said, "Now, Charlie. Tell our little fellowship what your man, Isaiah, saw that night on False River."

****

After Charlie had finished describing Isaiah's encounter with the ship and chasing it along False River, Monsignor dismissed the small group. Each was told their particular mission, many of which were to begin that very night.

As the group was dispersing, Monsignor nodded to Mamou. The old woman followed his lead discreetly. Without a word passing between them, Thomas left the rectory to wait for Mamou alongside his transportation. Thomas still drove a horse and buggy. It wasn't a religious observance, like the Amish, or even a spurning of modernity, Thomas just preferred a horse to horsepower.

Monsignor closed the door and bolted it behind him. He turned to Mamou. "There's something, *someone* you ought to see. Follow me up the stairs."

They both groaned as they climbed up the old rectory's narrow staircase. "We're just not as young as we used to be," Monsignor smiled back at Mamou.

"Speak for yourself, old man. I may be nearly seventy, but, if I'm not mistaken, you've still got a few hundred on me."

Monsignor didn't respond to Mamou's jibe. She could feel his mood suddenly grow cold as they crossed the upstairs landing and the visitor's bedroom. "You'll understand, I'm sure, Mamou. I didn't share this with the rest, because it's best that as few know about this as possible. I'm certain she's being hunted. Not sure how she survived in the first place, actually."

"Who is it?" Mamou asked behind him. "I'm sure nobody would expect a woman to be hiding out in the rectory."

In lieu of answering, Monsignor swung open the visitor's bedroom door without knocking. Behind the door, the woman rose from the rocking chair in the corner.

"Mamou, this is Nurse Jana. Without her, I'm afraid we could have never acted in time. She is proof to me of God's intercession to straighten our paths. She works at – err, *worked* at the abortion clinic. Jana, please, if you don't mind, tell Mamou what you told me."

The Tunnel

A tall, stooped man dressed all in black and wrapped in a black coat led a group of four men along the rim of the spillway. It was Monsignor, and behind him were Brian, Thomas, Smitty, and Charlie.

"So did you get to see Pudge homer last night?" Monsignor called back over his shoulder.

"Wha—? Oh." Smitty had been focusing on his footing as he and the rest did their best to keep up with the old priest. "Nah, grounded out, and then it was over. Pretty depressing, actually. Playing the Yankees, too. I didn't know you were a fan, Monsignor?"

"Ah, yeah," Monsignor said. "Since way, way back."

"What're you, a Cardinals fan?" Smitty asked, chuckling to himself. "Get it? *Cardinals*?"

"Smitty, that stinks." Charlie frowned, and then with a mischievous glint in his eye: "I'd think he was a Padres fan." Charlie burst out laughing.

"Whyy I oughta!" Smitty waggled his fist as his old friend.

"Actually, I'm a White Sox fan."

"Nice, Father. Shoeless Joe Jackson!" Brian added.

"Yeah, the *Black* Sox," Smitty added sourly.

"Mr. Jackson actually signed a baseball for me. It's in my office."

"Wha – ?" Smitty barked.

"But, how's that possible?" Brian asked. "He basically disappeared after the 1919 World Series and you almost never see his signature – he was illiterate. Did you run into him as a kid or something and somehow recognize him? He ran a store for a while, I think, in South Carolina or Georgia."

"Dang, Brian. You know a lot about baseball," Charlie remarked.

"Nah, Mr. Bonnette. I just know history – I know *you* used to play, too, back in the day."

"That was a long time ago," Charlie nodded, but was interrupted.

"How's that, Father? You never answered my question." Brian went back to questioning the leader of the little group.

"Steady now," Thomas said, grabbing Brian's shoulder and saving him from tumbling down the height of the levee.

Brian ignored him, single-mindedly pursuing his interview of the priest. "Father? When did you meet Shoeless Joe?"

"He was playing for the New Orleans Pelicans, as I remember."

"Shoeless Joe played in Louisiana?" Smitty guffawed.

"Yeah, for just a year," Brian offered. "One season. Led 'em to the pennant, single handedly. But that was, that was, uh, 1910. You must've been a tiny baby at the time."

Monsignor laughed. "No, I was a priest even then."

Brian stopped suddenly. Thomas nearly crashed into the back of him, but nimbly stepped out of the way just in time. Charlie and Smitty were not so lucky. They both tripped, and their hands sank deep into the mud to prevent them falling. "Sonofa!" Smitty growled. "What's the idear?"

"But that puts you at 90 at the very least! That's impossible."

"Only 90, huh?" Monsignor turned back and winked at the young man. Monsignor took the opportunity to stop and let the men recover from their collisions. Though clearly the oldest member of the group, his breathing was even. "There it is," the old priest pointed away down the curve of the levee.

"Down beyond the *bloodweed*?" Thomas asked. "That's interesting."

"You would know, wouldn't you?" Monsignor smiled knowingly at Thomas. He continued, "Gentlemen, can you see the dark spot near the bottom of the levee?"

"See what?" Smitty asked.

"Come on, then." Monsignor beckoned them. "We'll go a little farther then. It's the opening I told you about. You'll see it soon enough."

"Listen, here," Charlie said. "Can't you hear that?"

"He's seeing things. Now you're hearing things?" Smitty's tone was growing coarse.

"What do you hear, Mr. Charlie?" Thomas asked. His eyes seemed to hold more knowledge than he was letting on.

"It's just a … hmm, what's the right word? A whinnying, a whirling? A war— that's it … it's a warbling sound. Like someone's playing the saw in the old country jug-band." Charlie nodded, remembering for a time the sounds of his youth, late nights and revival tents. But then his smile faltered. As he stood listening, his mind began to phase out the warble, and another sound grew stronger. "Oh my God," Charlie said as his voice cracked with a sudden sadness.

"Yes," Monsignor said. "You've heard right. Think of it as the sound we're trying to prevent – to stop, and your courage will return."

At first, Monsignor's words had no effect on the old pilot. The man cradled his head in his hands, as though the sound had driven him to the brink of insanity. It had only been the space of a moment – or had it been a prison of a thousand years? If he had been asked at the moment, Charlie could not have answered with certainty. But Monsignor's words held a certain power over him, and in a few more moments his memories had faded and he was restored. "My God," Charlie whispered, drawing a thick tear from his eye. "What was that?"

"Like I said," Monsignor said, tugging on the man's arm to follow. "It is what may yet be."

"You heard the man," Thomas nodded and spurred Brian and Smitty back on their way.

After walking another hundred yards or so crossways against the slope of the levee, the five men with Monsignor in the middle were standing at the entrance of an improbable cave. "The sound has stopped for now, thankfully," Monsignor remarked.

"Mercy." Charlie shook his head.

"But it will return in waves the closer you get," Monsignor continued. It was the same hole Monsignor had discovered the morning he'd ended the torment of the massive alligator that had been skinned and left to rot. The mouth of it had smoothed some in the passing months, and the sod had yellowed in expanding rings around the cave's mouth. Dead ropes of segmented grass hung from the opening like bangs on a corpse. Inside, the tunnel quickly faded to blackness.

"The closer we get to where?" Brian asked.

"To the heart of the tunnels," Monsignor answered with a shrug.

Smitty looked down at his flashlight in suspicion. He was thumbing the on and off switch. Charlie looked over at his friend and knew instantly what he was thinking. "Why am I starting to think our flashlights won't take us very far? Monsignor, what if that kind of darkness, deeper in, can't be scattered by these little toys of ours?" He asked, wobbling the aluminum barrel of his flashlight between his fingers and thumb.

"Charlie, you surprise me," Monsignor smiled his half-smile. "For someone who never cared much for imagining and so-called fairy stories, you see farther than most. *He who hears the gallows, with eye that pierces shadows*," Monsignor mused. "That notwithstanding, I have prepared you for the deep darkness. Have each of you brought a crucifix?"

"You *would* ask two old Protestant codgers to pack crucifixes. That's nice!" Smitty grumbled. "I had to ask my neighbor for one," he continued glumly.

"Frances had a drawer full, blessed and everything. This one by the pope, himself!" Charlie said, holding up the crucifix pendant for the others to see. The others, too, had pulled out crucifixes from their packs or from chains around their necks.

"Good," Monsignor nodded in approval. He turned to see that Brian had unpacked a dozen or more crucifixes and was holding them proudly aloft like a knock-off Rolex salesman in Times Square. "And I see some of you have brought enough to share. Thank you, Brian."

"Yes, it is very important that the articles be blessed, and I will add my own blessing, but more important still, is the faith of the one who holds the crucifix. So long as you do not waiver in your belief in Christ, no harm can come to you." With that, he raised his arm in blessing.

"Unless there's a cave-in," Smitty muttered under his breath, as Monsignor lowered his head and spoke the words of blessing. As he did, the other four men watched in wonder as the sky turned from cloudy blue to white and back again.

"What was that?" Brian asked.

"A very special blessing," Monsignor answered, smiling. "Now, you four need to get going."

"Wait … you're not coming with us?" Smitty asked wide-eyed.

"So the old Protestant won't leave the side of the priest, will he?" Charlie laughed.

"No, as we discussed, I have to stay in town. Not only to protect those who remain, but also for what may come. But, I think you may find help along the way. Remember, *big* things come in small packages." The old priest smiled as though rummaging through long memories.

"Someone has to stay and protect the homefront, Smitty. Ain't it always this way?" Charlie explained. "Besides, he's gotta look after Jim, Anne, *and* the baby. Somehow, I feel like they're way more important than a couple old soldiers like us. I think, maybe, more important now than anybody in the whole world."

"Once more unto the breach and all that, eh?" Smitty nodded. "I can do that. I'm just starting to wish I'd brought old Fitz."

"What?" Charlie smiled broadly. "You mean *this*?" As he said it, he pulled a snap inside his leather bomber's jacket and slipped out a Colt New Service pistol from under his right arm where hung half of a double shoulder holster. "You know I can't shoot for crap with my left hand, anyway."

Thomas laughed from just inside the tunnel, "What else you got in there?" Brian was also now inside the tunnel, having followed Thomas. Charlie followed the two men into tunnel, talking about pistols.

"Hot dang," Smitty smiled. He took a moment to roll the snubnosed pistol over in his hands, inspect the cylinder, and touch the trigger. The front of the trigger guard had been removed. "*Now*, I'm ready to crawl down the bowels of Hell. Hey, Monsignor, how's about a special blessing on the tools?"

"Go with God, you youngsters. You know how to reach me if you need me, *really* need me."

****

"What the hell made this thing?" Smitty asked no one in particular. The four men were crouched walking in single file down a slightly-sloping tunnel.

"My question," Thomas whispered, "is why we aren't under water? The floor of this thing isn't even slick or soft."

"What's that circular pattern all along the walls?" Brian asked.

"You ladies sure got a lot of questions and I ain't heard no answers." The men all spun around at the sound of the new voice.

"Sonofa!" Smitty crowed. "Who in the world?"

"Or what?" Brian added.

While they had been focusing on the tunnel ahead, a fifth person had silently fallen into step behind them.

"Why, it's just a little girl," Charlie smiled uncertainly.

"Just a little girl?" Brian winced. "Don't you watch horror movies? A little thing like that is just typical. They come in carrying a sweet doll or an innocent red balloon, and then come the axes and the chopping off of heads."

The small lady clapped her hands to her stomach at Brian's words and laughed full of mirth. "You know, he's right. Sort of," she said.

"Drip?" Thomas said softly from behind the other men. "Is that you? It's been so – but you can't be, can you? You were part of my *childhood*." Even as he said it, Thomas gently pushed down on Smitty's forearm lowering his pistol.

"I've been part of many childhoods, I guess you could say. Mamou's, too. All up and down your family tree."

"Small packages, eh?" Smitty asked, smiling.

The men were slowly comprehending the small woman who stood before them. She was no girl, though she was barely larger than a toddler. She was barefooted and seemed to be covered in a dress of green leaves. A thick mane of jet black hair also clung to her small frame. The hair was streaked with a mossy green lichen. Emerald eyes twinkled between crow's feet. She seemed to be at once ancient and young.

"*What* are you?" Smitty grumbled in surprise.

"I'm not a what, thank you very much," the lady clasped tiny fists at her sides in offense. "I'm a *who*."

"I should have known," Thomas smiled. "I always found you near the bloodweed."

"*You* found *me*? I see." Drip smiled, shaking her head. "I've been keeping my eye on Monsignor and the young couple. Something truly awful has come to this place, and worse still, it's been making holes in my swamps and lakes."

"How far do they go?" Smitty asked. "Miles?"

"If we're lucky. I think we'll find out for sure tonight." She pushed against Thomas' knees and slapped Smitty's belly to get the men all walking again.

"So, are you a dwarf or something?" Brian asked, trotting up beside Drip. "How are you so small?"

Drip rolled her eyes, and ignored his questions. "Have you boys been watching the walls of the tunnel?"

"Why?" Smitty asked with a sudden quaver in his voice. "They're not collapsing, are they?"

"No, they're not, which is surprising in itself, but it's the reason why. Look at them." Drip kept pushing along against the backs of their legs to ensure they looked without stopping.

"It's just ring after ring of circles, like scales maybe," Charlie said.

"It's actually more of a spiral of circles or scales, as you call them," Brian corrected.

"Is that all you can see?" Drip said, waiting for the dawning of recognition.

Thomas was the first to comment. "Each scale is covered in a texture of some sort. Why? What's it matter?"

"That's not just a texture, Myron Thomas. It's the future."

"What?" Charlie cocked his head to the side. He dismissed the small moss-covered maiden, and pushed ahead of her in the tunnel.

Moving quickly, Drip walked straight up the man's back and down his front side again. As she crested the man's head, she kicked him square in his chin with her smallish foot. Charlie grunted in astonishment, and his glasses tumbled to the ground. He was soon bent over in pain, and spit out a wad of blood.

Humph. Drip muttered. "Tall and stupid."

Charlie got a good look at the walls of the tunnel as he bowed down in pain. As he did, his eyes slowly widened. He looked intently through the red haze of pain at the wall. He started shaking his head slowly and muttering to himself. Slowly, he staggered backward. The others were all staring at him in horror, Smitty especially. He had never known the man to fear anything. It was a common trait among former pilots. Former, *living* pilots.

Staggering backward, Charlie quickly ran into the opposite wall of the tunnel. His head was flicking back and forth all around him. "Mr. Charlie?" Thomas asked, trying to keep his voice steady. As the older man slipped down against the tunnel's rounded walls, he began to rub and scratch at his arms and legs madly, as if being consumed by a swarm of red ants.

"Oh, now. Don't let it touch your *skin,*" Drip called, dashing over to the man. He had begun to shriek with pain. He was pulling back at the sleeves of his bomber jacket, and screaming at his bare arms. Only his arms weren't bare, there were lines spreading across them. There were marks.

As soon as the men had seen the marks growing across Charlie's arms and then his face, as well, they began to see the scales of the walls filling with spiraling words. It was as if a thousand ghost hands were writing feverishly across the walls and across Charlie.

"Get it off. I can feel her hands all over me. Get *her* off!" Charlie screamed thrashing on the ground. Drip ran to him, pulling a silver thimble from inside her mossy dress.

"Get her! She's gonna finish him off!" Smitty yelled as the small woman ran past him to Charlie.

"It's not Drip that Charlie's yelling about, I assure you," Thomas said pulling back on Smitty's arm. "You really need to let her help. I promise."

Drip stood before the supine man and dipped her fingers into her little thimble, one-by-one, and seemed to anoint the man in dabs of the thimble's water. Her hands worked quickly – too quickly. The hands were just a blur of motion.

Slowly, the old man's body stilled and the marks faded from his face. The other men could not tell what was going on beneath the bomber's jacket. Even as the markings faded from the man's skin, they continued across and around the walls, overhead and under feet.

"My God," Brian said, closing his eyes. "What is this place? I couldn't before, but now, I can even feel the hands moving across the walls."

"I can hear the scratching of pencils and quills and – God – is it fingernails?" It was a sound like yellow, brittle fingernails cracking against dry stone. Smitty, too, was kneeling by Charlie's side. He helped lift the man into a sitting position. "God, it *must* be hell. Can you imagine? Damned to write your sins along unending tunnels for all eternity, like chalkboard sentences forever."

"God, I can see her now," Charlie blurted out. He crawled closer to Drip. He now felt with utter assurance that he wanted Drip on his side. "It's not the souls of the damned, it's just one solitary woman. But you should see how she moves. The body moves unnaturally, but she could be a millipede with the speed of her arms all reaching around her, endlessly scribbling.

"It's not her sins she's writing, either. Nor even ours, which could keep her busy enough. It's the *future*." And then mumbling to herself, "Gee, how many times do I have to repeat myself?"

"Who is she? I can't see her. Just shadows," Brian called out. His voice was cracking and he was slowly sinking to his knees.

"She is a sibyl, a prophetess," Drip said, pushing Brian back to his feet.

"Can you make her stop?" Brain asked. "It's terrible. The endless scratching."

"She can't stop, not ever. She'll keep scrawling feverishly across the scales in unending spirals forever. Come on, boys. Stop your gawking, and let's get out of here." Drip slapped at Thomas' knee which was near eye level for her. "I don't know whether I should be at the head or the tail of this little company."

Smitty helped Charlie get back to his feet and limp away down deeper into the tunnels. Brian eventually turned away from the phantom arms and hands. He moved quickly when he discovered he was about to be left alone with the terrible apparition.

The Bath

Sam would have been excited to learn that Monsignor's plan included him, too, despite his being the youngest member of the group by far, but he had other things on his mind. Edward Teach, LaColt's business partner and the only one of the two anybody had really ever seen, except for Jim, had not escaped Monsignor's notice. He was the black bishop piece that could strike from all the way across the chessboard. It was too dangerous, Monsignor knew, to forget this man by focusing all his attention elsewhere. Sam had been tasked with watching the man, if he was a man. When Sam took Erin to the clinic, as Monsignor had instructed, he had inquired about the man. He had been told by a nurse there that Teach was rarely, if ever, seen – that he seemed to keep odd hours. He would come in early in the morning or late at night.

During the next week, Sam rode his bike by the clinic and alongside the employee parking lot when the sun had not yet risen or after it had set. He took notes of the man's behavior and any oddities. He wrote all this down in a little black notebook he kept in his back pocket. All the while, Erin was getting worse and worse.

Erin was way past the point of being able to sit beside Sam in her backyard anymore. The sweet, endless days of their romance had ended. Erin wasn't able to do much of anything now. She was nearly full term, Sam estimated from Monsignor's count, and the baby still wasn't showing. Erin was growing distant, as well … far-away. The last several times he had knocked on the door, Sam had been told by Erin's mother that she had been taking a bath.

Sam, of course, didn't take the mom's word for it. Both of Erin's parents had grown dull and listless. It was as though the lights had gone out of their eyes. Sam was pretty sure neither even left the house anymore. This sort of thing was starting to happen all over town.

When told that the girl was taking a bath, he had gone around to the side of the house to stand under the second-floor bathroom window. He could hear the sounds of bath water running up there, as well as the squeak of knobs turning and the steaming up of the window. He had tried many times to throw pebbles at Erin's window or the bathroom window, but there was never a response.

Yesterday, after knocking long enough for Erin's dad to open the door, the dad had just stood there slack-jawed and staring out the door, never looking at the boy. "I'm here to see Erin, Mr. Bellefontaine."

"No," he had answered in a monotonous drone. "She's not available to come to the door."

"Yes, sir," Sam had readily agreed. "Thank you, sir. I'll just be going then. See you later." But, as he said it, Sam had just walked straight past the man, through the door, and up the stairs. Mr. Bellefontaine had just nodded and waved at the empty front yard, as he closed the door. It had hardly mattered, though, Erin had been asleep and he had been unable to wake the girl. He had just kissed her lightly on the cheek – he could feel no fever or clamminess – and left a flower for her on the nightstand.

Sam again used his trick to slip by Mr. Bellefontaine, leaving the man once again waving at an empty front porch. Sam couldn't believe it had worked twice in a row. Something was seriously going wrong in this town, and then pushed the thought from his mind. He was approaching Erin's room.

The upstairs hallway seemed a little longer today and the shadows all seemed more menacing. Erin's door was ajar, so Sam stepped through it into a grey afternoon haze. Erin was sitting at her bedside with a hand on each thigh. She was wearing her pajamas, a matching set of floral print shirt and pants. The shirt had been buttoned, but as by a child, without only one hole filled by a button and it was the wrong button. Erin's head didn't move when Sam entered the room. He saw instantly, through Erin's mostly unbuttoned shirt, that her belly, which had never really grown much, was flat again.

Sam sat down beside the girl on her bed, as his knees felt weak beneath them. He felt blood rushing to his face. "Erin," he said. "What's happened to you? To the baby?"

Erin never looked at the boy, but Sam caught the slightest glint of surprise in her eyes, as she noticed he was sitting beside her. "Oh," she said. "It was time for my bath."

Erin kept talking, smiling weakly and distractedly. "I lay down in the water. The water was cool. I had been feeling a twisting in my belly. It wasn't a good feeling." As she said it, she touched her flattened belly through her open shirt.

"There was a strange gurgling in the drain, and then the water turned dirty and it smelled. A piece of metal popped up from the drain." She laughed then. It was a haunted, far-away laugh that sent chills up and down Sam's spine. "And then," Erin turned and looked at Sam, and he could barely recognize the girl he knew. "And then," she repeated looking at him, "it came up, out of the drain. Like a snake or a tunnel or a worm. I didn't move. I watched it come closer to me through the water. And then, I don't know. I could feel the pulling, pulling, and the baby was gone. Taken."

Erin turned away from Sam. She turned to her former position, staring blankly ahead, as if the small amount of focus she had been able to muster had just dissipated. Sam's own vision seemed to dissolve into a red heat. He seemed frozen, too, watching the girl as she still held her belly through the open shirt. Suddenly, he found himself standing, transfixed, as well, to the same spot on the girl's closet doors. He wavered there for a moment, and suddenly was gone.

There were no outbursts of anger from Sam. His anger was deeper, stiller. It was fury, like a bezerker, but there was no madness to it. His mind was cool; his whole will bent upon his objective.

As he descended the stairs of the Bellefontaine house, he grabbed a bannister from the stairs as though it were a toothpick at the check-out counter of a restaurant. The bannister snapped off with a double bang, as the wood sheered against the grain. No one in the house seemed to notice. Sam was gone and out the front door, where, Sam saw, Erin's dad was still standing, dumbly. Had Sam stopped to consider it, he would have noticed the whole family's resemblance to automatons or marionettes, quietly awaiting the vitality of an outside force to act.

For the next several hours, Sam lost himself in a flurry of preparations. When he finally emerged from his mental bubble, his knapsack had grown much heavier. Sam had filled it with the wooden bannister, now sharpened to a point, a mallet, and his dad's revolver, as well as holy water and a pyx holding several pieces of the Eucharist. He had also tucked some rope at the bottom of his pack. Even though he suspected that bullets would be no help against LaColt, he thought a bullet between Teach's eyes would just about punch that guy's ticket.

He stood, staring at the ostentatiously wide and long trunk of one of the ugly yellow Jaguars. It was now dusk and nearly dark. He knew the car was Teach's. His hands moved to the trunk's lock. As his hand passed over the lock, the interior latch clicked and the trunk popped open, obediently. The boy slid into the spacious trunk and pulled it down above him, quietly. The inside of the trunk smelled of saltwater and dead fish. The boy waited there for three, maybe four hours, in the darkness, until the motor roared to life.

Monsignor's Plan

"My God!" Smitty finally called out after a long silence had fallen over the men. "This place must go on for miles and miles. Must've been two or three miles so far."

"It could've been a hundred miles or just one. I wouldn't know," Brian said rubbing the sweat from his forehead and flinging it off the back of his hand. "It's so strange. So *foul.*"

"The worse the smell, the closer we're getting," observed Drip, who had been for some time taken lead of the small company.

"We must've passed it already, then!" Charlie smirked.

"So, what was Monsignor's plan, again?" Smitty asked. "Was it just to explore the place? If it was, I say we bang a u-ey and head back. We've explored the hell outta this place."

"Yeah," Brian agreed with an expression of sudden realization spreading across his face. "Why does that mad old priest have us down here, anyway. Why hadn't I thought of this before? Did he actually *tell* anybody?"

"It's obvious, isn't it?" Drip snickered ahead of them.

"He told us about the earth, remember?" Thomas spoke up.

"The what?" Smitty said. He knocked at the shoulder of Charlie in front of him and mimed a shrugging expression.

"On the ship that Isaiah saw," Charlie added. "Monsignor believes that the ship was carrying, not just all of LaColt's crap, but earth – you know, dirt – from wherever he came from. He needs it or something."

"Upon your belly shall you go and dust shall you eat." Drip murmured. "We must sterilize the earth, so that he can no more seek safety in it."

"Wait, we're looking for *dirt*?" Smitty asked. "Well, look around, fellas, we've found it! We're surrounded by the stuff. And we must've passed branch after branch of this damn tunnel, how we know we're going in the right direction? It's like the friggin' Viet-Cong down here!"

"Drip told you," Charlie smiled. "We're following our noses."

"Speaking of our noses," Brian interrupted. "What's this new lovely stench?"

"Garr! It smells like rotten eggs." Smitty shook his head as his eyes began to water.

"Sulfur steam," Thomas observed.

"Like from a thermal vent?" Brian asked. "In St. Maryville?"

"Yes and no," Drip answered from the head of their column. "We're sort of in St. Maryville and sort of not."

"That doesn't make much sense to me, little lady," Charlie said from under a furrowed brow.

"There are mysteries hidden below St. Maryville that I'd rather not mention here in these tunnels. Things like universals, things that have always existed. Aren't you people always treating this town like it's the center of the universe or something?"

"I'm with Charlie. I've only ever seen dirt under the dirt." Thomas balked at the idea.

"Have you only?" Drip flashed a knowing look back toward Thomas. "Methinks the man digs and hides his great treasure. But it doesn't matter. Just know, not everything will make sense down here. It'll be like walking in myths and allegory."

"Well, that explains everything," Smitty snorted, as he and the company kept trudging along. After another hundred or so yards, the tunnel broadened into a dark expanse filled with steam. They could hear the quiet, heavy sound of moving water.

"Keep to the side of the cave and follow me," Drip whispered. "Don't go near the water, and don't let anyone wander away."

"What is that winding line of light over there?" Brian asked. "It looks like track lighting at the movie theater."

"It's the River of Fire."

"That's a river?" Thomas asked, amazed. "It can't be more than a few feet across. More like a stream."

"So this is hell? And that's the River Styx?" Smitty grumbled angrily. "Well, ain't that a peach."

"It's more than a mile across," Drip stated matter-of-factly, keeping a watchful eye on the men. "And no, it's the Phlegethon, though it runs near the Styx."

"Impossible," Brian scoffed. "No way it's so close. I think I could touch it."

"I wouldn't try it, Brian," Charlie instructed. "Just keep your eyes on the little lady."

"It would have to be miles and miles away," Thomas said in wonder.

"It is and more," Drip answered. "And below us, too. So watch your foo—" But even as she said it, scraping and scratching sounds erupted behind her.

"Wha—whoa-ah!" It was Brian – he had tried walking over to the river to prove its proximity.

The other men rushed to catch and steady Brian, who had nearly walked straight off the edge of the cliff, nearly invisible in the steamy half-light. Gasping for breath as his heart was racing, Brian bellowed, "A cliff? We're walking along – a cliff – and you didn't think – you didn't think it was important – to tell a man a thing like that?"

"She did tell you, you old goat. *Sheesh,*" Smitty scolded.

"How can a thing like that exist?" Charlie wondered aloud. "The whole Mississippi River would just disappear into it – and the Gulf of Mexico, too."

"Like I said, it's here and it's not here," Drip said, while her other ear twitched for sounds of pursuit.

"Like Schrodinger's cat!" Brian yelped. "And this cat just dropped one of his lives."

"Come on," Drip whispered darkly. "Let's get going."

Confrontation

Miss Tee-Eva had been bugging Sheriff's Deputy Dabadie for almost a week about the yellow Jaguars. They had been appearing here and there in St. Maryville for months. That Rock kid had been hit by one, but that seemed irrelevant to what had come after – if the hospital staff's accounts were to be trusted at all. But now, according to Miss Tee-Eva, they were prowling up and down the back roads of St. Maryville "bold as brass." People, she said, were disappearing. Whole families, even. "Why'd no one file no report? 'Cause thez all gone, tha's *why*."

The lady had always provided solid information, so the sheriff's deputy promised her that, next time he ran across a yellow Jaguar, he would investigate, as a personal favor to her. That had seemed to mollify her, and she slid him a sweet potato pie – "On the house, dear."

That same night, Dabadie's squad car was waiting in the parking lot of the electric company building on the outskirts of town. It was a typical spot for cops to park and wait, as the speed limit dropped down drastically just there. At night time, people usually took their time to adjust their speed, if they even noticed the speed trap at all.

So it was that, after three cars had sped through the speed trap – all of which he recognized as locals – the deputy watched as a yellow Jaguar going at a respectable 40mph, waited a reasonable distance after the speed limit sign before accelerating to the new speed limit of 55mph.

"Good enough," the deputy said to himself, knocking his squad car in gear and quietly slipping out of the parking lot. The deputy didn't flip on his lights or sirens. He didn't even turn his headlights on.

He followed the yellow Jaguar half-way down the length of the river. Dabadie was, without knowing it, taking the same course along the river as Isaiah had so many months before when he was following the black ship.

"The Sheriff's Deputy." Teach observed aloud to himself, as Sam listened from inside the trunk. His adrenaline had never stopped pumping. Red hot malice still burned in the boy's chest, while he remained still focused and collected. He lay there like a coiled spring, ready to pounce.

"He will likely ask to search the car," Teach continued, still speaking to himself. "As well as, I suspect, the trunk?" The man let the question hang in the air, unanswered, even as ice water suddenly coursed through the boy's veins. His jaws clenched to the point of splintering his teeth, but the pain gave him solace, somehow. The boy's thoughts fluttered along quickly. Teach wasn't trying to announce his knowledge of the stowaway and frighten him. Or, at least, that wasn't all he was trying to do. He was warning the boy. If Sam was discovered in the man's trunk, there would be complications. Delays. But tonight, Sam knew somehow, was Teach's night to die. If he stayed where he was, the officer would find the boy. He would take him away.

No, Sam realized, *that's not right.* Teach wasn't warning him to prevent the officer from taking the boy away. Teach would never allow the officer to escape with a mind full of suspicion, much less allow the officer to arrest him. Teach was warning the boy that, if Sam didn't hide, Teach would be forced to kill the officer and stuff him into the trunk along with the boy.

Moments later, the yellow Jaguar slowed and turned onto a gravel drive. It continued to slow until it stopped. Sam could hear the driver knock the gear shift into park and turn the key in the ignition, killing the loud, eight-cylinder diesel engine.

As Teach likely suspected all along, the squad car followed them into the lane, flipping on its headlights as it did. Unlike the Jaguar, the squad car thumped and rattled down the lane. Sam could hear the car's hydraulics straining over whatever had suddenly moved to obstruct the lane. The police car's engine revved again and again, as though climbing a series of sharp inclines.

The seam of the trunk door was suddenly illuminated as the police car pulled in behind the Jaguar. Sam could hear the squad car's idling engine, and he could hear as the sheriff's deputy shifted the car into park. There was a long, grating squeak as the deputy kicked open his car door and then the crunching of gravel, as he stepped outside.

"Please step out of the car," Sam heard the deputy announce over the car's CB loudspeaker. Sam listened as the deputy returned the mouthpiece to its hook, and removed something from the car, before slamming the door shut behind him. Sam had an image in his mind of the deputy leveling a shotgun at the driver's door of the Jaguar. It may not kill Teach, but maybe it could weaken him. *What are the chances that sheriff's deputies load their shotguns with blessed rock salt?* Sam wondered.

Sam listened as Teach actually cranked open the car's heavy doors and exited the vehicle. The man's feet made no sound on the gravel. Sam shifted into a crouched position in the spacious trunk. He disguised his movements with the sound of the opening and closing car doors, and later with the sound of their voices. He gripped the trunk's interior latch which, when pulled, would allow him to access the backseat, if he had enough time and was small enough.

There was a long pause, finally broken by Teach himself. His words seemed to reverberate in the mind, not as any physical effect of compression waves. "Good evening, officer. Is there a problem …" There was a pause, and Teach finally finished saying, "… sir?"

As Teach spoke, Sam could feel heat traveling from his mind and spilling over to the rest of his body. His hands felt suddenly warm and clammy. Sam's once-cool and collected thoughts grew restless. His mind began to flit from place to place. His thoughts grew non-linear. The boy's fever was rising in strides.

"Don't you usually travel by horse-drawn carriage, buddy?" The officer said. The crunching gravel beneath his footsteps seemed to have stopped by the car's back window. The cop, Sam realized, must have been holding a flashlight to the end of his shotgun barrel, as the outline of the little door between the back seat and the trunk was suddenly illuminated.

"Don't you need probable cause to search my vehicle, officer?" Teach asked in his subtly lilting accent.

"Let's just go with reasonable suspicion – sound good, boss?"

At this point, beads of sweat had begun to form and drop from his head, collecting behind his ears and dampening his hair. Sam thought it was the effect of Teach's voice. Then, he suddenly became aware of the stench of death which filled the trunk. His mind had been disciplining his senses up to that point, but was failing now. Sam could also feel, now, the oily residue which imbued the stiff carpet of the trunk. The fury and redness, so long held in check, was now tipping its banks.

Adoration Chapel

Monsignor's eyes suddenly flicked open. He was sitting slouched in the small Adoration Chapel on the first floor of the rectory. The room seemed to throb around the old priest. Monsignor looked around in confusion, but his eyes were quickly drawn to the Eucharist residing in the monstrance at the focal point of the room. He watched, breathlessly, as the small glass holder at the center of the monstrance's gold sunbursts, the receptable which held the consecrated bread, slowly filled with blood.

Monsignor sat up quickly in the rough upholstered chair, and then slipped his knees to the kneeler in a controlled fall. There was the brittle sound of crepitus as the old man's knees, legs, and hips erupted with little cracks.

The man dipped his scarred, wide brow to his clasped hands. Soon, the beads of his sweat turned ruddy and dark. A spreading red sogginess began to pool beneath the kneeler.

Winding Tunnels

The men were trudging along deeper and deeper into the tunnels. They followed Drip, their faith in her growing with every turn. All the while, the air was growing foul, more foul than even the sulfur steam of the River of Fire.

Thomas gasped. "*What?*" A face had appeared out of the darkness of the tunnel. It was a white face with a fixed expression of surprise. A mask. It floated backward from them, reeling away down the tunnel on legs of black cloth and staring at them as it retreated. There was a pitter-pat of feet which did not match the thing's footsteps. Had there been more light, its shadow might have revealed its true form.

Thomas stood against the curved walls of the tunnel, panting for breath. "What in the name of God?"

"Come *on*. I can't take this crap," Brian said, rubbing his fists against the sides of his head. "This place ... I feel like I'm losing it. I'm losing it." His voice faded into distracted ramblings.

"Drip, if we're gonna do something. Let's do it quick and get out of here," Charlie said, wiping the fog from his glasses with the hem of his untucked shirt. "I don't know how much longer we're gonna last."

"Until the job is done." Drip smiled. "More than that, and we'll be pressing our luck. Besides, that apparition means we're close. Those things are like flies caught in the cobwebs. They'll do you no harm, unless you let them."

The tunnel had been long and almost always straight up to this point, but now it started bending into tight turns. They wound way through a triple switchback. The walls tightened in on them in patches and they were slowed down.

"What the hell?" Brian wondered aloud, creeping closer to an edifice protruding from the tunnel.

"Well, that's different," Smitty said. "At least it's something different to look at."

"What is it?" Charlie asked.

"It's an altar," Drip answered with a sneer. "For rituals. Dark ones. I can smell remains of things slaughtered there. Years and years and years worth of waste. It makes my stomach turn. *And* it pisses me off."

The rest of the men continued past the altar with looks of curiosity mixed with disdain. They passed several more altars like the first one.

"This is the crypt. We're nearly there," Drip whispered. "Be quiet, we don't know what we'll find."

But after she had said it, the sharply-turning tunnels nevertheless began to wind endlessly, as though they were trapped in a great labyrinth of unholy altars.

I can see him yet

"You're Mr. Teach, aren't you?" Sam could hear the officer ask. "Kinduva funny name, isn't it?"

"I must admit I prefer it to being described by my beard." Teach answered cordially. "You're Sheriff's Deputy Vincent Samson Dabadie, are you not? Yes, Miss Tee-Eva has told us much about you. Of course, we've known your family for some time, haven't we?"

When the officer next spoke, his voice was clearly rattled. "Please open your trunk, Mr. Teach."

Teach then rattled his keys like a chain of old bones. Had Sam's mind not been roiling with fever, he might have thought it odd, as he had not heard Teach remove the keys from the ignition. Nevertheless, it was all he could do to stay focused on the little door between the backseat and the trunk, as the world began to swirl around inside his head. "I will need to unlock the trunk by hand, officer. There is no automatic trunk release. Please step aside."

"Watch it, buddy," The officer replied. "Your mention of Miss Tee-Eva has made my trigger finger awful itchy."

"Of course, bud-dy," Teach replied in his mocking Bristol accent.

As the keys jangled like dry bones at the trunk latch, Sam raised the lever, gently lowered the seat forward into the backseat, and slid his body and knapsack through with one graceful motion. He could hear the trunk open behind him just as he raised the seat back into place. When he was safely in the backseat and out of sight of Teach and the deputy, all the movement finally caught up with him. The rising fever broke its banks. His brain was spinning within his skull, and he teetered on the verge of blacking out.

He somehow timed the opening of the backseat door to match the sound of the trunk slamming shut. He left the passenger door ajar behind him as he spilled out onto the gravel drive. He scrambled as quietly as he could to the front of the Jaguar, where he could watch Teach and the deputy, only he forgot about the shadow he would cast passing in front of the headlight.

The sudden contrast of Sam's silhouette, black against the illuminated oak trees, must have startled the two men. The deputy leveled his shotgun at Teach, and Teach, a blur of motion, had grabbed the shotgun, tossed it aside, and wrapped his massive hands around the deputy's neck, all before Sam's shadow had finished passing in front of the Jaguar's headlight. When next he looked, the deputy was dangling and wriggling in Teach's grasp like a stuck insect.

Sam's hands pulled madly at his knapsack. He could physically feel the passing of the precious few seconds he had to act. Teach was exposed. His attention, at least most of it, Sam thought, was directed to the deputy. Besides that, Sam knew, it was only a matter of time before Teach squeezed, snapping the poor man's neck like so many twigs.

His blinding focus came back to him just then. He took the sharpened bannister in both hands, and leaping, through his whole body, stake first, against Teach's back. He aimed for a spot inches to the left of the man's protruding spine. In his mind's eye, Sam could see the stake disappearing into the thick weave of the man's coat and sinking deep into the man's flesh. But just inches from the stake making impact, Sam's head was snapped violently backward. There was a blinding flash across his vision and he was thrown backward. Something slammed him down to the ground hard.

Sam couldn't speak or yell. Only a single miserable squeak chirped out of his throat. He thought he saw Teach turn in his direction and toss the deputy's limp body aside. There was a horrible sneer outlined by the man's black beard.

As Sam tugged at his neck, he realized he was being dragged by a noose. It was his last thought before he succumbed to unconsciousness.

****

The boy awoke with surprise. He had thought he was dead or worse. He looked around and concluded from the jumble of rope around him that he had probably been pulled upward by the noose, until mercifully, he had been dropped. And then he saw the ghost.

The Lady in White was running straight for him. Her white dress fluttered around her, and her eyes were terrible. The eyes glowed like pale starlight sunk deep within the emaciated face. He tried to scream, but pain exploded his throat. He could not speak, as the cartilage of his vocal cords was likely torn.

Then he noticed, the other one. The slave woman smiled down at him hideously as she hung from a noose, swinging back and forth beneath a thick live oak limb. It was she, he knew, that had dragged him by the noose, a soul damned to torment others as she had been tormented and killed.

He would have asked himself how he came to be lying on the ground and not dead, but a blinding fear overtook him, as the ghosts came nearer to him. The lady in white was reaching toward him, as if a single touch and Sam would forever share her damnation. The swinging hanged slave woman was also approaching, as the oak limb bent to her will. Sam, by now, was horribly injured. Even if he could move without eruptions of intense pain, he was frozen within his skin.

The Lady in White reached him first. Her touch was icy as her hands slowly climbed his legs. Her face pulsed between her former beauty and the emaciated hag. Sam was still frozen, and now, as her hands reached closer and closer to the boy's head and heart, he could feel a numbing death spreading across his lower members.

With the woman's touch, the boy slipped into a gray mist of restless dreams. He was running endlessly through the live oaks. Sometimes, he would trip over one of the severe roots, which rose to meet him. He would hear the crack of his ankle, just before the crack of his skull and a little staccato of the rest of his bones. Sometimes, he would just throw himself at one of the thick trunks, like a piece of exquisite crystal. He would see himself lying on the ground in a thousand different pieces, and then he would be running again.

He was always running, always crashing. There was no escape and no hope.

And then, something changed. Sam couldn't figure how many days, how many years, how many thousands of times he had felt all his bones break. "I can see him yet," he would later say, "walking through the gray mist."

It wasn't Teach, coming to finish off the boy by his own hands, though Teach was there when he awoke. Sam could see clearly again. The fever had finally broken, though his clothes were soaked with sweat.

No, it was another. The white light of the ghosts became like shadows before the new figure. The ghosts squealed in horror, as the piercing light of the new figure seemed to rend holes in their incorporeal bodies. They turned to flee back into the nothingness and the live oaks, but they were stopped in their tracks. It was Teach. The yellow Jaguar had disappeared, and the driver was again standing before his carriage. He had cracked his long whip twice, once against each of the ghosts' backs. The three of them turned to face the blinding light of the newcomer. Sam thought he recognized a scarred brow in the midst of the light. *Could it be?* He wondered.

But there was no time for idle thoughts. Sam knew he had been given a second chance. His fever was gone, and though his throat was still badly damaged and he may yet be full of brittle, broken bones, there was no time to waste on pain. He circled around the encircling shadows. He saw the deputy was alive, but cowering behind his squad car, unable to believe what he was seeing. Sam moved to where the Jaguar had been, where the carriage and the horses now stood. Though the car had transformed, his knapsack had remained, and the stake was not far from it. He had time enough this time to collect the mallet from his knapsack. He would not miss his mark twice.

When Sam turned back to the shadows encircling the newcomer, he saw that the new light had only grown in intensity at the shadows' approach. Light from light shot out from the figure. The ghosts dissolved in the light, and in a moment, Teach was alone before the rising tower of light. The tips of Edward Teach's black beard erupted into little flames. His shadow loomed larger as the light grew brighter. Teach launched his great arms around the figure like two living tree limbs, seeking to crush the newcomer. As he did, he exposed his back to Sam's stake. The boy rushed forward with blinding speed.

In one motion, he set the stake and thrust all his remaining forward momentum into the swinging mallet. The stake sank deep in the man's flesh, clearing the space between his ribs. Light began to seep first from the wound and then cracks slowly spread outward from the wound. Soon, the light – the newcomer's own light – was shining straight through Teach's crumbling body. His arms and head sloughed off his body as blocks of ash and dust. In a moment, he was just a pile at their feet.

The boy looked up into the light, and shielding his eyes with his hand, he saw again the scarred brow. He saw, too, Monsignor's face smiling down on him. Neither was able to speak. Sam smiled back, before staggering backward and collapsing, finally succumbing to his injuries.

The Girdle Breaks

In their growing exhaustion, they were rocked suddenly by a stabbing pain in their minds. It came from not far above them, where the old plantation home stood. Their weakening knees buckled beneath them. Slowly, they rose back to their feet. Drip, who had remained standing throughout, helped Smitty get back on his feet.

"Don't know how much more of this …," Smitty paused amid labored breathing. "How much more of this, this fat, old Yank can take."

"Buddy," Drip smiled. "I think our way just grew a lot easier. Will you follow me around one more turn?"

As the group followed the small lady around another sharp switchback, the tunnel widened suddenly. They followed her, one by one, into another dark place. Though they could see only very little, the room felt large, but not nearly as large as the river valley of the Phlegethon.

Drip tapped her tongue in her mouth and little claps of sound skittered around the room's periphery. The shape and size of the room suddenly became apparent to the men. There was a high ceiling and thick stone walls. Their feet – now accustomed to the soft curve of the tunnel floor – felt the cool of paving stones.

The men groped around the room. "So you're saying this is where Monsignor planned for us to go? The dirt's here?" Brian asked.

"Must be," Smitty answered. "Smells like a dead rat's arse."

Charlie grumbled, "*Sonofa.* I think my toe just found the first crate."

"Yessir, here's another," Thomas called out. "Now what?"

A number of eyes fell on where they had last seen Drip. "Why didn't we think about any of this before setting off on this damned dirt hunt?"

"We're just sma't like that," Smitty answered.

"We could drop it in that River of Fire," Thomas suggested. "That would purify anything." As he said this, he was feeling around the crate he had found. "But I don't see us moving these things. These wooden crates must hold a cubic yard of dirt each. And –" he grunted, feeling along the edge and seams of the wood. "I don't suppose any of us were smart enough to bring a crowbar?"

"Wait … we can't just pull the lids off?" Brian said with mounting disappointment. "That's just great, it'nt it?"

"If we could somehow push the boxes off that cliff back there, I'm betting they'd open all on their own," Charlie said with a smirk that no one could see.

"Let's get after it then," Thomas said with grim determination. "There must be twenty or more of those things in here. The four of us men can each take a side, but it'll take hours of work, and we ain't got no food and no water."

"It's hard for a lady to get a word in edgewise 'round here," Drip said haughtily, stamping her small foot. The men had begun knocking around the crates and prying at the lids, all to no avail. Slowly, they turned toward the shadow of the diminutive figure.

"Please tell me you've got an easier alternative," Smitty said, already breathing heavily. "It's been a long time since Air Force PT."

"Didn't Monsignor send you with some holy water?" Drip asked. "He practically sanctified the entire spillway a little while ago turning all the frogs to madness. We could've just grabbed a puddle-full on our way in …"

"No, no," Charlie interrupted. "You're right. How stupid of us. I've got the bottle he gave me right here."

"Me, too," Thomas smiled, eyes downcast, as he pulled a thick bronze pyx from his own pocket. "He gave me these consecrated hosts, probably no more than ten. 'Spose I can break them into smaller pieces, and it will have the same effect."

Smitty and Brian, too, each pulled bottles of holy water out of their pockets. "He said I might need this," Brian nodded. "That little bugger seems to have thought of everything."

"He would," Drip said. "Never misses a trick, that man. He knows where all the chess pieces lie and where they're all going, turns and turns ahead. Wouldn't doubt if this is all just pregame moves, for all that – and if it weren't Monsignor who drew Mr. LaColt here in the first place."

"Wait ... you know about LaColt?" Brian asked.

Drip rolled her eyes in the darkness with such exasperation that the men could almost hear it. "I've brought you to that monster's lair, haven't I?" A blush spread across Brian's ears more than his ebony cheeks.

"Alright, let's get to it," Charlie said. "Can we just sprinkle the water on top, or do we still have to pry off the lids?"

"I know I'm burying a piece of host in each box," Thomas answered.

"I think you'll find that most are already pried open, but best to finish the job," Drip answered.

"And how do we do that, exactly?" Smitty complained. "I think I've already ripped off a fingertip trying."

"Do I have to do everything myself?" Drip replied with emasculating disgust. "Fine. If I must, I must." They watched as her shadow moved about in the darkness.

"I wouldn't go after it like that, little miss," Thomas cautioned. "You might hurt ...," but he didn't finish the sentence. As they listened, Drip was hopping from one box to the other, like so many lilly pads. One by one, they heard the crates creak open.

"How'd she ...?" Smitty muttered. Thomas just shook his head and Charlie laughed heartily. "Must be one of those feminist things."

Drip's broad smile sparkled in the half-light of the room. She stood with her hands on her hips, as the men uncorked their small glass bottles of holy water and splashed their contents on the black, rocky soil. Thomas, for his part, dug out little holes and pressed pieces of the Eucharist into each box of soil. Towards the end, he was having to blow at the end of his fingertips.

"What's happening?" Charlie asked, coughing.

"They're smoking!" Brian shouted in surprise, as the dirt within the boxes began stirring with vents of hot air. The heavy wooden crates began to shake, rocking across the stone floor. Cracks of wood echoed through the crypt, as Drip's tongue tapping had done earlier.

"The evil is losing its potency. It's being exorcised," Drip observed.

"All because of some drops of water and bread?" Smitty asked incredulously.

"All because of the sacrament that made Monsignor a priest," Drip corrected.

"You mean *every* priest has this power?" Smitty asked in wonder. "You know, maybe I should become Catholic. God, Carol would kill me." Though his wife had been dead for several years, he still spoke of her as though she were merely waiting at home for him.

"At least you'd be resurrected after it was all said and done," Charlie laughed, patting his friend on his back.

"Drip, what's happening?" Brian asked. "I'm beginning to see you." Red light was starting to fill the crypt.

"This can't be good," Charlie said looking around at the room.

Smitty stared in wonder at the walls of the crypt which were filled with awful carvings. "Somebody must've taken notice of our mischief."

"This is an evil place," Brian shuddered, as his eyes focused on one of a set of six stone carvings. Six hieroglyphs. There was a stone pyramid with feathered animal-faced gods at their pinnacle. Streams of children rose to the top of the pyramid on one side and then blood streamed from the other side. But there was something funny about the pyramid. It was *inverted*.

Then, Brian's finger traced another set of six hieroglyphs, and then another. "Pharaoh," he whispered. The stone was carved with images of more pyramids, but these beside the great river. "Herod," he whispered again, as the light flickered against a depiction of the slaughter of the innocents beneath a star.

"Drip, what's happening to the wall?" Thomas pointed behind Drip. The red light seemed to be spilling from this one wall alone. The whole wall glowed red.

"It's alabaster," Brian answered. They could hear his voice quavering, and he was shaking visibly. "I've seen windows of it in the villas of Rome. Before there were glass windows, you see." His voice was growing distant. "The light that filtered through alabaster windows … heavenly," he whispered.

"Behold," Brian continued, only his voice had entirely drained away. It had been replaced by a deep darkness. "The creature's mouth."

Just as Brian had described it, the red light glowed in and through the wall. But it was not heavenly. The wall seemed to melt into a screen. What at first appeared to be a large carving across the whole wall, they slowly realized, was actually a view of something shuddering and twisting in the distance. Beyond the wall, there was a great expanse of flesh.

"Brian?" Smitty asked in confusion. Without a moment's hesitation, Drip again hopped across the room. Only this time, she landed squarely atop Brian with her small foot nestling neatly between his eyes.

To the men, Brian was standing there one moment and laying crumpled on the ground the next with Drip standing atop. "Carry him," she said. "We've gotta get out of here and *now*."

"But what is it?" Charlie asked. He had ignored the whole incident. His eyes remained fixed on the vastness beyond the wall. "A mouth? I don't …."

"Don't look like no mouth I've ever seen. Looks like a huge funnel, maybe." Thomas, too, was transfixed.

"My God, it *is* a mouth. Can't you see the veins?" Charlie was shaking his head back and forth in disbelief. "It's flesh and tissue and … teeth. Rows and rows of teeth like a sharp, like a funnel – yeah – but a mouth, too."

"What's that, then – the esophagus?" Smitty asked. He was pointing to the fleshy tube which led from the bottom of the mouth like a stretch of intestine and away below them. "It's impossible. It's too big, and it's not connected to anything."

"Yes, it is," Drip answered. "The Phlegethon. It's the mouth of the River of Fire."

"Rivers don't have *actual* mouths," Smitty said dismissively. "That's just a term, a geography term. Besides the mouth should be at the end, not the beginning."

"Smitty," Charlie said. "Open your eyes. What lies beyond that wall doesn't give a crap for your logic and reason. It knows only madness. You're looking at a mouth, a great disembodied mouth, that could eat, not just all of us, but entire football fields and aircraft carriers."

"Before you get all philosophical – whatever it is – we ain't got no time for it," Smitty said pulling at the arms of Thomas and his friend. "I don't care if it is the size of the Grand Canyon."

Drip, too, was tugging at the back of Thomas' pant leg. "I've got to agree with Smitty on this one. It's time to go. *Really* time. Thomas, get over here and carry Brian." Thomas, a man of thick build, lurched backward at the motion of Drip's small hand.

"More like Carlsbad Caverns than the Grand Canyon. Or a tornado made of guts." Charlie was still trying to describe the hideous thing, as though hypnotized. "There're just no words for it. No, there are *six* words."

"Time to go, Colonel," Smitty said, as the larger man bear-hugged his friend, plucked him off the ground, and carried him out of the crypt behind Drip and Thomas, who was carrying Brian.

The Possessed

"Has he been acting strange, dear?" Mamou asked. She was taking off her coat at the front door of Honey House, or so Anne called her house. It was yellow, though, if you asked her, Anne wouldn't remember precisely why she had so christened the house.

"He's been mostly sleeping, all day, everyday. He's been that way since we all met at the rectory. Sometimes, I think, he gets up to do some work he's brought from the office. It's like he's sleep walking, but he seems to be a very efficient sleepwalker."

"And at night?" Mamou asked, as she made her way to the kitchen. Working in the kitchen was her way of working through difficult times and decisions. She would have the place humming like a forge and billows before long.

"Always around 3AM." Anne answered. She was leaning backward, rubbing her spine up and down, as her belly swelled in front of her. "That's when the weird things happen. He gets up and sits alone in the den and the darkness. The river. He talks about it swallowing him. Mumbles, really. His dad, you know, drowned in it. Even before, he would sometimes scream out in his sleep. But it's worse now. I don't think he can wake up for the nightmare anymore."

"And how are you?" Mamou asked, deftly shifting the conversation. "I bet you're feeling every one of those thirty-eight weeks, aren't you?"

Anne rubbed her lower back as she spoke, absentmindedly. "It's funny, you know. When the baby kicks or presses against my bladder, if I just say 'ouch' or wince a little, the baby will stop."

"What do you mean, dear?" Mamou asked from the stove. The kitchen was already beginning to fill with the warm, buttery scent of roux in the frying pan.

"It's like, oh, I don't know. It's silly. Nevermind."

"Speak up. If you're saying you've found a way to ease the pains of pregnancy, let me know – let the whole human race know, child. We haven't had an easy pregnancy since the Garden. And with Eve being born of Adam's rib – wouldn't you know – a man was one of the only people in history to have an easy pregnancy. Lord knows it had to be just so."

"It's just – I think – I *really* think she hears me. That she can *understand* me, too."

"'She,' huh?" Mamou smiled. "So you think the baby's a girl? Why's that now?"

"It's like I was saying … I think we're communicating some kind of way."

Mamou had turned to her daughter and was staring at her with a knowing look, all at once far away, too. "Really?" She said, cocking her head to one side.

"Mamou, yes! I really do. *And*, you'll definitely think me a mad woman after this, but I think I've even seen her smiling against my belly. Like she was putting her face to a window pane."

"Dear, listen to old mama," Mamou said, putting down her wooden spoon and putting her hand to her aproned hip. "Can't say as I know all the ins and outs, but, if what you're saying is so, the child must be protected at all costs."

"Why, mama?"

"Your child is a special child. Yes, I think I've known it myself, too, all along. And, all the while, the monster is prowling for babies. Why it picked St. Maryville, of all places. It's odd to you, isn't it? Of all the bigger cities? Lots of places aborting children by the thousands. Why here, you see? Unless it's a moth, scarcely aware it's being drawn to the flame. But, there's more here besides, Lords knows."

Mamou slowly came out of her thoughts, and looked backed to her child.

She saw the look of confusion on her daughter's face, and thought better of saying more. "*Oh* child," she said. "Let's get you sitting down. You've been on your feet too long in this hot kitchen."

****

"Let's see if he'll eat something," Mamou said raking a spoon through a bowl of gumbo she had made. "There's plenty of spice in it. If he doesn't eat it, it'll at least make an impression. Dear, will you please say a rosary while I do this? It might be just enough to keep whatever-it-is at bay, while I try to feed him."

Together, Anne and her mother entered the master bedroom of Honey House. It was a wide room that had once been a porch. Jim was laying on his back. His chest hopped up and down, as he took quick, shallow breaths. "He certainly looks like he's got the devil in 'im," Mamou said, as she pulled a chair around to the side of the bed. She kept an eye on the crucifix hanging above the bed. "I remember that from your wedding. It's good that it's hanging there."

"He keeps knocking it down, and I keep putting in back up." Anne frowned, and her face suddenly collapsed into tears. She quickly put the back of her hand to her eyes to catch the tears before they could fall onto her husband.

"Let 'em fall," Mamou said. "It'd do him good." As she took her daughter's hand into her own broad hands, she noticed that her daughter's long sleeves were hiding long, terrible scratch marks.

"Do you – do you think I'll ever get him back, mama?" She choked the words out where they wanted to lodge in her throat.

"I won't roll it in sugar for ya, honey. I think we'll be lucky if we – if some of us – escape with our souls intact, and maybe our lives." Mother and daughter exchanged a long, hard look. "Now, let's see if we can get this poor boy to eat something."

As she said it, Anne unzipped her small brown felt rosary bag and pulled out the strand of mother of pearl beads. Without getting up from her chair, Mamou lifted her son-in-law to a sitting position. She did it so naturally that an onlooker would hardly notice her immense strength. "That's a good boy,"

210

she said. She clanked a worn silver spoon against the white ceramic soup bowl, and slowly pushed it into the man's mouth. After two strong swallows, his body began to shudder.

"What kind of spice did you put in that bowl, mama?" Anne asked between Hail Marys.

"Some cayenne, lots of garlic, and a pint of holy water," the older woman smiled.

"And a silver spoon?" Anne smiled faintly.

"For good measure," Mamou smiled warmly. Just then, the smiles were wiped from both of their faces. An animal started snarling just behind the bedroom window above the bed. The window panes rattled and the crucifix started rocking slowly, side to side, like a pendulum.

Jim started coughing. It was gentle at first, but his body was soon rocked with pain and involuntary spasms. He was bent down along his outstretched legs. Jim was straightening his torso along his legs, as though any bend caused terrible pain. He winced with pain at every cough as the rocking of his body curved his back.

Anne watched in horror as the veins in her husband's eyes began to rupture and the white sclera began to fill with blood. "Mama," she cried. "Make it *stop*. He can't ... He's *dying*. Help him, please!"

Mamou had put her fist to her own mouth, feeling the panic and helplessness rise in her throat. Her daughter's sobs became inaudible beneath the wretching and coughing. Blood began to splatter out of the man's mouth as his body racked involuntarily. He screamed in pain. As he did, the metal pins began to fall from his throat and out of his mouth. The red smears began to spread across the white of his sheets.

Anne was rocking back and forth in pain and grief. Her jaw was locked in a silent scream, and she looked to Mamou imploringly. Mamou took her daughter's hand in her large paw of a hand. "You just hold his hand, dear. No matter where he is or what he's feeling that'll bring him comfort. This has to come out of him, no matter what's left afterwards. And you say that rosary, girl. Don't you stop, no matter."

Mamou stopped talking and looked to the windows which stood in a row at the back of the bedroom. Anne didn't think about or even notice her mother's almost-predatory movements until the growling began. The great woman rose from the bedside, grinding her back molars. "You just mind my words, Anne. If you remain steadfast, the two of you just might get out of this. Even now."

"What are you doing, mama? What's making that terrible sound?"

Even as she gave Anne her parting instructions, Mamou was moving slowly along the row of windows, like a prowling animal. "I'll be back in a minute or in the morning – you just do your job."

A barking growl of some huge predator banged like a thunderclap against the bedroom windows. It was followed and even squelched by an equally powerful roar from within the bedroom. Anne thought the sound had come from near her mother. Could it have come *from* her mother? She was distracted for a moment by her husband's continued vomiting. A huge upwelling of blood and black miasma splattered across the bed and even onto her lap. She tightened her grip around her husband's hand and her rosary beads. When she looked up again, her mother was gone. As her husband was racked by anguished heaving, she barely noticed as the house continued to rumble beneath her, as some titanic struggle rolled its way up and down Pennsylvania Avenue and into the woods beyond.

Leaving the Tunnels

Isaiah Harris fished every time he got a chance. He was sitting along the edge of one of the borrow – called "barra" pits – located along the levees which formed the Morganza Spillway. There was nothing fancy to his rig: Isaiah sat on an overturned galvanized steel bucket holding a long red cane pole. There was a basket of crickets, too, humming and popping beside him.

Typically, Isaiah avoided this particular spot, because there was a slippery concrete shelf which disappeared into the water nearby. At least two children he knew of had died here. That Devereaux boy, for one. It was thought that the kids had been playing along the concrete and had somehow slipped into the water. Either they had hit their heads on the concrete, or they'd just slipped in and had been able to climb back out on the slime-covered concrete, and had died of exhaustion. Some of Isaiah's boys had stopped fishing this spot afterwards. Isaiah knew those boys of his wouldn't leave a good fishing hole, even if it meant sitting still in a pile of fire ants, so he, too, had avoided the spot. Until now. Recently, there hadn't been a fish to be found *anywhere*. Pretty much, Isaiah thought, nothing since he'd seen that damn ghost ship in False River.

In his desperation, he had climbed down the levee to fish along the upper edge of the concrete wall. Though he was teetering over the edge of the wall, he was staying as far as he could from the shore and the black water. Usually, lake and swamp water was brown and cloudy in these parts, like the Mississippi's own water. But this water, Isaiah observed, seemed darker still despite being completely unclouded. He wondered just how far the builders had dug to construct this wall and whether it had grown deeper still.

Isaiah's cane pole shook as he shivered violently. He had caught a reflection of his face in the water. He seemed to scowl back at himself, sneering. "Oh, Lord, why'd I think to come down here."

Before he could look back up the slope of the levee to measure his path out of here, Isaiah felt a strong tug on his line. Already, his cane pole was bending low. "That ain't no nibble!" Isaiah said aloud, despite himself. "One fish, and I don't care if he's a bass. I'm outta here."

Isaiah arched his back backward, pulling up on the pole and the twenty pound test line attached to it. There was no reel on a cane pole. The pole was used either to pop the fish out of the water or else drag them to the shore. There was no popping this fish out of the water. It was just too big. Isaiah scrambled to his feet and began dragging the cane pole and his catch into the shallows. He wasn't able to budge the fish very far. Standing, he turned back and watched as his line sliced up and down through the water. He had begun to wonder why the fish hadn't splashed him, cresting the surface of the water, when he first sensed the danger.

There was a flash of white in the depths of the black water. "Ain't no fish belly, there." He made to drop his cane pole and scramble back up the hill, but he realized he couldn't move. His booted feet had sunk deep into the turf beside the black water. It must have happened when he was pulling on that line. *But how could that be?* He asked himself. *The line would've just snapped clear off!*

And then he saw them. Hands. The hands of a child were pulling on his line, pulling it *down*. He had seen them peak out from the depths. He felt a momentary surge of Samaritan rise up in him to save the drowning child. Then, he realized with disgust the rotting stench that had also risen from the black water. And Isaiah saw the hands were slimy white, but he also knew, somehow, that they were the hands of a black child.

Isaiah felt his muscles pushing against his jaw to scream and realized, suddenly, that his whole body was frozen in place, not just his sunken feet. He desperately wanted to drop the pole and run, but instead he was holding the pole solidly in place. With jagged movements, the hands climbed higher on the fishing line. The line was sinking deep into the soft white flesh of the child's hands, as though into soggy dough, but the hands kept pulling up, up on the line.

Soon, the child's bloated white eyes bubbled out of the water. The eyes were like hard-boiled eggs, but shriveled like pruned fingers left in bathwater too long. Isaiah felt his stomach lurch inside his frozen body, and the vomit dripped and sputtered from his clenched, immobile jaws.

The child was now hanging on the fishing line swinging slightly from side to side, as though playing on a climbing rope. It stared at Isaiah with unseeing eyes, and began reaching for him. It reached suddenly for him with both arms outstretched, as if it were his own child reaching for daddy. It lost its balance and slipped from the fishing line, falling onto the water.

Isaiah breathed a quick sigh of relief when the thing fell, but the relief was soon stifled in his throat, as the child simply fell flat onto the water's surface without sinking. Having climbed out of the water, it could no longer sink into it. It began again groping towards Isaiah, scurrying with its jerky, dislocated movements.

Isaiah realized with ever-widening eyes that another pair of hands had begun climbing up the fishing line, even as the first pair of hands began tugging blindly at his boot. Soon, two of the soggy child creatures were pulling and tugging at his boots. The second wore the remnants of a red and blue striped shirt, but was otherwise naked like the first.

Isaiah watched, unable to move, as the small, bleached squishy hands ripped open his thick rubber boots like they were damp tissue paper. The first one began tugging at his second toe. Isaiah could feel the carpals and metacarpals attached to the toe twist within his foot as the cold white hands tugged. He had never stopped trying to scream.

Just as the second child was about to pluck off his kneecap, as if it were dried gum hanging on the underside of a school desk, the black water shook. Before Isaiah saw anything, he heard the awful gurgling roar. At the sound of it, the children with the dead eyes shimmied backward quickly and excitedly back into the water. They disappeared into the inky blackness, though their eyes seemed to remain for moment, staring up at Isaiah.

Even as the black water began to shudder, Isaiah could feel his muscles loosening. He was soon able to move again, and began tugging at his boots which had sunk even deeper into the mud. The bank on which he stood was a small peninsula of land which perched along the concrete wall. The ground, itself, seemed to be slipping into the black water, just as soggy babies had.

The roar came again. Isaiah looked back along the length of the black pool beneath the sloping concrete wall. The sound was deep and throaty, almost as if one massive slab of concrete was being dragged against another. There was a black shape moving at the far edge of the pool where it disappeared into a cypress and willow forest. Isaiah blinked and began tugging madly at his boots.

He had seen something more than the great black predator stalking towards him. He had seen that it was not black, not exactly. It had no color. The dim half-light did not even touch the form. It had the look of hole or even a tear in reality, itself. One glimpse had inspired madness. Isaiah gave up on his boots and let himself fall backward onto the levee's slope. As he fell, his feet popped free of the boots. His clean white socks looked almost comical as he scrambled away from the shore. He looked back and saw that the roaring beast, at first over a thousand yards away, had already covered half the distance. It was moving with impossible speed, but appeared to be only slowly stalking the poor, trapped man.

Finally, the man's throat and lungs allowed him to peel off his long-awaited scream. It was mostly just a garbled explosion of air from his chest, but the word "help" was also discernable.

The beast was almost upon him, stalking slowly but with impossible speed. Isaiah, resigned to his fate, just knew somehow that he would be swallowed whole by the shadowless form, that the darkness itself would tear him to shreds, not any fangs within the thing's mouth.

"What the hell?" A voice yelled from behind Isaiah, somewhere up the levee. "That sounded like Isaiah."

But Isaiah didn't have time to hear or recognize the voice. The creature was upon him. He watched as the black formlessness swept over him, leaping.

He felt his own existence shudder, as though torn by a mouth full of icy teeth. But then it was gone. It had never been him. He had not been the prey. It was past him, prowling up the levee.

"Good Lord!" Another voice hollered. "Drip, *no*. Watch it!"

"Ephpheta!" A small voice bellowed.

The creature leapt away, roaring as though it had been slapped. Its outline rose up slowly and menacingly on its haunches.

"Mr. Charlie? That you?" Isaiah leapt up and ran to the tunnel entrance, sliding and slipping in his white socks. He ran to where Charlie was and squeezed in the tunnel behind him. "When the hell this here tunnel get here?"

"Just now, I think," Brian observed.

"We just can't catch a breath-ah!" Smitty said, huffing and puffing as he leaned against the curved entrance, or rather exit, of the tunnel.

Drip was standing on a log now just beyond the tunnel. Her hands were raised to her hips. The thing was prowling back and forth. Without taking her eyes off of it, she yelled back at the others, "I think you boys better get going."

"What? And leave you with that thing?" Thomas asked in indignation. "I think *not*."

"Put that down, Thomas." Behind her back, Thomas had picked up whatever weapon was nearest him. "Even if you could get at your entire arsenal, you couldn't do anything to this thing. Remember hearing about that boy at the Ennis Clinic? I was the one who first found him after the attack. *That* is what attacked him. This thing is beyond any of you, you understand? It looks black, right? Like a jaguar, but that's just the blackness, the emptiness. I can stall it, which is more than I can say for any of you. It's all we got."

Smitty, no longer out of breath, sidled up behind her. "We haven't come this far, little lady, still thinking we're getting out of this with our lives. We're not leaving you, not no-how."

"Actually," Brian said. "One of us *has* to get out of here, if at least to tell Monsignor what we've found and done. I'll volunteer for that."

"How gracious of you," Charlie growled from behind clenched teeth. But there was no more to be said, the creature had stopped stalking back and forth when all the men had finished lining up behind Drip, even Isaiah and Brian.

The creature bounded towards them, then suddenly slowed again, as if marking the inevitability of the outcome. It seemed to mess with their eyes as it approached. As it got closer, it didn't increase in size naturally or even steadily. They found their eyes had trouble focusing on it, and could see it clearly only in their peripheral vision.

"In odorem suavitatis," Drip continued. "Tu autem effugare, diabole; For the judgment of God is at hand."

The creature's head was knocked to the side as by an unseen force, but it continued forward unfazed. It growled as it had before, the sound of concrete slabs grinding together.

"I wish Monsignor was here now. He would be far stronger than me against this sort of thing."

Though it was still thirty yards away or more, the thing leapt suddenly into the air and was upon Drip in a flash. There was no slowing of time as it arched through the air, and their brains dumped adrenaline into their blood. It was just there, as if it had been toying with them all along, like cat and mice.

The men watched as the thing pounced on Drip, smothering her beneath its belly or devouring her in a single bite – they could not see. Smitty, in a fit of rage or tremendous courage, launched himself against the beast, hollering at it and leveling one thick upper cut into the side of the thing's head. Smitty's blow may have even blinded the creature, had it been corporeal. But Smitty watched in horror as his first dissolved before him. The man's hand had slipped into the shape's black nothingness. An icy chill racked the man's body and he lost consciousness falling face first into the creature's horrible skin.

Or, he would have, had Drip not escaped the initial onslaught – to the surprise and astonishment of all the men – and been there to knock his falling, limp body in the opposite direction. She had moved fast to escape, as fast as the creature – at the speed of thought – but it had been too fast for the men to see. Too fast for Smitty's hand.

But all that was inconsequential now, for Smitty was rolling unconscious down the levee, while the creature turned to face the men and Drip. With one sweep of its tail, a single two-inch cross section of flesh could be removed from the men's bodies, halving them. The creature had other plans for the men, apparently, because it began lowering its jaw inch by inch until the jaw's touch scorched and erased a bit of turf. Then, slowly, it did bring its tail to bear, encircling the men and cutting off their escape back down the tunnel.

Drip planted herself between the men and the creature's mouth, standing tall just above their knee caps. As the men nudged forward away from touch of the creature's tail they inadvertently edged their small protector closer to the creature's waiting maw. The creature's mouth stretched nearly ten feet from snout to jaw, seemingly unhinged like that of a colossal snake. It seemed to have prepared some deeper darkness for the small company.

Eyes like stars twinkled at them from within the creature. It was like looking into the end of the universe, that thing that would at last consume the last black hole. The creature did not breathe, but there was a strong wind gathering all about them, as the creature passively devoured the atmosphere.

Right when Charlie had begun shifting forward, ready to volunteer to take the first step into nothingness, if it could save his friends for only a moment, the creature was rocked. It shook like it had shaken before, at Drip's words, but more somehow – as though it had been physically attacked by another predator.

The men all bent low as the tail came slicing over them. Thomas lost some of his shirt and a slice of his shoulder blade, and Brian would always, from that day onward, bear a Friar Tuck balding pattern, but they were not seriously harmed. The jaguar tumbled jaw over tail and nearly consumed itself. It raced haphazardly across the island pockets of the spillway, often leaving only an in rush of water in its tracks. Whole trees collapsed into its outline, as it tumbled around furiously, growling thunder as if it was being attacked.

"Good *night* – what's happening to it, Drip?" Charlie asked.

"I think," she stammered, and then laughed. "I really think it's been attacked!"

"By what?" Thomas asked. "There's nothing out there that I can see. Fleas?"

"Not *what*, but *where* you should be asking. I think this thing was appearing here and somewhere else at the same time, and it's being pummeled some-*where* else."

"But how? What could possibly be fighting that thing?" Brian asked bewildered. "It's emptiness with form."

"Well," Drip smiled. "Maybe, something's somethingness is more than its nothingness. I, for one, would like to think it's fighting a great bear."

Thomas turned to look down at the lady, who was winking up at him. He smiled back, "Would that be a great *mamma* bear?"

Regroup

They had all piled into Isaiah's little white truck, leaving behind a load of janitorial equipment to do so, including a floor buffing machine and some heavyweight vacuums. They all sat for a second catching their breaths. Thomas was the first to regain his bearings. He looked around the cab of the truck. Then, a little more frantically, he turned to look into the bed of the truck.

"Wha – where is she?" He frowned.

"Where's who?" Isaiah asked, distractedly. He was busy shifting the truck back and forth between drive and reverse, trying to rock his small truck out of the mud.

"Drip – she's gone!"

"Gone?" Smitty said. His voice was muffled until he slid open the small back window of the truck's cab. "Nah, she was just right here." Smitty turned to point to the back of the truck and stopped.

As they bickered among themselves, Thomas turned to look out the passenger side window of the truck. He caught sight of something out of the corner of his eye. He jerked his head in surprise, though no one noticed – not even Brian who was squeezed in beside him.

In the shadow of the trees where they leaned over the still waters of the borrow pits, there was the outline of a small figure. Drip was waving to him. She had put a finger over her lips. In another instant, she was gone. Her smile seemed to linger after her. Her part in this tale was now over.

****

A short while later, Isaiah had managed to liberate his truck from the mud. Thomas had similarly managed to unburden the other men of their worry over Drip. They drove down off the levees and were passing through the small town of Morganza, which straddled the railroad tracks for half a mile or so.

"Isaiah!" Smitty banged on the cab's back windshield. "Mister Isaiah!" Smitty continued motioning that he pull the truck over at either the gas station or the diner.

"Hey, what's the big idea?" Brian complained, as he sat crammed into the front seat. "We're not nearly far enough from that animal-thing for my liking. No one's stopping this truck until we're back in St. Maryville!"

"To hell with that, I need a beer. And maybe some of that cherry pie they sell over at the diner."

"If this truck stops, I'm taking your other hand myself!" Brian continued.

"Sit still, Brian," Thomas said, who was sitting opposite Smitty near the cab. "Some supplies wouldn't be a bad idea at all. I know Isaiah, at least, could use some more boots."

Brian didn't move from his spot when Isaiah slowed in front of the diner to let Smitty out. Thomas got out with him, helping the injured man over the side of the truck. Thomas leaned into the cab of the truck after Isaiah finished rolling down the window. Isaiah sat at the wheel, driving with bare feet. He had taken off his soggy white socks, and tossed them somewhere in the bed. "I was thinking I'd help Smitty get cleaned off, and I don't want to stand between him and a beer and pie." Thomas said leaning in the window. "Why don't y'all stop by the sundries store and pick up some boots and socks for Isaiah, and maybe fill up?"

Charlie nodded, "That's fine, but I say we had back to the Rectory, ASAP. I'm anxious to check in with the others, and I want to get back to holy ground."

"What he said!" Brian bellowed morosely from the middle of the cab. "Pie? Are you kidding me?"

"We should move quickly," Charlie agreed. "Our list of enemies seems to be growing."

"Well," Isaiah said. "You've got friends, too, Mr. Charlie. I can be plenty useful once I gets some boots on these feet."

Thomas nodded, tapping the windowsill, and turning to follow Smitty into the diner. The diner was a one-story brick building with a green and white striped awning flanked by bright red Coca-Cola medallions. A long white sign above the awning read, "Home Made Pies, Lunches, *Short* Orders." The truck tires crunched against gravel and oyster shells, as Thomas swung open one of the green double screen doors to Melancon's Café and disturbed the bells hanging there. As his eyes adjusted to the somewhat dimmer light, he prepared himself for the scene created at the sight of Smitty's injury and appearance.

What he found was more surprising still. The café *was* full. Stone-faced and pale Morganzans filled the tables and high-backed booths. The café was usually a raucous place, since everybody knew or was related to everybody else in Morganza. Friendly jabs and how-do-you-do's were usually flying from one side of the café to the other, like so many flies chased by shoo-flies. But the quiet of the tomb reigned this morning.

Smitty was already sitting at the linoleum coated, soda fountain counter. Though beer was usually not served until sundown, Smitty was already enjoying a slice of cherry pie and a glass of beer, one hand at a time. The old Boston man smiled at Thomas as he entered and sighed, "A few bites was all I needed. Think I can already feel that hand regrowing!"

Thomas sat down at the green vinyl cushioned swivel stool beside Smitty, slowly, and without answering. "You don't think there's something suspicious about this place?" Thomas leaned over and whispered.

Smitty stopped chewing and slowly poked an eye across the café and back to his waitress. She was just standing there staring at Thomas slack-jawed, awaiting his order. Everyone else in the diner was staring forward, mindlessly. Smitty turned back to his pie slowly and kept eating so as not to attract attention. "What do we do?" He asked Thomas, as he tried to stare forward blankly.

"I think we eat some pie," Thomas answered.

****

223

"How the hell did this happen?" Smitty asked, banging his stub against the rectory's long oak table. The vibrations rattled the pie tin which lay in front of him. The flesh had sealed up almost immediately after his hand had dissolved into the jaguar-shaped creature. There had been little to no blood loss. "You're telling me this stuff has spread across the whole parish?"

"Would've thought ain't no way, but after seeing that whole diner in *Morganza* …," Thomas said, rubbing his forehead in frustration. "Can only imagine what's going on in St. Maryville."

"I knew Miss Dot wasn't the only one," Anne added. She was leaning heavily against the table and rubbing her swollen belly. She was also holding a cold compress to her forehead. She had called Monsignor to her and Jim's house, not long after Mamou had disappeared and the animals had rolled through the neighborhood like twin tornadoes. He had evacuated them both to the rectory, which was quickly becoming the town's last sanctuary. Jim lay convalescing in the same guest bedroom that Nurse Jana had recently occupied.

"If we kill LaColt, or LaColt *and* Teach, do we get the people back?" Charlie asked Monsignor, who was again sitting at the head of the table as he had the night before.

"Look, it's easy. We just pack up, get out of Dodge real quiet like, and let the fire burn itself out," Brian said.

"I will not force you to stay here, Brian, but I can almost guarantee that you would not be allowed to leave the parish alive," Monsignor answered. Brian's face paled, and he sat back, sullen and mollified for the moment. "And maybe, Charlie. I think we have at least an even chance of freeing the people."

"Okay, so what *do* we know?" Charlie said, looking up from his arms crossed in front of him. Isaiah had been happy to join the rest of the group at the rectory. He had even dropped by Charlie's house on the way to the rectory – to Brian's constant jawing – to pick up Frances, his wife, who was currently splitting her time between tending to Anne and to her grandson, upstairs.

"We know the jaguar is injured," Thomas said raising a finger. "Or possibly, *both*. Whatever Drip meant by that. I wish we still had her with us."

"Right, so do I," Charlie agreed. "We also know the soil is no good to LaColt anymore."

"So we got them massholes cornered. Right?" The confidence in Smitty's voice rapidly dissipated, as he heard the words spoken aloud.

"Feels like we're the ones cornered, don't it to you, Monsignor?" Thomas asked.

"Perhaps we're at our most dangerous, then, as well," Monsignor said, crooking his half-smile.

Each of the stout hearts gathered around the table quickened a bit at Monsignor's words. Anne straightened up and the burden of her belly seemed to ease. Even Brian seemed to find his courage as he squared up his shoulders and leaned in.

"I think I know what we have to do." There was a new voice at the table, and everybody turned to look at her, as though surprised to find her sitting there. It was Nurse Jana.

He Will Give the Devil His Due

The yellow Jaguar slammed against the curb and jumped over it onto the sidewalk. There was a popping, splintering sound as the car's front end plowed into the white picket fence of the Bellefontaine home.

"Sorry about that," Sam whispered, as he crawled out of the passenger side of the car. His driving experience was pretty limited up until now. He really wasn't sure how he had managed to drive the stolen car all the way from Parlange plantation, much less how we had been able to remain conscious despite the blinding pockets of pain erupting here and there across his body. As for what he had seen at the plantation, he was trying his best to push those images out of his mind. The pain was very useful as a distraction.

He pushed the door of the sports car open with his good arm and spilled out of the car onto the pavement. He meant it to be sort of a controlled fall, but his right arm collapsed on him. The sudden movement banged his brain around in his concussed head. A jolt of nausea welled up inside him and he vomited. Blood and bile sprayed across the pavement.

He eventually dragged himself upward along the side of the car. He was able to stumble over to what remained of the fence and use that as a crutch. He was dragging his right leg limply behind him, and his right arm, too, seemed to be hanging at a funny angle. He was still wearing his backpack.

"Sam?" A voice asked in hushed tones.

Sam whirled around, looking for the source of the voice. He couldn't hear too well because of the thudding in his head. The voice could've come from anywhere – maybe even from *Erin*.

"Sam, it's me. You look terrible." It was Elton, not Erin, Sam finally saw with a thud of disappointment. The smaller boy had emerged from the far side of a live oak tree on the other side of the street.

"Elton?" Sam looked at the boy suspiciously.

"Yeah, it's me. What's going on? The whole town is –"

"Zombified?" Sam asked.

"Yeah, I guess that's it. My mom – I don't think she recognized me. Sammy, what's going on?"

"Your mom?" Sam asked.

"Yeah, she totally kirked out on me – like I was a burglar or something."

Sam had dragged himself all the way to the bench on the Bellfontaine's front porch. He sat down with a sigh of pain. "How'd you find your way here?" Sam asked Elton, who had been following him step for step.

Elton got a faraway look in his eyes for a moment and then answered. "I saw you. A couple blocks back at my house." He turned pointing in a direction generally behind him. "I ran the whole way to catch up with you."

"You ran, huh?" Sam asked, growing distracted. He was trying to listen for noises inside Erin's house.

"Yeah, probably three or four blocks I followed that weird car of yours."

"Wow," Sam nodded in mock surprise. "All that despite your asthma and you weren't even breathing hard."

Elton didn't respond. The faraway look had returned to his eyes.

"Listen, buddy. Can I lean on you a bit to get in the house?" Sam raised his arm to indicate what he meant. Elton nodded agreeably.

"Yeah, yeah. Sure, friend," Elton said returning to himself.

Sam sort of hopped along beside Elton, letting his limp right leg drag between them. They found the front door to Erin's house was open. "Well, that's probably not good," Sam said with mock humor.

Sam decided not to announce his arrival to the house at large. He limped into the living room beside Elton. It was dark. The blinds were not open and the lights were off. Sam scanned the living room, allowing his eyes time to adjust to the dimness.

Elton turned in surprise, as Sam suddenly gasped. "Jeeez-*zus*," Sam said through clenched teeth.

It was Erin's dad. Mr. Bellefontaine was just standing against the wall. His back was to them. Sam thought the man's nose might actually me touching the wall, as if sent there by an elementary school teacher. "I thought I was done being scared," Sam whispered.

"How about we just let that man be?" Elton whispered back.

"No, help me sit him down in that armchair over there. I've got some rope in my backpack."

Elton helped Sam turn the middle-aged man away from the wall. Sam gasped again when he saw the condition of his face. He thought at first that the man had been crying and that mascara had run down his face, but mascara didn't make any sense for a man. His eyes were closed, but his cheeks were stained and burned with some black substance. He wasn't breathing, but he walked easily enough. The boys were able to lead him over to the armchair and sit him down without any resistance.

Sam tied him up the man's hands and feet and then tied him to the chair. He used one long length of rope for all of it. He didn't want to cut up his rope any more than he had to. His experience tying people up was pretty limited, but his instincts were good. When he was finished with Mr. Bellefontaine, he cut off the remaining length of rope.

"Elton, how about you take a seat, too?" The other boy had just been standing by the chair while Sam tied up his girlfriend's father. He had that faraway look again. "There. Right there is good." Sam instructed as he staggered behind Elton, guiding him to the other armchair.

"So what's next, friend?" Elton asked as Sam plopped him down onto an orange and brown plaid cushion.

"We just hang tight for a bit." Sam answered as he began tying Elton's wrists and ankles together. All while he worked, Elton never questioned what Sam was doing.

"There," Sam said, breathing hard to catch his breath. He allowed himself to collapse backwards onto the Bellefontaine's brown couch. "So Elton, how exactly did you run into your mom? She's been dead since you were a kid.

228

She and your dad. You live with your grandma. And 'kirked out'? I don't think so."

Elton turned to Sam and stared at him with that same faraway look in his eyes. Sam shivered. It was like looking at a puppet made from Elton's skin.

After a moment of silence, Sam began struggling to shift his backpack onto his lap. He winced as he was forced to turn his right arm and shoulder. He looked inside the pack and rummaged among his remaining supplies. He stopped. He still needed to check on Erin upstairs. *The stairs.* He thought, groaning in anticipation of the pain. He turned his neck to take a look behind the couch to where the stairs led up to the darkness of the second floor. "This day just keeps getting better," he complained aloud.

Just as he was about to turn back around, he caught a glimpse of movement at the top of the stairs. There was a flash of white. Sam was suddenly rooted to the couch, unable to move. *It's her. She's back.* He thought to himself as his heart started pounding in his aching head.

It was the Lady in White, the lady who haunted the alley of oak trees at the plantation. She was slowly gliding down the stairs. She was reaching for him. *She's following me. No. I never left.* His vision shuttered between the stairway at the Bellefontaine house and the front stairs at Parlange.

His body began to rock with sobs. It was despair. He had shut it away in the attic of his mind. He thought he had locked it up there for good when he had escaped the plantation with his life. But now. It was all just a mirage. Maybe he was being punished for leaving the dead cop behind. The words 'He will give the devil his due' echoed through his head.

As he watched, the Lady in White descended the stairs. She was gliding towards him. He was locked in her gaze and he couldn't run, couldn't even move. His eyes locked on hers. As he watched in horror, the woman's beauty kept fading and returning. The ghost's face emaciated over and over again, but always at the end the tree struck. Her face was lost in a terrible time loop, at the end of which her softened skull kept bursting inward. The mix of enchanting beauty and then ruin and then gore – it was all too much. His heart was beginning to beat too quickly. There was a heaviness on his chest and now he couldn't breathe fast enough. His heart was going to explode.

And then it was her face, too. The girl's. *His* girl's. It was Erin's face. She was added to the ghost's endless loop of faces. This is how he would be punished. He finally understood. This is how he would be punished for getting back too late, for failing to save her. The devil would get his due.

But then, the other one's face began to skip out of the loop. The ghost's face was leaving and, along with it, her broken face. In another minute, even the flowing, mouldering white of the ghost's bridal gown was gone. The gown had been replaced by the floral print of a matching set of Laura Ashley pajamas. It was Erin. Not just a spectre of a dead girl, but her, really her.

Sam felt like the fingers of a giant fist were slowly uncoiling from around his rib cage – or rather, the looping coils of a serpent. He could breathe again. Then, he could move again. The devil, that old son of a bitch, Sam snarled, would have to wait.

Just as Sam was able to raise himself up from and around the couch, the ghost lady's transformation was complete. Erin hung suspended for a moment at the foot of the stairs. One hand lay lightly on the first bannister, balancing her and keeping her upright. And then she, too, was released. She collapsed on the floor.

****

Sam had tried calling the rectory to ask Monsignor's advice before he began, but there was no dial tone. The line was dead.

He had run out of rope, so he wasn't able to tie up Erin. He didn't really want to tie her up, anyway. Instead, he somehow managed to lift her limp body and place her on the couch. He had wrapped her body tightly in a bedsheet and tied the opposite corners together to form an 'x' of knots. It would at least restrain her if someone or something else took control of her body.

"Sorry, Mr. Bellefontaine," Sam said, as he popped open the small golden box he had carried in his backpack. They were all three of them – Erin, Elton, and Erin's dad – possessed to varying degrees. He was sure of that. Sam had decided that he would try to purge their bodies of whatever it was that had taken control of them. He liked Mr. Bellefontaine the least, but, Sam thought, he also looked to be the furthest along. There may even be just a shell of him left, and Sam was worried this was about to get really gross. Either way, Mr. Bellefontaine would be the guinea pig.

"Sir, if this ends up being your last moment on earth, and if we – your daughter and me, I mean, sir – somehow survive, I'd like to ask for her hand in marriage. Okay?"

Sam then looked around sheepishly to see if anyone was watching him. Erin and Elton both seemed to be sleeping. "I can't believe I'm doing this." And then he gently placed his hands at the sides of Mr. Bellefontaine's head and rocked the man's head back and forth to signify his consent.

Sam picked the golden box back up and cracked one of the thin wafers inside it in half and then in quarters. The boy held up the wafer before the man's face and said, "Behold, the lamb of God, who takes away the sins of the world." And then he pressed down on Mr. Bellefontaine's chin and placed the wafer inside his mouth and on his tongue.

He prayed that it would work. He was desperate to save any of them, but especially *her*. Sam had recited about a quarter of the "Our Father" aloud, when he first noticed the acrid scent in the air. At "give us this day our super-substantial bread," he saw the slim line of smoke trailing from between Mr. Bellefontaine's lips. The man's eyelids fluttered open. Up to this point, he had kept them tightly shut except for the trails of black leaking down his cheeks.

The eyes flashed open and Sam staggered backwards, tumbling over and across the coffee table. His right leg collapsed beneath him and he fell hard against the side of his ankle. He felt a sharp pop as he fell. Despite the searing pain, he was still able to lurch forwards to catch what came.

Even as he was falling, he realized what was happening. The pop in his ankle wasn't nearly as bad as the sickening feeling in his stomach. Smoke was spilling out of the man's mouth, as if a chimney had been thrust up into his esophagus. But it was coming from somewhere else, too. It was also coming from underneath Mr. Bellefontaine's jaw and chin. From his vantage point sprawled across the floor, Sam could see a black pie shape forming above the man's Adam's apple. A tongue of flame licked out from the hole burning through the base of the man's head.

The smell of the man's burning flesh filled the room. It smelled like roasting meat, and Sam noticed shamefully that his stomach ached at the smell. As the hole grew wider, Sam was astonished to see a flash of whiteness falling through the opening. Whatever it was, it was about to fall onto Mr. Bellefontaine's lap and renew its burning descent. Sam lunged forward to catch the host before it could further destroy the man's corrupted body. He felt bits of tissue grinding inside his ankle joint as he dove forward.

For the next several minutes, he just lay across the Bellefontaine's mustard-colored shag rug. He teetered there at the edge of consciousness as waves of pain crashed against his broken body.

This single test had been enough. Plenty enough. Sam understood now that he was powerless to free his friends' trapped souls. Their bodies were nothing more than pillars of ashes awaiting their last breeze.

He could, however, keep them from getting into more mischief. They would stay tied up for now, and if he could manage it, he would also try barricading the doors. He just hoped Monsignor and the others were getting close.

He was stuck here for now, but he knew he wasn't helpless. There was something more he could do, besides just keeping his friends bound. His pain was beyond excruciating. It was beyond unbearable. Snatching a glimpse down at his ankle, he saw that the bone had begun to protrude from his skin. He needed to stay conscious and awake, somehow or another. If he could do this, he could offer himself up as sacrifice for the success of Monsignor's small band. He could give them strength in his weakness.

The Bellefontaine house gasped suddenly with the force of a cold wind. He turned to Erin, almost reflexively. She was staring at him. Her mouth was moving, though Sam wasn't sure the sound was actually issuing from it. He could hear her voice, though. He could hear it clearly. She kept repeating the same words over and over again. Without knowing why he was doing it, he started counting the pattern. There were six of them, six words.

At the Gates

After finalizing their plans, they had gathered together every last scrap of salt in the rectory and the church, and Monsignor had said Mass. Then, he had asked that they wait while he headed upstairs and tended to Jim, asking only that the nurse and Thomas follow him upstairs. He asked that the two others wait on the landing. The old priest sprayed holy water on the young man in two straight lines forming the shape of a cross. The younger man's eyes had flicked open at this. Monsignor sat down heavily in the chair at the side of Jim's bed. He began twisting the chain of his crucifix back and forth, as he had before. The room filled with swirling points of light.

Jim stared fixedly at Monsignor for a few minutes. He did this without breathing, or so it seemed. During all this, Monsignor's heart beat like a trip hammer. The priest was feeling the onrush of events, as though stones were being laid one by one atop his chest, being pressed to death. A crisis was waiting at his doorstep and the seconds, when each one counted dearly, were draining away.

Gradually, Jim's eyes closed. His breathing slowly returned, visible as a gentle heaving of his chest. Monsignor wiped great beads of perspiration from his forehead with a handkerchief and lowered his crucifix. When Jim re-opened his eyes, he did not seem like the same man. His pupils were fully dilated, like two pools of viscous tar.

Monsignor motioned to the others to join him at the bedside. He then raised his hand, motioning for silence. "Where are you?" He asked Jim.

The answer came in an odd neutral way that contrasted sharply with the man's evil appearance. "I don't know this sleep. It has no place it can call its own."

"Focus," Monsignor continued, careful to keep his voice at an even, almost monotonous pitch. "Describe your surroundings."

"It is black as pitch. The great coil surrounds us. The river, below the river. The bodies sink into the mud, endless mud, below the river. But there is earth. I can feel it at my mouth."

"What do you hear?" Monsignor asked, and the others could feel the strain in his voice.

"The sound of the men stamping overhead. The innocents are carried below. There is water, too, far and through the earth. Water lapping against the posts."

"What do you feel?" Monsignor asked, speaking the words slowly, as though in agony. Thomas came behind the old priest, as though to steady him.

"I am still, so very still. It is like death."

"More." Monsignor commanded, gasping. "Tell me more."

"My hide was torn. Rent by the bear. Why here? What else lives beside the river?" The voice faded away into a deep breath as of one sleeping. The eyes flickered, and then were closed once again.

Monsignor fell back in his chair, as though he was able to finally release a great weight. He sat with his head lolling backward for several minutes until his breathing again became even. He turned to the nurse and Thomas, and again wiped the great beads of perspiration from his forehead. A large puddle of sweat had formed in the deep cleft of his forehead, and he caught it before it could fall across his face. He smiled at them in exhaustion, "The sly old fox. Can we be sly, too? Maybe, but maybe that's not the way. Nevermind, anyway. Tell me, Nurse Jana. Where was he? Do you know the place?"

The nurse turned away to Jim, who now appeared to be sleeping peacefully, perhaps exhausting for the moment his connection to the other one. The nurse looked back to Monsignor, and nodded. "If I didn't know better, I'd think he was describing the room I found under the clinic. The one with the hole."

"Do you, Jana? Do you know better?" Monsignor asked.

She looked down, almost ashamed. "No, I don't, Father. That's the place. I feel sure of it, somehow."

"So be it. Thomas, you will lead what is left of our little fellowship to the clinic."

"I will go, too," The nurse said, adamantly. "I have unfinished business there."

Monsignor looked at the young woman for a long moment. "I think it would be better, Jana, if you stayed here." Then, raising his arm with effort, "Joachim, here, needs tending to."

"I'm sorry, Father. I must go."

The old priest nodded sadly. "Thomas, you and the others must leave immediately. We cannot wait until morning. Another night, and I think all our advantage will be lost."

When Thomas came back down the stairs with Jana and Monsignor following, there were still a couple hours of daylight left. "It'll have to be enough," Monsignor had said, and gave all present a final blessing.

****

A piece of metal glinted in the reds of the late afternoon sunlight. It was the brass poker from Monsignor's fireplace. Sensing what was coming, Smitty had asked Frances to tie it to his forearm and what was left of his hand. Charlie's wife had done her job thoroughly, as she always did, tying the implement against Smitty's forearm in three separate places and then wrapping the whole forearm in duct tape. Smitty had slapped it when it was finished. "It's harder than a cast, Frannie! Fine job."

It was only a short walk between the rectory and the LaCour Building, just a straight stretch of sidewalk. There were no O.K. Corral dramatics, as they came down the street. Instead, they walked nearly one-by-one down the sidewalk, trying to attract as little notice as possible, except for Smitty's increasingly odd appearance. Thomas was wearing a blue canvas backpack with Garfield the Cat emblazoned across the front of it, which had been found in the church's lost and found. The bag was filled with paper bags of blessed salt, as much as could be scavenged from the rectory, as well as containers of holy water. Between them, they were each also carrying an odd assortment of water bottles, including a military-issue canteen and a rubber hot water bottle. These were all filled with holy water. They would have used water balloons if they had had any.

They were seven in number, Thomas, Charlie, Smitty, Brian, Jana, Isaiah, as well as the full-bellied Anne. She could not be restrained from going when she learned, or rather *inferred*, that there may still be a way to save Jim. Charlie and Isaiah walked on either side of Anne. Thomas, her brother, walked in front of her. Frances left Jim's side to pray in the adoration chapel on the first floor of the rectory. It was just as her aunt had done decades earlier, the night of her death, at the approach of an oncoming storm.

Minutes later, their procession was standing before the LaCour building. They had tried not to look into the restaurants and shops as they passed, but they couldn't resist a careful peak. In each, the people sat black-eyed and staring. As they looked up and down Main Street, they were amazed at the feeling of emptiness. Though there were people, there were no cars. The street was completely empty. Tumbleweeds could have rolled on by, and it would have seemed perfectly fitting. It seemed like a model town built to test the destructiveness of an atom bomb. The people seemed like no more than mannequins. The air, though, was tinged with a sickly green, and it was elsewhere clear that nothing was right about any of it. There were sounds, barely audible, echoing across the empty street. It could have been the cracking roars of the jaguar or the babble of babies or unbounded, uncontrolled laughter. It could have been in the streets or in their minds.

Slowly, they gathered their wits together, and looked in anticipation to the nurse. She was to show them to the back entrance. They were prepared to either pick or ram their way in, whatever it took.

They stood at the gap between two buildings, a restaurant and the abortion clinic. The windows of the restaurant looked as they would on a typical Friday evening. People were seated at the tables.

"Gah, the place is packed," Smitty said. He was just brazen enough to stand at the big picture window, as all the eyes slowly latched onto him.

"Chère Mamma's hasn't been full like that for a while."

"Notice anything funny about it?" Charlie asked. He was looking at their reflection across the picture window. It was distorted.

Smitty looked deep into the restaurant. He stepped back and looked across the front of the building. The old man bunched up his bottom lip and shook his head. "Nah, same old, same old, except for those jerks staring at us. It's just Chère Mamma's."

"Only it isn't. Not anymore," Charlie said looking away.

"Whatcha talking 'bout? Says right there, bold as brass." He had raised his arm to point at the name of the restaurant, which was typically emblazoned in gold paint on a stretch of reclaimed cypress wood. Only now it wasn't. "But how can that be? Wasn't never … Melancon's?"

But it was. The name of the restaurant had changed, but that wasn't all. As Smitty looked now again into the depths beyond the window, it *was* a different restaurant. It was now a restaurant from another town. Smitty looked away in disgust at the impertinence of the thing. As he did, his eyes alighted on their reflections in the wide window, the ones that Charlie had noticed almost immediately.

"What'n the hell?" Smitty yelled too loudly, so that it seemed to echo amidst the roar of the other sounds.

"Just don't look at them," Charlie said, beginning to pull on his old friend, on his good arm. "It's just a trick and no good can come from lingering."

"But it's us, Charlie, you and me. Only we're young again, if you can believe it."

"Young and hideous," Charlie said, beginning to pull on the much heavier man with violence. He soon found that Smitty had become immovable. "Thomas," he called. "Isaiah. Quick."

Smitty was quickly losing awareness of the men and voices beside him. He was transfixed to the images of youth staring back at him. But they weren't staring back, not exactly. It was their same faces, at least as they had been once, but it was the tar eyes staring back and the thin, mask-like flesh.

"Come on, buddy. Nothing to see here," Thomas said as he picked out a consecrated host from inside the Garfield pack. He let it rest in his palm and shine in one of the few patches of sunlight still poking through the clouds. It, too, reflected in the window, and the phantom reflections seemed suddenly dark and more grotesque. They faded away in muffled protest and were gone. The window now stood without any reflections in it whatsoever. It was just flat and empty, like the faces beyond it.

Smitty shivered as though he had just forgotten something important, and started walking again. The other men let him go, and they were all standing at the entrance to the alleyway between the restaurant and the clinic. There were no scattered pools of sunlight in the alley, as there had been in the street.

It was dark and the sidewalk quickly terminated into an earthen path.

Jana led them down the alleyway to the entrance, which she had last approached from the opposite direction, from the employee parking lot. The ground was formed of packed trash. Many years of trash lay compacted under their feet. Old bottle caps winked at them from beneath mouldering food scraps and choked weeds. The door was not far down, but their passage through the alley seemed interminable. They knew it was a bad sign, the last in a long, seemingly-endless parade of bad signs, when the door swung open at the nurse's barest touch.

"Feels like the traveling carnival fun house," Smitty remarked in a rare whisper.

"Something wicked this way comes," Anne agreed, nodding.

"Of course," Nurse Jana said, smiling grimly. "The lights would be out." She toggled the light switch back and forth a few more times.

"Flashlights out," Thomas directed. When they were all through, Thomas asked the last man, Brian, to see if he could secure the door. "Lock it, barricade it, whatever you can do."

The lights were not completely out. There were lights marking the doorways that kept flashing, each at varying frequencies. Nurse Jana carried a flashlight, too, and led them past several of the first doorways, down a couple twists and turns of the hallways. "This is where I begin guessing. This place is a maze, and – call me crazy – I'm pretty sure the hallways shift from here on in."

"Ain't no way all these doors'n corridors fit in the building I was just looking at," Thomas observed.

"Remember what Drip said about the tunnels and that river," Charlie said from Anne's side. "That they were sort of here and not here, real and not real."

"I don't doubt it," Jana agreed. "I'm taking you to a basement that I swear was on the first floor. No stairs, nothing. You may even find a door to the tenth floor on this floor."

"Or the 666th floor," Smitty snorted. "Brian, you still back there?" He called backward, looking into the face of a flashlight that he hoped was still being carried by one of their own.

"Still me, but I'm pretty sure I won't last much longer. Last guy never does."

"Something's not right," Isaiah said.

"Sor-*ry*, chalk it up to my dark sense of humor, I guess."

"No, not you, Mr. Brian. My money's on you, too," Isaiah chuckled. "The floor's not right. Y'all feel that?"

"Feel what?" Smitty asked. "The carpet?"

"No," Charlie said. "Listen to him. He's on to something."

"I cleaned a lot of floors for you, ain't I, Mr. Charlie?"

"No doubt, Isaiah. Ain't no one better than you. Tell us what you're thinking."

"You say there's a basement underneat' this floor, right?" Isaiah asked.

"Yeah, hey," Thomas said. "That's right. Jim was talking about people 'stamping overhead' when we were upstairs."

"So what?" Smitty burst out.

"No basement under this floor," Isaiah answered.

"Huh?"

"Just listen, Smitty. It sounds like a slab foundation under us, no basement."

"So, what?" Smitty snarled. "There could be a reinforced concrete slab roof down cella."

"Yeah, but what's he mean about 'stamping overhead'?" Thomas asked.

"Who cares? Now, listen to me," Smitty insisted. "Everything in here is designed to mess with your senses, your mind, your everything. Stick to the job. Get in, get out, just like in the war."

"Maybe you're right, Smitty," Thomas answered.

"Of course, he is," Brian barked. "Ours not to reason why; ours not to make reply."

"Into the valley of death rode the *Seven Against Thebes*?" Thomas asked.

"Ayuh, always knew you weren't no bumpkin," Smitty smiled.

"I'd rather 'The Cremation of Sam McGee,' myself," Thomas said opening a doorway and shining his light into it. "The Artic trails have their secret tales." As he said it, he looked away from the dark room and closed the door behind him. If he looked back into the room, he would have seen a pair of eyes glowing purple in the darkness.

"Johnny Cash's version?" Charlie asked.

"One of these days, we'll find the end of all these tunnels," Brian said, spinning his flashlight's beam around on the floor in front of him. The others let that be the final word on the subject for a while. Only the closing and opening of doors echoed through the hallways. Soon, they were all wishing their silly chatter had continued, even if it was terribly unwise. Slowly, there came again the light tinkling of sounds just beyond their senses, the ghostly laughing of children and the inky roars of phantom beasts.

"Sonofa—!" Nurse Jana cried out, after perhaps twenty turns and switchbacks in the endless maze of corridors. "*Come* on."

"What is it? What do you see?" Thomas rushed forward to stand beside the nurse. His flashlight's beam crossed over hers, and they were soon both looking at the same heart-breaking sight.

"Hey, Brian," Thomas called back, switching off his flashlight. "Remember when I asked you to lock or barricade the entrance?"

"Right, yes. A first rate job, as I remember. Why?"

"I'm hoping you're wrong, but I'm guessing not." Soon, they were all bunched up in a clump in the hallway, and Brian was trying to see over their shoulders. The door stood slightly ajar, and the last rays of daylight hovered at the jamb. They could see where Brian had carefully laid a line of blessed salt across the threshold. The door had not been pushed inward, the only direction its hinges allowed. It had been thrown outward. The steel door had been bent outward, rolled open like a sardine can.

"Not good. *Not* good."

"Yeah," Smitty nodded. "If I get out of this, I'm becoming Catholic. That's not just salt."

"If it is, then to hell with it." Anne laughed, despite herself. When the others looked at her, as though she might, too, be possessed, Anne just waved her hand, dismissively, "It's uh … just a quote."

"Jana," Thomas said. "You ever see any other doors, maybe on the *outside* of the building? Maybe there's more than one way to skin this cat."

"Yeah, okay," Brian nodded, gulping down a mouthful of spit. "I'll start by barricading the alleyway." He stepped forward, holding his own bag of blessed salt above his head.

"Look at this guy, eh?" Smitty said, tapping Brian on his shoulder as he passed. "Suddenly he's Sir Richard, the lion-hearted. Not for nothin', but things are looking up."

Brian disappeared, turning right around the twisted hulk of the metal doorway. He reappeared a moment later, heading back toward the Main Street end of the alleyway. After a moment, they heard as Brian *psst*-ed back at them. Thomas and Isaiah squeezed through the ruined door. Thomas turned to see Brian waving his hand frantically for them to come over and see something. Isaiah crept slowly towards Brian. Thomas, however, was slipping the canvas Garfield pack from his back. He wanted first to make sure that the other side of the alleyway had been properly sealed. After walking a couple steps, he stopped short, watching as a mob of people poured into the small employee parking lot from every possible direction. They had the same blank-eyed stony faces as at Melancon's diner, both of them.

Thomas looked down in panic to see if Brian had already laid out another line of salt at this end of the alleyway. He thought he knew, then, exactly what was making Brian so excited on the other end of the alley. A sudden rush of relief washed over Thomas, as he saw that Brian had already accomplished the task.

But something was wrong. He watched in horror as the oncoming swarm of people did not stop at the line of consecration. The first person walked several feet past the hosts and then stopped. He lowered his head to where

Thomas had taken a knee, prepared to draw a fresh line of salt. The man, Thomas thought he remembered him as the bearded manager of the Tractor Supply store on the other side of town, looked down at him with tar swirling in little pools where his eyes should have been. Thomas watched as the tar poured down into the man's skull. He thought he saw something there. It was something mysterious and wonderful. A little light tugged at him, inviting him into the liquid depths. But suddenly the little light turned red and hot.

Thomas felt as if he had been suddenly released. He fell backward onto his heels as though pushed. A fire grew in the other man's eyes and began spilling across his face. The fire spilled out like the long legs of spiders emerging from tiny holes. The veins in the man's head pulsed with light. The man's feet, too, started to shine. It was the plastic of his worn-out black sneakers. The shoes were melting.

The oncoming mob retreated back behind the line of salt, but many of them carried what seemed to be a cloud of heat with them. Thomas should have thought to retreat behind what remained of the metal door, but he sat transfixed by the change coming over the face of the bearded man.

In the growing heat, the man seemed to come back to himself for a moment. But it was too late. The flesh had already begun dripping from his fingertips. The bones that remained behind glowed red like coals. Before it was all over, the bearded man looked to Thomas, as if to plead for help, but there was nothing Thomas could do. He couldn't even move.

A breeze passed through the alleyway, swirling the mirage of heat growing before Thomas. The slight shudder of wind seemed to knock violently against the bearded man. What remained of him toppled over. Thomas was reminded of videos he had seen of demolition crews imploding cast-off casinos in Las Vegas. The man seemed to collapse at multiple levels at once. In a flash, all that was left was a glowing heap of molten bones.

Now that he could see behind the bearded man, Thomas saw that the others that had crossed the line of consecration were likewise disappearing into showers of melted flesh and bones. One of the human candles – it was a woman in shorts – collapsed against another member of the crowd. She sliced straight through a tar-eyed nurse in scrubs. The two halves of the nurse tumbled away in opposite directions.

The mob did not swell with hatred or retreat further in fear. It just reformed beyond the line. All of the faces wore the same blank expression.

Thomas rose shakily to his feet. He was deeply disturbed by the power he had just seen demonstrated. Though the face of the bearded man would haunt him for the rest of his life, he shoved it all away. He moved slowly back towards the other end of the alleyway, putting his finger to his mouth as he passed the ruined door. The others were startled at Thomas' re-emergence from the other end of the alleyway. It had only been a moment, but he was now as grey as a week-old corpse. He was covered in a veil of ash.

Soon, the three men, Brian, Thomas, and Isaiah, were standing bunched together at the Main Street end of the alleyway. Under happier circumstances, it would have reminded them of Alvin, Simon, and Theodore peering around a doorway. As they watched, people poured out from every building, doorway, and side street. Two huge columns of people poured in from both ends of Main Street, and they could hear the quiet pounding of another group coming down New Roads Street. It was like a scene from a St. Maryville Mardi Gras parade, except for the lack of voices of any kind. The only sound now was the shuffling of thousands of feet, but even that couldn't overcome the eerie echoes of children laughing and animals growling somewhere in the distance.

"Brian," Thomas whispered. "Do you think you can complete a line of salt around to the other side of the building before we're surrounded?"

"You sure you couldn't find a braver man for this?" Brian asked.

"I'll comes with ya," Isaiah said, tapping the man on his shoulder, and taking Thomas' blue canvas Garfield backpack.

"Make it more than an arm's reach from the building, okay?" Thomas said. The two men nodded and burst out from their hiding place at the end of the alleyway. They began leapfrogging each other as they poured sections of a continuous line of salt across the front of the building.

Thomas trotted back to the door, quietly. "What is it? What're those sounds? Why are you covered in soot?" Anne asked, frightened by her brother's return. Charlie and Smitty were both still standing at her side, and

Jana was holding the flashlight backward into the hallway to make sure nothing came from behind.

"It's pretty much my worst nightmare, correct?" Smitty asked.

"Ayuh," Thomas said, imitating the older man's New England accent with just a hint of a smile.

"Come on, Sissy," Thomas said, taking the pregnant woman by the arm. "We may still get out of this."

"Holy Mother of God," Smitty almost shouted as they walked into the alleyway.

"What in the hell?" Charlie said, coming out of the door and looking upwards.

"*That* wasn't there a second ago," Thomas said, hurrying them along. Between the two two-story buildings that marked the alleyway and even above, there rose a great black stripe across the darkening sky and sunset. Rotted, black sails hung from gaffs and crossbeams.

"It's Isaiah's ship," Charlie answered. "Can you believe it? It would be amazing, if it weren't so damn frightening. Like the USS Constitution or something."

"Ah, pissah," Smitty said, stopping suddenly in his tracks.

"What?" Charlie and the others turned to look at him.

"Nothing, nothing," Smitty said, literally poking them forward with his new arm. "Charlie," he said confidentially. "It's the *tower*."

"What's that, Smitty?"

"It's a tower, you know, *in the water*."

Charlie turned back at him suddenly. "You mean, your dream? The water tower?"

"Right," Smitty nodded. "The water tower on *Parent* Street." As he said it, they reached the end of the alleyway to see the swarming throngs of people filling the street.

"Does this mean we're about to see that black hole under the water tower?"

"S'pose it does," Smitty grimaced. "And a whole lot of blood."

"Mercy," Charlie said, shaking his head. Looking down the front of the LaCour building, they could just see Isaiah and Brian rounding the corner. A clear path lay ahead of them, but Thomas worried how the presence of a pregnant mother might affect the crowds of people. Just as he had feared, the stony faces of the crowds, as one, swung to stare at Anne when they broke cover from the alleyway. Hundreds of eyes, some just dilated and some already swirling with tar, were upon the mother in an instant.

"Take her," Smitty called to Thomas, as Anne fainted. "My arm's no good for holding her." Smitty took over the lead in their little phalanx. He thrust the brass poker towards an approaching man, as a threat, but the man didn't move or try to dodge. Instead, the brass poker disappeared into the man's stomach. Smitty pulled it back out straightaway, confused and horrified by what he had done. "My God," he whispered, as the man's clothes began to flutter and collapse. The man's face and body dissolved before them, and a second later, there was only a small pile of clothes resting on a pair of wingtips. The man's cufflinks and belt, as well as some dental fixtures, clattered to the ground and rolled away.

"Smitty, what you got tied to your stump, exactly?" Charlie asked, bewildered. "You just ghosted the president of the bank."

"Monsignor blessed it," Smitty said, staring in wonder at the brass poker. "This Catholic stuff, I tell ya."

"Just watch it, okay?" Thomas asked. "These people – we know most of them – and this thing, whatever it is, might still be reversible."

"Yeah, sure," Smitty said, still staring in wonder at his arm.

As the small, huddled group rounded the corner of the LaCour Building, they were struck by the smell. They saw, too, that Brian and Isaiah were halfway down the building and could go no farther. The empty lot between the LaCour Building and Miss Tee-Eva's, which faced New Roads Street, had filled with staring faces. The two men trotted backward to meet up with the group, running along the overgrown weeds and grass of the empty lot.

As they did, Brian stopped suddenly. For a moment, he tottered in empty space with a look of confusion on his face. It looked for a moment as if he had tripped. Isaiah didn't even notice Brian was no longer at his side until it was too late, and then he only knew by reading the faces of the others. A look of sheer terror spread over Brian's face as he fell to his knees. And then, in the blink of an eye, he was gone.

They gasped. "Stay here," Thomas said, getting Isaiah to take his place holding Anne. Thomas crept toward the spot where Brian had suddenly disappeared, hugging the brick wall of the LaCour Building, as the crowds began to tighten up and press in. Arms were reaching across the line of salt, trying to grab at Thomas and the others. Within seconds, the arms began to dissolve even as the bank president had done at the front of the building. The people kept pressing in, oblivious to their danger. Many of the people were now standing armless, like defanged sentinels with searching eyes. Much longer, however, and the crowds would just topple over the line of salt or melt on top of it, dissolving it.

Anne, now regaining consciousness, began whispering something. "The signs," she said, and kept repeating it.

"What is it, darling?" Charlie said. "What're you trying to say?"

Anne's eyelids fluttered, and she spoke only with great effort. Nurse Jana was fanning her to give her fresh air amidst all the stale air spilling from the slack jaws of the mob as well as the pit. "The signs disappeared into the ground," Anne said with effort. "Jim – he leaned them against the building. And—" she said sleepily, almost dreamily. "They disappeared. Down. Into the ground."

One of the crowd reached for Smitty, as his arm accidentally crossed over the salt line. It may have even been Tee-Eva's daughter, no one knew for sure. The hand that touched Smitty's prosthetic poker dissolved on impact.

The crowd was starting to moan. It was low at first, almost white noise, but it was gathering in intensity.

"She's talking about a way in, I think," Jana said. "I think we have to follow Brian."

Just then, Thomas trotted up from behind. "I think we can follow Brian." They all turned to him. "What?" he said. "Come on. There's, uh, another tunnel."

"I hope it's wider than Brian," Smitty said, tapping his belly.

"For Anne's sake, too," Charlie said, as he lifted her from the wall and Isaiah moved in to help.

Soon, they were all standing over a narrow grass-covered pit in the ground and holding their noses.

"God, that's an awful smell," Smitty moaned.

"It's like what the whole town has been smellin' like," Thomas observed, "but concentrated."

"Are we sure we're not just jumping into something's mouth?" Jana asked. "Something with really terrible breath."

"Dangle a leg in it, and see if you get it back," Smitty suggested.

"I don't know, Mr. Charlie. Maybe I'll just stay up here and keep the line?"

"It *would* be good for somebody to finish the salt line," Thomas offered. "You know, complete the ring around the building. Or just keep it intact."

Charlie looked to the thickly-muscled black man. "I don't know, Isaiah. You're like a son to me. If something happened to you, I—"

"Mr. Charlie, I do this for myself. Not for you. It's not on you. Some things you just gotta do."

Charlie nodded. "Here, take this," He said, handing Isaiah his own sack of blessed salt. "It's a big building. How're you gonna get around it?"

Nurse Jana threw her legs down into the hole, and hovered over the opening for a few seconds, supporting herself on her haunches. She nodded, "Just feels like a hole." Thomas hurried in after her, and Smitty followed, ready to catch Anne when Charlie and Isaiah lowered her in. Anne stirred as they lowered her into the hole.

"Don't worry about me, Mr. Charlie. I cleaned this building dozens of times, back when, before they started killing babies here. I know my way."

"Isaiah, the more I think of it, the more I think you're the man of the moment."

"Yes, sir, Mr. Charlie. That's me. Superman. Don't worry about a thing." Isaiah helped the older man down into the hole and looked around, suddenly feeling less heroic now that he was alone. He picked up Charlie's and his own bag of blessed salt and went to work. "You heard the man, people. Back off and let Isaiah do his work. I don't want to hurt you, but just make me a path and we're okay." He had to yell to be heard over the gathering moan.

Had Isaiah looked backward to the building at his back, he would have noticed it change. The brick building had grown far past its original two stories. It had also darkened. Its shape changed, growing hideous features. The mindless throngs pressed in to worship, eyes lifted to the revealed black idol. The black idol looked out upon the city and the crowds with eyes of liquid tar.

The Basement

They stood around the dirt hole in an old and mouldering brick wall, collecting themselves and letting their eyes adjust to the darkness of the basement. "Why do I feel like that was too easy?" Jana asked.

"Man, I'm glad y'all didn't leave me alone down here." Brian's smile was a white smear across a darkened muddy face. "I tried crawling back up the hole, but it was impossible."

"What do you mean, little buddy?" Smitty asked. "It was *maybe* a foot drop."

"Yeah, what're you talking about?" Charlie said, kneeling beside Anne. "We should have never brought her down here."

"No, you people don't understand. Not only is it a *much* longer tunnel than it feels like. I've been down here at least half an hour. I'm guessing you followed me almost straight away?"

They all slowly looked to each other. Someone eventually nodded at Brian. "Yeah, that's what I thought. Something wanted us down here. Let's just hope that its gamble pays out for us."

"Where is *here*?" It was Anne. She was waking up. The place seemed to be invigorating her.

They looked around at the basement, what they could see, anyway. It was dark and illuminated chiefly by the strange blue light along the far wall, where there was a sink and racks upon racks of jars filled with a blue preservation liquid.

"That's where I came in the last time," the nurse said, pointing to a doorway. "Oh my God, what are they? I rushed out too quickly last time to get a good look. What are in those jars?" Jana walked, stumbling in the half light, toward the pool of blue light, which was filtered and colored by the contents of the jars. She stopped short of the racks, as soon as she could see their contents. She put her hand to her mouth, and began sobbing. Thomas came from behind her, and put a tentative hand on her shoulder. "I knew it, somehow I knew it," the nurse stammered between sobs.

The jars were filled, not just with the blue liquid, but with the bodies of aborted children. Thomas couldn't see all the small bodies, but enough to realize what they all had in common—or *did* have in common. All the babies were deformed, somehow. One child, only because he could see his eyes clearly, Thomas recognized as a baby with Down's Syndrome.

"No, don't. Anne, you shouldn't see—" Thomas said suddenly, realizing that Anne had approached from behind.

Tears streaked down Anne's face. "All of these children. *All* of them would've been loved and nurtured at El Arca. There was a place for them," she cried, letting her head fall into the crook of her brother's arm. "Thomas?"

"What is it, Annie?" Thomas said, kissing his sister's head somewhere beneath her mess of tangled curls.

"I think I'm beginning to understand," she answered.

The nurse turned to her, "What do you mean? 'Understand'?"

"Hey, uh, gentleman and ladies?" Brian called out, interrupting the conversation. "Can you turn your attention to the rest of the basement for a moment?"

Distracted by the blue light and the racks, they hadn't had time to register the black expanse which filled the rest of the basement, much less, that it was moving.

"When I was here, before," Jana said, backing up against the old brick wall. "There were men, or the bodies of men, at least. They had heads like animals ... *birds.*"

"Wait," Brian said. "You mean they were twitchy or something, *moving* like birds?"

"No," Jana laughed miserably. "I wish. I thought they were holding doll parts at first. But no, they wore medical masks over their feathers. They had bright beaks. Wheelbarrows and shovels of 'doll parts.' They were shoveling it all in *there*." She pointed at the black pool. "But," she shook her head slowly. "It wasn't a pool. It's *not* a pool, even now. There are teeth."

The surface of the black pool was moving, almost churning. There were shadows, lighter shadows, bobbing just beneath the surface. Finally, they could hear small splashes of water. They could see things, though they knew not what, crawling out of the pool. They looked like giant, crawling grub worms in the flickering blue half-light of the basement.

"No," the nurse cried, bending double. She vomited at the sweet smell of water-logged, rotting flesh. It filled the basement. And there was more, too … it was the sound of children laughing. So long it had remained at the edges of their consciousness. Now, it echoed loud and clear against the walls of the basement.

"Get back," Charlie yelled. "Get over here, all of you," he shouted to Anne, Thomas, and the nurse, as he tugged at the loops on Brian's knapsack. He unceremoniously grabbed a handful of the salt and scattered it in a circle near the wall, wide enough for all of them to shelter in. Thomas hurried Anne over, but the nurse was too traumatized to move. The babies' little hands knocked her down, and then, slowly, irresistibly, they began dragging her sobbing and screaming into the black pool.

"That's right, my dear ones." A new voice suddenly echoed through the low-ceiling basement. A woman stepped out from among the shadows of the basement. Purple light flashed across her eyes. It was Fletcher. "She must be made to understand your dignity and value, isn't that right?" she cooed. "Carry her down. Purify her."

"No," the younger nurse said, choking on a mouthful of dirt and rot.

"But, yes," the older nurse entreated. "Yes." Nurse Fletcher was now kneeling before Jana. Her long skirt and shoes remained ghostly white despite the muck. Fletcher clutched her hands together in prayer as she watched the younger nurse being dragged away by a dozen little hands.

"No," the younger nurse insisted. Her waist was over the edge. She could feel the heavy wetness surrounding her. It was so cold. She felt teeth begin to tear at her legs. Gathering up every last bit of will that remained, she lunged forward suddenly. She tore against her own body and all the little hands. One last gasp.

Her hands clapped together around Fletcher's like an iron vice. The older nurse was caught completely by surprise. The strength of all the little hands was now added to Jana's. Fletcher was lifted completely off her feet. One bone white shoe remained mired in the mud. Fletcher was thrown sideways over the black pool, as she careened helplessly around and over Jana.

It all happened too fast. There had been no time to realize what was happening, let alone act. The rest were all horrified, almost catatonic, at witnessing the young nurse's violent struggle. Suddenly, there was just a white nurse's cap skimming across the surface of the black pool like a paper boat.

A terrible silence followed the last screams, the strangled gurgles of air, as the two nurses were at last pulled under. "Now, we are only six," Brian remarked with horrible insensitivity, finally breaking the silence. "The number of the beast, and just in time to meet him, I'm sure."

"No," Anne said, embracing her belly. "We are seven."

Slowly, the soggy-white grub worm creatures — the babies, some white and some black, but all now pale, as from long time spent living underground – swarmed around the ring of salt. About this time, men began filing into the room from the door that the nurse had once stumbled through. These were the men who wore thin masks and drove the garish yellow Jaguars. Beneath their masks, the pools of liquid tar and the decayed or chewed away lips lay poorly, clumsily disguised. The bird men came, too, further confirming the nurse's story. They hummed instead of chirping; one long, low chirp, possibly.

At some unseen signal, one of the men pulled on a rusted iron lever which stood in a slot along one of the walls. There was a clattering of gears and ironworks, and then a sucking sound. Smitty tapped their arms and gestured to the black pool. The black liquid, whether it was tar or simply fetid water, was slowly draining away.

Soon, they could see the teeth the nurse had described. As the pool drained away, they could see the rows of teeth, spiraling down. The sides of the pool were quivering flesh, and the flesh quaked as it swallowed gulp after gulp of the dark, stinking liquid.

"It's the mouth we saw," Brian said, nudging the men beside him who had been with him in the tomb. "You can almost smell the sulfur as it belches." As they watched, the flesh down in the depths of the wide mouth quivered. As it gulped down the black pool, it tugged at the metal hooks that kept its lips pinned to the basement's soggy floor.

"My God, the salt," Brian continued. "Look at it. It's dissolving. Well, here we go then." The pale, fidgety man was strangely serene and observant. They all were. Even as the pool drained away, grace welled up within them from the infinite recesses of their souls. This was especially true of Anne. The men began to forget the danger and monstrosities that, they now saw, surrounded them and blocked every possible exit. Instead, they slowly turned one by one to Anne.

The last man to turn to Anne was Smitty, who was frothing with righteous anger and threatening the men, beaked or lipless, with his new brass arm. Charlie nudged his old friend in his prodigious belly. Smitty turned slowly. As he did, his face transformed from the bluish tint to a reflection of the golden glow. Smitty's features softened in the new light, and he seemed to grow younger, healthier, more robust.

As they watched, Anne seemed to radiate. Despite the low ceiling of the basement, they seemed to see the sky and endless clouds reflected in the pools of light beyond Anne. A golden light pulsed from her head. "My God," Charlie said shaking his head tremulously. "This must be what the artists meant by halos."

"Sissy?" Thomas coughed, not wanting to even blink. A man not accustomed to crying in his youth, his eyes welled with tears. From then on, the tears would always flow easier. "Sissy? Where are you going?"

Anne had left the protection of the salt circle, but she bent down, as she did, to collect the salt. As she did, it formed into circles of bread. She looked, all at once, like a little girl collecting flowers and a queen commanding legions. Bands of the low-men fell upon her, four or five each clasped at her arms and her neck. Despite this, she stood up, raising her hands to her breast. As she did, golden light seemed to rise up through the creatures' capillaries. Steam welled up inside their translucent masks, clouding them. As the steam whistled through the open pores, they collapsed as empty suits and crumpled masks onto the filthy floor of the basement.

The bird creatures, likewise, dissolved into golden light, but out of their little piles of clothing and wristwatches, fluttered coveys of birds. The birds took wing and whirled about the low-ceiling basement looking for a perch. Eventually, they settled under the bluish light along the racks which held the jars of the disabled babies. They began pecking away at the glass jars.

Anne turned back to the four men, and their knees grew weak below them. Never had any of them seen such beauty. She put her hand out to Smitty. He gave her first his good hand, but she shook her head. He slowly raised his stub to her hand. "Don't be ashamed of this, Warren. This is a very brave hand."

As they watched, she wiped the duct-tape reinforced bands from his forearm, as though they were no more than dust. She took from her ankle the worn friendship bracelet that Miss Frannie Pearl had given her and that had managed to cling to her throughout everything. She put it around Smitty's handless wrist. When she next took him by the hand, they were all startled, especially Smitty, as none of them had noticed his hand return.

She took each of their hands, even Brian's, and said, "Behold, I am the handmaid of the Lord, and generations will call my daughter blessed. For me, though, for now, I must go down and choke the dragon. He cannot bear the ones born unstained." And she smiled, and walked backward.

Behind her, rivulets of saliva began coursing down into the mouth from pores beneath the fangs. Even so, the giant, lipless mouth began to quake with such ferocity that its flesh was beginning to rip from its moorings in the floor. The hooks were exposed that held the great tunnel to the River of Fire in place. The men collapsed to the floor as the jaguar roared with intensity great enough to splinter the timber crossbeams and posts supporting the building overhead.

Thomas scrambled toward his sister, despite the quaking of the ground and the thunderous roar, pleading with her to stop – that there must be another way! But his sister's radiant face was implacable. Thomas threw himself to the edge and watched as his sister, the living image of sublime beauty, plummeted shining into the abyss.

He would have fallen, too, had Smitty's new hand not caught him by the arm. Smitty and Charlie, both, helped the sobbing man back to his feet. The whole place was shaking violently as the mouth continued to quake and the timbers began snapping. The four men ran to the door, just as the glass jars – every last one – fell from their racks and broke open along the lines created by the birds.

The men rushed past the pitiful bodies, but Brian called to them: "Holy Water, give me your bottles!"

"Are you crazy?" Smitty called. "The whole place is collapsing!"

"Give 'em to me. I'll baptize them, and they'll be free."

"But you can't—!"

"Shut up, of course, I can. *Anybody* can in an emergency."

"But she said–," Thomas called to him over the din, thinking over what Anne had said. "It knew not to eat these, because they wouldn't sin."

"Whatever, there's still original sin. No exceptions, well, except for— nevermind," Brian called out, unscrewing the hot water bottle, and spraying two cruciform lines across the bodies. "I baptize you in the name of the Father, and the Son, and the Holy Spirit."

"Amen! Dammit," Smitty roared, and grabbing again with his new hand, he dragged Brian's smiling face away by the scruff of his thin neck.

"No exceptions? Except …" Thomas' words were cut off by the roar of the collapsing building.

****

As they leapt from the collapsing building, the four men somehow landed in the empty lot where they had left Isaiah, not in the side alley, as they had expected. They looked back to the collapsing building. Their hearts sank at what they saw. It was the black idol, and it seemed to be laughing at them from high above. Even as their ebullience suddenly collapsed into despair, they backed into Isaiah. He was lying huddled on the ground and shaking in pain.

The poor man had been burnt badly. It had likely been wave after wave of the melting bodies falling into him. His hands groped blindly for them. "Mr. Charlie, is that you? I did all I could, but wasn't enough. Not near enough. They's keep on coming."

Charlie supported his old friend so that he did not fall, but there was no where to go. The idol was at their backs and the crowd was pressing in. Little remained of the lines of salt now.

"There!" Thomas shouted. "Do you see it?" He was pointing at something moving in the crowd.

"See? See what?" Smitty yelled annoyed. He was half-wishing he still had that rod for an arm, when he pushed his new hand into the face of one of the oncoming hoard. The thing's skull collapsed inward softly. The person had turned into a tower of ash. The ash crumbled inward and then toppled into the wind as the crowd pressed it. "Would'ya look at that!" Smitty yelled, as he began thrashing his arm around to protect the others. "I'm like blessed Buckaroo Banzai."

"Not just you, Smitty," Charlie said pointing along with Thomas. "Look there, here they come. Must be the saints come marching in."

The mobs stilled suddenly. They stood for a second, staring blankly forward, then some power seemed to crack inside them. They became hysterical. They began pouring over one another, like roaches fleeing the beam of a flashlight. The men were all knocked down beneath the sudden onslaught. Many of the feet trampling over them, seen in flashes and glimpses, were bare, as though the people had been called out of their homes. Many of the people in their flight folded like animals and dropped down to all fours.

They would have been crushed under the clawing hoard, but the weight above them slowly cleared and they found themselves alone inside the eye of the storm.

But they weren't alone. A circle had been formed around them by someone, several someones.

They were scrambling back to their feet slowly and painfully. Charlie had been stomped hard in his right eye and was clutching that side of his head as he looked around in confusion. Brian was clutching his groin. "*Gahhr*," he shouted. "Those little … must've been five of 'em. Right in my. *Piss.*"

"Where's Anne?" Somebody asked. It was one of the El Arca community members, a young dark-haired lady with Downs' Syndrome.

"Rose for the lady," Wally answered or asked, no one knew for certain which.

"She's gone. For now," another voice answered. It was Miss Peggy, who had just recently lost her battle with cancer and died. None of the men knew this and they barely noticed her changed state amid all the confusion. "But don't you worry about her."

The El Arca community members had formed a protective circle around the men. They stood protecting the men, but doing their best to do no harm to the mob, as well. Every time one of the mob collided with one of the El Arca residents, they evaporated, leaving just a pile of clothes to fall softly against their backs or at their feet.

"All the world loves M&M's," Chris was shouting in fear. "Pure milk chocolate joy for everyone!" He was pointing wildly at the black tower and was moving back and forth erratically.

Smitty and the others turned back to the black tower. "What the'ell's that kid talking about?"

"He's saying it's all about to come down, that's what," Brian explained. "Ah, *Jeez.* I was really feeling safe there for a second."

They were all frozen in place, staring helplessly up at the liquefying and crumbling structure. The idol's liquid eyes seemed to stare down on them, hanging disconnected from time. Brian understood in that instant the purpose behind the murals which still stretched across the side of the Lacour building. The harvest, he thought darkly, and the town – *the town was always the harvest, the children of the town.* In that same millisecond, he noticed a little historical oddity. He hadn't noticed it before, so nobody had. The farmers' faces – what looked like the faces of men – were not. It wasn't just artistic license. Their eyes were just black holes, little black pools.

Then the tar started spilling from the idol's eyes. The idol's black tears splashed down from its face. The massive head lurched forward above them. "Run!" Thomas bellowed.

The idol's obsidian head roared down on them from its perch. It seemed to hang in the air endlessly and it slowly relented to gravity. It roared as it plummeted to the ground. They tried to run on instinct, but it was pointless. The head, like a meteor, shattered as it crashed into the ground. Shards of crystalline tar, like grape shot, hammered at their backs.

The earth growled beneath them. Smitty tried clinging to the ground with his new hand as he and the others were tossed upward by the impact. Thomas blacked out and felt the tar sweeping across his consciousness.

Thomas' next memory was the ringing in his ears. He opened his eyes slowly to see the others slowly climbing to their feet. The El Arca community members stood as though unmoved by any of it. As they looked around, they saw that thousands still filled the streets. The city's streetlights cast pools of light onto the cowering crowds, illuminating hundreds at a time, but the lot where the men and El Arca stood was empty. Almost.

"What the frick?" Brian yapped, noticing an enormous shadow that seemed to be spilling outward from his feet.

"Behind you," Thomas whispered.

They were all slowly turning to face it. There was a giant form that seemed to be emerging from what remained of the idol's broken head. It was black, but it seemed as though stars shined from deep within its hide.

Brian screamed when he had turned to face it. "It was an egg! A giant *egg*."

"No, you idiot. Shut up," Smitty scolded him between clenched teeth. "It *saved* us from that falling chocolate crap or whatever that kid said."

Brian wasn't listening. He was turning to run. The giant form shifted its weight and tumbled towards them. Smitty staggered backwards, as did all the others. The ground for the second time groaned in protest.

It was the bear. It had been standing high on its hind legs after deflecting the fall of the idol's head. It dropped now to all fours. Even standing on all fours, it was still well over twenty feet tall. Standing on its hind legs, it would have been taller than any building in St. Maryville, save the towering idol, itself. It roared, shaking and splitting the windows in their sills, and the crowds fell back.

The bear was not in the act of devouring them, gulping them down two or four at a time, like a handful of Chris' M&Ms, Brian eventually realized; it was protecting them. Just as the El Arca community was protecting them.

Suddenly, the silent, stony faces of the hoards began to soften. The bear's roar had blown away the last wisps of power that had possessed the crowds. The faces began tightening and hands went to their heads and eyes. They were all suddenly aware of a throbbing deep in their skulls. This was quickly forgotten as they took in their surroundings.

They began screaming in terror. As the fog began to pass from their minds, whatever torment they had been trapped in for the last days and weeks, even entire lifetimes for some, was replaced by the monstrous form of the bear. Though the men could sense somehow that the bear was good and posed no harm, in their renewed primal state, the hoards were thunderstruck.

Suddenly, the bear reared back and bounded away onto the Regions Bank rooftop. Two of the columns that supported the front portico of the bank building cracked on impact, but the bear was gone. It had disappeared into the night.

There was a short period of quiet, as the crowds, suddenly very sleepy, began to dissipate. Charlie returned to Isaiah's side who was still lying on the ground, but now he was still. Charlie rolled the larger man onto his back. "Isaiah," he yelled. "Isaiah! Wake up, *dammit.*"

"He's dead," Brian was saying, shaking his head.

Smitty slapped the younger man with his new hand to silence him. "Put a sock in it, kid."

Isaiah wrinkled his eye lids. "Yes, suh, Mr. Charlie!" Brian and Smitty both gasped in surprise.

"Stay with me, son. You're in shock," Charlie said lifting the much larger man into his lap, so he would be angled upwards. As he did, Isaiah slowly took stock of the others and watched as the crowds retreated. "Look, Mr. Charlie," he said. "It's Mr. Gremillion. Call to him. What's he doing?"

Charlie looked to where Isaiah pointed and saw his business partner. Mr. Gremillion stared back at them without expression or comprehension. The mustached man slowly turned and walked away like a displaced ghost.

The rush of events suddenly caught up with Isaiah, who noticed with surprise that he was still alive. At this, he tipped his head back and started laughing. The sound shocked the others out of their stupor. The laughter seemed to mean something to each man. It was a deep, infectious laugh, and they were all soon overcome by it. Even the sadness of losing Anne was passing away. The memory of her beauty was so strong, so palpable, as to be almost living, or better than.

"Quiet," Thomas shouted, who had begun to start smiling, despite himself. Even that nascent smile fled from his face. "Quiet! All of you. *Listen.*" They all froze. Thomas ran off, disappearing into the rubble of the former LaCour Building. There was very little of the building left, as much of it had collapsed inward, filling what was left of the hole, what had been the demon's mouth. Above it all, they could just hear the cries of a newborn.

As they listened, Monsignor, Frances, and Mamou came walking up through the almost sleep-walking crowds. Mamou was carrying Jim in her arms. Smitty hurried over to his grandson. Charlie did likewise, helping Isaiah lift himself into a sitting position.

"We had to come," Monsignor said. "Jim is free now, but his body is failing. You would have missed him. The end is very near now for him. I think he wants to rise and meet his bride."

"Sweet boy," Frances said, wiping the sweat-drenched hair from her grandson's forehead. "I think it was all he ever wanted."

Just then, a pile of debris collapsed behind them, the last of the murals. It was Thomas. He, too, was carrying someone. The sound of the newborn's screams, though soft, echoed across the empty intersection of the one-intersection town.

"I think," Thomas said, smiling and dripping with fresh tears, which would forever remain close at hand. "There may be one last thing Jim wanted before leaving us."

"His daughter," Mamou announced. Her voice was still massive, rising from her very toes, like the roar of a bear. "The sweet baby."

"Behold," Monsignor said, his eyes fixed on the newborn. "The seventh word."

Jim's eyes rustled under his lids. They opened weakly at the sound of the newborn's approach. A smile spread across the young man's pale face. With his last ounce of strength, he raised his hand to the girl, and laid his palm gently on her heart. The newborn quickly quieted down. At her father's touch, the newborn even opened her eyes. For one fleeting instant, their eyes met. With his last breath, the dying father called to his daughter. "Immaculata," he said.

And then, with his last, Jim lifted his hand from his daughter to Thomas' shoulder. "Your father," he said. And then he died, the smile still upon his face, as though he could still see his daughter's face.

Epilogue

People would later say they saw several garishly-colored Jaguars speeding out of the parish along Highway 1. One, however, remained. It was rolling slowly through the dispersing crowds. The people wore confused looks on their faces. Their hair was matted and slick against their faces, as though they had just awakened from a very long and restless nap.

Sam was again behind the wheel of the vehicle. The hood of the vehicle seemed to stretch out impossibly far ahead of him. He kept clanging into the people as they staggered away from the center of town. Though he knew they were a long ways from being able to hear him, he kept muttering apologies under his breath.

He couldn't have driven faster even if the streets had been empty. He couldn't use his foot to press down on the gas or the brake because of the compound and ugly fracture of his ankle. He had grabbed a brass-handled cane from a vase standing in the foyer of the Bellefontaine house as he left. He was using the cane and his left hand to mash down on the pedals.

Erin and Elton were sharing the passenger seat beside him. Erin was nearest to him. Even though the bones along the entire right side of his body were all in bad shape, he still enjoyed the brush of Erin's arm against his own.

Erin and Elton were in roughly about the same shape as the people staggering around the sides of the Jaguar. Thankfully, they had had enough wits about them and motor control to help Sam limp back to the car. He had tried convincing both of them to drive, but that had been a fool's errand. Sam let his mind drift back to moment they had finally awakened. After Erin had finally stopped her mad mutterings and sank back into herself, Sam had just known it had been the last he'd ever see of her. But then it happened. She had come back. They both had. Erin's father, too, had briefly regained consciousness, and – much to Sam's relief – had fallen back asleep. His wounds would need to be tended to very soon, but Sam needed first to understand what had happened. He knew the others must have succeeded, somehow.

****

Brian had continued to pester Monsignor about all the dead children, including those in the jars, that must be buried beneath all the rubble of the collapsed LaCour building.

"I can't baptize the dead," Monsignor had insisted gently. Brian was still in shock after the traumatic events of the day and wasn't quite in his right mind. "I can only bury them."

With that, Brian had dragged the elderly priest away from the rest of the group, who were still mourning over Jim's body. Nearly Jim's whole family had been there in his last moments, even Isaiah had known Jim since he was a little boy.

Brian and Monsignor stood at the rim of the crater that had once been the LaCour building. The size of the crater revealed the reality that no one had been able to see until the final unveiling.

"How long had it been here, Monsignor, under our noses?" Brian asked.

"Well, I'd hardly say 'under' our noses. It had become a colossus, certainly. The black idol, the monument to evil, it had been here for quite some time, slowly fouling the air. I wish I could say something like this is rare, that St. Maryville is an anomaly because of this, but this is not why St. Maryville is a place set apart. Now that you have seen one, Brian, you will see others, and other things that are hidden. There is so much that people do not see. Sometimes I wonder if it's better that way."

Brian nudged again at Monsignor's elbow. He had in his hand one of the leftover bottles of holy water, which he passed to the priest. "Bless it, please. Make it holy ground."

Monsignor began to recite the funeral rite over the pit. He knew it all by heart, having said it many, many times over his long years. He began by sprinkling the holy water and reciting John 11, "I am the resurrection and the life, saith the Lord: he that believeth in me, though he were dead, yet shall he live: and whosoever liveth and believeth in me shall never die."

Monsignor and Brian looked up suddenly as the town's last Jaguar rolled to a stop on the far side of the crater. Sam saw Monsignor's hand raised in blessing and guessed at what was happening, though the rest remained a mystery for now. He shoved the cane down so that it was pinned between the seat and the brake pedal. He then used his left hand to shift the car into park and turn off the car's ignition. Monsignor nodded to Sam and the other two with his crooked smile and pressed on with the recital of the funeral rite. At the sight of that crooked smile, Sam could no longer hold back the tears and emotions he had so long kept in check.

Jim and Anne's baby had begun to cry ever more loudly after becoming an orphan, as though she knew somehow what had happened to her father. The baby suddenly grew quiet within Thomas' arms, as Monsignor was finishing the funeral rite. The others looked up in the sudden quiet.

There was something moving in the slanting rays of the setting sun. Many somethings were visible in fading light. Brian gasped suddenly. "Sweet Jesus," Isaiah whispered.

They were suddenly surrounded by children wearing white gowns. There were children of all ages, running here and there, playing in the half-light. Many of them were just learning to crawl. They were sometimes difficult to see as they passed in and out of the light. Monsignor and the others would later say the children could only truly be seen from out of the corner of their eyes. For the children, they were all ghosts.

They understood suddenly why Jim and Anne's baby had stopped crying. It was not the ghosts of the children. It was Jim and Anne. They were both standing above Thomas, who was still kneeling beside Jim's body. At the sight, Frances fell back against her husband, but Charlie caught her. Charlie, for his part, was staring wide-eyed, trying to freeze his grandson in his memory. He knew this would be his last glimpse of his grandson. The ghosts of Jim and Anne seemed unable to take their eyes away from their daughter.

Brian nudged again at Monsignor's side. Monsignor shook his head, unable to speak for the tears issuing from under his deep brow.

"It's time, father," Brian insisted and Monsignor nodded. The old priest cleared his throat to finish the Rite. "Rest eternal grant unto them, O Lord," he announced in a booming voice.

Brian answered, "And let light perpetual shine upon them."

****

As silence began to fall on the town and the rising ghost of dust began to fade over the fallen idol, a sound erupted from the heavens and for miles in every direction, surrounding the lake, the town, and the river. Had the daylight remained, they might have seen great plumes of dust and steam erupting in a great ring around the town, forming a circle ten miles or more in diameter. Something massive shifted in the ground, and the course of the river shifted. The spillway flooded and St. Maryville, at last, became an island. A sound like horns or trumpets or great tectonic earthworks bending and snapping shook the air and the ground. It lasted maybe an hour, throwing every person within a hundred miles to the ground, clutching at their ears. And then, there was silence: the long silence.

www.ingramcontent.com/pod-product-compliance
Lightning Source LLC
Chambersburg PA
CBHW052040240626
47153CB00006B/2170